THE TEMPTATION
OF ANGELIQUE

Gold Beard's Downfall

BOOK TWO

SERGEANNE GOLON

THE TEMPTATION
OF ANGELIQUE

Gold Beard's Downfall

BOOK TWO

Translated from the French by
MARGUERITE BARNETT

UNABRIDGED

PAN BOOKS LTD : LONDON

Originally published 1969 as *La Tentation d'Angélique* by
Editions de Trévise.

© Opera Mundi, Paris 1969

First published as one volume in Great Britain 1969 by
William Heinemann Ltd.
This edition published 1971 by Pan Books Ltd,
33 Tothill Street, London, S.W.1

ISBN 0 330 02595 3

*Made and printed in Great Britain by
Cox & Wyman Ltd, London, Reading and Fakenham*

CONTENTS

PRINCIPAL CHARACTERS

Angélique, Countess Peyrac: an aristocratic French lady of the seventeenth century; after an early marriage to the Gascon nobleman, Joffrey de Peyrac, by whom she had two sons, Florimond and Cantor, she becomes separated from her husband whom she believes has been executed for sorcery. She herself regains favour at Court as a result of her second marriage to her cousin Philippe du Plessis-Bellière, who is killed shortly afterwards. In order to escape the King's attentions she flees the country and is captured on the Mediterranean by the Berbers and imprisoned by the Sultan Mulai Ismail at Meknès in North Africa. There she is rescued by her fellow-captive, Colin Paturel, who accompanies her across the desert to Ceuta. She is taken back to France by the King's agents but escapes and leads the people of her native province, Poitou, in their uprising. She is condemned to death and once more obliged to flee France with her youngest child, Honorine, and a party of Huguenot refugees. On reaching America she is reunited with her long-lost husband, Joffrey de Peyrac, and with Florimond and Cantor. Together they survive their first winter in the inland fort of Wapassou, in the mountainous country of Upper Kennebec near the Canadian border. When spring comes they set off down river to visit their settlement of Gouldsboro at the mouth of the Bay of Fundy, then known as Frenchman Bay.

Joffrey de Peyrac: a high-born Frenchman. His great learning and considerable fortune arouses the envy of King Louis XIV, who contrives his ruin and has him condemned as a sorcerer. After many adventures, he is reunited with his family and disembarks on the shores of Maine where he founds the colony of Gouldsboro. By setting up inland mining communities to exploit the vast mineral resources of the region, he established a claim to a large part of the territory of Maine, then known as Acadia, the sovereignty over which was disputed between France and Britain.

Colin Paturel: often referred to as the King of Slaves at Meknès, Angélique's rescuer from captivity in North Africa. (See above.)

Florimond and Cantor: Joffrey's and Angélique's sons, aged seventeen and fifteen respectively at the time of the action.
Honorine: Angélique's four-year-old illegitimate daughter.
Yann le Couennec: Joffrey de Peyrac's equerry.
Kurt Ritz: a Swiss mercenary in Peyrac's employ.
Rose-Ann: an English child whose life Angélique has saved.
Piksarett: chief of the Patsuikett Indians.

French Canadians:
Baron Saint-Castine: a friend of Peyrac's.
François Maupertuis and Romain de l' Aubignière: trappers.
Adhemar: a buffoon.

Settlers in Gouldsboro:
Gabriel Berne: leader of the Protestant community.
Abigail Berne: his young wife.
Monsieur and Madame Mercelot: paper-makers.
Bertille: their daughter.
Monsieur and Madame Manigault.
Madame Carrère: the innkeeper.

PART FOUR

Jack Merwin's Sloop

CHAPTER FORTY

THREE DAYS before all this, to the north of Casco Bay, a ship on the sea. One ship among so many others. But the sea is so vast and the islands so numerous that the ship seemed to be alone as it crept along like a hunted animal, constantly in peril of the treachery of current and rock. Keeling over to the leeward she would round a promontory, melt into the shadow of a cliff, reappear in the sunshine, sometimes escorted by the scent of flower-strewn shores, sometimes rising and dipping in salt-laden squalls.

Human forms could be seen along the beaches of the islands, waving their arms as they ran along, shouting. There were boats and bigger ships hidden in the creeks, some tacking as they sailed or fished on the far side of some rock, while others only appeared after the ship had gone by.

It was for ever alone amid the labyrinth of those 365 islands in Casco Bay. From Maquoit Point, the ship had followed the coastline southwards.

The last part of the night had left Angélique exhausted, after trying to devise a thousand and one ways to escape from Colin.

That morning he had come into her cabin. She had slept but little and felt weary and heavy hearted, but determined to make him set her free.

But he had anticipated her request.

'Follow me, Madame,' he had bade her coldly.

He was calm and distant, still imposing, with all his weapons slung about him, and she followed him out on to the deck. Some of the crew were loitering about, ostensibly performing their usual morning duties, but above all trying to catch a glimpse of Gold Beard's prisoner, and Angélique saw a boat lying up against the hull of the ship, pitching up and down with a straw bollard to protect it from collisions.

It was an English sloop, one of those big boats that constantly plied from bay to bay, from village to village between New York and Pemaquid or still farther. Its master, a powerfully-built, gloomy-looking man, must have been hailed that morning by the French filibusters of the *Heart of Mary*, and no one knew precisely what his views were concerning the booty with which they were busy filling his sloop. But, accustomed as he was to navigation in these waters, he must have learnt that it was prudent to show circumspection when dealing with undesirable visitors from the Caribbean. Angélique leaned forward and saw a large number of passengers on board the sloop, among whom she recognized the Reverend Patridge's bulldog-like face, that of the devoted little Miss Pidgeon, young Sammy Stoughton, and Adhemar, whose wails of protest filled the particularly limpid air of that wistaria-coloured dawn.

'Well! Falling into the hands of pirates now! It certainly looks as if I collect disaster . . .'

The wooden bar across the gang port had been removed and a rope ladder hung from the opening.

'So that's that!' Colin remarked in a stifled voice, standing close to her and speaking to her alone, 'We had better part, had we not, my dear? The skipper of this boat tells me he is sailing to Penobscot. So if the wind is good and he cuts straight across east-north-east, you will be there in four days at the outside . . .'

For all his efforts and his good intention, he could not help addressing her in the familiar form; and she realized that every time he felt her close to him it would be as it had been in the desert, when he was the only one in the world to look upon her and to take her in his arms . . .

She looked up at him in an attempt to make him understand what she felt – friendship and gratitude.

She was overjoyed at the thought that within four days she might be with Joffrey again, and her nightmare over.

She would be able to breathe again and straighten out her thoughts. Once back with her husband again, reassured by his beloved voice, so sweet to her ears, she would try to sort things out. They would talk things over together . . .

Colin's face contorted in pain at the dazzling smile she gave him.

'Ah! You love him, I can see . . .' he murmured.

But she scarcely heard him.

She knew she must not give way to emotion and that she must escape as soon as possible.

She must seize this present opportunity before he changed his mind. Already, because she recognized how characteristic was this open, generous gesture he was making in releasing her, she felt an indefinable sense of regret grip her heart.

She took her bag from one of the sailors and threw it unceremoniously across her shoulders.

She was still barefoot, but what did it matter! What did one need shoes for on the slippery deck of a sloop? At the last moment she almost inquired after Slitbelly, the man she had operated on, but resisted the temptation, for she did not wish to lose a single second. She refused help from a man who offered to assist her down the rope ladder, and called out gaily: 'Thanks all the same, friend, but I've knocked about the Mediterranean, you know.'

Colin laid his hand on her shoulder, unable to contain himself as the moment came to see her go. He stared intently at her and, with his astonishingly clear blue eyes that still looked almost childishly youthful in his heavily-lined and tough-looking face framed in the pale hair and beard which he had tried to turn into a symbol of fear, he tried to take in everything about her. He seemed to be attempting to hold her image fast as one does a ghost, a phantasmagoria of the mind, as if she were not completely real. And yet she had the feeling that he was not only thinking of his passion for her, but of something still more urgent, more outward, something even more serious that pre-occupied him. Twice he seemed on the point of speaking.

'Take care,' he whispered at last, 'take care, my lamb . . . there are people who wish you no good . . . No good at all! . . .'

Then he let her go, and she made her way swiftly down the rope ladder, arriving near the prow just as the captain pushed off from the ship with a shove of his boathook, heedless of the fact that Angélique stumbled and almost fell into the water.

Nonetheless she gave him a cordial greeting in English, to which his only response was a glance as expressionless as that of a dead fish. Another Puritan, no doubt, who considered any young, laughing, and . . . tousled woman the very incarnation of the Devil!

Angélique sat down happily beside Adhemar and Sammy while a young ship's boy with tow-coloured hair unfurled the jib and the boom-and-gaff mainsail and the captain rowed his craft away from the corsair ship to pick up the wind.

And thus it was that this little sloop, the *White Bud*, began to tack back and forth among the islands of Casco Bay, sailing in solitude from one wave crest to another like a lovely wheeling bird.

There were three other passengers on board the boat which had rescued Angélique, her French soldier and her English refugees.

There was a pedlar from the colony of Connecticut, a little black boy acting as his assistant and . . . a bear. It was this bear that Angélique noticed first, her glance irresistibly drawn towards a wise, appreciative and amused expression she felt light upon her, although unable to determine whence it came.

It was the bear. She suddenly caught sight of it, lying beneath the false afterdeck where it had made its den. With its sharp nose between its paws, it stared at her with tiny shining eyes. The pedlar immediately introduced the bear to her:

'Mr Willoughby . . . Believe me, milady, I could not wish for a better friend than this animal.'

His own name was Elias Kempton, and in less than an hour Angélique knew everything about him. Born in Massachusetts, he had set out from the little colony of Newton at the age of eight with his parents and about a hundred of the other inhabitants. Led by their pastor Thomas Hooker, a man of liberal views who disliked the harsh oligarchy of the Puritans, they had made their way through the forest until they came to a river with broad, calm expanses of grey water, the Connecticut. On its banks they had founded Hartford, where before there had been nothing but a small Dutch fur trading post. Now it was a pleasant town, godly and gay, that made its living from the sea. It was not easy to till the land on the banks of a river like the Connecticut, for the current constantly tempted you down towards the river mouth, towards more fertile soil . . . so at the age of twenty Elias had set off with a bag filled with wares and his bear, Mr Willoughby, had followed him.

'I brought him up and we have never been separated since.'

He told them how the bear would accompany him on all his journeys, which occasionally gave rise to complications, but it helped to create a relaxed and happy atmosphere with his clients, who were generally slow to part with their shekels. The bear could dance and perform a few tricks, but he was best of all at wrestling. The strongest lads in the villages used to take him on, and he was a good sport and always gave them a chance, but eventually a friendly, almost casual swipe of one paw would send the young fighting cocks reeling.

'Willoughby . . .' said the Reverend Patridge thoughtfully, 'but I think I knew a pastor of that name somewhere near Watertown.'

'Very likely,' the pedlar admitted. 'My friend here looked so like that worthy clergyman, who used both to terrify me and amuse me when I was young, that I gave him his name.'

'A decided slight,' Thomas Patridge replied sharply, deeply offended. Then he continued, in a threatening tone: 'You could find yourself in serious trouble . . .'

'Connecticut is not Massachusetts, saving your pardon, Reverend. Our people are more liberal in their outlook and enjoy a good laugh.'

'It's a land of taverns,' growled the pastor, 'rum drinkers from birth.'

'But we do have our own constitution and we do not travel on Sundays to please the Lord.'

Looking pleased with himself Elias Kempton drew from his pockets twists of tobacco, pictures, lace, and some small watches. He had everything imaginable to catch the interest of the settlers in the farthest flung outposts in the land – or rather their wives – and as he had coasted round every smallest inlet of every bay in the region, he knew better than anyone what could be found in this or that place, what was lacking in some other, what would bring a sparkle to some young girl's eyes, and a disdainful pout to the lips of another, what would enchant some child or some grandfather, or bring the radiance of pure joy to the humblest log cabin in the form of some treasured or useful object.

He said he was making for Bartlett Island to the east of the Penobscot, in search of the woollen cloth dyed a particularly brilliant shade of indigo or red for which the place was famous. For there the sheep grazed on a hundred different varieties of flowers and the inhabitants of the island bartered catechu with the ships from the Caribbean.

'But that island must be close to Gouldsboro,' Angélique remarked, resolved to go and make some purchases there herself.

Elias Kempton knew Gouldsboro from hearsay, but had never done business there, as his usual class of customers, settlers' wives, had hitherto been lacking in those parts.

'Oh there are women there now, and I shall be your first customer,' Angélique assured him.

Delighted, the pedlar fell to his knees, but only to measure her feet there and then, for he was also an itinerant shoemaker and promised he would make her a marvellous pair of shoes of the softest leather, with laces tipped with copper to protect them from wear. Up in the north on Fox Island, there was a solitary old Scott who tanned the most supple skins for him. Provided, of course, that he found all those English folk alive, for they might well have been scalped by the Indians meanwhile.

Taciturn and disdainful of the passengers, the captain gave his full attention to the management of his craft. Once again it fell to the agreeable pedlar to inform his new companions that the aforesaid skipper answered to the name of Jack Merwin. He had discovered him in New York, and, although a moody man, he was a remarkable pilot.

And it was indeed true that Jack Merwin steered his boat among the shining, perilous currents and over the foam-crested ocean shelves with an easy, deft skill, which to the trained eye bordered on the miraculous.

Apart from a few manoeuvres with the jib which he instructed the boy to carry out, he managed the boat alone, handling both the tiller and the big square mainsail, sometimes holding the sheet taut with his big toe.

If the weather stayed fair the passage with him promised to be a fast one. But after some hours Angélique was alarmed to see that the boat was still heading obstinately south. She questioned the captain, but he pretended not to understand her imperfect English. Then the Reverend Patridge solemnly enjoined him to reply when he was spoken to. He condescended to mutter out of the corner of his mouth, his eyes turned in another direction, that to get out of this maze of blasted islands in Casco Bay without losing your boat or your life, the quickest route was to head down towards Portland, and to pick up the current that ran between Peaks Island and Cushing Island, the latter of which was known as the White Hat. Until the White Hat was sighted, he concluded, they must follow the coast southwards. Young Sammy opened his eyes wide in an attempt to catch sight of this famous White Hat.

Shocked by the lack of respect shown him by the English salt, in spite of his being a clergyman, the Reverend Thomas began to eye the man with suspicion, muttering something or other about his probably being a Virginian, that all the members of that colony were jail-birds and other riff-raff, and just because they had grown rich with their Virginian tobacco there was no call for them to bring their godless ways up to Massachusetts Bay. And so he went on in an aside, to relate the history of Virginia to Miss Pidgeon, while Adhemar, who grasped something of what was being said, began to wail:

'If the fellow is a convict, and he certainly looks it, he will maroon us all on some desert island . . .'

16

'There are no desert islands in these parts, my poor friend,' Angélique reassured him.

And it was indeed an extraordinary thing to be so utterly alone between sea and sky, between rock and shore, and yet at the same time to see all about them a kaleidoscopic collection of sails, flotillas of canoes, wooden villages, a dockyard, the timber ribbing of cod-fishing vessels under construction, a distant convoy of big-bellied ships, and to see along the beaches groups of men gathered about a fire dressed in tawdry finery, busy melting down pitch, seal oil or whale oil in huge cauldrons, while others in woollen caps bustled around their outstretched nets and their oyster baskets, and to see others again, in black pointed hats and dark doublets, their wives dressed in blue or black with white coifs, searching among the rocks for shellfish or clustering around their soup pots, which were all that remained to them of their homes.

For over half a century the permanent inhabitants of the Casco Bay archipelago had consisted of a motley collection of Scots, Irishmen, Englishmen, and even French Huguenots, to which were added, in the cod and tunny season, fleets of fishermen from St Malo, Dieppe or Boston, whalers from the Basque coast, and now, in these tragic, torrid late June days, refugees from along the coast.

In fact the entire bay was swarming with refugees from the Indian massacres. Everywhere lay ships loaded with pewter mugs and plates, Bibles and old muskets. From the lower Kennebec and Androscoggin the Abenaki torches had left a trail of fire, and – after Newehewanik – Brunswick, Freeport, Yarmouth, Falmouth, Portland, and, still farther south, Saco and Bideford had gone up in flames. When, towards evening, the boat reached the mouth of the little Presumpscot River, two miles from Portland, the stench of still smouldering fires and of rotting corpses came to them from the land on the fresh breeze, mingling with the tang of the pine woods. A small island rose up before them, decked in a variety of evergreen, a picture of harmonious colour and line. Apprehensively the occupants of the boat watched the spray-crowned rocks in the estuary growing ever closer, until they were pitching and tossing a few cables' lengths from the island, and the passengers cast anxious glances at Jack Merwin, who seemed totally unconcerned. This cold man sailed as the fancy took him.

During the course of the day he had often come in close to this island or that, almost to the point when it seemed he would run the vessel aground. Then he would scan the beaches as if looking for something or someone, and Angélique began to think that he must be searching for someone he knew among the refugees, which was proof in itself that he was not a Virginian. Occasionally he would hail another ship, and inquire about the advance of the Indians to the coast . . .

CHAPTER FORTY-ONE

THERE, quite suddenly, close to the shore of the island, he took in sail and the boat began to roll aimlessly, being driven gradually in towards the shore by the swell. The little island looked like a crown of emeralds in the rays of the setting sun that made the brilliant, glossy pine needles shimmer with blue and green tints. In spite of the roaring of the surf and the wind, the celestial music of innumerable singing birds seemed to come to them from the island.

'That is Mackworth Island,' the pastor said in hushed tones, 'the Paradise of the Indians. Be careful,' he added, turning towards the owner of the boat. 'I would not be in the least surprised if the island was infested with savages at the moment. They come from inland via Lake Sebago and the Presumpscot River. This is their ancient paradise, or so they say, and they have tolerated the presence of Englishmen here. Last year, that damned Frenchman from Pentagoet, Baron Saint-Castine, seized the island with his savages. They joined forces with some other Terratines heading down from Sebago and massacred all old Mackworth's sons and those of Richard Vines and of Samuel Andrews as well; since then the island has been deserted . . .'

No sooner had he uttered these words than the boat, rounding a headland, came upon an inlet in which glistened a number of reddish-brown canoes lying empty in tight-packed rows on the beach. In the golden light of evening, these frail bark canoes caulked with balsam and resin, shone like the transparent wing-sheaths of giant cockchafers. At the same moment the sky suddenly grew dark as if a storm cloud had obscured it, and darkness literally fell on earth as thousands of birds suddenly rose up in flocks from the island trees, and swept across the sky in a dense twittering, and screeching cloud.

Dumb with horror in the sudden, shifting darkness they saw

thousands of red ghosts rise up among the red pine tree trunks – a great multitude of Indians with hideous, painted faces.

With one accord they clasped one another in terror, and later Angélique remembered that she had clutched to herself not only Sammy but Elias Kempton the pedlar from Connecticut. There lay the boat, tossed hither and thither by the waves which were gradually carrying it nearer and nearer to the bar that enclosed the beach.

Angélique cast a terrified glance at Jack Merwin, who, like a man suddenly awakened from slumber, grasped his rudder, and, with alacrity that made up for his earlier rashness, hoisted the mainsail in a flash and whisked his boat out of the treacherous surf. But, having done this much, he still showed no haste to get away, and, after sailing for a short distance on one tack, he went about and headed once more for Mackworth Island, keeping just out of bow shot, but sailing so close to the shore that no detail of the Indians' trapping escaped them, and they saw the entire company of Redskins forming a terrifying, motionless tableau, against the background of the trees, the branches and the rocks of the island. The vast, circling cloud of birds over their heads still held them in a sinister, noisy twilight. Jack Merwin continued his inspection of the Indians, sailing up and down the beach. Was it defiance, curiosity, or provocation? He would have been a clever man indeed who could have read Merwin's thoughts from the expression on his face.

Then, still with a kind of nonchalance, he signalled to the boy to hoist the jib and set his course south-east, drawing away at last from Mackworth Island, the legendary Indian Paradise.

Little by little the sky grew brighter again, and soon only a few gulls remained to escort them on their way.

Angélique was trembling almost as much as the English people. She did not know whether it was an illusion or an obsession but she could have sworn that in the yawning darkness that had suddenly engulfed them she had seen among the trees the mocking face of Sagamore Piksarett.

'You're a reckless one, Jack Merwin,' the pedlar remarked sharply. 'It's three weeks now that I've been travelling with you and putting up with your macabre whims, and I can't stand much more. Every time we skim past some rock or you decide to sail just as a storm is breaking, I think my last hour has come ... And what about Mr Willoughby, the poor creature! Can't you see he's pining away with fright? His skin is hanging off him. He hardly stirs now, he can't even dance any more ...'

'Just as well if he doesn't stir again,' growled Merwin. 'What use do you expect us to have for a dancing bear on board this boat?'

And with supreme disdain, he spat into the waves.

Angélique could not help laughing, a natural reaction after the fright she had had. And it had to be admitted that they were a somewhat picturesque band on board that cockleshell. The Negro boy, entwined in a red homespun cloak, looked rather like a round, black radish and his white eyes were almost starting out of his head.

And where was Adhemar? Had he fainted? No, he was being sick over the side of the boat. He had never been able to endure the sea.

'And while you were busy parading back and forth in front of that assembly of red snakes, Jack Merwin,' the pedlar continued soliloquizing, for he had a lot to get off his chest, 'did it ever occur to you that a flotilla of their canoes might suddenly have come paddling round that point and taken us from the rear?'

But the skipper seemed no more put out by the little man's recriminations than he would have been by the prick of one of his needles.

In a sudden burst of curiosity Angélique took a closer look at the skipper. Beneath his faded red woollen cap he had long, very dark hair. His features were nondescript and not very clearly delineated, and he had a long face. His complexion was manly, neither swarthy nor ruddy by nature, the kind of complexion found in men of European extraction, maintained by good health and lightly tanned by the sea breezes.

He looked forty, give or take a year or two. His eyes were dark, rather like mercury, beneath heavy lids that often dulled their brilliance, giving him a vacant, unintelligent look.

He chewed continuously a quid of tobacco, but when he spat into the sea he did so with an air of casual distinction.

Under his open-necked coarse linen shirt and his waistcoat with its horn buttons, his shoulders looked narrow but powerful. He wore trousers of drugget – a tough, extremely hard-wearing woollen cloth made for sailors – and the legs were cut off below the knees. His calves were like cables of plaited rope, and he did everything with his calves and his feet.

Angélique thought to herself she did not care for this man Merwin, and considered that Colin had not made a good choice in stopping this particular boat. But he probably had had no option anyway. Colin . . .

Gold Beard! She felt her heart tighten, a brief moment of shame, of fear. Their day at sea had been so full of varied impressions that her memory of Colin had begun to fade. Deep down, she felt a sense of relief that things had ended this way, but inasmuch as she now felt secure against her own weakness, the illogicality of her feminine nature caused her an occasional pang of regret, a vague sadness. Colin ... the depth of those blue eyes intoxicated by her presence, the strength of his primitive embrace. Something she knew, something which belonged to her alone. Her secret place. Why could one not love according to the dictates of one's heart and one's body? Why should the quality and strength of one's love depend on so difficult a choice? As if the dispersal of feelings and the gift of oneself condemned one never to know them in their fullest intensity. Was it the truth, or was it a mere illusion, left over from her early teaching, that made faithfulness to her husband the foremost of all the obligations of honour for a woman. Was she not burdening herself with pointless constraints? If she had given in to Colin, what a delectable moment she would have enjoyed ... and Joffrey would never have known anything about it.

She felt herself grow red at her own thoughts and felt humiliated by the mere fact that she had formed them within her.

Impatiently, she shook her head in the wind.

She must forget ... forget at all costs.

Mackworth Island was fading into the distance and looked more than ever like a crown of brilliant jewels in the mint-green dusk.

'Look! Look! I can see the White Hat,' shouted little Sammy.

The Old Whitehead was an enormous granite dome that crowned little Cushing Island, rising fully 150 feet above the sheltered entrance to Portland Harbour.

The fresh waters from inland, endlessly churned up with the ocean brine at their point of contact, formed a soapy lather that was tossed into the wind by the everlasting ebb and flow of the tides and spattered in fringes of white foam across the grey granite brow of the rock, lending it, as they dried out, the appearance of a huge hat or the head of an old man with white locks, according to the prevailing light.

On drawing nearer, it was possible to differentiate between the snowy cover of foam and the equally thick deposits left by seabirds nesting or perching on every available rock face. And it was through a kind of white blizzard that they made their approach, discovering the island with its teeming life beneath this downy plumage.

Here one could truly say that in these last days of June – a June bright with intense, short-lived blooms – every beach was swarming with Puritans and with seals, while above them the birds wheeled, joyously, and that anyone attempting to disembark among the skuas, seagulls, terns, and seamews, anyone trying to set his foot down on a rock white with foam or feathers might equally well bump into a waddling seal or a grave Puritan dominie draped in a Genevese cape, both equally solemn, severe and indignant at finding themselves in such company, but equally determined to make the best of a bad job. Eggs were trampled on in their nests, piles of clams, scallops, lobsters, crabs, oysters and mussels, lying beside the fires on a carpet of seaweed were trodden underfoot, and to be heard one had to have a voice more shrill than those of the assembled birds of the sea.

'Don't come here! Don't come here,' cried the refugees as they saw the boat approaching the shore. 'We have no food and there are too many of us already. There will soon not be enough shell-fish for everyone and we have too few guns and too little ammunition!'

Merwin went about some distance from the shore, and little Sammy Stoughton cupped his hands round his mouth:

'There are no end of Indians over on Mackworth Island,' he cried in his thin childish voice that carried across the roar of the surf and the shrieking of the birds. 'Mind they don't come and kill you all . . .'

'Where do you come from, laddie?'

'From Brunswick-Falls, on the frontier.'

'What has happened up there?'

'They are all dead,' the little boy called back in his thin voice, and the words floated away like the notes of a flute.

The tide was high and the boat was able to sail a considerable distance up the bay where landings were made, but Merwin, faced with a volley of protest from the first occupants of the island, made no attempt to land. Once again he was content to examine everything about him curiously and attentively.

A fat woman with her skirts hitched up high, searching among crevices in the rock for lobsters, hailed him as he passed.

'Are you from the coast?'

'No, I come from New York.'

'And where are you making for?'

He pointed with his chin towards the north.

'Gouldsboro.'

'I know that place,' said someone, 'that's at the mouth of Frenchman Bay. You will get yourselves scalped by the French and their savages . . .'

Jack Merwin grasped the tiller again and steered the ship towards the mouth of the little harbour, but as he rounded a rocky point, another woman rushed towards him gesticulating, dragging behind her a girl with a small bundle of possessions.

'Take her with you,' the woman shouted, 'she has no family left, but I know she has an uncle up there somewhere near Frenchman Bay, on Matinicus Island, or on Long Island this side of Mount Desert, I'm not sure which. Take her with you . . .'

The woman gave the girl a shove and the bewildered child leapt into the boat just as a wave carried it out to sea.

'Old fool!' Merwin exclaimed, roused at last, 'what do you take me for, a custodian of orphans? I've better things to do than to worry about these Bible-bangers, the Devil take the lot of you!'

'You talk like a heathen,' retorted the woman from the end of her rock, 'and you have a Devonshire accent too. Belphegor gave you a doubly hard heart at the hour of your birth . . . But take the child to safety, or your evil deeds will choke you, however far away you may be, that I wager.'

Merwin, whose anger had made him rise to his feet, seized the tiller again and only just managed to avoid a sharp rock projecting from the water.

'Old fool!' he growled again, 'if they have Hell on their side what are they waiting for to conquer the whole world?'

'The woman is right, your words . . .' began the Reverend Thomas, but the boat shipped a wave and interrupted the argument by soaking them all, whereupon Merwin set the boy to work bailing out.

The sea was growing rough and the vessel plunged deeper and deeper between the waves. Merwin had to concentrate so hard on handling it that it was out of the question to return to White Hat Island to put the orphan girl ashore. A pearl-grey and pink mist heralded the evening, one of those long-drawn-out June twilights that would hang over the sea. It was essential to find a haven for the night. Fortunately Merwin seemed to know the locality and sailed along the coasts of Peak Island, the next in the series, then Long Island, next to which came Chebeague

Island. Halfway along the eastern coast of Long Island he turned his boat in towards a shingly beach, in an area that seemed less thickly populated. He sprang down into the water and made fast the boat in a rocky cleft, then made for dry land, leaving the ladies to get ashore as best they could. This they did without worrying about getting their feet wet, for, after long hours of sitting and standing still, it was delightful to paddle in the cold water and stroll along the sands. The girl from Cushing Island, whose name was Esther Holby, was telling her tale of woe to Miss Pidgeon, while Mr Willoughby, the bear, emerging from his shelter, made his way up the beach, pointing his nose towards the smell of the woodlands. Angélique saw that he was a huge, slow, gentle creature. He went off to forage among the tree roots, although Elias Kempton called him back from time to time to avoid alarming other people in the area.

As Angélique listened to young Esther she began to feel considerable respect for the poor child. Suddenly thrown into the midst of strangers among whom she had discovered a French Papist and ... a bear, she had shown not the slightest dismay but had accepted her situation with considerable dignity. When disaster befalls the English they do not jabber about it as the French so often do. Rather it is as if a stone had been dropped into a deep well, whose surface is even stiller than before.

As Angélique listened to Esther telling how she had seen her father, her mother and her brothers scalped by the Indians and her little sister taken away into captivity, she felt like wringing her hands and weeping for the child.

Merwin came back carrying armfuls of branches and lit a fire. Then he filled a cast-iron pot with water, threw in a piece of salted pork and set it to boil. His movements were neat, those of a tidy man, accustomed to living alone. With astonishing rapidity the tide went out, uncovering an expanse of land brown with seaweed and glistening with innumerable tiny pools as far as the eye could see.

Little English children came out of the woods and began to look for sea-shells among the exposed rocks.

Dusk was falling behind the black trees and both sky and sea took on the hue of a ripe orange that grew gradually darker and darker until it had been transformed into a brilliant pink glow that seemed as if it would never fade. The children leapt from rock to rock humming a refrain then, pleased with their gatherings, they came over and held out their baskets to the newcomers. Merwin bought two pints of scallops and clams from them, and Angélique asked them to sing the refrain she had heard them humming before, which, as a little girl born on the island told her, was a song the shellfish liked. Then their fresh, rhythmical voices rose up, giving the lie to threatening misfortunes. Among them were many refugees from the coast, delighted by this escapade into the Bay, far from the toils of farm work or long hours spent in study at the meeting house, and they were by no means backward in stressing and proclaiming with conviction:

'Clams is physic the whole year through, come eat my clams, bid the doctors adieu.'

To thank them for being so obliging, the pedlar called his bear and, to the great astonishment of the children, the animal stood up on its hind legs and made them a deep bow, then, on being asked to choose the prettiest little girls or the most impish, or the most pugnacious of the boys, he complied, appearing to think the matter over, to hesitate, and finally placed before the chosen person a cloth flower, a trinket, or a coin.

Soon quite a crowd had gathered around the strangers' fire, and Elias Kempton, seeing an athletic-looking man with muscular arms among the spectators, asked him if he would care to measure his strength against the bear. It was a good clean fight: the man was allowed to use his fists and Mr Willoughby undertook not to use his claws. With the skill of a born actor the bear pretended several times to stagger beneath the man's blows, then, just as the fellow was beginning to think the victory was his, the animal knocked him flying with a mere flick of his paw . . .

After much laughter and applause, the pastor led them all in prayer and the gathering broke up.

CHAPTER FORTY-TWO

ANGELIQUE was unable to sleep, for the night was cold and she could not get warm, even by sitting close to the fire. The others had wrapped themselves up, some in coats, some in cloaks or blankets, and the pedlar and Mr Willoughby were snoring in unison clasped in one another's arms. Angélique envied the little man from Connecticut, who must have found his rustic friend's fur warm and cosy.

Henceforth she must resolve that wherever she was, she would never go to sleep without having three things to hand – her coat, her pistols and her shoes, and that her very first move, even before opening her eyes, would be to seize these indispensable objects; and only after this would she concern herself with what was going on about her, whether it was a pirate raid or anything else. Because she had not reacted quickly enough, the night had caught her with half-naked arms in her fine frieze bodice, and the cold chilled her to the marrow although the air was so dry it almost cracked.

She got up and began to stroll along the beach. The air was crystal-clear and vibrant, and the sleeping island breathed a harmonious plaint in deep, singing intakes of breath, a mingling of wind, murmuring voices, the sound of human breathing, the clamour of seals and the roaring of the surf . . .

As she moved away from the camp where Jack Merwin's horn lantern cast a yellow glow that served as a landmark, Angélique made her way towards another glow she had glimpsed through the trees, that lighted a larger, neighbouring beach. She had been told that the island boasted a 'singing beach' which could be heard when the wind blew from a certain quarter when it sounded like a sweet melody or the footsteps of an army on the march . . . Was this what she heard, a hallucination of souls in torment, or the approach of Indian canoes pursuing their prey through the maze of islands? . . .

The light she saw was not the fatal decoy she had imagined, but only the brilliance of the long June night, so slow to die, as it stretched out over the earth its green, phosphorescent awning . . .

A colony of sealions lay along the beach, and the big bulls, called the masters of the beaches, stood out here and there, dark monolithic creatures, gazing out towards the shimmering sea, watching heaven knows what, while the smaller and blacker glistening females lay coiled around them . . . They were a peaceful people, full of grave innocence, troubled by the comings and goings of human beings in these their private domains where they had ruled for so long, and she caught herself looking at them with a kind of tender pity. So as not to disturb them, Angélique made her way along the edge of the wood and the big bulls turned their thick, moustachioed heads towards her. During the previous century a traveller had described the seals with some surprise: 'Their heads are like those of dogs, but without any ears, and their coats are the colour of the brown homespun worn by mendicant hermits, like the habit of our Minim Friars.'

Angélique had read this when she was a child and had dreamed of sailing to America ... and now, here she was, on this godforsaken American shore, a woman who had reached her middle years, no longer the dreamy, excitable child from the old château of Monteloup, and yet she felt as if little had changed within her. 'Our characters are formed in the cradle ... We can only change by disowning ourselves ...'

What exactly was meant by disowning oneself? Now, Joffrey had never disowned himself ...

She crossed her arms over her breast and rubbed her shoulders and forearms to warm herself up. Only last night she had been aboard Gold Beard's ship and Colin had taken her in his arms. She shivered even more at the memory of it ... But all that had already become just a rather disturbing dream which she must endeavour to forget, to bury, to efface.

At the far end of the beach lay the skeleton of a whale that had been washed ashore, a giant, macabre frame of a translucid, snowy whiteness, in the luminous night – a forest of bones with a pearly sheen; and through its arching vaults, as if marked out in chalk against the night sky, she could see stars trembling on the horizon.

Angélique, startled, shuddered still more violently.

Then a woman appeared and came towards her, pale and white in the milky brightness.

'Thou art cold, sister,' she said in a gentle voice. 'Here, please, take my coat. Thou canst return it at sunrise.'

Unaccustomed to this solemn use of the familiar form of address which she had not had occasion to hear the English use except when addressing themselves to God, Angélique looked at the woman without being quite sure that she had before her a living person.

'But what about you, Madame, will you not suffer from the cold?'

'I shall share my husband's coat,' the woman replied with an almost celestial smile. Then, laying a hand on Angélique's brow, she added:

'God bless thee!'

When Angélique got back, she saw that Jack Merwin was seated on a rocky promontory as if keeping a lookout.

As she reached the encampment, more comfortable now

under the charitable stranger's cloak, she stopped a few paces away to look at him.

The man intrigued her more and more. That morning, when she had seen him for the first time, she had taken him for a rough, common sailor, but here, considering him in meditative posture, it became apparent to her that he must be one of those exceptional natures, that often find refuge and concealment on distant seas. His immobility was so complete – he was not even chewing his everlasting quid of tobacco – that an almost disturbing quality of solitude emanated from him, and appeared to burn within him like a fierce, brilliant flame.

He must be some erstwhile pirate, she thought, possibly even a man of noble birth? A man weary of his crimes, who seeks to forget and be forgotten by dangerous companions of yore . . . Is it for them he is on the watch, them he fears, them he seeks, pursued himself by remorse or fear? Or is he the youngest son of some great impoverished English family who thought that a life of adventure would make him a prince. And, weary of the company he found on ship board, gave everything up to return to the solitude of the sea . . .

He must also have been sadly crossed in love, for I sense that he loathes women . . .

The curve of the man's shoulders seemed as if turned to stone. It was as if his soul had left his body like an empty envelope to wander abroad. What could he hear, what was he discovering in the secret moments of his absence? Was it the Indian canoes he saw coming towards him across the luminous sea?

It was a strange night, full of undefined dangers, tender, poetic spells, and possibly evil incantations too.

Angélique felt a desire to snatch the man from his strange lethargy which she found almost frightening.

'What a lovely night, is it not, Mr Merwin?' she said in a loud voice. 'A night that invites meditation, do you not find?'

Was he asleep? His eyes were wide open, but his pupils seemed blank and empty, and yet after a few seconds he turned his head towards her.

'The beauty of this land fascinates me,' Angélique went on, driven by an impulse of which she was no longer in control, in order to attempt to establish some sort of communication with him. 'One can breathe freely here . . . I don't know how to explain it . . . It is something unknown, gone for ever from Europe, to such an extent that the very idea seems alien, and one only discovers it on reaching these shores . . . A mysterious and exciting thing that I can only call ... the very essence of liberty ...'

She was thinking aloud, aware of the fact that the thoughts she was trying to put into words were complicated and obscure, and that as she tried to express them in her still hesitant English, it was highly likely that the sailor would not understand a thing. So she was almost surprised to see that on the contrary she had managed to draw him away from his dreams.

She saw his features quiver, his eyes flash, then his face relaxed and set in a sardonic, scornful smile, while his dark eyes threw her a piercing glance of detestation, almost of hatred ...

'How can you dare to utter such words, to make such judgements?' he asked in his drawling voice which he seemed to delight in making still more slurring and vulgar.

'How can you talk of liberty, you, a woman?'

And he gave a scornful laugh. And behind him she thought she could see the glow of a sneering, enemy face, the face of some superior being, who despised and rejected her ... A demon! That was what lay hidden beneath this strange exterior, a demon on the prowl amongst men ...

She stepped back, overcome by a chill sense of numbness, and began to walk away from him.

He called her back peremptorily.

'Wait a minute,' he cried. 'Where did you go just then?'

'I went for a short walk because I was cold.'

'Well, don't go off again for any more midnight revels in the forest, because I intend to leave at dawn and shall wait for no one.'

'What a coarse brute!' said Angélique to herself as she lay down beside the fire.

That's all he was, just a coarse beast. A coarse brute in an Anglo-Saxon mould. 'A land which has given birth to a race of swashbuckling ruffians. The most tiresome barbarians in the world ...'

She wrapped herself in the cloak lent to her by the woman with the glistening eyes. They are all a bit mad, these English!

'You speak of liberty! You, a woman! ... You a woman!'

She could hear his contemptuous voice.

'You ... a woman ... you ... a woman.'

And in spite of herself, in the weary hours of the night, she felt dreadfully alone, overwhelmed by forces that nothing could ever overcome. How foolish of her to think that she could attack them!

Fortunately there was one man on earth whose companion she was and who loved her . . .

'Joffrey, my love,' she sighed.

Then she fell asleep.

CHAPTER FORTY-THREE

WHEN SHE AWOKE Angélique saw that a thick fog had enveloped everything and that it must already be fairly late, since the sun, which could just be made out through the mist, already seemed high in the sky.

Jack Merwin had once again become to all intents and purposes an ordinary, grumpy man and was busy stowing a number of kegs of drinking water away on his boat. This was a good sign, for it showed that the skipper intended to make a long trip without intermediate calls and would probably resist the temptation to go on pottering about among the islands. He had also somehow managed to unearth half a large, circular cheese and some wheaten bread, so his passengers ran no risk of dying of starvation *en route*.

'The fog has delayed our departure,' Miss Pidgeon explained, 'so we let you sleep on, my dear!'

'I must find the kind woman who lent me her cloak,' Angélique replied.

But Jack Merwin suddenly urged them all aboard at once.

'How in the world do you expect to navigate in this pea-soup?' Kempton protested. 'It will be the death of us.'

'Death! You are crazy,' wailed Adhemar, who was beginning to understand more and more English. 'Oh! Madame, do stop him putting out to sea. Last night I had a terrible dream, and I feel sure that it is about to come true.'

Adhemar was a simple-minded man, and in France, in the provinces, it was commonly believed that the simple minded have the gift of second sight.

'What was it you dreamt, my poor boy?'

'You were drowned, Madame, and I could see you right at the bottom of the sea where everything is green like a Venetian lamp, with your hair streaming out behind you like seaweed.'

'Oh! Stop it for goodness sake!' cried Angélique. 'You can never open your mouth without spreading alarm all round you.

And in any case you ought to be pleased to see me drowned since you take me for a She-Devil.'

'Madame, don't say things like that,' Adhemar stammered, crossing himself several times.

The pastor gave him a sidelong glance and pinched his lips. He had had more than his fill of this Papist company, to which had now been added the presence of Merwin, obviously a godless and irreligious man. He was half minded to remain on Long Island but Miss Pidgeon dissuaded him by saying that if he wished to be reunited with what was left of his flock from Brunswick-Falls he must go on to Gouldsboro.

'Come along now, get aboard,' Merwin growled, adding an expression in English unfamiliar to Angélique but which seemed to imply something halfway between 'you spineless lot', and 'you good-for-nothings'.

But in spite of all his urging no one seemed in a hurry.

'You have the cloak of a Quaker woman there!' the Reverend Patridge suddenly remarked, pointing to the garment Angélique was attempting to hand to him. 'You did not speak to a member of that infamous sect, did you? You wretched woman! That could put the salvation of your soul in great danger. You are right, Miss Pidgeon. It would not be right to remain in a place where there is a risk of meeting people of that ilk – although I thought that New England had been cleared of them all, but I suppose we shall have to hang a few more to deter the others.'

'But I don't see why people should be hanged whose only crime is to lend their cloaks to those who are feeling the cold,' Angélique protested.

'But the Quakers represent a serious threat to public order,' the pastor replied.

'Yes,' chimed in Miss Pidgeon, 'they refuse to raise their hats even to the King himself, and they call him brother, and say "thou" and "thee" to him. They claim they are in direct communication with God.'

'Irreverence personified,' the pastor shouted.

'They refuse to pay tithes to the churches . . .'

'There must be no tampering with doctrine,' the pastor went on, and he was about to embark on a long sermon when Jack Merwin exploded. First he swore roundly two or three times, calling them bloody fools, an effective phrase, for Miss Pidgeon and young Esther gave shrieks of horror and covered their ears.

'Blasphemer!' roared the pastor.

'Shut up, you contemptible dolt,' said Merwin with genuine

hatred in the expression of his bitter mouth; 'you are incapable of opening your mouth without causing trouble and confusion.'

'And what about you, unhappy wretch? I realized from the start that you were a godless man, a son of Lucifer, of him who dares to look his God in the face and say: I am your equal!'

'It would be better if an ignorant fool like you did not take it upon himself to judge his fellow men; you're more than likely to make some sorry mistakes.'

The Reverend Thomas could not tolerate it that a common sailor, as like as not from some convict colony, should speak to him in such a tone of voice and employ such language in front of weak women whose conduct largely depended on the confidence they felt in their pastor. To tolerate being thrown in this humiliating fashion from his pedestal meant running the risk of plunging simple, faithful souls into doubt. Before devoting himself to the study of theology, Thomas Patridge had been an energetic young man and a keen boxer. He had kept his strength, and now that he had recovered from his wound he was still a formidable opponent. He grabbed Merwin by the collar of his shirt and would have crushed his face with a terrible punch had not the latter, also a nimble fighter, freed himself with a sharp blow with the edge of his hand across the wrist that held him. The pastor let out a roar and his face went purple.

Angélique threw herself between the two men.

'I beg you,' she said with all the authority at her command, 'I beg you, gentlemen; you are losing your wits.'

She held them back forcibly, with one hand on each of their muscular frames, and could feel their seething anger ready to explode like the rumblings of an active volcano, but her imperious glance prevailed over their feelings and she succeeded in holding them apart.

'Pastor! Pastor!' she begged, 'try to forgive a man who has not received the same spiritual benefits as yourself. Do not forget that you represent a God who condemns violence . . .'

The pastor had become ashen with the effort he was making to control himself and as a result of his pain, for Jack Merwin's blow had almost broken his wrist.

Jack Merwin had also grown waxen, a vein at his temple throbbed violently and his eyes looked even more steely and inscrutable.

Beneath her fingers Angélique could feel Jack Merwin's heart thudding irregularly, and at that moment he once again seemed human and vulnerable.

'And you are not sensible either,' she said to him, as if scolding a child. 'It is not the act of a good Christian to insult someone invested with ecclesiastical authority. And furthermore, this minister is wounded; only a few days go he was half scalped by the Indians.'

The sailor's eyes made it clear that he thought it would have been a good thing if they had finished the job.

It was the Reverend Thomas who gave in first.

'I defer to you because you so wish it, my lady, although you are a Frenchwoman and a member of a scandalous religion, Babylonian and fanatical. I bow to you because you have shown yourself to be our friend. But as for him . . .'

'He too . . . he too has shown himself to be your friend. He has taken us all on board his boat and is taking us to Gouldsboro, where we shall be safe and out of danger at last.'

She maintained her hand on Jack Merwin's chest until she felt his heartbeat grow calmer and he stepped back, breaking away, once more master of himself.

Once the quarrel was over everyone took his place in the boat, including Mr Willoughby. As they left the harbour the fog was lifting and they saw a great crowd of people on the beach waving them goodbye, including the Quakers in their round hats and big white coifs standing apart from the others as if plague ridden, but no less cheerful and demonstrative.

As they sailed past them Angélique shouted a message about the cloak which she had left with a helpful woman on another beach.

Then they passed the tip of Clipp Island and then Jewell Island. The latter was the farthest out to sea in Casco Bay, and consequently farthest removed from any possible attack by the Indians, but the people were already at work organizing its defences with a speed that did credit to the local leader, Captain Joseph Donnel.

Settlers from Boston, Freeport and Portland whom he had fetched himself with his little fleet, were working night and day, men and women, on the fortifications, and after less than a week it was already a small fort with crenellated ramparts rising above the one point on the island where boats could land. Lime kilns had been set up to make mortar from shells for packing the interstices between the planks and beams, while another group was busy sowing wheat and cultivating the soil against the possibility of a long siege. The children had been sorted out as they landed, all those old enough to handle a knife, whether boys or girls, being dispatched to help with the heavy work of clearing land or fishing, while the little ones, under the supervision of a few of the women, disported themselves, pink and naked, in the icy sea among the seals and porpoises.

This information was obtained by the occupants of Jack Merwin's boat along with a final basket of shellfish before they headed for the open sea.

Then they were out on the ocean, all blue, white and speckled with gold, and nothing but the occasional sail glimpsed here and there.

Angélique rejoiced at the open horizon. The islands had disappeared. They continued to head east-north-east, every puff of wind in the sails carrying them farther from the imperilled coast and closer to Gouldsboro.

The day passed quickly, stories from the pedlar alternating with Bible readings by the pastor. During these readings Angélique watched Merwin out of the corner of her eye, but the skipper of the *White Bird* – for such was the boat's name –had resumed his expression of disdain and chewed away nonchalantly at his plug of tobacco, contemptuously spitting out jets of brown saliva whose lengthy trajectory was greatly admired by Sammy and the little Negro boy, Timothy.

There was always something going on to amuse the passengers. For a long time a white dolphin followed the boat; it was as big as an ox and as lithe as a grass snake, and kept falling back then racing forward at top speed, greatly amused by the children's shouts and appearing to give them a mischievous glance each time from its piggy little eyes.

Towards the middle of the afternoon Monhegan Island hove into sight. This is an isolated island, a considerable distance out to sea, south of the Damariscotta archipelago and the coast of Pemaquid. It is also known as Sea Island because it stands alone, like a single precious stone, its pink and blue cliffs wearing like a diadem its forests with their countless varieties of wild flowers. It is also called Wolf Island, for at one time it had abounded in the animals, which also explains why it is called the Island of the Mohicans, for that is the name of a great Indian tribe that took the wolf as its emblem.

But, at the time with which we are concerned, there were no wolves left on the island, or Mohicans either for that matter.

The island was now inhabited by a considerable number of Basques, Bretons and Normans, Swedes and Dutchmen, Spaniards and Portuguese, Englishmen and Scots, and flotillas of ships from the whole world over made their way into its narrow fiord, opposite the granite hump of Ramana Isle.

As the island came more clearly into sight the passengers noticed a huge black cloud hanging over it, a cloud that seemed even darker towards the west, and they fell silent, their hearts struck with fear.

The dark cloud seemed to be standing still, sometimes assuming the shape of a flat mushroom with pointed extremities, then suddenly reforming again.

'Is that smoke?' murmured Angélique.

Even Merwin for once seemed intrigued, but he said nothing. Young Esther, who had been brought up on the sea coast, was the first to explain the mystery. The cloud consisted of birds, she said, which had come together from every direction and were wheeling over Monhegan, no doubt attracted by some particular choice prey.

She was not wrong, for as they drew nearer, they began to hear the piercing cries of thousands of wheeling birds.

Later they learned that a Basque ship had harpooned a whale in the waters off Monhegan and towed it to the island where the crew was loading the oil into barrels.

CHAPTER FORTY-FOUR

Skilfully Merwin steered the *White Bird* among the jagged tips of rocks just breaking the surface of the water, and guided her smoothly up a narrow passage that scarcely merited the name of creek but which ended in a tiny sandy beach that sloped up towards the forest.

He leapt waist deep into the water and pulled the boat in until he felt its keel brush the sand. Then he climbed on to the nearest rocks in order to make her fast, and, making haste himself, he signalled to his passengers to leave the boat.

'Look lively! Don't hang about here, get up into the forest,' he called to them.

He knew the dangers of lingering on the east coast of Monhegan Island. Obediently they made haste at the sound of his voice and ran up the beach, carrying their bags and the baskets containing the remains of their meal.

'Quicker! Quicker!' cried Merwin, although it was not clear why.

It was at that moment that the catastrophe occurred.

The ground swell that comes crashing up the steep cliffs of the Black Head and the White Head on the eastern shores of Monhegan Island is a devastating thing.

It steals up on you treacherously and never from the expected direction, hurls itself upon you, then straight away draws back, clutching its prey.

It began with a tall, snowy spout of water that sprang up to the right almost in front of the group of women and children, like a geyser suddenly gushing from the ground to bar their way. The water showered down over them and as they were still looking to the right another wave crept up silently behind them, round backed, huge and glistening, and engulfed them all. They fell to their knees pell-mell, were dragged down the beach with the ebb, then, suddenly released, most of them promptly got to their feet again, and clinging to the rocks, gathered their floating possessions together, and hastened once more up the beach. Some were even laughing at the unexpected soaking, but Angélique turned and glimpsed little Sammy's head bobbing up and down in the foaming waters at the mouth of the inlet. Without a moment's hesitation she ran along the promontory and plunged into the water just as the retreating tide brought the child towards her. She met him halfway and seized him.

Then the sea swept them away in a demented dance. Looking towards the coast Angélique could see at the far end of the rocky promontory – the point she had just left – the tall figure of Merwin, who had quickly made his way to exactly the right spot. In a frenzied gallop the sea hurled them back towards him.

'Catch him!' Angélique shouted, throwing the little English boy in Merwin's direction.

He caught the boy literally in mid air. For her part, Angélique had tried to grasp a rock but the pull of the sea had been so swift and irresistible that once more she found herself carried out to sea in the frothy layer of intertwining trails of foam. The troughs of the waves sucked her down as if a hole had suddenly gaped beneath her, then all of a sudden she would find herself at the top of a foaming crest that was so high that she thought that she was going to be hurled like a cannon ball at a point halfway up the cliffside. Her skirt, now saturated with water, was beginning to weigh her down like lead and she found she could no longer move her legs to keep herself on the surface. Then once again, with a convulsive lurch from the depths of the abyss, the waves brought her back towards the land. Hurled towards the promontory where Jack Merwin was standing she saw him draw nearer at a fantastic speed. He was now alone at the extreme point of the peninsula, having placed the rescued child in a safe spot.

He was alone, gigantic and sombre in the wind that tossed his long black hair, sombre against the bright sky flecked with wisps of white foam, and his red woollen cap stood out like an approaching beacon. She held out her hand towards him, ready to grasp his, but, contrary to all her expectations, instead of moving, he remained motionless with crossed arms.

He did not offer her his hand. Angélique's fingers clutched at the empty air, scraped along the craggy rocks, too weak to get a grip on them, and as the monstrous suction of the waves drew her back once more, she gave a cry. It was the cry of a child, a cry of frustration and astonishment ... 'If only he had held out his hand to me that time, I could have made it ... *He did not hold out his hand to me.*'

Saltwater filled her mouth and she began to choke. Summoning all her strength she fought to keep calm in order to remain afloat and let herself be carried by the current which sooner or later would bear her back to the shore. Her only hope lay in those swirling waters that plunged ceaselessly into the caves at the foot of the cliffs, whose walls thundered with the pounding and made the inlet echo with a sound like gunfire.

A black wave engulfed her, rolling her over and over in a furious torrent, and Jack Merwin's eyes suddenly appeared again, this time close beside her.

Then she understood.

He had not come there to save her, but to see her die.

For he wished her dead.

This resolution was written all over his inscrutable face with its two burning eyes fixed on a world beyond this, seeming to stare right through her, through that poor battered, bruised female body, that the sea sought to rend to pieces, and which was already nothing more to him than a mere piece of flotsam.

As she discovered him to be thus in one last crazy flash, he seemed even more demoniacal than on the previous night, and a cry of agony rose from her tortured depths.

'Joffrey! Joffrey!'

Her cry was one of despair. Deep down inside her a voice called 'Joffrey! Help! Help! The demons are trying to kill me . . . They are here! . . .'

Then in a flash of lucidity, she added:

'Dirty swine of an Englishman! . . . I should have been on my guard against him.' You a woman he had said, and here he was, delighting in watching her die, a woman!

She began to struggle violently as panic gained the upper hand, and only sank farther and farther. Suddenly she felt as if something had seized her from below and was dragging her down to the bottom. She gave a kick to reach the surface again, and realized with horror that her skirt was caught between two rocks, while the water rushed back and forth over her, tossing her this way and that, but still held fast in the trap. Her temples were drumming as if they would burst, and every time she struggled madly to escape from the grip of the rock she was brought up short, and could not reach the air. The legendary monster that lurked in caves by the sea now held her in its claws, kept her close to its den, held her prisoner as she spun round under the blue-green water, among the seaweed that bound her hand and foot.

She could hold on no longer. She was about to open her mouth to breathe, to breathe in death.

Then a sudden jerk freed her. Her skirt tore, and she could see the light of day once more. But she was exhausted and scarcely managed to take a breath before disappearing once more.

The bitter spittle of the waves rolled over her, pummelled her, devoured her, crushed and powerless.

'No! No! I don't want to die! . . .' she cried, despairingly within herself, 'I don't want to drown . . . it is too horrible. Joffrey, Joffrey, I must see you again . . . I don't want to remain alone, far from you, at the bottom of the sea . . .'

Had not Adhemar seen her in a dream that night, tossing at the bottom of the sea, deep in the green gulf, with her hair trailing behind her like seaweed . . . alone . . . alone . . . gone to sleep for ever . . .

Something struck her on the temple. It was like a nail brutally hammered into her head. A rock she had struck, whose blow had awakened her, thrust her for a brief moment up to the surface again.

A dazzling vision in the sunshine, and still that same motionless standing form erect over her – which suddenly came to life, stooped, and dived.

38

A mirage!
She was sinking, sinking, vanishing for ever.

CHAPTER FORTY-FIVE

SOMEONE WAS dragging her up the beach by her hair. Angélique felt her body gradually liberated from the viscosity of the sea, become as heavy as lead and begin to score a deep furrow through the pebbles of the beach. She was covered in grazes, bleeding and inert, while Jack Merwin, likewise exhausted, hauled her up the beach as he would have hauled a boat or a dead animal.

He only came to a stop when he had passed the last band of seaweed right up beside the trees, where the sea could no longer reach them. Then he too fell to the ground beside her, and in her half-conscious state she could hear his breath wheezing like the bellows of a forge.

It had been a terrible struggle, in which she had clung convulsively to him, and he had had to strike her in order to stun her, and in which the sea, twenty times over, had borne them so far from the shore that it seemed no more than a phantom shadow, unattainable. They had finally come ashore some considerable distance from their point of departure.

Angélique's lungs seemed to be on fire, and it was in vain that she tried to breathe, for with every movement she had the impression that her chest would burst.

She tried to raise herself on her hands and knees like a dying animal making a last supreme effort to get to its feet. Groping blindly, she clung to the man beside her, as a wave of nausea swept over her and she began to vomit uncontrollably. The salty flood seemed to corrode her throat as it came up, and she collapsed on her side.

Jack Merwin stood up. For a moment he had been overcome with exhaustion, but now he was once more master of himself. He threw off his filthy waistcoat and cast it aside, then removed his shirt and wrung it out, before doing the same to his red cap, which he put back on his head, and hung the twisted shirt round his neck.

Then bending down towards Angélique, he grasped her

upper arm with one hand, forcing her first to her knees, then to her feet.

'Go on! Walk! Go on!'

He hustled her along, now pushing her before him, now pulling her along, and his voice sounded different, full of contained anger but also a new note of emotional turmoil. She managed to take a few steps, but was unable to lift her feet from the ground without a superhuman effort. The world was spinning, giving way beneath her, and she fell back face downwards in the sand which stuck to her cheeks.

'Joffrey! Joffrey! ... "They" are trying to kill me. "They" have always wanted to kill me.'

Merwin tried to get her on her feet again, but she kept falling down. She was crying and vomiting, and her throat and the back of her nose hurt so much that she thought she could feel them bleeding. She was shivering and her teeth were chattering, and she kept wiping her face unconsciously as she sobbed 'Leave me alone ... Leave me to die ... I don't mind dying here ... but not in the sea ... I didn't want to drown, it's too ghastly.'

Jack Merwin had walked on without waiting for her, then he turned round with a look of exasperation at seeing her once more lying on the ground, and retraced his steps. He seemed to resign himself to the situation and, reaching a decision, took hold of her once more; but this time he stretched her out full length, face downwards, with arms extended and head turned to one side.

Then taking his knife from his belt he slit open her dress right down the back, and tore away the saturated cloth sticking to her ice-cold flesh, cloth that had already been torn to ribbons against the rocks. He laid her bare to the small of her back.

Then he placed his two hands at the base of her ribs and began to press down on them rhythmically, which immediately made her feel better. Her breathing, assisted by these regular movements, grew deeper and less disordered and she was able to take in some air.

Then he began to massage her back vigorously with the palm of his hand, and bit by bit the freezing blood in Angélique's veins began to circulate again. The twisting pains inside her began to ease, her nerves calmed, her teeth stopped chattering uncontrollably, and a gentle warmth flooded through her as her thoughts floated, vaguely wandering but calm.

'This man is as evil as sin ... but his hands are good ... yes his hands are good ... How good it feels! What a blessing! Oh what a blessing it is to be alive!'

The world had stopped spinning and grown solid and sweet beneath her outstretched body.

'He will have all the skin off my back if he goes on like this ... Has he noticed the fleur-de-lis branded on my shoulder? I am frightened ... does it matter? He too may be a bandit, a gallows-bird ... supposing he betrayed me ... No! He's an Englishman. He probably doesn't even know what the fleur-de-lis means ...'

She was feeling much better, and sat up unaided.

'Thank you,' she murmured. 'I am sorry!'

'Everything all right?' Merwin asked briefly.

'Yes, more or less!'

But she had overestimated her strength for once again the black veil came down over her eyes, and she let her head fall on to Jack Merwin's shoulder. The shoulder was bone hard but had a gentle, reliable curve. A man's shoulder.

'How comfortable that feels,' she murmured in French.

Her mind was wandering; she became aware of her naked-ness and in an instinctive gesture of modesty she tried to cover her bosom with the remaining shreds of her bodice.

Merwin put one arm round her shoulders and his other hand under her knees and picked her up effortlessly in his arms. Angélique thought she had become a child again. Nothing more could harm her, and the roar of the sea grew fainter as he went striding off with her down a track through the woods. He could not have walked for long, but she was unaware of anything, for she must have fallen asleep. She did not lose consciousness but rather sank into a brief, deep sleep from which she awoke feel-ing completely rested, only a few minutes later. She found herself sitting on the ground leaning against a tree trunk, with her head resting on her knees, while above her Jack Merwin's authoritative voice was instructing young Esther to take off one of her petticoats and her chemise for Angélique to wear. The girl ran off behind a bush and came back shortly after-wards to hand over the two items of clothing to Angélique, who, in her turn, went off into the woods to change.

The English girl's skirt and chemise still retained some of the warmth of her body and made Angélique feel better. She rinsed the sticky sea water and sand from her hair in a nearby spring that gushed up from the moss and then made her way back to her companions. The worthy Elias Kempton had lighted a small fire to warm Sammy who was swathed in the pastor's coat, and they all stared wide-eyed at her, for they had thought they would never see her again.

'Sit close to Mr Willoughby, Mistress de Peyrac,' the pedlar insisted. 'Yes! Yes! You will see, he will keep you warm.'

'We must be on our way,' Merwin cut in. 'We shall be able to get help on the other side of the island.'

So they set off one behind the other through the pine trees, which were like pillars in a cathedral. The night was warm and dry and crackling with electric sparks. But was it night? ... A pale turquoise sky still shone through the trees.

'It's Midsummer night,' Adhemar said, 'the night when the sun never dies, and when the bracken blooms with a tiny rust-coloured magical flower that only lasts for a few hours. They do say that people who see this flower bloom never come back ... Let us hurry out of this wood. There is so much bracken here and night is falling ... Midsummer night ...'

Angélique walked on like a sleepwalker. She was half dead with sleepiness and the pit of her stomach still felt ice cold.

Merwin cast an occasional glance in her direction.

'How are you feeling?'

'Quite well,' she replied, 'but I think I would feel better if I could have a good swig of rum or something hot to drink.'

As they rounded a bend in the path, the village on the west side of the island came into view at last, caught in the light of the setting sun, and the clamour of the birds and the shouts of fishermen burst upon them, together with the stench of rotten fish and melting fat.

A farmhouse built of logs appeared on their left at the entry to the village.

Standing on the threshold, Jack Merwin called out to the occupants, but as no one replied, he and the others went inside without further ado. Taking for granted the sacrosanct laws of hospitality prevailing in these distant colonies of the New World, that authorized anyone lost or starving to treat any dwelling that Providence threw in his way in these deserted lands as his own, he went straight to the wooden dresser, took from it a blue and white china bowl and a pewter ladle, walked over to the hearth and lifted the lids of the various cooking pots.

From one of these he served a brimming, piping hot portion of clams and scallops, and from another he took three boiled potatoes, then poured some milk over the mixture from another pot that stood warming among the ashes.

'Eat that,' he said to Angélique, placing the bowl before her on the table, 'eat it quickly.'

Then he went on deftly handing out soup plates to all and sundry as if he had spent his whole life dispensing soup to the poor.

CHAPTER FORTY-SIX

In time to come Angélique was to make no secret of the fact that she had never tasted anything more delectable, more delicious, more comforting, than that shellfish soup which she ate in the poor farmhouse of some settler on Monhegan Island, after she had narrowly missed being drowned.

Thus it was that she made her acquaintance with the national dish of the region between Cape Cod and the northernmost point of the gulf of Saint Lawrence, taking in the Bay of Fundy and Nova Scotia. The French, Canadians and Acadians, call it *chaudrée*, the English *chowder*, that heavenly, nourishing soup which is a blend of all that is most delightful along those shores – the potato, that grows wild in America, health-giving shellfish from the fertile, motherly sea, and milk, delectable, delightful product of the Old World, a reminder of distant, grassy lands, a luxury in this new country, so hard to tame, that is surprised to see a few exiled cows as they graze, somewhat out of place, on the verge of the Indian forest lands . . .

All these things are to be found in that bountiful bowl with the delectable smell.

Add to this a juicy onion, a pinch of pepper or nutmeg, a few cubes of salt pork, and at the last minute, a knob of butter per portion . . .

It should have been round a clam chowder in a silver tureen – or a gold one, why not? – that the treaties should have been drawn up that decided the fate of this part of the world. Everyone would have been the gainer.

They ate hungrily and not a sound could be heard save sighs of contentment and the smacking of tongues.

'Hello there! Make yourself at home, you English,' said a voice in French, and they saw a big peasant woman standing on the threshold.

'Ho there! Whatever is that, gentle Jesus?'

'It's but a bear,' muttered Kempton as he lapped up the last drops of his soup.

'I can see that, you great oaf! But do I have to have a bear right in my very house? Has my house become a kennel? Am I supposed to offer him some soup too in one of my beautiful plates that my good mother brought all the way from the Limousin forty years back without breaking a single one?'

'Madame, are you French?' Angélique asked her in the same tongue. 'Is this an Acadian household by any chance?'

'Well, perhaps it is now, and perhaps it isn't. I couldn't tell you what we are exactly here in Monhegan ... I myself come from Port-Royal on the Acadian Peninsula where I landed at the age of five with Monsieur Pierre d'Aulnay's party of recruits, but that was ages ago. When I was twenty I married our neighbour, a Scot called MacGregor, and we settled together on Monhegan and have been here nigh on thirty-five years.'

Jack Merwin questioned her in English, asking her whether the Indians had tried to launch any attack on the island and whether there was any trouble in Penobscot Bay. She shook her head and replied in English which she regularly spoke, although with a strong French accent.

She told them that the Indians, Mohicans, Tarratines, Mic-Macs, and Etchemins from Penobscot and Dariscotta were still at peace. This time they had not unearthed the war hatchet, for the great French nobleman who ruled over Gouldsboro had managed to persuade all the white men in the Bay, and especially that little hothead Saint-Castine, not to have anything to do with that wicked campaign. Only last week her man, old Mac-Gregor, had gone off with his three sons to Popham Point to meet 'the great Lord of Gouldsboro' and together with all the white men from the area and the chief sagamores from the neighbouring lands they had made an alliance, exchanged promises, and smoked the peacepipe together. The Lord of Gouldsboro was strong and wealthy; he had his own fleet and money to burn. He had promised to protect anyone against their own governments who found himself in difficulties for having undertaken to keep the peace. And quite right too! People here had had just about enough of being made to dance like a lot of puppets in accordance with the whims of the Kings of France or England, who took good care not to set foot in the colonies themselves.

Angélique had grown red with emotion at the mention of the name of her husband, Count Peyrac. She plied the good lady with questions from which she learned that after Joffrey left the mouth of the Kennebec he had made his way back towards Gouldsboro. So there was every likelihood that she would find him there, if they reached it tomorrow, which seemed likely since the sea remained calm in spite of the equinoctial tides.

When she discovered who it was she had welcomed into her humble cottage – the great Lord of Gouldsboro's very own wife – Mrs MacGregor clasped her hands together in rapture, dropped a deep curtsy as her mother had taught her to do to nobility, and danced attendance on them all, speaking now in French and now in English according to whom she was addressing.

Angélique told of her mishap, how she had almost been drowned as they had landed on the island, and the woman revealed that this was an almost daily occurrence. Every family had more members drowned than alive; that was how it was!

'I'll fetch you some good clothes, Madame,' she concluded in a voice devoid of emotion.

'You wouldn't have a pair of breeches for the man who rescued me, would you? He is still soaking wet.'

'A pair of breeches? No, there's nothing like that here, my poor lady! My menfolk wear nothing but their big plaid wraps, tartans they call them; a Scot would not feel right unless he went about with a bare behind, saving your presence. But the assistant from the shop, Mr Winslow, our neighbour, who comes from Plymouth, should be able to help these gentlemen find what they want.'

And she sent the men off with the bear to her English neighbours, retaining only the women and children, among whom was the little black boy.

'A real little jack-in-the-box, popped straight up from Hell, is that kiddy there. But it's Midsummer night, isn't it? This is the night when all the brownies and hobgoblins come out ... Look! Look how light the sky is still ... At midnight the Basques will light their fires and dance.'

For people were gay on Monhegan, in spite of all the drownings. Furthermore the Basques from Bayonne had harpooned a whale two days previously.

After a desperate struggle during which the whale's tail had sent whole boats flying and one man had been killed, the catch had been brought in, under a screaming cloud of birds of prey. The whale, already cut into pink and white slices by the whalers' knives, still floated in the water between the anchored boat and a small, quiet sandy beach upon which three huge cauldrons had been set up. A fortune lay there bobbing up and down on the tide at Monhegan and it was pieces of gold that the sailors handled in their imaginations with the cubes of fat they threw into the cauldrons. Some of them were busy bringing up buckets full of spermaceti from huge cavities in the whale's head, a white oily substance used in the manufacture of the most expensive candles, while the whalebone would be used for the manufacture of clothes, feather tufts, plumes, bodices and fans . . .

The tongue, the choicest morsel, would be salted and served on princes' tables, while the blubber would provide broth for the poor during Lent. The bones would be transformed into beams, joists and fencing posts.

The great harpooner Hernani d'Astiguarra, who was also captain of the little 150-ton ship, swaggered, proud as a peacock, around the harbour leaning on his harpoon as an Indian leans on his lance. As soon as the first star began to tremble in the firmament and the contours of the forest loomed dark against the green sky, they would stop work and light great bonfires along the beach, for it was Midsummer night and they had to dance and leap over the fires.

Meanwhile Angélique had been negotiating with Mrs Mac-Gregor the purchase of a sealskin coat, quite enchanted by the velvety softness of the fur.

'I have nothing with which to pay you just at the moment but as soon as I reach Gouldsboro I will send you a purse containing twenty crowns and a small gift, the choice of which I will leave to you.'

'Listen,' said the old lady, 'we have all we need here and there's no need to go to all that trouble. They say you have the power of healing, and if you could get my grandson Alistair on his feet again, that would be payment enough. It would be a blessing for the child too.'

So they went to see young Alistair. Mrs MacGregor had had twelve children, and her surviving sons and daughters, who had all married on the island, made up a family of considerable size. In order to avoid jealousy between the national saints of the two Franco-Scottish families, the children had been given French and Scots names alternately. Thus a Leonard preceded an Ogilvey and an Alistair was followed by a gentle Janeton.

A few days earlier a strange thing had happened to young Alistair; as he ran across the rocks to escape the high tide, he had tried to leap across a crevice. This was no occasion to miss his footing as there was a sixty-foot drop below. He just managed to save himself from falling on landing on the other side, and since then a terrible pain prevented his putting his feet to the ground.

Angélique immediately saw that as the boy had gripped the rock face with his toes he had torn the main tendons under his arches. Coaxing them back into position was a painful business but after an hour of massage the boy placed a timid and incredulous foot on the flagstones again, delighted that it no longer hurt, then, going to the other extreme, said he thought he would be be able to dance the crossed sword dance that very evening, which Angélique told him firmly he was not to do. He must rest, so that the ligaments could unite. She called for some good woodchuck grease, which was something all self-respecting housewives always kept a pot or two of in stock, and after a final massage left the boy leaning on a stick. At least he would be able to attend the festivities.

A considerable crowd, draped in tartan, hooded and wrapped around in red and green or green and black – for there were two clans, the MacGregors and the MacDuffs – wearing blue berets with pompons, had watched the miracle. And intermingled with these bright costumes were the dark coats of the English traders and settlers. Their families were descendants of the first inhabitants of Plymouth in Cape Cod Bay – the Pilgrim Fathers – and, like old Joshua whom Angélique had met at Houssnock, they all had, in spite of their strict ways, a certain sprightliness about them which was not at all to the liking of the Reverend Patridge. There were also two families of Irish fishermen, and one of French origin, called Dumaret, who claimed to hold the record for drownings. But then, in this land where, as soon as a child can stand, it dashes into the waves astride a plank of wood, how could it be otherwise? These people constantly sail from island to island, in a region where the sea is even more treacherous than elsewhere, and one day, especially around the age of fourteen or fifteen – an age which knows no fear but still lacks experience – these indefatigable vagabonds of the straits get drowned.

In the Dumaret family the old granny always had a premonition of disaster. Whether by day or by night, she would be seen to rise and begin to fold and put away the clothes of a boy who was at sea. 'He has just been drowned,' she would say.

Angélique heard all kinds of tales as she was taken round the hamlet and the various farms. Her visit did great honour to the island and the healing of young Alistair completed the legend. Some sailors from Dieppe who had landed with two boats to replenish their stocks of drinking water mingled that evening with the population, and the whole place buzzed with a strange lingua franca, consisting of a mixture of Indian dialects, a bit of French from Saint-Malo and a smattering of English. Some peaceful Mic-Macs, who were related to some of the inhabitants of the island, began to make their way out of the forest, placing furs and game at the doors of the houses, then squatting on the heights, anxious to participate in the Paleface festivities. Most of these Indians were very tall, almost giants, with square, copper-coloured faces.

Towards ten o'clock in the evening Angélique decided that she had made sufficient sacrifice to the vanities of this world and that she must snatch a little sleep before the fun began.

She had managed to get a good hot bath at Mrs MacGregor's and the sweltering night air had dried her thick hair, but she was overcome with weariness.

So she wrapped herself up in her beautiful sealskin coat and sat down away from the others, leaning against the roots of a great oak.

Tomorrow she would be in Gouldsboro. Would to God the sea remained calm.

Below her things were growing more and more lively round the houses and along the beach, where firewood was being piled up.

Casks and tankards were brought out, and bowls laid on trestle tables. The night was getting on but the big Midsummer fires were not to be lighted until the last moment, at midnight.

Some children rushed by holding hands, sweeping Timothy the little Negro boy, Abbial the ship's boy and Samuel Corwin along with them.

Monhegan, the eternal, Monhegan the mother of all sea-going peoples, was living through another magical night and its heart could be heard beating in the dull thud of the swell pounding the cliffs and the first beats of the drums rehearsing a dance at the Basque encampment.

Into this narrow fiord, driven by the mist, towards the year 1000, ships with dragons on their prows had once glided, discovering then as now the granite cliffs covered with flowers. And since that time, on the grey stone, mysterious markings kept fresh the memory of the Vikings' visit, those Normans with golden beards and hair. After them had come John Cabot, Verrazano the Florentine sailing for France, the Spaniard Gomez, the Englishman Rut, a French priest called André Theot, Sir Humphrey Gilbert, Gosnold, Champlain and George Weymouth and John Smith who, in 1614, had been sent on a mission 'to explore North America for gold and whales'.

The island's history was long, crowded and multi-coloured. The isle of the Mohicans breathed its stirring saga in the varied cries that rose through the night air in the Gaelic lilt of Irish and Scots voices, in the earthy smells, in the oaths in every imaginable language, and in the laughter of men, women and children, and the costumes from all parts of the globe – Scots tartans, red basque berets, black Calvinist hats and the satin neckerchiefs of the handful of buccaneers from Barbados, and the multi-coloured woollen caps of sailors from every port in the world.

The crickets, hidden in the grass, played their endless, high-pitched saraband, and along the saffron-coloured horizon, where night was at least beginning to fall like a dark froth from the green firmament, sails, still more sails passed by.

And then suddenly there was nothing left: the sea was deserted, the coast was empty. Angélique was alone gazing out at the sea and the abandoned beach. Why are there so many ports along this coast whose names suggest desertion, abandonment? The names sound like the tolling of a death knell. All is empty, all has faded and gone – the whales gone, and the shoals of cod and sardines, those great silver shields on the surface of the sea, the vast clouds of birds along with the seals in their Minim's robes, the white porpoises, the blue sperm-whales, the fierce grampus and the gentle dolphin . . .

But it is not only that which is so sad . . . A sense of discouragement grips one's heart, an infinite nostalgia seizes the soul . . . a dull feeling of despair in the deserted creeks . . .

Too many memories, too many battles, too many massacres, too many drownings, too much greed, too many passions, too many souls wandering in hate and desolation, forgotten, gathered together weeping and lamenting in the mists, in the wind, in the spray of the waves, borne hither and thither by the gigantic, terrible tides that are swallowed up in the bowels of the earth, whistling and wailing as they go.

So many deserted shores . . .

Shimmering, fine mists that rain down heavily on the cedar forests, on the green pine needles, on the glistening foliage of maple and copper beech, falling on fields of wild lupin and rhododendrons, on lilac trees beside a ruined house, and on roses growing in a forgotten garden.

Land of ghosts – French, English, Dutch, Swedish, Finnish, Spanish, Breton, Norman, Scots, Irish; pirates, peasants, fishermen, whalers, trappers; Puritans, Papists, Jesuits and Recollects; Indians, Etchemins, Tarratines, Mic-Macs, Malacites, where are you all? Where are you, ghosts of Acadia, land of a hundred names, kingdom of creeks and peninsulas, of leafy haunts with a sail passing by?

The smell of the woods and the smell of the seaweed, the smell of the Indians, the smell of scalps, a smell of burning, a smell of the seashore, a smell that wafts off the sea, and off the land, that surrounds you with incense, that makes you numb, and over it all a relentless, cold gaze watching you die . . .

A wailing broke the silence, a peculiar, shrill wail that startled Angélique out of her sleep and out of the nightmare she was having and made her straighten up once more with beating heart at the foot of the tree where she had drowsed off.

'What's that? Are they killing a pig?'

No, it was only the Scottish bagpipes beginning to play down on the beach.

A few paces away Angélique noticed that Jack Merwin was sitting looking towards the shore where the big bonfire had just been lighted, while the Scotsmen danced over crossed swords or wrestled with the black bear.

'I had a dream,' Angélique said, almost to herself, 'people fought so much among themselves that these lands became deserted and forgotten.'

Then she noticed that she had spoken in French.

Jack Merwin's back remained as motionless as the rock. He sat with his forearms resting on his knees and his hands hanging limp, and she noticed for the first time that in spite of their calluses they were long, aristocratic hands.

The uneasy feeling she had often had when she looked at him came back to her still more forcibly, with the memory of his extraordinary behaviour in refusing to hold out a hand to her as he watched her in the throes of death with his cold, relentless eyes.

Whatever had possessed him to allow her to sink and go through that terrible struggle and then to dive in when it was almost too late and save her life at the very last moment, at the cost of a superhuman effort? He was a very strange man. Perhaps he was mad, after all!

'Give me your hand, Jack Merwin,' she said suddenly, 'and let me read your fortune.'

But he threw her a furious glance and clasped his hands tight together as a clear indication that he intended to keep them to himself.

Then Angélique gave a sudden laugh. She really must be still half asleep to have dared to show even that degree of coquetry and provocativeness to a hostile misogynist like him. Her own heart was like a ship with billowing sails, ready to speed towards the horizon, and she was delighted by all the hurly-burly including even the wailing bagpipes.

'It is so wonderful to be alive, Merwin. I am so happy . . . You saved my life.'

Merwin scowled, his hands still clasped firmly together. In any case, listening to her talking to herself like this, he considered she must be mad.

Then she laughed again, intoxicated by this June night, spellbound by its endless strident sounds.

Louder even than the bagpipes, came the rhythmic call of the fifes and drums.

Angélique leapt to her feet.

'Miss Pidgeon, Mrs MacGregor, Mrs Winslow and you, Dorothy and Janeton, come, come . . . Let us go and dance the farandole with the Basques.'

And she seized them by the hand, drawing them along with her as she ran down the slope.

CHAPTER FORTY-SEVEN

THE BASQUES advanced one behind the other, bare footed and on tiptoe, capering and whirling as they went; they were prodigious dancers, full of grace and vigour, and the glow of the fires shone on their poppy-red berets.

A tall supple fellow spun round and round in front of them, holding aloft a tambourine with copper jingles which he tapped with his nimble fingers.

When Angélique and her companions entered the ring of

firelight the men gave them a noisy welcome and made room for them at their sides.

'By Saint Patrick,' cried the Irishman Parsons, 'that divvil of a lass is getting our womenfolk to join in the dancing!'

'I have heard tell things about her,' the Englishman Winslow replied. 'They do say that she is a She-Devil.'

'A She-Devil!' old MacGregor roared with mirth. 'Hold your whist, you know nothing about it. She's a fairy! I used to meet them on the moors in Scotland when I was a child, and I recognized her straight away. Let it go, neighbour, let it go. Tonight is the mad night. The very sound of those Basque flutes makes my feet itch. Come and dance too, neighbour. Tonight is the mad night.'

The farandole went on weaving its sinuous way among the bonfires, the houses, the rocks and the trees.

Every woman, old or young, grandmother, mother, girl or child must join in the dancing on Midsummer night. The tall harpooner, Captain Hermani d'Astiguarra, held out his hand to Angélique and drew her into the dance, his eyes never leaving her face. He soon discovered that she knew most of the traditional steps of the Basque farandole and, once back on the beach, he swept her into the centre of the circle. There, yielding to the spell of the exciting music she danced with him a multitude of complex, dashing yet graceful figures traditional in the Basque country.

At Toulouse, in Aquitaine, Angélique had danced the majority of these figures, for in the château they were preferred to the excessively stiff and formal Court dances. Joffrey de Peyrac had often taken his young wife to the Basque country, in the Pyrenees, to attend the big popular festivals, where in her capacity as Suzeraine, she had happily joined in the merry-making of her vassals.

One by one these memories came back to her as the frenzied music continued.

Young Esther's short skirt made it easy for Angélique to kick her legs high in the lively measures, and she laughed gaily as the irresistible Basque captain swept her along, treading so lightly she scarcely touched the ground, her golden hair at one moment streaming out behind her like a banner, then striking against her cheek and swathing her face in a silky net.

He spoke to her sometimes in Basque and sometimes in French whenever the figures of the dance brought them together and his steely arm encircled her more and more possessively with each encounter.

'A fairy rose up out of the sea for Midsummer night,' he said. 'Monhegan is a happy island. It is all so much magic, Madame; how can you possibly know our dances?'

'Because I am the Countess de Peyrac de Morens d'Irristru.'

'Irristru? ... That's a name from our part of the world.'

'Yes indeed.'

'Are you from Aquitaine, then?'

'Yes, by marriage.'

'And what is your husband doing leaving you to wander about alone at the ends of the earth?'

'He is not very far away, so take care, sir.'

'Madame,' he went on in Basque, 'you have the loveliest figure, and the trimmest waist that I have ever held in my hands and your eyes are intoxicating ... Do you know the wine-harvest jig?' he went on in French.

'I think so.'

'Then come along.'

He drew her wildly into the dance and spun her round until she was giddy; the deep blue sky swung across the red flames of the bonfires, and joyous faces bounced up and down like so many balls before her eyes.

'I've had enough,' she cried, 'my head is spinning.'

He came to a halt but not before he had lifted her off the ground and whirled her several times round.

Everyone clapped and Angélique laughed as they passed her the goatskin flask from which one was expected to pour the wine straight to the back of one's throat without touching the flask with the lips. A further burst of applause greeted this new exploit.

Farther up the hillside, the Reverend Patridge who disapproved of such goings-on, and the sailor Jack Merwin, who was in no mood to participate, sat leaning against a tree trunk contemplating the scene with the same sombre, reproving stare.

Angélique caught sight of them and burst into peals of irrepressible mirth; the two of them were just too comical for words.

Her gay laughter encouraged the others to yet more mirth, and everyone began to dance again, the adults in pairs and the children in a ring, with the bagpipes supporting the drums, the *bourrée* of Limoges intermingled with the Scottish jig and the Cornish brawl, while the less agile or exhausted members of the party kept time by clapping to the music.

Occasionally one or other of the dancers would collapse beside the trestle tables to quaff a mug of beer or take a long swig of wine. All the ships in the harbour had brought out the supplies they held for special occasions – Spanish wines from the Caribbean, French wines and a rough wine with a strong bouquet from the wild vines on Matinicus Island. The drinkers switched from one to another and the sunshine of so many continents, mingling in their glasses, gave them a glorious feeling of warmth in the pits of their stomachs and put lightning into their calves, although later they would be left perilously weak.

Sitting at the tables were two old ladies from the island one of them being Granny Dumaret, who had the visions of those about to be drowned – tirelessly opening clams and oysters with their busy knives.

Monsieur d'Astiguarra reminded Angélique of the correct way to eat 'loubinkas', a favourite dish of the Béarn and the Basque countries.

He had taken good care when leaving Bayonne to stock his ship abundantly with strings of these highly spiced little sausages, which were eaten fried, each one being swallowed burning hot, and followed up immediately with a raw oyster – the height of gastronomic bliss – a burning sausage and a cool oyster. Then a few moments dancing, followed by a draught of Jurançon wine. Then another of those diabolical sausages, so highly flavoured they made your eyes water, and a green, ice-cold oyster, swimming in its salty juices, drunk straight from its iridescent shell. The dancing, the laughter, the rhythmic clapping of hands, the amber-coloured wine with a flavour as strong and vibrant as the piping of the fifes . . .

Some of the revellers sat down, some fell to the ground . . . some began to giggle uncontrollably, some did not feel very well and looked rather pale, but no one paid much attention.

Up above them, beside the houses on the edge of the wood, sat the Mic-Mac and Mohican Indians, looking almost as serious as the Reverend Patridge, as they watched the Paleface revels. There seemed to them to be little point in drinking wine, which did not make you really drunk, and they thought that firewater alone had divine and magical properties. When they had accumulated sufficient brandy from the ships in exchange for the furs, then they would organize a great carousel somewhere deep in the forest; then they would go mad and be reunited with the Spirit of Dreams. They would not be content with just laughing and dancing stupidly like the Palefaces ... and eating nothing but a few shellfish ...

On the stroke of midnight, the first man to leap the fire shot out of the flames like a black devil.

Then one by one the other Basques, with legs like steel springs, leapt over the flames, feet spread wide, arms raised, every jump being greeted with a cry of fright and admiration from the spectators.

'The Devil is powerless for a whole year against anyone who leaps over the Midsummer fire,' said Hernani d'Astiguarra.

'In that case I shall jump too,' cried Angélique.

'But women can't do that,' one of the Basques protested, shocked at this break with tradition.

'So you'd abandon women to the devil, would you?' Angélique retaliated, pulling the man's beret down till it touched his nose.

She was a little foolish and a trifle tipsy, but what of it? This was an opportunity that might never come her way again and was something she had always dreamed of.

'It's all right for *her*, *she* can!' Hernani said with considerable force, his eyes full of smouldering passion as he gazed at her. 'But your hair, Madame ... you must take care of your hair,' he added, laying a caressing hand on Angélique's head – a gesture she was scarcely aware of in the fever and intoxication of the moment.

'Have no fear! I was born under Sagittarius, the sign of Fire, whose children are the cohort of the Violent and the legion of the Salamanders and can pass with impunity through flames. I MUST jump! Monsieur d'Astiguarra, your hand!'

He led her to within a few paces of the crackling fire, and everyone fell silent.

Angélique kicked off the shoes she had borrowed from Mrs MacGregor. Beneath her bare feet the sand felt cool, and the roaring flame rose up before her, tall and golden.

Angélique, who had also partaken of the scalding 'loubinkas', of fiery wine and the salty tang of the sea, felt as if she herself had become a flame about to crackle and leap into action.

Hernani handed her a small flat flask, which she sniffed, recognizing the smell.

'That is Armagnac from the Piquepoul vines! ... A thousand thanks, sir!'

And she took a long draught of the brandy.

Everyone was watching her. No one remembered her name very clearly but the things that had been said about her floated hazily in their befuddled minds.

As she stood there barefoot and ready to leap forward, she looked to them like the incarnation of some goddess, not altogether of their world, and yet dominating them by the quiet independence of a creature who was sure of herself.

They could see that her slender waist showed no sign of fragility, that her graceful shoulders, in spite of their elegance, bore witness to a life rich in experience and struggle, and they sensed, by the glint in her eyes, that in challenging the flames she wished, so to speak, to set a seal on so many other infernos through which she had passed.

But Angélique herself had no such thoughts, for her mind was entirely bent on this difficult and fascinating ordeal.

At first it had been a kind of yearning of her body, overwrought by the heat of the night, to leap into the air — the living body which that very day had almost died, and now among the writhing flames she seemed to see a resplendent, fearsome face calling to her, the mythical spirit of Midsummer night, a dazzling succubus whose hair was now dusky blue now purple, the She-Devil!

The tambourine began to beat. Hernani d'Astiguarra grasped Angélique by the hand and launched her forward, faster and faster . . .

The golden wall rose up before her.

Gripping her tight, Hernani lifted Angélique up into the air, and as she leapt forward, she felt the hot breath of the fire, passed through its shifting, incadescent drapery, felt the fleeting nip, the glowing red whirlwind that sought to wrap itself around her and hold her fast, then she made her escape, landing on the other side in the coolness of the night, where another of the Basques was waiting to pull her to safety still farther away, out of all danger.

Two others rushed forward and beat out the smouldering edge of her skirt with their palms.

There was a slight smell of singed hair, and Angélique shook her locks.

'It's nothing! I got through, thanks be to God!'

'You make me ill!' cried Adhemar bursting into tears. 'What would have happened to us all if you had fallen in? Wasn't the water enough for you to die in without having the fire as well?'

He was dead drunk.

The music began again, in a somewhat confused and jerky manner, and the tall Hernani ran his harpooner's arm round Angélique's waist and drew her to one side.

His black eyes shone like two carbuncles, and he spoke to her in Basque with a note of urgency in his voice.

'Meeting you is an unforgettable experience, Madame. You have ravished my soul. We shall finish the night together, shall we not?'

Angélique shook herself free in order to see him better, and her astonishment was due less to the overbold proposition he had just put to her, than to the fact that he had spoken in Basque, which should have been completely unintelligible to her.

'What an extraordinary thing,' she exclaimed, 'but . . . I appear to understand Basque! Me, Basque! That incomprehensible gibberish that no one seems able to learn unless born on the banks of the Soule! . . Did your Armagnac contain some magic potion, Monsieur d'Astiguarra?'

'No . . . but . . . is it not a fact that you, Madame, speak some of the Acadian Indian dialects?'

'I am in fact familiar with the Abenaki tongue as spoken in the Kennebec region.'

'That explains the mystery. Our tongue and that of the Indians are related. I presume that, both starting out from Asia, our races went round the world in opposite directions, the Indians ending up here and we in Bayonne. When my forefathers hunted whales in these regions, they had no difficulty at all in understanding the savages and often, entirely without study, we were able to act as interpreters between them and the missionaries.'

Once again he made to draw her towards him.

'And so, if you understood my bold proposal, Madame, what is your reply . . .'

She placed two fingers over his lips.

'Hush, sir! On Midsummer's night people say many foolish things, but they should not do them. It is a time of fairy enchantment, not a time of realities.'

The time seemed to have come for all respectable ladies to retire, and Angélique with Miss Pidgeon clinging to one arm, and Mrs MacGregor in tow on the other, the latter herself supporting one of her daughters to whom her little girl and a whole bevy of children were clinging, not without difficulty climbed the hillside towards what looked vaguely like a group of houses at the top.

Their slipping and sliding set them laughing till the tears ran down their faces and their sides ached with laughter.

A dour figure of righteousness, the Reverend Patridge, loomed up before them, and thundered:

'Miss Elizabeth Pidgeon, I heartily condemn your present behaviour. You, so pious . . .'

'Oh leave the poor creature alone,' Angélique cut in, in a voice that struck her as a little hoarse. 'After all, she has had her fill of horror and suffering over the past two weeks! She has every right to enjoy herself a bit now that we are out of danger!'

She swung the giggling Miss Pidgeon round her in a circle, and began to dance once more.

'I shall take you to Gouldsboro, darling, and there you will be safe . . . Mistress MacGregor, may we rest beneath your roof?'

'Yes, my dears,' sang Mrs MacGregor, who was three sheets in the wind; 'my house is at your disposal.'

They lay down to sleep on kelp-filled mattresses laid out on the living-room floor. No sooner had they found a comfortable position to sleep than a group of sailors banged at the shutters, shouting for women.

Old MacGregor leapt to his feet and took up station in the doorway, his shirt tails flapping and musket in hand, shouting that he would shoot full of holes anyone who dared disturb the ladies' rest.

After this all was calm, and then came the dawn.

Thus ended the crazy Midsummer night on Monhegan Island, the shortest night of the year, the pagan celebration of the summer solstice, with fires lighted along the hills and the beaches, the night in which the bracken burst into flower in the undergrowth, when old Shapleigh goes off into the forest of the New World to pick wild vervain . . . Juno's tears, Mercury's blood, the joy of simples . . .

CHAPTER FORTY-EIGHT

THE THIRD DAY of their journey dawned. The morning after the night before . . . A mist that might at any moment turn to rain hung over the island, heavy with the smell of burnt-out fires and dead fish. Only the seagulls, the cormorants and the shrikes had resumed their chattering calls. 'It's our turn now!' they seemed to say somewhat spitefully.

As Angélique made her way down towards the landing stage with Adhemar and young Samuel, Mrs MacGregor's daughter ran after her, with her two little girls aged eight and twelve following behind her.

'Take them with you, would you,' she said, puffing and blowing, 'take them to Gouldsboro. I understand there is a school there, where they can be taught to speak good French like my grandmother's and learn their prayers. It is three years now since we had a pastor here ... And as for knowing their letters, the poor creatures! They are more likely to learn how to blaspheme here!'

With Dorothy and Janeton in tow Angélique felt a certain embarrassment as she presented herself at the landing stage.

'I shall pay these children's passage when we reach Gouldsboro,' she said to Jack Merwin, who merely looked away with the distasteful look of a man whose boat was being treated as a kind of rubbish dump.

Yawning and somewhat unsteady on their feet, the other passengers on the *White Bird* took their customary places, then at the last moment Captain Hernani loomed out of the fog, every bit as lively as the previous day, and placed something heavy on Angélique's knees.

'That is for your friends in Gouldsboro,' he said. 'I know they are from Charentes, and will know how to appreciate it ...'

It was a white oak keg full of the very best Armagnac, a priceless treasure!

Merwin was already pushing his boat out, and Angélique scarcely had time to thank the friendly captain.

'Come and see us in Gouldsboro,' she cried out.

And they watched him standing there, blowing kisses to her, until the bright red of his big beret had faded into the mists.

Accustomed to the whims of the English captain, Merwin's passengers had embarked as soon as he had given the order to do so. But they soon realized that it had been sheer madness to put to sea in a 'pea-souper' like this.

Fortunately none of them was in much of a state to reflect on the matter. Lack of sleep had made them all drowsy, and Angélique, for her part, was delighted at their hasty departure. That night they would be in Gouldsboro, and nothing was going to spoil her mood of happiness, neither the wretched weather, nor the dark sea, nor the even more louring looks cast by the Reverend Patridge, who was sulking with Miss Pidgeon, while she gazed at him with a repentant expression, nor even Jack Merwin's expression, which was even colder and more hostile than usual.

She found the two little Scots girls adorable with their little round, roguish faces peeping out from the voluminous red-and-green-checked plaids in which they were swathed from head to toe. They both clung tenaciously to their little bundles consisting of large kerchiefs tied round a few possessions, and the younger girl clasped a simple Indian doll made from corn husks with cheeks dyed red with raspberry juice and dried grass for hair.

Angélique thought of Honorine and of the bright grace of childhood.

The fog was growing thicker, and Merwin had set the ship's boy the task of sounding the fog horn. As the lad puffed and blew into the enormous shell, the shape of a large fishing sloop loomed up, drifting towards them. There seemed to be no one on board, but as the vessel approached, a terrifying cry rent the air, a Redskin war cry. And as they all sat petrified, the barrel of a long pistol appeared over the side of the sloop and an unseen man called to them in French:

'By the Blessed Sacrament, are you Englishmen?'

'We are French! We are French!' Angélique and Adhemar replied hastily.

The sloop came alongside the *White Bird*, and threw on boat hooks which brought the vessel to a halt. It was an Acadian boat from the mainland in search of some English capture.

A youthful, beardless, sunburnt face, framed in long black tresses, beneath a felt hat adorned with eagle feathers, suddenly appeared from nowhere and two dark magnificent eyes swiftly scanned the passengers in the sloop.

'Ho! ho! I believe I see a fair number of Englishmen among you!'

He revealed himself in full. A silver crucifix and several medallions jingled on his soft leather jerkin, which was fringed in the Indian style. On his belt he wore a cutlass and a hatchet, while in his hand he held a riding pistol with a mother-of-pearl butt. Behind him appeared a row of hang-dog faces, looking very much like those of a lot of wreckers, with three or four Mic-Macs among them wearing pointed black bonnets decorated with pearls.

Their young leader looked suspiciously at Angélique, and his eyes narrowed.

'Are you quite sure you are French and not English?'

'And you,' she retaliated, 'are you quite sure you are French and not Indian?'

'I,' he exclaimed indignantly, 'am Hubert d'Arpentigny, from Cape Sable. Everyone in Acadia and in Frenchman Bay knows me!'

'And I, young man, am the Countess of Peyrac and I think that everyone in Acadia and in Frenchman Bay knows my husband!'

Quite unabashed, Hubert d'Arpentigny sprang down into Jack Merwin's ship.

While, on his mother's side, he had a grandfather who had been a great sagamore of the forests, his paternal grandfather had been one of King Louis XIII's equerries and had taught him the manners of the French Court, and he kissed Angélique's hand very elegantly.

'Madame, I recognize you by your reputation – beautiful and daring! Nothing could be further from my mind than to cause you any harm. But it seems to me that you have among your companions here a handful of Englishmen – just what I want to put up for sale as hostages.'

'These people belong to me and it is my task to take them back to my husband, Count Peyrac.'

Young d'Arpentigny heaved a deep sigh.

'And ... have you no supplies, no wares on board this sloop? The winter has been a hard one in our lands and we are still waiting for one of our company's ships to bring us supplies from Bordeaux. If it turns out to have been wrecked or seized by pirates we shall find ourselves completely destitute.'

'So you indulge in a bit of piracy from others,' Angélique replied, doing her best to hide the barrel of Armagnac that Hernani d'Astiguarra had given her. 'I am terribly sorry, but you will find nothing here. We are as poor as Job.'

'Indeed! ... You there, English captain, move aside and let me have a look in the well-deck.'

With a peremptory gesture with the barrel of his pistol he signalled to Merwin to move out of the way, while his companions continued to hold their ship close up against the sloop, exchanged a few jokes in Indian language, made eyes at young Esther, and furtively scrutinized Angélique while laughing outrageously at the heretic pastor.

Angélique was beginning to wonder how it was all going to end when she saw young d'Arpentigny leap back on board his own ship and sweep off his hat respectfully and repeatedly to her, with a grin that stretched from ear to ear.

'Off you go, Madame; you and your hostages are free. God speed!'

'A thousand thanks, Monsieur. If you are in difficulty before the harvest time, come to Gouldsboro.'

'I shall most certainly do that. Monsieur de Peyrac has always been generous to us. And you, you are every bit as lovely as they say in Frenchman Bay. My day has not been wasted . . .'

'What a young lunatic!' said Angélique with a shrug of her shoulders.

Then they found themselves alone once more, tossing up and down in the fog.

Jack Merwin, grumbling, hoisted his sails once more, and tried to get his bearings. The pedlar wiped his brow. If the Acadians had rifled his stock, he would have been ruined.

'Milady, thank you. Had it not been for you . . .'

'Please do not thank me; it was not my doing.'

She did in fact have the impression that the young pirate lord's sudden change of heart had not been due solely to her presence. Was it the discovery of Mr Willoughby in the well-deck that had driven him away? No, certainly not, for a man like Hubert d'Arpentigny would never have allowed himself to be intimidated by a bear, tame or not!

She found herself looking about her, and even up into the air. These French Acadians who spent as much of their lives on the water as in the forests might have sensed some impending storm, seen some indication as yet invisible to other eyes, that enjoined them to make for shelter as soon as possible.

She already thought the sea was getting rougher, and Jack Merwin had apparently reduced speed, no doubt reluctant to sound the fog horn any more for fear of attracting further pirates. So he put himself athwart the wind, tacking back and forth through the mist, concentrating all his attention on avoiding obstacles.

Angélique looked at him anxiously.

'Shall we reach Gouldsboro tonight?' she asked him.

He appeared not to have heard her.

Fortunately the fog was beginning to brighten. It became translucent like porcelain, disintegrating into long gauze-like strips, then suddenly the horizon appeared, glittering like enamel and sparkling with colour. The sun was still high in the sky, the sea still furrowed with huge waves, blue-black and tipped with white, but the coastline was already in sight, and there was something about its green outline that reminded her irresistibly of the country around Gouldsboro.

Angélique's heart gave a leap.

She could think of nothing now but of their swiftly approaching reunion, and sat gazing out into the distance, heedless of her companions' expressions of satisfaction, as they too foresaw the end of the journey.

'Joffrey, my dear love!'

An interminable time had passed since they had been so unexpectedly separated.

Over and above all the difficulties that had since arisen along her way, she feared that some immaterial obstacle might still appear, something that could not be fought against, like ill fortune. She would not feel completely reassured until she was with him once more, able to touch him and hear his voice. Then everything else would be effaced. How well she knew his way of looking at her, that look in which she could read that she was beautiful, and in his eyes, unique, alone, that look that enclosed her in the enchanted circle of his love. He possessed in the highest degree the gift of isolation and separation that is the prerogative of men when their hearts are full of the gladness of love. This clear-cut aspect of the male character had sometimes shocked Angélique, for she was a woman and in her everything mingled together, feelings, passions, anxieties and desire, like the deep waters that swirl where a river joins the sea.

Such is the nature of woman, forever seething with an excess of different sensations. She did not always follow him, but she needs must follow him and he had the gift of forcing her to do so, for at such moments it seemed as if he had nothing else to do than to love her and to prove it to her. So successful was he in persuading her that all doubts, fears and dangers stopped short on the threshold of any room in which they were to make love, so skilled was he in drawing her with him into a world in which they were alone, their hearts and bodies filled with joy and wonderment.

She also knew that she would make no mention of Colin to him at first. No! Later ... Afterwards ... When she had won her way back into his heart again, when they had discovered one another again in the intoxication of abandon, when she had been refreshed in the freedom of her body offered without restraint to the sweetness of his caresses, when she had savoured the intoxicating delights of lying naked and defenceless in the warmth of his arms.

Angélique's eyes met Jack Merwin's gazing at her.

How long had he been watching her? How many of her thoughts had he been able to read on her face as she sat daydreaming?

Then almost immediately he looked away, and she saw him spit a great jet of tobacco juice out into the sea. Still calm and meticulous, he took the quid of tobacco from his mouth, slipped it into his woollen hat as was the sailors' custom, and put the hat back on his head. There was an air of finality about these familiar and homely gestures which she was to understand only later. Then he seemed to sniff the wind.

As if he had come to some decision, he stretched out his gnarled leg with its big toe as prehensile as a crab's pinchers and seized the mainsail sheet with greater strength than if he had been using his fist. Coping alone with the rudder and the other topping lifts, he brought the heavy boat about, laying it almost flat upon the water, and caught the wind on the quarter, sailing close enough to keep the ship steadily under way, but avoiding by a hair's breadth taking the wind head on.

Angélique gave a cry.

It was not this brilliant manoeuvre which, had it been carried out by a less skilful man might have had them all in the water, that had caused her exclamation, but the fact that she had just seen how close they were to the shore. They could make out the lines of trees passing by and hear the surf breaking at the foot of the cliffs.

On the other hand the two pink hills familiarly known as the Mount-Desert Bulbs, behind which lay Gouldsboro, were beginning to vanish into the distance towards the east.

'But you are not going in the right direction,' Angélique cried. 'Gouldsboro is over there. You are sailing away from it.'

Without replying the Englishman continued on his way, and very soon the Bulbs disappeared.

The *White Bird* veered north-west and made its way into a large bay crowded with islands. Young Esther, who had once visited her uncle on Matinicus Island, recognized the bay as the one at the mouth of the Penobscot.

Angélique glanced at the sun to judge the time. It was still high in the sky. With luck, and provided that Jack Merwin did not hang about too long, they might still, thanks to the long June evenings, reach port before nightfall.

'And now where are you taking us?' she asked him.

She might as well have been speaking to a block of wood.

They sailed up the estuary for about an hour, and when the boat then headed off to the left up a narrow, shady river Angélique could not help exchanging a glance of exasperation with Elias Kempton. Both of them felt a murderous desire to hurl themselves on the skipper, Jack Merwin, overcome him once and for all, and seize the tiller.

In the shelter of the trees the wind dropped, and became a mere warm, light breeze, that pushed the boat very slowly upstream. Merwin furled the sail, took hold of the oars, and soon after guided the boat towards a willow and alder-shaded beach. Beyond, pines, oaks, maples and beech trees mingled in luxuriant disorder from which rose the warm scent of the summer undergrowth. The smell of the sea did not reach this far inland, and there was the buzz of wild bees.

Merwin jumped into the water, that came halfway up his thighs, and hauled his boat up towards the shore where he made her fast.

'You may disembark,' he said in unruffled tones. 'We have arrived.'

'But we should have been at Gouldsboro tonight,' Angélique shouted, beside herself. 'Oh! This damned Englishman infuriates me! . . . He drives me mad . . . You are a . . .'

She was looking for an adequate way to express her feelings about this block-headed individual and could not find the words . . . especially in English.

'You are utterly unreasonable, Jack Merwin,' she went on, forcing herself to remain calm. 'You must be aware of the fact that a terrible Frenchman lives hereabouts, who is much given to cropping English hair, Baron Saint-Castine by name, and that if he and his Etchemins come upon us I am not at all sure I shall have time to make myself known to him and them before we are all killed.'

'Do you hear what she says?' the pedlar added, 'you damned fool. The place stinks of Frenchmen and Indians, and we are defenceless. Do you want us all to be massacred?'

'Just come ashore,' Merwin repeated, utterly indifferent.

Mr Willoughby the bear had followed him willingly, for he loved the smell of the land. There must have been wild honey in the offing for he stood up on his hind legs and began to claw at the trunk of a pine tree, making excited little grunts.

Sighing, the other passengers did as they were told. The place spelt no good to them, and they felt heavy-hearted.

Intrigued, they watched Merwin's goings on. After getting his bearings, he kneeled down at the foot of a tree and began to dig with his hands through a thick layer of leaf mould between the tree roots.

'What's he doing?'

'Has he got some treasure buried there?'

'He might well have. Many pirates hide their loot along these shores.'

'Hi there, Merwin, you damned scoundrel,' the pedlar exclaimed, 'how's your fortune made up, Spanish doubloons, Portuguese moidores or silver pesos?'

The sailor made no reply but continued digging. Under the layer of leaf-mould he came upon a screen of interwoven branches which he removed, followed by some moss and stones. Then at last from the depths of the hole he drew out a largish parcel wrapped in old skins and oilcloth. Another smaller packet followed and the Englishman stood up, satisfied.

'Good! Wait here for me,' he said, 'I shan't be long; while I am away, get something to eat. There's still some cheese on board and some bread and a flagon of wine Mrs MacGregor gave me.'

So pleased was he to have found his parcels in their hiding place that he had become almost amiable.

He repeated:

'Wait just a minute!'

And he went off into the willow thicket. Angélique began to discuss matters with her companions then, exhorting herself to be patient, went back to the boat to fetch the provisions. They might as well eat. The place seemed completely deserted and a long way from anywhere. If they did not stay too long they had a chance of getting away before the savages of the region sensed their presence.

It was no use getting angry. They simply had to put up with the captain's caprices and his sudden changes of mood. Given his impossible character, the dangers of the war, and bearing in mind that three days before they had all been prisoners of Gold Beard in Maquoit Bay, it had to be admitted that the voyage had been particularly swift and had gone as well as could have been hoped.

She returned to her companions and with Sammy's help began

to set out portions for each person on a big flat rock. They began to eat in silence. Then, towards the end of the meal, as Angélique looked up to ask someone to pass her the wine, she saw all the English sitting deathly pale, open-mouthed, wide-eyed with fear, staring fixedly at something behind her. It cost a tremendous effort to bring herself to turn round and face the new danger.

From among the willows whose long, greenish-gold leaves trembled in the wind, a Jesuit in a black soutane had just made his appearance.

CHAPTER FORTY-NINE

ANGELIQUE'S FIRST REACTION was to jump up and position herself between the terrified Englishmen and the newcomer. Her second reflex sent her eyes to the priest's crucifix to see if it bore the ruby by which Father d'Orgeval's was distinguished. But she could not see it, so this priest could not be he.

The priest in his black robe, standing motionless in the shadows just a few paces from them, was a very tall, thin man, clean-shaven, and his dark hair hung loose over his shoulders. His high black turn-down collar with its white bands encircled a long, muscular neck, under a head whose features were both noble and distinguished. One of his arms hung stiffly at his side, but his other hand, resting on his chest had two fingers clasped round the end of his crucifix, which hung from his neck by a black silk ribbon, as if he were introducing it to them.

Two dark, fearless eyes stared at the petrified group of men and women as if trying to rivet them to the ground like so many hypnotized animals.

Finally he moved and came out from under the shade of the trees into the full glare of the sunlight on the little beach. Then Angélique noticed that, beneath the hem of his soutane, which was crumpled and creased, the Jesuit's feet and ankles were bare. And those bare feet seemed somehow familiar to her.

'Hello, all of you, how do you do?' came Jack Merwin's voice. 'Don't you recognize me?'

Transformed into pillars of salt, Angélique and the English people uttered not a word in answer to this greeting, which, by some piece of witchcraft or some hallucination, had seemed to issue from the Jesuit's mouth.

He continued to advance towards them while they backed away from him until they found themselves standing at the very edge of the water.

Seeing their terror, he stopped again.

'This,' he said in English with the ghost of a smile, 'is the treasure I removed from its hiding place a few moments ago – only my poor soutane, which I left here when I set out, and which I am at last able to put on again after eight months' absence.'

Then, turning to Angélique, he went on in French:

'Are you so astonished, Madame, at my transformation? I had the impression you had begun to suspect me.'

'Merwin,' she murmured, 'you are Jack Merwin?'

'The very same. And I am also Father Louis-Paul Maraicher de Vernon, of the Society of Jesus. So you see it can happen that a damned Englishman can change into a cursed Frenchman, even a shocking Papist.'

A hint of humour brightened his transformed face. He went on to explain:

'Last autumn my superior entrusted me with a secret mission in New England. My sailor's disguise was only one of many I was forced to assume down there in order to fulfil my mission without running the risk of being recognized. Thanks be to God I am now back safe and sound in the territory of French Acadia.'

He spoke polished French but it still bore a trace of an English accent, out of sheer habit, since for many a long month he had spoken nothing but that language.

'But ... are you French too?' Angélique stammered, quite unable to overcome her astonishment.

'Indeed I am. My parents came from the Auge region, but I have spoken English since I was a child, as I served as a pageboy to the English royal family during its exile in France. Later I went to London to perfect my knowledge of the language.'

In spite of these urbane explanations Angélique still found it hard to take in the fact that it was Jack Merwin, the skipper of their boat, who stood before her. She stood transfixed, and as he saw her half-open mouth and her uncomprehending eyes, he could not help laughing.

'Come, Madame, do not be so astonished! Some of your

remarks made me quite anxious, but I see now that I had nothing to fear. You never guessed my true identity.'

It was the first time any of them had seen Jack Merwin laugh. Yet paradoxically it was by that token that they finally recognized him. Yes, it really was the skipper of the boat that had brought them who stood before them now in his black robe, so reviled and so feared, the same man who but shortly before had nonchalantly chewed his quid of tobacco while his muscular foot struggled with the billowing sail, as he pottered from island to island, curious, taciturn and solitary . . .

In a flash, Angélique saw into the depths of Jack Merwin's personality which had so intrigued her.

But, of course! Of course he was a Jesuit!

How was it she had not noticed the fact sooner? She had been brought up in Catholic convents, so masterfully governed by the members of the most lofty and powerful religious order of the time – every week all the pupils had to make their confessions to one of the reverend fathers, hiding nothing of the shadows on their consciences – how could she ever have allowed herself to be taken in?

How was it that with so many clues, not even a shadow of suspicion had crossed her mind?

That night, sitting on the rocks on Long Island, so 'far away' that he had quite frightened her, *he had been praying* as only the sons of Saint Ignatius know how, and what she had interpreted in him as abstraction or lethargy had been rapture, mystical rapture!

And when he had handed out their food on Monhegan how was it that she had failed to recognize that quick deftness that characterizes all members of whatever religious order, irrespective of their rank, who, ever since the days of their noviciate, have been accustomed to serve the poor their daily ration of soup?

And that very day, had not the sudden change of manner in the young Acadian nobleman, Hubert d'Arpentigny, been due to the fact that he had penetrated the English seaman's disguise and recognized him as perhaps the very missionary who had prepared him for his first communion in days gone by. The priest must somehow have indicated to him that he should say nothing.

Mr Willoughby went up to the Jesuit and sniffed at him then, recognizing the familiar smell of the skipper of the *White Bird*, rubbed himself against his soutane, and the Jesuit father's hand stroked the bear's big soft head.

'Actually, we are already acquainted, Mr Willoughby,' he murmured.

For many a long day since they left New York they had shared the same shelter of weather-beaten planks on the treacherous seas. Mr Willoughby's friendliness finally convinced the most incredulous among them, and their morale collapsed. They were plunged in gloom, realizing that their fate had been decided, and that they had lost. Angélique was incapable of uttering a single word. Never had she felt so mortified and, reflecting on the consequences that this impersonation would have for her and her companions, she no longer had the heart even to laugh at herself for being so utterly and completely taken in. She wondered whether it had been pure chance that had brought the craft of the alleged Jack Merwin alongside Colin's ship or whether, yet again, she had fallen into a trap.

She hung her head, defeated, and a bitter furrow creased the corner of her lips.

The Jesuit turned towards the Englishmen.

'You have nothing to fear,' he said in English. 'Here you are under my protection.'

He walked to the edge of the water, lifted his eyes towards the trees, then cupping his hands round his mouth, gave an Indian call which he repeated several times like a signal.

The leaves began to stir and shortly afterwards a horde of noisy savages appeared, some crossing the river in the shallows while others came down the hill. They fell to their knees before the Jesuit, asking for his blessing and showing every sign of friendliness towards him. And of course the great sagamore Piksarett appeared, proud and boastful.

'You thought you had escaped me,' he said to Angélique. 'But I always knew where you were; I followed what was happening to you and Black Robe has brought you back to me. You are my captive.'

Some of the savages laughed as they ran their hands over Elias Kempton's scant remaining hair, while he seemed more dead than alive with fear, and his tame bear growled threateningly.

On seeing the bear some of the Indians drew back and pointed their spears at it, while others seized their bows. But the Jesuit calmed their agitation with a word. Seeing him lay his hand on the bear's head, the Indians looked at him with reverence, but nothing a Black Robe ever did astonished them.

'Fort Pentagouet, under the command of Baron Saint-Castine, is not far from here,' Father de Vernon told Angélique. 'Would you be good enough to follow me, Madame, and we shall make our way there.'

'Ah, good,' Adhemar's voice suddenly exclaimed as they began to climb the hill, 'are you, Father, by any chance a brother of Jack Merwin's? You don't half look like him. Where's he got to, by the way? It's about time we set sail again! 'Bout time we got away from here, because, here, you know, with all these savages . . .'

CHAPTER FIFTY

'JUST LOOK, FATHER,' said Baron Saint-Castine, pointing emphatically at a wall covered with English scalps, 'am I not a loyal officer in the service of God and His Majesty? I have campaigned with my Etchemins and my Mic-Macs against the English heretics more than enough to win myself a place in Heaven. Could I ever be reproached for being lukewarm in matters of religion, I who brought about the conversion of the great Mateconando chieftain and his children, I who even stood godfather to them since there was no one else on this godforsaken coast to perform this Christian duty at the time they were baptized.

'And yet now Father d'Orgeval, your superior, writes to me reproaching me acrimoniously with what he calls my evasion of duty, or even betrayal, over this matter of the new holy war into which he has just launched the Abenakis. In the first place, I would like to say that I consider that this campaigning has been started prematurely. The Indians are still busy trading and planting their crops, which are vital matters for them.'

'A crusade can suddenly become a matter of urgency,' replied Father de Vernon, 'if it is carried through with the help of every available staunch heart. It may be that your . . . evasion of duty . . . will result in the campaign lasting longer than it should, thus preventing the Indians from doing their bartering and sowing their crops before the winter season.'

'Well anyhow my Indians will be spared that,' Saint-Castine replied sullenly.

'Do you not consider that it was their DUTY to fight for the God in whose name they have been baptized?'

It was the day after their arrival at Pentagouet. The three of them were sitting in the main hall of the Pentagouet outpost finishing the midday meal that had brought them together.

Angélique sat at the end of the big wooden table, Father Maraicher de Vernon in the middle, while Saint-Castine was pacing up and down in some agitation, all the feathers of his Indian headdress a-quiver.

A thick mist that had come up with the dawn had enclosed them all in a grey, opaque world, pierced only by the heart-rending cry of invisible seagulls, like the wailing of lost souls.

The French outpost was a modest building.

Saint-Castine had placed at Angélique's disposition a small room which must have been his own, but she had spent part of the night in a lean-to shed where the Englishmen had been shut up, doing her best to cheer them, for they were plunged in gloom.

Now that they had fallen once more into the hands of the French they would doubtless be taken off to Quebec and sold to those terrible Canadian Papists. Unless of course Baron Saint-Castine managed to negotiate with Boston to buy them back. The Reverend Patridge could rest assured that his co-religionists, for the most part notables and magistrates, would not abandon him, even if it meant clapping on a tax to raise the sum necessary to buy him back, but Miss Pidgeon, who had no family, would find herself doomed to lifelong captivity, the most painful aspect of which would be the necessity daily to resist all solicitations to adjure her faith and be baptized a Catholic.

Being all worn out, they did finally get some sleep, after partaking of a little maize and fish, and Angélique sat thinking for a long time how she could get a message to her husband.

In the end everything began to go round and round in her head. By what piece of ill-fortune had Colin stopped, that morning, the very ship carrying the disguised Jesuit back to Acadia, after completing his period of espionage. Had Colin known the identity of the English captain who chewed his quid of tobacco and spat so expertly into the sea? ... Was that why he had murmured: 'Take care, they wish you ill?'

Piksarett's darting shadow seemed to hover ubiquitously over all her peregrinations. He had been at Maquoit the day before Gold Beard's ship cast anchor; she had thought she caught sight of him on Mackworth Island and now here he was waiting for her on the banks of the Penobscot.

Having made up her mind that she must speak to Saint-Castine, she did not have to seek him out, for the very next day he himself came to invite her to join him and the Jesuit in a meal.

The priest had been very busy ever since their arrival the preceding day. Informed of his coming by their drums, the Indians poured in from all sides, for they considered it better to be baptized by Black Robe than by the modest, worthy Recollect monks.

High Mass had been sung, and the prisoners had heard the distant sound of plain chant.

During the meal, Baron Saint-Castine kept winking encouragingly at Angélique. 'Everything will be all right, have no fear' he was trying to tell her. Nevertheless, he kept a close guard over his tongue in front of the Jesuit, who, after saying grace, ate frugally and unhurriedly, his eyes downcast. Then the debate began. Castine claimed that he had never refused his help to the Reverend Fathers in their heavy, uninspiring task of converting the Indians and bringing Catholicism to North America. By way of proof he showed him his monstrous collection of red, brown and blond scalps which, hanging from wooden pegs, covered the whole of one wall of the room with a stale-smelling, repulsive layer of human hair. They had been mounted on little wicker rings, to which they had been sewn with pieces of gut like beaver skins, and hung up to dry beside the cabin doors of the Etchemin, Tarratine and Mic-Mac braves. Then, when they were ready, they had been brought to Fort Pentagouet, and handed over to Saint-Castine, who had thanked the Indians in the name of the King of France and given them small gifts in return.

'When I think how many of these heretics' scalps I took myself!' said Saint-Castine, with the pained expression of one whose devotion to duty has passed unnoticed. 'My score was always double that of any of my braves.

'And, what is more, Father, this year we have been at peace. It was clearly understood, when you met Father d'Orgeval and Jean Rousse before you left for New England, that no move was to be made against the heretics until you got back, since the point of your mission was to discover some pretext to break our treaties. And then Father d'Orgeval goes unearthing the war hatchet, as we Indians say, more than ten days before your return!'

'No doubt he had found better grounds for doing so than any I might have brought him,' Father de Vernon retorted without emotion. 'He is guided by God and I have rarely seen him embark on any course without weighing all the consequences.'

'I think I can tell you why he began this war without waiting for you,' Angélique interrupted.

Father de Vernon, who throughout the entire conversation had addressed his remarks entirely to Saint-Castine or had sat deep in thought looking down at the remains of his frugal repast, slowly turned upon her the cheerless, enigmatic glance that she knew from her experience of him as Jack Merwin.

'Yes,' Angélique went on, 'I am certain that Father d'Orgeval saw an opportunity to have me taken prisoner by the Canadians when I went alone to the English village of Brunswick-Falls to the west of the Kennebec, and he immediately declared war, knowing that a few days later I would have reached the safety of Gouldsboro and that any such action would no longer be possible.'

To her astonishment the Jesuit nodded in agreement.

'Yes, that is indeed what must have happened. What were you doing in that English village, Madame?'

Angélique gave him a defiant glance.

'I was taking a little girl, whom we had bought from the Abenakis, back to her family.'

'So you, a Frenchwoman and a Catholic, considered it right and proper to take an innocent child back to that nest of obscurantist heretics, when fate, nay, Providence I should say, had decreed that she should have the opportunity of discovering the true light of Christ in Canada?'

At first Angélique made no reply, for she could not get used to hearing Jack Merwin speaking in this manner, but eventually she retorted with a half smile.

'The nest, yes! Children are like birds. However poor their nest, that is where they like to be.'

'So you opposed God's will for the child,' he broke in severely. 'And ... how is it that after this ... ambush, you were not taken off to Quebec?'

'I fought,' she replied angrily. 'I fought for my life and my freedom.'

Then remembering the disdainful look he had given her in the moonlight on the beach at Long Island she repeated: 'my freedom!'

'So you fired on the soldiers of Christ?' he went on.

'All I did was fire on savages who were trying to scalp me.'

'But ...'

'And I was lucky enough to be able to come to an agreement

with Sagamore Piksarett, your notable convert.'

The Jesuit frowned. This seemed to him the more incredible part of her story.

'And why, in your estimation, Madame, should Father d'Orgeval wish to take you prisoner and have you sent to Canada?'

'You know that as well as I do . . .'

'I am sorry, Madame, but I don't. I left these parts several months ago, during which time it has been extremely difficult for me to keep in touch with my superior. My life among the English was dangerous, for had they discovered that I was spying for Christ and the King of France they would undoubtedly have given me a hard time of it. At the time I set out you had only just landed at Gouldsboro.'

'But you already regarded us as thorns in your flesh, if not as actual enemies, settling as we did at Gouldsboro with much greater means at our disposal than most settlers have. What a wonderful opportunity to discredit my husband's name and hold him up to the fanatical execration of the people of New France by the revelation that his wife was the incarnation of the She-Devil,' Angélique retorted bitterly.

'That you must know about, I feel sure . . . The visionary nun described a settlement by the shore, which could have been any one, but which ill-intentioned people insisted could only be Gouldsboro . . . Did she not see the horses we brought with us in the symbol of a unicorn, the mythical animal the She-Devil was riding when she first appeared? And when I rode into the back country, the similarity between the two scenes was obvious and the Canadians fell to their knees in terror. And yet all this was pure chance . . .'

'Yes,' the Jesuit father replied thoughtfully, 'when diabolical processes are set in motion, it often happens that chance seems to favour those through whom Evil is being perpetrated.'

'But who is perpetrating Evil in all this?' cried Angélique, and why must it be I who has to be your She-Devil? After all there are other women in Acadia on to whom you could have pinned the name as well as me. Was it not you, Saint-Castine, who mentioned a woman somewhere in the depths of Frenchman Bay renowned for the debauched life she leads and nicknamed Marcelline-la-Belle?'

The Baron burst out laughing.

'Oh no, not her. That would be too funny. She is just about capable of bearing children to every ship's captain that comes ashore, and she can open clams faster than any other woman in the Bay. They say she can get her knife between the two halves of the shell and split it open before the preceding shell has reached the ground ... She's a juggler, I grant you that.'

'And might not this skill also be considered magical?' Angélique asked with a laugh. 'What do you say, Father?'

But Jack Merwin remained icy, refusing to be drawn into lighthearted discussion of so serious a matter. He seemed to be considering the suggestion, then shook his head.

'Marcelline Raymondeau? No, she is not intelligent enough.'

'So a She-Devil has to be intelligent, does she?'

'Indeed she does! If you think about it. Who, next to God, is more intelligent than Lucifer, the Lord of all Demons?

'It is a well-known fact which has often been observed that succubi, that is to say She-Devils, when incarnate in a female body, have great difficulty in hiding their brilliant intelligence during their sojourn on earth. It has even proved possible sometimes to unmask them by the predominance of this particular quality – which is so rare in women.

'Let us not forget that the most important of all the infernal spirits, Behemot, the Beast, Mammon, Cupidity, and Abadon, the Exterminating Angel, are capable of possessing succubi.'

'I've got it,' cried Saint-Castine as if suddenly inspired. 'The woman we are after must be Madamoiselle Radegone de Ferjac, who is governess to the children of Monsieur de la Roche-Posay at Port-Royal on the Peninsula. She is as ill-natured as a weasel, as miserly as your Mammon, and as ugly as the seven deadly sins.'

But once again the Jesuit shook his head.

'No, you are on the wrong tack. What you suggest is out of the question because you are talking about an ugly woman. It may be that the femininity of these succubi cannot manifest itself in any other way, but it is a fact that they have never been known to inhabit the body of an ugly woman.'

'And what about witches?'

'There's more to it than that. Witches are only human beings who have dealings with the Devil, whereas the infernal spirit that enters the body of a woman or becomes incarnate in her at her birth is truly a demon, one of the fallen angels that followed Lucifer in his fall from Heaven at the beginning of Time.'

'But you cannot think that of me, it's impossible,' cried Angélique, wringing her hands. 'I have done nothing, nothing to deserve so horrible a reputation.'

'And yet the prediction is quite specific. It speaks of a woman who is very beautiful and seductive . . .'

'Am I so beautiful, then?'

Her disturbance was such that it removed all coquettishness from her question, and young Saint-Castine gave her a broad smile of admiration.

'Yes, Madame, you are. But I shall not accuse you for that . . .'

'And seductive? . . .' Angélique went on, turning towards the Jesuit. 'Come, Father, I spent more than three days in your company . . .'

He looked down at her with his mercurial gaze, sometimes sombre, sometimes sparkling, and sometimes expressionless, a gaze in which one could read nothing, and thoughtfully stroked his chin.

'Seductive? . . . I don't know . . . but captivating, yes . . . On Midsummer's night at Monhegan . . .'

Angélique, fearing that the blushes she felt covering her cheeks might reach her forehead, interrupted him.

'Yes indeed! Midsummer night . . . since you mention it . . . What could anyone possibly reproach me for? I laughed, I drank, I danced, granted. But since you were present, you can bear witness that I did nothing dishonourable. Is the Catholic Church going to prove as strict as the Reformed Church in matters of merrymaking? I grant that had I known who you were and what you did . . .'

It was his turn to interrupt her smartly:

'Really? Were you really not in any way suspicious, Madame? I was occasionally anxious about your shrewd eyes.'

'Oh no, not at all! Have no illusions about that. At the very outside I thought you might be the erstwhile captain of some pirate ship, or the youngest son of some noble family seeking his fortune . . . So you can see for yourself that, alas! I am no sorceress in spite of the powers with which I am credited. Had I known, as I said, who you were, a Jesuit, I should certainly have been less . . . exuberant, more careful. But beyond saying this, I have no regrets . . .' For a moment her mind went back to that wonderful night.

'How can I explain the delight I felt on that lovely June night, after all the danger we had been through . . . Had not death itself laid its hand on me that very day? You know that better than anyone, you who rescued me from the sea . . .'

Then she broke off, as she realized that it had been in fact that very same priest sitting there now with one hand on his crucifix who had dragged her by her hair up the beach, had brought her back to life, and had carried her in his arms back to the fire.

Never had Angélique felt so embarrassed in all her life as she tried to find words that would not land her from the frying pan into the fire, when she noticed a tremor in Father de Vernon's lips, a fleeting sparkle cross his eyes and a shadow of a smile on his stony features, and she guessed that he was trying not to burst out laughing.

In fact since the beginning of his conversation with her he had been laughing. He had been laughing inwardly, enjoying her embarrassment and confusion, as he made her say all kinds of silly things.

'And you are making fun of me again,' she exclaimed.

'Well, I must say . . .'

And he began to laugh openly. Then he looked at her ironically, but with a certain warmth as well, and for the first time she discovered the spark of humanity hidden behind those severe eyes, and thought she glimpsed a look of friendly complicity.

Could she hope then that during those three days she had spent on Jack Merwin's boat between the bear and the little black boy, he had really got to know her? He did not think that she was a She-Devil. She could read that in his eyes.

'Let me go free, Merwin,' she murmured warmly, reaching out impulsively towards him.

The priest immediately looked away, his heavy eyelids drooped forthwith and he resumed his haughty expression.

'But . . . you may go, Madame, who is stopping you? You are not my prisoner, as far as I know . . . You are only Piksarett's . . .'

CHAPTER FIFTY-ONE

SEEN IN the evening light, Gouldsboro was already a small town.

Thus did Angélique discover it the next evening, as she glimpsed in the distance, through a veil of light drizzle, the winking lights of the houses grouped about the port, spread out along the shore and climbing up to the very top of the cliffs.

The boat danced up and down on the black sea, in which the lights, yellow and white from lanterns and candles, and red from the huge bonfires that served as beacons to mark the dangerous reefs, shone back in a thousand glistening reflections.

The Acadian conducting them said he would put in towards the west side of Gouldsboro and that he wanted to set off again immediately for Pentagouet. Father de Vernon had offered them the use of his boat for the final stage of their journey home, and once Angélique, her English protégés, the little Negro boy and the bear, had been set ashore at some point along the Gouldsboro Peninsula, the man was to make his way back immediately.

Angélique delighted in the smell of the land, and of the village borne to them on the wind.

'I shall see you again in Gouldsboro,' Piksarett had promised her, just before she set out from Pentagouet. 'Don't forget that you are my prisoner and that I have to claim your ransom from your husband.'

But apart from this reminder of their relationship, he had shown himself very liberal, for reasons known only to himself, and had allowed her to set off, after giving her his solemn blessing, literally as well as metaphorically, for this great sagamore invested with supraterrestrial powers enjoyed pontificating and was only too happy to distribute, after the manner of the Black Robes, his protection in the form of a large sign of the Cross.

The fog cleared towards the beginning of the afternoon, thus enabling them to set sail. Father de Vernon and Baron Saint-Castine accompanied them down to the Pentagouet shore. The Jesuit retained the golden-haired lad who had served as his ship's boy; the boy's name was Abbial Neals, an orphan Merwin had picked up on the quayside in New York. No one knew whether he was of Irish, English or Swedish extraction, but be that as it might, he was to be baptized.

At the last moment someone came down with a large trunk, into which Baron Saint-Castine had hastily piled part of his collection of English scalps.

'Monsieur de Peyrac has told me of his plans to go to Quebec,' he explained to Angélique, 'and I thought I would ask him to be so good as to take this present from me to the Governor with him. I hope that it will create a good impression, and that those in high places will stop accusing me of not being sufficiently keen to fight the English.'

They also found room for the barrel of Armagnac; then the helmsman, an Acadian farmer, took the tiller, while Sammy, who had served his apprenticeship in seafaring during the past few days, helped him with the sail.

Very soon, the pearly curtain of rain masked the shapes of the treees, and hid from their view, standing on the shore of a lost river, in the heart of the American forest land, the tall figure of a man in a black soutane, a man whose name had been Jack Merwin.

CHAPTER FIFTY-TWO

How MANY TIMES since the previous evening had Joffrey de Peyrac turned over in his mind the terrible tidings he had received?

The night had passed without his moving; he had remained sitting at the table, his head resting on one hand and his eyes closed.

How many times during the course of that night had he heard the echo within him of the rough, mocking voice of the Swiss mercenary?

'Her name? ... I don't know. But when he was making love to her he called her Angélique! ... Angélique! ...'

And every time the same spasm of pain gripped him.

And then there had been Yann's words, which had thrown a little more light on the situation – if one could talk of light among the gloom of these intrigues which had suddenly drawn a hideous mask over his beloved's face:

'They were kissing one another like long-separated lovers ...'

Was this the key to the mystery, the explanation of her shocking betrayal? A former lover? A man from her past, from that part of her life which she no doubt missed – when she had been free, her life easier, when she had been free to satisfy the desires of her delightful body as she wished, without fear of the anger of a jealous husband.

He could see now how it all must have happened ... the stranger, a man from the past, hearing the name Angélique and learning that she was in the neighbourhood, had sent a message to her at Houssnock, and she, under the pretext of a journey to the English village, had taken advantage of Peyrac's absence and set off to meet her lover. Then an accomplice had met Peyrac on the Kennebec and given him false information to keep him away from her more effectively, and for longer ...

No ... it did not tie up. There was something else ... And Angélique appeared to him as she had been that last night at Wapassou, when she had raised her head to listen to the wolves howling, and the last glimmers of the aurora borealis had lighted her face, so that her complexion exactly matched the pale pink of the sky. The lustre of her dreamy eyes, inscrutable and wondering, had sent a tide of adoration coursing through him, for in those eyes he had read the certainty that she was a unique woman, unlike any other – his, and his alone.

How naïve and presumptuous he had been! What an arch fool! How had he failed to see that she was a mere wanton, with a life rich in experience, magnificently endowed with all the witchcraft of her sex, a woman who played upon the things that made her so different from the rest in order to permit herself, whenever desire or pleasure urged, to be just like the rest – unfaithful, weak-minded, without honour or memories ... Nothing is sacred to such creatures ... nothing but the pleasure of the moment, and the hope that afterwards a smile or a glance will serve to obliterate the wounds they have inflicted ... It is so easy to win back an infatuated man, so tempting for that man to believe what a pretty mouth tells him – that she loves him ... that she has always loved him and none but him! Yes, in spite of everything, in spite of her betrayal ...

From time to time he would be filled with a mad hope. It was all just a bad dream, Angélique was about to arrive, she would appear, and in a few words would explain everything ... and he would find her again, entire, pure, his friend, his lover, giving herself to him alone, caressing and passionate, as she had been in the solitude of the woods, during the winter, snug in their big bed, or in the springtime, when they had walked together among the wild hyacinths, feeling free and intoxicated by the renewal of this wild landscape over which they reigned, triumphant sovereigns, and he would look at her with rapture, and kiss her over and over again, until he could bear it no longer, then sure that they were alone ...

Angélique's eyes upturned towards the trees reflected the fresh green of the new leaves, and she would say with a laugh: 'You are crazy, my dear lord ...'

Then she was his. His alone, and had pleasure through him alone ...

This was how it would be when he found her again ... It could not be otherwise. But then his thoughts stumbled like a blind man against the indisputable reality of the facts:

'When he was making love to her, he called her Angélique! Angélique!'

A blow, a muffled cry. Every time the memory of these words shook him, made him double up as if he had been pierced by a razor-sharp blade.

He could not stop his mind returning constantly to the same point: she had been seen, naked and languid with pleasure in Gold Beard's arms!

The idea of doubting poor Kurt Ritz's story had never so much as crossed his mind. The straightforwardness with which the fellow had told his tale was the direct consequence of the fact that he had no idea it concerned his master's private life. And the wine he had been given to drink on an empty stomach, had for a brief moment dulled his perceptions, making him all the more frank. Had he been sober, he might have noticed the general embarrassment, grown wary, and cut his story short, for he was by nature a cautious man.

No, there was no doubt about it. Kurt Ritz had been an eye-witness of the scene as he made his escape. One night, when separated from her husband, Angélique had abandoned herself to the caresses of a strange man. She had been caught unawares, she, the wife of Count Peyrac, his wife, in the arms of the pirate Gold Beard, and there was no way round that . . .

In Joffrey de Peyrac's eyes, the other woman, the Adorable one, was fading away . . . Only the Stranger remained – the woman he had once suspected her to be, the proud, sensual woman, who had lived a full, free life, the play actor, the more skilled for being only half conscious of her own wiles, finding them natural and necessary.

Life had left its mark on her and in facing its difficulties she had blunted her capacity for affection. Nothing mattered to her but the gratification of the moment. The dominance Angélique had over all men, did it not come precisely from her intimate understanding of them? She knew men too well, she was too close to them . . . With a smile, with a word, she had them at her beck and call, be they lords or rustics. Her skill was no doubt due to her having been far too long and from too tender an age the victim of men. But now it was too late, the harm was done, the terrifying truth was there. Now she was stronger than any man, feared nothing from them, and took those she desired . . . She liked all men, any kind of man, such was the secret of her charm and her unfailing hold over them –

except possibly those who made themselves ridiculous by their infatuation with themselves and their military superiority, like that fellow Pont-Briand. She had not deserved much credit for repulsing him – she did not like him. But what about Loménie-Chambord? Peyrac had noticed the warmth between the two of them, and he began to wonder whether the virtuous gentleman had not deceived him beneath his own roof? For was she not capable of dragging a saint down to hell?

Angélique! Angélique!

The red mist of vengeance clouded Peyrac's eyes.

To set sail, come up with Gold Beard's ship one night ... climb aboard, surprise the two of them, kill them ...

It cost him a superhuman effort to take a hold on himself again.

Day was breaking over Gouldsboro. The mist transformed the countryside into a cold, deserted waste, echoing with the mournful call of conch shells across the bay.

Only a few miles away Angélique was waking up at Fort Pentagouet. In a few hours' time she would embark, joyous and impatient to see her husband again, and by night she would be there to stand before him.

Utterly exhausted, Peyrac saw in the depths of his heart a shattered image. He was so weary that he no longer sought excuses for the truth which he must face in all its bitterness; and he at last accepted that he must see her as she was, cheap and deceitful ... like the rest ... a woman just like them all!

CHAPTER FIFTY-THREE

DAY HAD dawned with all its heavy tasks upon which human lives depended.

Count Peyrac set off towards the port. Alone in the white, muffled world, in which he would henceforth have to walk alone, with this astonishing sense of bereavement, this unexpected wound, the depths of whose pain he had not yet fully plumbed ... Angélique! ...

As he made his way down to the beach he began to feel a burning impatience to do battle. It was this that gave him strength to stand upright, and it occurred to him the fog was a blessing, for he well knew that not one of his ships was ready to put to sea that day and give chase to the pirate. The fog would protect him from acting with ill-considered haste and would enable him to lay his plans with care. Tomorrow or the day after he could begin his hunt to the death, and then nothing would stop him until he had come up with Gold Beard and killed him with his own hands.

The fitting out of the *Gouldsboro*, the chebec and two other luggers anchored in the harbour was immediately put in hand.

Obsessed with his ideas of vengeance, he received at first with indifference, then with irritation, the news brought by some Indians that two English ships were in distress off Shoodic Point. Let them go to the devil, English, French or whoever they were.

Then he pulled himself together.

Let it never be said that a woman had made him forget his duties and responsibilities, that a woman had so unmanned him as to render him indifferent to the lives of human beings which he alone had the power to save.

Gouldsboro, which he had created, was the beacon of Frenchman Bay. Everyone looked to it to provide aid, life, and counsel. Oh! how little it all mattered to him, suddenly. But he must not flinch, not for a single moment. The slightest sign of wavering on his part would bring the entire structure down.

And those who knew already, what were they expecting of him? Had he lived so long, and triumphed over so many pitfalls, in order to doom and destroy it all in a few hours for the sake of a disastrous love affair?

The long habit of strict inner discipline, an innate sense of responsibility which had always, throughout his already long career, marked him out as a leader, a man apart from the common herd, came into operation within him and helped him to bear up.

Bear up! . . .

Promptly he went on board his ship, mustered his crew, set off for the disaster area, and was successful in rescuing the little fleet which the State of Massachusetts had dispatched to Frenchman Bay to avenge the Abenaki massacres fomented by the French. One of the ships was commanded by the Bostonian Phipps, the other by the English admiral Bartholomew Sheringham himself.

Back in the shelter of Gouldsboro Bay the English admiral was only too pleased to accept Count Peyrac's generous hospitality. Very elegant, in a powdered wig, and his sword at his side, he made no secret of the fact that he had little appetite for this expedition deep into Frenchman Bay in pursuit of an invisible adversary, constantly liable to vanish up some creek. But these damned French had to be taught a lesson. An undertaking must be obtained from the Quebec Government to restrain their hordes of dedicated savages. It happened that they had heard that Monsieur de Ville d'Avray, the Governor of Acadia, was touring up the Saint John river, visiting his best friend, Monsieur de Grand-Bois. If he could be penned up and taken prisoner, it would be an excellent thing for the English Government.

Peyrac had little difficulty in convincing Admiral Sheringham that the expedition could have no other outcome than a declaration of war between the French and the English, since any pretext to extend the conflict would be welcome in Quebec, and that he would do better to join Peyrac in hunting down the pirates that infested Frenchman Bay and hampered the activities of the English as well as Portuguese and French codfishers during the annual season.

But Phipps, the Bostonian, quite a number of whose relatives had been scalped by the Canadians and their Abenakis, refused to give up the chase, and set sail again as soon as the fog had lifted. All the same, since he was acting on his own, and no longer in the company of the British admiral, the diplomatic implications of his action would be less serious and the battle in the Saint John river less bloody. Peyrac, after considering all possible means of defusing the bomb, summoned the local Etchemin chieftains and their principal Mohicans.

He agreed with them that messengers bearing two wampum necklaces should be sent to the Malecites and the Souriquois in the east: let them, if they had to, help the French to whom they were bound by ties of friendship and family, but without killing any Englishmen if possible. If the war hatchet were disinterred in Frenchman Bay, it would be of little advantage to the local tribesmen, who had already suffered heavy losses during the cruel winter famine, and who would be left to protect them from bands of raiding Iroquois, a constant threat in the summer months?

Having sent out these words of wisdom, he entrusted Cromley with the task of warning the few scattered Englishmen clinging to their plots of land at the mouths of the St Croix and Machias rivers.

Old Salprice would no doubt refuse to leave his little fort, but the Strington family at Merchnaisby would find it in their interest to take refuge in Gouldsboro for the month of July.

Each and every one of these measures had at first cost Joffrey de Peyrac a superhuman effort, then little by little he had come to carry them out automatically; and the performance of these essential and inescapable tasks acted as a temporary balm to his open wound, conferring a kind of oblivion.

And yet, in spite of the bustle and activity of that day, no other in his life had ever seemed so long, so dreary and so cruel.

Meanwhile, he was supervising the preparation of the ships for the expedition that was to set out the following day against Gold Beard.

He must not weaken.

His revenge too must be carried out in a level-headed manner, without losing sight of the general interest. He had no right to do otherwise.

And yet, what did the others matter, what did his work matter, what did life matter . . . *without her?* . . .

That evening he again convened the same people as the day before, in order to continue the council meeting which had been so dramatically interrupted by the arrival of Kurt Ritz, and he asked the admiral to join them.

With the exception of the latter, who was unaware of the painful and embarrassing nature of the situation, they all entered the room with downcast eyes and circumspect tread.

Peyrac sat waiting for them behind the carved table, on which had been placed his ink stand, his pens, a sand-box, his measuring instruments and, as on the previous day, his maps spread out to view.

He begged them cordially to come in and take their places.

At the sound of his voice, so calm, with that slight hoarseness to which they had grown accustomed, they looked up, and in spite of his normal appearance, gave a shudder.

He was wearing a magnificent costume of ivory satin slashed with scarlet moiré and with tiny diamond-shaped pleats each held in position by a pearl stitch. Every movement revealed a gleam of red. It was a costume that had been brought from London on the *Gouldsboro*, together with his tight-fitting red knee boots and his gauntlets. Peyrac preferred the English style of dress, which, favouring as it did the doublet and hose and soft leather boots, suited his roving life better than the French-style jerkin and vests and boots with very wide turn-down tops. On the other hand, the pearl-studded lace of his cravat and cuffs was in the French fashion.

His thick black hair, framing his weather-beaten, scarred face gave him the air of a pirate and contrasted disconcertingly with the refinement and elegance of his dress, while the lighter patches of hair at his temples gave an unexpected softness to the dark skin of his sun-and-wind-tanned face. Was there a touch of pallor lurking beneath that brown skin, a trace of emotion under those impassive features, or of suffering behind that bold, penetrating gaze that came to rest upon them and did not turn away? No one could have guessed it! It was they who looked down and seemed to suffer acute embarrassment.

'A lesson,' the filibuster Gilles Vanereick was often to repeat later, 'a lesson, that's what that fellow Peyrac gave us that night! A lesson to all us men, who seem destined by nature and from the moment of birth to be cuckolded one day ... I tell you, that never did a cuckold face the world with such superb dignity!'

'Gentlemen,' Peyrac said to them, 'you know that I must needs go to war and I do not know what fate Heaven has reserved for my arms. Now at every point on the horizon a storm is brewing. The least I can do is to leave you with the full knowledge of a situation which your courage, your good sense, and your skill will help you to face. And, I would add, your desire for peace. We have no enemies. In this can reside your strength.

'I am speaking particularly to you, gentlemen from La Rochelle, for it is into your hands that I shall shortly commit the fate of this establishment and its land defences. Monsieur d'Urville is to accompany me, as will Monsieur Vanereick, and our English ally Lord Bartholomew Sheringham, in pursuit of the pirate who has already caused us all a great deal of trouble. He must be got rid of once and for all. So we must concert our plans for defence, pursuit and attack. And first we must take stock of and allocate the ammunition we have at our disposal.'

Absorbed in their calculations and plans, they did not see that the night had fallen. A Spaniard entered to light the candles in the candlesticks and in the wrought-iron chandelier that hung from the ceiling.

Little by little, they became caught up once more in the routine of life and forgot the incident of the previous evening. Consequently, they thought at first that it was only the return of a bad dream when the same sentry as the night before poked his head round the door with the same alarmed expression and called to Peyrac:

'My lord! Someone to see you!'

But this time it was not Kurt Ritz, haggard after his escape from the pirate.

This time it was She.

As they turned round, they saw a dazzling apparition; framed against the dark backcloth of the night, they saw HER! ...

CHAPTER FIFTY-FOUR

DAZZLING IN her beauty, she stood looking at them with a radiant smile on her lips. And swiftly her eyes sought out, at the far end of the room, the tall figure of Count Peyrac. Joffrey! Wearing a costume she had not seen him in before. He was there ...

Everyone present, petrified, looked at her in utter silence.

The golden, velvety sheen of the big sealskin cloak she wore draped about her heightened the warm tones of her flesh and, standing out against the night, her hair shone so golden that it looked like a halo.

It was little Laurier Berne who had escorted Angélique to the door of the main hall of the fort where he knew his father and the other notables, in company with the filibuster captain and the English admiral, were holding council with Count Peyrac.

She just did not know the place, so much had Gouldsboro changed. That almost deserted shore of the previous year was teeming with life, so full of activity continued into the dusk that she might well have thought she was in some other settlement, had she not very soon encountered her friends Abigail and Séverine Berne.

Her impatience to join her husband as soon as possible and to make sure that he was in Gouldsboro prevented her from noticing the embarrassment and coolness of the two women's welcome. It was only later that she remembered and understood why. But young Laurier had appeared with a basket of shellfish on his shoulder, and had thrown his arms around her neck with all the irrepressibility of his ten years. 'Dame Angélique! Oh! Dame Angélique! How marvellous!'

At her request he had guided her through the winding streets of the new Gouldsboro. As they reached the fort they passed a man carrying a halberd.

'That's the Swiss mercenary,' Laurier had whispered. 'He arrived here yesterday evening . . .'

'Hi, you there! Haven't I seen you somewhere before?' Angélique called, struck with uneasiness on perceiving the grim look the man gave her as he went by.

'Yes indeed, Madame!' he replied. 'You have seen me before.' There was a note of contempt in his Teutonic voice.

But Laurier had already led her up the wooden steps and the council chamber door stood open before her.

In complete silence – a crushing silence which immediately struck her as unusual – she walked into the room. There were faces she knew, faces turned to stone . . .

'Monsieur Manigault, how do you do . . . Oh! Master Berne, how pleased I am to see you again . . . My dear Pastor, how are you? . . .'

All these Protestants in their black jerkins, all these motley strangers, a French filibuster, an English officer, then a Recollect father in grey homespun . . .

Not one of them, not a single one, made any reply. No one . . . no one . . . Their eyes followed her. And all these people . . . they just stood there like so many wooden figures, Joffrey like all the rest of them, motionless, watching as she made her way down the room.

Now she was standing before him and her eyes sought his in vain. And yet he was looking at her with a fixed gaze that was both strange and sombre. A nightmare! Joffrey bent down over the hand she held out to him but she did not feel his lips on her skin, it was merely a show of politeness.

She heard herself ask in a faraway voice that seemed to tremble as she spoke:

'What has happened? Has some disaster befallen Gouldsboro?'

Then everyone came to life, and one by one they bowed and left the room. No one thought to smile. In the same atmosphere of catastrophe as the previous day, the same ceremonial began all over again.

Once outside, Gilles Vanereick said, gasping for breath: 'Was that her?'

'Well, who do you think it was?' Manigault growled.

'But she's . . . she's wonderful! She is marvellous! . . . That changes everything . . . Gentlemen, how do you expect so beautiful a woman to help making conquests wherever she goes, how could she help succumbing occasionally to the love she stirs up in people? . . . It would be immoral . . . I myself feel . . . Oh! my God, what will happen now? It's terrible! I hope he doesn't . . . No, she is too lovely for him to kill her . . . My legs are giving way beneath me . . . I am a very sensitive man, you know . . .' and he was obliged to sit down on the sand.

CHAPTER FIFTY-FIVE

'WHAT IS going on?' Angélique repeated, turning towards her husband. 'Has someone died?'

'Possibly! Where have you come from?'

Looking up at Peyrac's clouded brow and icy expression, she tried to understand.

'What do you mean? Where have I come from? . . . Did Yann not get here? Did he not tell you that . . .'

'Yes he did! He told me . . . he told me you were taken prisoner by Gold Beard . . . He told me a lot more too . . . and so did Kurt Ritz.'

'Kurt Ritz?'

'The Swiss mercenary who has been working for me, and who was also taken prisoner by Gold Beard last month. Ritz managed to make his escape three days ago. Before doing so he saw you on board Gold Beard's ship. He got away one night by climbing down the poop . . . The window was open . . . He saw you . . . on board the ship . . . in the chartroom . . . with him . . . WITH HIM . . .'

Joffrey de Peyrac spoke in broken phrases, his voice muffled and terrible, and with every word the truth began to dawn in Angélique's mind.

Paralysed by this overwhelming sense of surprise and terror, she could see the truth advancing towards her like a monstrous but real beast, ready to pounce and baring its claws to rend her to pieces . . . The man! . . . The man whom she had seen making her escape that night in Casco Bay . . . That had been the Swiss mercenary, one of Peyrac's men . . . and he had seen her . . . he had seen Colin enter her room and take her in his arms . . .

'The window was open,' the strangled voice went on as if far away ... 'He saw you, Madame! You were naked ... naked in Gold Beard's arms and responding to his kisses ... to his caresses ... to him! ... To him! ...'

What had he expected to hear by way of reply? An exclamation of indignation, vehement denials, possibly a laugh? But no! ... silence!

Nothing but silence! The most terrible thing to suffer after such words.

And in the silence that fell drop by drop, every second adding its leaden weight to the one before, Joffrey de Peyrac thought he would die of distress.

Time was passing. The moment had passed ... to retrieve herself. Every second had fallen like molten lead, setting its seal on the inevitable. Confirming her guilt, which was still manifest in her sudden livid pallor and the hunted look in her wide, startled eyes.

Angélique's brain was quite incapable of gathering two thoughts together at once. Everything jangled together in a dreadful fog.

Colin! Colin! ... She must tell him that it was Colin ... No! That would make matters worse ... He had already hated him before all this.

If she had wanted to, she would have been quite incapable of offering the least explanation, of uttering a single word. Her throat would not let a single sound through, and she was trembling from head to foot. She began to feel faint and had to lean against the wall and close her eyes. And seeing her lower her eyelids with that tender, pained and secret expression that always moved him to the depths and occasionally irritated him, the Count's anger was unleashed.

'Don't lower your eyes!' he shrieked at her, almost breaking the table beneath his fist, 'Look at me!'

He grabbed her by the hair, and forced her head brutally backwards.

She thought that he had broken her neck. Leaning over her, his burning eyes scanned the face which he could no longer read, a stranger's face. He may have been speaking, she did not hear him. 'So it was true! You! ... You! You whom I had put on so high a pedestal!'

He shook her furiously in his mad desire to smash the false image she was holding out to him and find the other woman, his beloved.

Then suddenly he struck her with the full force of his raised arm, so violently that Angélique's head was knocked sideways and struck the wooden wall. A red mist came down over her eyes. He let go of her and pushed her away from him. She did not know how she managed to remain standing.

Joffrey de Peyrac walked over to the window, and looked out through the panes at the damp night, breathing heavily in an attempt to regain control of himself.

When he turned back towards her again, his wife was still standing there motionless with closed eyes. A thin trickle of blood had begun to run down from one side of her delicate nose.

'Get out! Get out!' he said in an icy voice. 'I loathe the sight of you. Get out, I say! I don't want to see you ever again! I don't want to kill you . . .'

CHAPTER FIFTY-SIX

SHE LURCHED and staggered on, bumping into corners and unfamiliar pieces of furniture in the semi-darkness of a room fitfully lit by the pale light of the moon as it came out between clouds. Her desire to hide, to vanish for ever had sent Angélique deep into the heart of the wooden fortress, and rather than face the gusty wind outside and the busy life of the village, or the terrible solitude of the open country where she would find no refuge from hostile creatures, the instinct of a wounded beast that seeks out its burrow in order to die there had borne her through corridors and stairways to the door of this huge, private room, and without recognizing it, she knew that this was 'their room', the one in which they had made love the previous year, the one in which she had dreamed of finding herself alone with him again.

She groped around, stumbling against sharp corners, and finally came to a halt in the middle of the room, where, in the midst of the infernal chaos that had crushed her, she became aware of the first sound perceptible to her – the intermingled sound of two people breathing, a sound that encompassed her and which, she only realized after a moment of fear, was none other than the echo of her own convulsive breathing and the sound of the surf outside, beating upon the rocky spur below the fort.

She was alone.

The fear which for an instant had swamped all other sensations, now left her only to be replaced by the crushing certainty of an irreparable catastrophe. One half of her head felt enormous, having acquired a shapeless excrescence like the lumps one sees on pumpkins, which seemed to radiate pain down one side as if the swelling were made of red-hot iron. She raised one hand gingerly to it and encountered an area of flesh devoid of all sensation. There was in fact no swelling but the mere touch of her fingers sent a terrible stab of pain through her. In the same flash everything came back to her with merciless clarity. Colin! ... His arms about her, his hands exploring her body, his lips taking possession of hers in a kiss that went on and on ...

The man, hiding outside, had seen all this by the light of the candle ... And now Joffrey knew ... and was accusing her of the worst. How could she make him understand, how could she explain things to him, how could she get him to accept that? ...

Were she so much as to mention the name of Colin, he would kill her. He had almost killed her once already that evening. She had felt this in the depths of her petrified flesh and had been incapable of reaction, unable to make the slightest move to defend herself. He had the power to annihilate her, to reduce her to nothingness. Because for HER, HE was everything!

She remained thus in the dark, scarce breathing now, for fear that she might awake not only the terrible physical pain, but shreds of the terrible vision she had had – Joffrey! Joffrey! His terrible face, and the glint of his doublet in which he moved, one caught a glimpse through the ivory satin pleats of that scarlet lining, as if she had caught sight of an endless stream of drops of blood, the shedding of tears of blood. Blood was flowing now, down her face. Her fingers were smeared with it and when she ran her tongue over her numbed lips they tasted salty. She tasted the blood with a kind of incredulous stupor. He had struck her! ...

He had struck her and she deserved it! A bottomless chasm had yawned beneath their feet ...

She remained there with straining senses in the blackness and trembled in every limb as she thought of this gaping crevasse, then once again fear rose up within her and a thousand demons seemed to surge up out of the abyss and creep towards her with glistening eyes, sniggering ...

It had all happened too soon, just when she had really come

to believe that their time spent at Wapassou had permanently renewed the bonds between them, and that their love was unassailable and indestructible.

It had come like a hurricane, like an earthquake, yet it had come stealthily and treacherously.

A beast spawned by hell, whose cruel eyes she had not noticed in time, had slithered towards them and had launched its attack.

She had been caught in a trap – they both had – a trap whose exact nature and functioning she did not understand, but whose jaws she now felt begin to crush her inexorably. So artful had been its approach that she and Joffrey had been struck to the heart at the very first blow.

'Joffrey! Joffrey! Please come! ... Don't leave me alone! I'm frightened!'

The room was teeming with dangerous shadows, as she began to measure the insurmountable barriers that had risen up between her and him, her beloved husband whom she had mortally offended.

A hand was clutching at her throat, half choking her, suffocating her. In order to prevent herself fainting she pressed her two hands to her swollen mouth, both to stifle the cries that sought to burst forth and to awaken, through the pangs of intolerable suffering, her fast sinking consciousness, until the combined effect of pain and a shattering vision of all that she had lost, her grief at both broke out into child-like sobs of despair ... 'If he doesn't love me any more ... If he doesn't love me any more ... what will become of me?'

CHAPTER FIFTY-SEVEN

THE MOMENT he had just lived through seemed to him to have been the most terrible of all his life.

Two men within him, frenzied and beyond control, had divided his being. Had he not driven her away, would he have been able to resist for much longer his overwhelming desire – as strong as his desire to kill her – to take her in his arms? Two separate beings within him had, throughout those terrible minutes, shared his body, his blood, his soul, so that he was torn in two – into a being bent on revenge, and one thirsting for adoration and sensual delight.

His veins were filled simultaneously with hatred and love.

And when he had seized her by the hair, had his hand not felt its fine silkiness, its soft warmth, and when he had bent over her, over that upturned face, over that forehead as broad and smooth as a beach of silvery sand had his lips, as they spat out their cruel words, not longed to lay themselves on hers in a passionate kiss? . . . And had not the thought flashed through his mind:

'What a lovely forehead she has! . . .'

And so, rent by these cross-currents of desire and anger, he had stood humiliated, trembling with rage against the woman to whom he owed this revelation of another side to his own character, who had forced him to see himself capable of blind violence, of irresistible lust, and of a degree of craven indulgence capable of abandoning itself to the prompting of the senses and to feelings contrary to all reason . . .

So superb a creature for love! . . . That was what he had thought. That was what they had all thought, when she had appeared to them on the threshold of night, and the obviousness of her beauty and her femininity had struck them like a blow, to such an extent that in a single moment all rancour, indignation, scorn and suspicion had vanished, leaving these men surprised and subjugated and with thoughts only for the indescribable enchantment of her presence.

So superb a creature for love! . . . Oh! you male idolaters, sensual idiots that you are! Ever ready to kneel before the goddess!

An unreflecting impulse brought Joffrey de Peyrac outside into the silence of the night.

Clouds scudded across the dull silver of the moon, against which stood out the black outlines of masts bobbing up and down in the harbour. The light of a few fires danced in the wind, and this, with the slow movement of an occasional sentry was the only sign of life.

The world was dead.

Where was she? 'Angélique! Angélique! . . . my love!'

He went back into the fort and sprang silently up the wooden staircase. He could hear her through the door, sobbing. And he stood there, consumed anew by a wild flame, his body tensed until it ached with the torment of temptation. He wanted to push open the door, to go in, to find himself alone with her, to bend over her, to grasp her, to clutch her to his heart, and to forget, to forget in the joy of their movements, their caresses, the murmur of their voices, of their intermingled breaths, of their kisses, and passionate whispered words 'My love! My love! It doesn't matter! I love you!' To forget, to forget it all ...

He came to himself again in the downstairs rooms, where the wax in the torches had burned right down, leaning his forehead against the window through which the pale light of dawn was beginning to shine.

No, Angélique would not be the cause of his downfall, he would not become the thrall of an unworthy woman.

No, never!

Why was she crying so loudly up there? Had she not known what she was doing when she let another man, the stranger, make love to her? She, whom he had thought of so highly! Had she not known what she was destroying? ... No she had not. She had not known! ... She was a woman, an irresponsible woman, just like the rest!

They want to have everything, and they destroy everything!

'I should never have forgiven her before ... They are all the same! ... All the same! ...'

At high tide he would set off out to sea with his ships, he would find Gold Beard, even if he had to chase him right down to the Caribbean ... and before he killed him with his own hands he would snatch from that unknown and hated face the veil of the past. He wanted to know what kind of a man it was to whom Angélique had shown the face of a mistress.

'Oh! If only I could pluck her from my heart! I shall do so if I have to.'

Such a superb creature! ...

The *Gouldsboro* had brought her dresses from France!

He walked over to a chest at the end of the room and opened the lid. He picked up watered silks and the daintiest of lace, while his fingers ran mechanically over the dress, smoothing the heavy folds of skirt and bodice into the shape they would have assumed when inhabited by a woman's body.

'How lovely she would have looked in this! That silver cloth with the pinkish tinge draped about her regal shoulders! I would have taken her to Quebec with me ... and she would have won the hearts of all! ...

His fists clenched on this shadow of womanhood that seemed to fade and collapse expiring beneath his grasp.

In an uncontrolled gesture he lifted the crumpled stuff to his face and stood there for a long time, as if lost and far away, nostalgically breathing in the delicate fragrance of flowers and femininity that came from the sumptuous finery.

Through the morning mist, figures came running towards him.

'My lord! God is with us. The ship of that cursed Gold Beard is not far off... He has just been sighted in the archipelago.'

PART FIVE

Gold Beard's Downfall

CHAPTER FIFTY-EIGHT

THERE WERE a large number of children in Gouldsboro always running about barefoot in a merry band, the little girls' hair streaming out from under their round bonnets or white coifs, the boys' heads uncovered, skirts or breeches tucked up so that they could paddle more easily in the pools, climb into boats, leap about on the beach, chase seals; as they gulped down shell-fish and gulls' eggs, or sucked at a flower – a whole troop of them in company with a crowd of little naked Indians, popping up here then there, constantly on the wing.

They glued their little faces curiously to the weatherboarding of the shed in an attempt to catch a glimpse of the captured pirates through the cracks, then ran off to the harbour to admire the beautiful painting that rose and fell on the stern of the *Heart of Mary*, the ship captured that morning, then they rushed off to fetch spring water from the forest and knelt down to give the wounded a drink.

The sun was going down in Gouldsboro on the defeat of Gold Beard the pirate.

That morning Angélique had been awakened by the distant rumble of gunfire.

Her soul and her body was aching with pain and she did not know where she was; it was quite a time before she realized she was in Gouldsboro. Then she took a look at her swollen face in the mirror. All down one side it was black and blue, and one corner of her mouth was swollen. She could only turn her head with difficulty. She had looked round the room and discovered some clothes in several linen chests, which she herself had folded away in the autumn before they left the fort. She dressed and did her hair, her mind still numb. She must find some pomade, some balm, anything to disguise her disfigurement.

Pushing back the shutters, she had caught sight of a number of ships sailing under the lee, near the edge of a rain-washed sky, against whose grey background, from time to time, a red flash could be seen. Then the dull thunder of the explosion reached her. A naval battle was taking place off Gouldsboro, apparently involving three or four ships attacking a single adversary which, after skilfully disengaging, fled under full sail, pursued by the others, and was soon outside Angélique's field of vision.

Soon afterwards a woman's voice called to her from somewhere inside the house.

'Dame Angélique! Dame Angélique! Where are you? Ah! Here you are! God be praised! Come! Come quickly, dear lady! There are wounded men, and blood everywhere!'

Angélique recognized the little woman as Madame Carrère from La Rochelle who had emigrated to the New World the year before with her ten children and her husband, a barrister.

'What is happening? Why are there wounded men?'

'They've just been settling up with that damned Gold Beard.'

'Who are "they"?'

'Monsieur le Comte, the filibuster Vanereick, the English admiral, all of them, in fact, who swore to make that scoundrel beg for mercy! They heard this morning that he was on the prowl among the islands, and Monsieur le Comte immediately set sail and gave chase. They cornered him and forced him to give battle, and Monsieur d'Urville has just brought news of victory.

'But it seems that when they came to board her, it was sheer slaughter ... The ships are coming back to harbour with their prize and all the wounded. Monsieur de Peyrac has sent word to us that you were here and that you must be warned to get ready to care for the unfortunate victims.'

'Are you sure that it was my husband who asked you to tell me this?'

'Of course! What could we do without you? Apparently the surgeon on board the *Fearless* has been wounded too and is unable to perform his duties. As for our doctor, Parry, you know him. He isn't much help when faced with slaughter like this ... Good Lord! Whatever has happened to you, you poor creature! ... You are in a mess.'

'Oh, it's nothing!'

Angélique raised her hand to her cheek. 'I ... I was shipwrecked off Monhegan Island and was hurled against a rock ... Wait for me, I'm coming. I only have to pick up my bag and put a few essential instruments in it. Have you any spare lint? ...'

Methodically, she gathered together everything she thought she might need, moving like an automaton, while her mind buzzed with agonizing thoughts.

Colin ... Colin had died by Joffrey de Peyrac's hand ... If only she had said something yesterday evening ... if only she had had the courage to speak ... But no, that had been impossible! She had been unable to say anything, to explain anything. And now Joffrey de Peyrac had killed Gold Beard ... and he had sent for her to tend the wounded ... So he did at least remember her existence. But why? Was he planning some further revenge? What if he threw Colin's body in her path. She could never bear that. She would never be able to help falling to her knees and taking Colin's big bearded head between her hands and weeping.

'Oh God!' she begged, 'let Joffrey not do anything so terrible. Oh God, how has it come about that he and I should so suddenly be such bitter enemies?'

She tumbled down the stairs behind Madame Carrère and ran towards the place where the villagers were laying out seaweed-filled mattresses, leather buckets of fresh water, and blankets. The first of the wounded were being unloaded from the long-boats and laid on the ground, moaning or swearing colourful oaths.

The remainder of the morning was a nightmare during which Angélique could think of nothing but cutting into flesh, sewing up or cleaning out wounds, dressing them, running from one man to another, calling for assistance, organizing a field hospital, sending children off in all directions to fetch herbs, bandages, water, rum, oil, thread, needles and scissors.

With her sleeves rolled up and blood-stained to the elbows, for hours on end she did nothing but perform emergency operations, taking upon herself the responsibility of diagnosing the gravity of wounds, and indicating what kind of treatment should be given and what remedies prepared. Very soon she found the old order forming itself about her once more. She recognized the women who spontaneously placed themselves at her disposal: Abigail, diligent and efficient in spite of her pregnancy; Madame Carrère active, the young women prompt and docile, courageous in the face of death and suffering, just like their elders. Suddenly she found Aunt Anna beside her, passing her her surgical instruments, precise and attentive, and old Rebecca comforting a dying man.

A young lad followed her everywhere carrying a large copper basin which he kept filled with fresh water for her to wash her hands and soak bandages in. It was only after a while that she recognized him as Martial, Maître Berne's eldest son.

All at once, she had resumed her place among them. But while she busied herself about her tasks with her customary diligence, her feelings, as raw as an open wound, noticed certain tiny details in their behaviour towards her. A faint suggestion of contempt in their voices, a sudden tightening of the lips, a hostile glance ... It was perhaps only an impression ... No! The people of Gouldsboro knew ... everyone knew.

And yet Madame Carrère had been straightforward and cordial with her. But Madame Carrère had never been a scandal monger. The rumour she had heard in Gouldsboro that Countess Peyrac had deceived her husband with the pirate was one she refused to pay heed to. The furtive eyes that followed Angélique that morning as she worked away indefatigably, were busy calculating the extent or the possibility of calumny ... But the most terrible thing about it all was that there was no question of calumny, but of truth ... or rather of half truth. She had lain in Gold Beard's arms, she had responded to his caresses. She would have liked to have shouted out for all the world to hear that she had not been guilty. She would have liked to have persuaded herself of the fact, to have become once more as she had been before. She bent over the men's wounds with infinite gentleness and infinite compassion for she felt within herself too, an open wound, every moment more painful, and she would so have welcomed a compassionate hand laid upon it. But no one would do that for her.

'Ah! Madame, save me,' implored the seriously wounded.

But as for her, to whom could she beseech – 'save me'?

Her pain was of the kind that merits no compassion. And at times it shot through her so cruelly that it left her almost paralysed.

'Joffrey does not love me any more... How could I have done this to him, when he is so kind, so wonderful? How could I have humiliated him thus in the eyes of the world? ... He will never forgive me. He has asked me to care for the wounded ... why? But of course, because he needed me. His men come first, his resentment next ... That is typical of him. But afterwards, he will drive me away, he will repudiate me. He will never want to see me again. He shouted: "I never want to see you again."'

But in spite of everything, she felt as if having to work for him like this, as it were at his side, was in a way like a truce between them. The thought that he had sent for her was like a gleam of hope.

He had sent for her. He had remembered her. So she did still count for something. She resumed her task with renewed vigour.

The poor unfortunates who moaned in pain as she bent over them, reassuring, encouraging, thought they were seeing an angel from Heaven come down to them, and as soon as she laid her hands upon them, they grew quiet.

'Is that Count Peyrac's lady?' asked all those who did not know her.

'Yes,' the others called out. 'You'll see, she'll make you better.'

And all this confidence around her stirred Angélique's courage, gradually dulled her inner torment, helped her to lift her head once more, to hold fast, although she was aware of her own swollen face, now covered with sweat.

She listened carefully, in the hope of overhearing some snatches of conversation about the course of the battle.

But no one mentioned Gold Beard's death.

Only the horrible, bloody combat between the crews of the various ships which had taken place after the *Heart of Mary* had been boarded. 'And Monsieur de Peyrac was the first to jump.'

Towards the middle of the morning the ships entered the harbour, encircling their prey.

Listing heavily, bereft of her masts, with a pall of smoke hanging about her like an ill-boding cloud, Gold Beard's ship came to rest against an island in the middle of the bay.

Then it was the turn of the prisoners to be brought ashore in longboats and they began to file up the beach, escorted by sailors from the *Gouldsboro* and soldiers from the garrison.

Monsieur d'Urville had them taken to the barn where maize was stored, a rough-and-ready building but fairly large and with only one door, which would make it easier to mount guard.

One of the captive pirates was yelling like a man possessed as they dragged him up the beach.

'Let me go, you dolts, you murderers. I'm wounded, I tell you, seriously wounded at that! You'll kill me!'

Angélique pricked up her ears at the sound of this shrill voice, and recognized it as that of the unspeakable Slitbelly, the man she had operated on in Casco Bay.

She made her way towards the men and said:

'This good-for-nothing is telling the truth. You mustn't make him walk! Lay him down there.'

'Ah, there you are at last, and not too soon either!' Beaumarchand moaned. 'Where did you get to, Madame? You shouldn't have left me like that, with this seam across my belly.'

'Be quiet, you loathsome creature! You could have gone to the devil a hundred times as far as I care, after the foul trick you played on me.'

She nevertheless examined the man and noted with satisfaction that Aristide ·Beaumarchand's monstrous scar looked healthy enough and seemed to be mending. A miracle indeed since his companions on board the *Heart of Mary* seemed to have paid precious little attention to him since they had taken him back on board.

'How I missed you, Madame! I certainly did miss you!' he repeated. 'They left me to die in a hole full of rats, like so much rubbish!'

She changed his dressing, bound him up with strips of linen like a newborn babe, and left him for the time being on the sand.

A little later she knelt down beside Monsieur de Barssempuy to attend to his shoulder, which had been slashed with a cutlass. He was the gentleman, second in command to Gold Beard, who had taken her prisoner at Maquoit. Today his face was black with gunpowder and he looked weary.

'What about your captain?' she whispered to him, 'Gold Beard, where is he? What happened to him? Was he wounded or killed?'

He threw her a bitter glance and turned his head away.

Her nagging fears continued, and she felt paralysed with anxiety.

The sun had reached its zenith, and the heat added to her distress and fatigue.

At that moment someone came to fetch Madame de Peyrac, asking her to be so good as to come on board the pirate ship to see whether ... among the more seriously wounded, there were any whom they could risk moving to dry land and which among the rest it would be best to allow to die where they were.

She went on board a longboat, accompanied by Martial, who carried her emergency bag, a small barrel of fresh water and the copper bowl. At the gangway she was met by a man in a black doublet full of holes and singed with gunpowder, wearing a moth-eaten wig in an oddly lopsided fashion, who led her limping to the battery-deck.

'I am Mister Vanereick's surgeon, Nessens. A cannon ball fell on the storeroom where I was operating ... As for my colleague on board the *Heart of Mary*, they found him stone dead beneath a pile of bodies. So you see the wounded would have been in a nasty fix had you not happened to be in Gouldsboro, Madame. As soon as it was known that you were there, the wounded cheered up, and I gave orders to evacuate as many as possible so that they could be placed in your charge since I was hampered in the performance of my work. Such is your reputation that people have begun to hear about you overseas. As for me, I have had to content myself with clearing up three ships today. But there are a few unfortunates here about whom I find I cannot reach a decision . . .'

It was difficult to move about the ship, for the deck was tilted at an alarming angle. Some barrels of cider had been pierced and the place was awash with sour-smelling liquid mingled with blood. They floundered and slithered through this noisome mixture and had to cling to anything available in order to make any progress.

But orders had been given to prevent the damaged ship from sinking and they could hear the gangs of men at work calling to one another.

'This was the ship that was most heavily damaged,' Nessens explained. 'Four of us came alongside her: Monsieur de Peyrac's chebec, the *Gouldsboro*, the *Fearless* and the English ship. Shortly after this the little yacht *Rochelais* arrived too. It was a good policing operation we carried out, half those bandits are out of action.'

The surgeon was a man in his thirties. When, back in France, he realized that, although a qualified surgeon, he had no right to practise because he was a Protestant, he found that the only possibility open to him was to become an exile and take up the dangerous profession of surgeon on privateers. After he and Angélique had examined the dying men, she suggested that she might dress his wounds for him. Furthermore, noticing that his limp came not from a wound but from a dislocation of the hip he had suffered in a fall during the bombardment, she reduced the dislocation and massaged it firmly to help the bruised, stretched sinews back into place again, and when he left her he was almost his active self again.

As she crossed the deck to re-embark, not without difficulty, a feeble voice called to her:

'Madame! Señora!'

The man who had called her was lying, half crushed against the ship's rails, hidden by coils of rope that had fallen across him. He must have been overlooked until then in the disorder and confusion after the battle. She freed him and dragged him a little higher up the deck, propping him up against the base of the mizzen mast. Looking at his waxen face and his huge black staring eyes she thought he seemed familiar.

'I am Lopez,' he breathed.

'Lopez . . . Lopez?'

She searched her memory. Then he helped her, with a ghost of a smile on his grey lips:

'You remember . . . Lopez! . . . Over yonder . . . the bees.'

She remembered. So he was one of the filibusters she had sought to defend herself against by hurling a hive full of bees at their heads. Now, after being picked up by Gold Beard's ship, his last hour had come.

'It's my stomach,' he murmured. 'You'll do for me like you did for Beaumarchand, won't you, eh? You sewed him up again, I saw you. And now he's running about as lively as a rabbit . . . I . . . I don't want to die, milady, if you please . . .'

He was still young, this bit of a boy from Portugal. A miserable wretch from the Lisbon quayside, brought up to the age of twelve on dust, sunshine and a handful of figs. And after that, life at sea. And that was all.

As a pure matter of form Angélique slit open his breeches which had already become distended by the crushed and putrefying flesh, filthy with blood, pus, cider, and sea water. Already the hollows round the man's eyes had told her the worst. Even if he had received attention in time, he could not have been saved.

'You'll do something for me, won't you?' he repeated.

She gave him a reassuring smile.

'Yes, my lad. First I'm going to give you something to ease the pain. Swallow this.'

And between his lips she slipped one of her last remaining pills, made of mandrake and Indian poppy seed.

He was unable to swallow the pill but kept it on his tongue and it began to make him slightly drowsy.

'Are you a good Christian, my lad?' she asked again.

'Yes, Señora, I am.'

'Then pray to the Good Lord and the Blessed Virgin while I make you better.'

She took his hands and crossed them over his chest and held them there, transmitting her life and warmth to him in this final contact with the world he was leaving, so that he would not feel alone as he crossed the last threshold.

His leaden eyelids opened again.

'Mamma! Mamma!' he breathed, staring hard at her.

She released his hands, now chill and lifeless, closed his eyes, and covered his face with the scarf she had hastily tied that morning about her shoulders. She had never managed to remain indifferent to violent death in battle, to the sudden metamorphosis of one who had lived, laughed and moved about in the sunshine only a few hours earlier, whom a single blow could change into an amorphous mass, vanished for ever from the earth and soon from the hearts of those about him. Although she herself had on occasion killed with her own hands, the senselessness of death and its irreparable cruelty still continued to cause deep pain to her feminine sensibility. And although she knew how worthless a creature this poor man was who had just completed his sojourn on earth, in spite of herself she found her eyes filling with tears.

CHAPTER FIFTY-NINE

As she stood up she found herself face to face with Count Peyrac, who had been standing for several moments, watching his wife bending over the dying man.

Gilles Vanereick, who was accompanying him on his final tour of inspection, had been the first to notice her blonde hair, like a vision of sweetness after the rough hours of battle; he had laid a hand on the Count's arm and both of them, interrupting their inspection, had stood there watching her as she bent over the cavernous face of the dying man and they had overheard her compassionate voice murmuring: 'Say your prayers, my lad ... I will make you better ...'

Then they had seen her cross herself and take off her scarf to cover the poor boy's face, while tears glistened on her eyelashes.

When she caught sight of Joffrey de Peyrac she was so disconcerted that Vanereick felt sorry for her. Painfully, she turned away under the pretext of rinsing her hands in the basin young Martial held out towards her.

'Have all the wounded fit to leave the ship been sorted out by you, Madame?' Count Peyrac asked her, without any particular inflection in his voice beyond a note of distant calm.

'This one is dead,' she replied, pointing towards the out-stretched body.

'Yes, I can see that,' he replied dryly.

She obstinately refused to let him see her face with its blue bruise which had embarrassed her the whole day long. It was the first time she had seen him since the terrible scene of the previous day, and she felt a sensation of icy cold as if she were suddenly faced with a stranger ... A wall had sprung up between them.

The Flemish gentleman accompanying Peyrac seemed a gay, lighthearted fellow. His yellow jerkin, adorned with knots of ribbon that streamed out in the wind, his red ostrich feathers, and his lace revers and cravat were in the gaudy taste of the Caribbean filibusters. On the other hand, his jolly face was marked with streaks of blood which obliged him to half close one eye.

In order to give herself a countenance Angélique turned towards him.

'Can I do anything for you, Monsieur?'

Gilles Vanereick, delighted at the prospect of getting to know her better, eagerly acquiesced.

She sat him down on an upturned barrel, and as Joffrey de Peyrac began to walk away, she gently cleaned his wounds for him, asking herself meanwhile with what kind of weapon they could possibly have been made.

He pulled a wry face and yelped like a puppy.

'You do make a fuss for a gentleman of fortune,' she told him. 'Any one as faint-hearted as you shouldn't get involved in battles.'

'I am the captain of the *Fearless*.'

'One wouldn't have guessed it.'

'But you see, I was never wounded in my life before, dear lady! Ask anyone, they will all tell you that Gilles Vanereick always gets off without a scratch.'

'Not this time, anyway.'

'But yes, this time too. The wound you are dressing with your dainty fingers is no war wound, far from it. I owe that to Ines's fury last night.'

'Ines?'

'My mistress! She is as jealous as a tigress, and she has the sharp claws of one too, and took umbrage because I kept going on about how dazzlingly beautiful you were.'

'But I do not know you, sir.'

'Oh yes you do ... I was in the council chamber yesterday when you made your appearance. But I shall forgive you for not having noticed my humble person, for I know you only had eyes for Monsieur de Peyrac, your husband, who is also my dear and much revered friend from the Caribbean.'

Angélique, who was winding a bandage round his forehead restrained her desire to pull his hair by way of vengeance for his irony. Vanereick's dark eyes were peeping up at her from under the bandage, full of admiration, but quick enough to have noticed the blue marks across one side of her lovely face, which he had not seen there the day before.

Apparently, or so he assumed, there had been a violent domestic scene, and the couple were still sulking with one another, but this woman was too beautiful for things to fail to sort themselves out. A little jealousy adds spice to a passionate love affair. He had seen worse with his Ines. And, like Peyrac, he did not like sharing either. But this was the kind of accident one had to risk when one got involved with such beauties, endowed with nature's every gift to delight the heart of man, including the gift of arousing other men's lust.

This woman too, this crazy, footloose Countess of Peyrac, she possessed this gift and knew how to make the most of it, and it was just too bad for Peyrac!

With trembling nostrils, as she delicately sponged his scratches, Vanereick revelled in her fragrance, so close to him, delicate and elusive, a fragrance like fresh-mown hay – the delicious fragrance of woman, a true blonde, which made him long to explore more fully the mysteries of her golden skin.

Taking advantage of his status as a combatant in an enfeebled condition, he had managed, as he sat down, to slip one hand around Angélique's hips. She had a magnificent figure, but he could only brush it, for she immediately moved away.

He told himself that naked, she must reveal the most opulent curves, and yet her gracefulness and the suppleness of her movements made her seem slimmer than she really was with her splendid body hidden beneath her clothes. The practised eye of the merry corsair envisaged the perfect shape of a body which, from the nape of the neck to the small of the back, must express a perfect harmony of line. A cross between Venus and the huntress Diana. And certainly very strong! This he realized when she brought his reverie to an abrupt end with a simple pressure of her wrist, bringing him sharply back to his feet, as she might have done to a bit of a boy whom she judged a trifle spineless.

'There you are now, quite recovered from the spite of the lady Ines, my friend. Tomorrow there won't be a trace left!'

With his swollen eye he gave her a knowing wink.

'I trust that the same can be said of you, lovely lady! I see that the planets Venus and Mars collided yesterday in the heavens and that we were both victims of this squabble between the gods . . .'

Angélique suppressed a grimace, as she felt a stab of pain down the left side of her face. She had done so much since the morning that her despair had begun to fade. Through a natural reaction of her irrepressible nature, her optimism was beginning to get the upper hand, and Vanereick's remarks about a squabble between the gods of love and of war had almost made her laugh.

Seeing her less distant in her bearing, he went on:

'Listen,' he whispered, 'I understand about love, and I am not a man to be hard on any lapses a pretty woman might make even if I am not the one to benefit. Would you like me to give you news of Gold Beard?'

Angélique's face froze and she threw him a glance of anger, humiliated to find him ranking her with casual indulgence among women of easy virtue, and humiliated also on Count Peyrac's behalf. Now she was sure that Kurt Ritz's confidences had not been kept secret and that everyone was gossiping about her escapade and his humiliation.

And yet, tormented at the thought of what might have become of Colin, she could not refrain from murmuring:

'Yes! What did happen to Gold Beard?'

'Well, to tell the truth, no one knows. He has disappeared!'

'Disappeared?'

'Yes! An extraordinary coincidence! You see, he was not on board when we attacked his ship and it was his second-in-command who organized the defence. Some say he left the ship during the course of the night in a little dinghy, without saying where he was going, nor when he would be back. He instructed his lieutenant, Barssempuy, to remain within sight of Gouldsboro but to keep hidden in the archipelago, until he himself returned with further orders. Whether he went off to reconnoitre, to see how best to attack Gouldsboro this time . . . But we stole a march on him. As soon as dawn broke Monsieur de

Peyrac's chebec surprised the *Heart of Mary* lying at anchor. First we pursued her, then we boarded her, then it was hand-to-hand fighting. And now our Gouldsboro men have won! As for Gold Beard, wherever he might be, his reign over sea and ocean is finished for a long time, I imagine!'

'I see. Thank you, Monsieur.'

Angélique returned to the harbour. The sun seemed as if it would never fall below the horizon. The clouds of dust and smoke had softened to gold and sulphurous yellow, while the heat, which had been overpowering in spite of the incessant wind, began to grow less intense at last.

Attracted by the noise of gunfire, the Indians had come out of the forest, bringing furs to trade with the ships, and game which was more than welcome in view of the considerable number of extra mouths to be fed. The English and French sailors and filibusters, even the wounded who were still mobile, rushed off to engage in barter with the Indians, so powerful was the attraction of fur trading along these shores and the lure of the money that could be made. They bartered anything they had, their caps, their tobacco, brandy, earrings, even the wooden or pewter spoons, which, along with their knives, were the most precious items of equipment in a sailor's life.

Through the weather-boarding of their lockup even the prisoners shouted to the Indians to come closer, and passed them various baubles to barter.

It was on this occasion that Angélique discovered among the captives another acquaintance from Maquoit Point.

After a battle in which so many worthy men had died, of course a man like Hyacinth Boulanger had had to survive. He had been making a thorough nuisance of himself and he had already had to be knocked out twice in order to keep him quiet.

'He's a buccaneer, so let him do some buccaneering,' Angélique decreed. 'At least if he does that, he won't be a nuisance, and might even make himself useful.'

She scolded him roundly:

'And don't let anyone regret having left you alive, you wretch! If you would rather have your wrists and ankles fettered than make yourself useful, that's up to you, but I would like to make it clear that you had better do as I say since the only alternative to behaving yourself will be to find yourself hanged like the dangerous good-for-nothing that you are.'

'Do as she says, Hyacinthus!' Aristide called across from where he lay. 'You know it's no use arguing with her, and in any case don't forget that she did sew up your blood-brother's belly!'

Subdued, the hideous butcher indicated that he had understood and went off swinging his ape-like arms to collect some green wood with which to prepare fires for smoking the meat. Angélique found two or three others who were buccaneers by trade among the crew, and sent them off with Hyacinthus Boulanger to a small beach apart from the others, under custody of an armed guard, with instructions to skin and joint the stags and does which the Indians had brought, and then to roast some of the meat and to smoke the rest.

The tasty smell of roasting meat that soon began to permeate the golden evening air reminded her that she had eaten nothing all day, nor since the previous day and even then ... Goodness, yes! Her last meal had been the one at Pentagouet on Penobscot Bay, which she had eaten with Baron Saint-Castine and Father Maraicher de Vernon, alias Jack Merwin, the Jesuit. Ages ago! ... It all seemed very remote and she sensed that she had still not reached the end of her troubles.

Then suddenly she felt hungry.

Her encounter with Vanereick had made her feel a little more cheerful. Now that she knew that Colin was not among the casualties, she felt better. Vanereick was probably right after all. Was it necessary to make such a fuss, to destroy two lives, even several lives, for such a trifle? Joffrey was no easy husband to face, but she would have to tackle him and overcome her fear ... 'I shall say to him ... Well! I shall tell him the truth ... that I have not betrayed him to the extent that he believes ... that Gold Beard is Colin ... He will understand ... I shall find the words to make him understand. Things are already better than they were yesterday. We are working together at the same tasks again. Life has forced him to remember me, to remember all that unites us. Haven't we been through other battles, other periods of separation ... other ... betrayals? ... And we got over them, have managed to love one another in spite of them, even more than before.'

After all they were no longer children with all the intransigence and inexperience of youth. Life had ridden roughshod over them, and had taught them to appreciate the value of true feelings, to know what one should accept or sacrifice in order to preserve the best and most priceless things.

And there were too many people depending on them. She must tell him that too. They had no right to weaken, no right to let these people down. She thought of her children, especially Cantor, who might well put in an appearance at any minute now.

Someone had told her that her youngest son had gone back to Casco Bay to look for her, and she had felt relieved that he was not present. But soon afterwards it had been announced that the *Rochelais* had returned just in time to take part in the naval combat that morning, and was still patrolling among the islands.

For Cantor's sake, too, she must explain things to Joffrey and be promptly reconciled, before all kinds of rumours and tales reached the ears of the sensitive lad. That very evening she would endeavour to catch Joffrey on his own.

But the day was not yet done, and she still had a thousand things to do. Close to Madame Carrère's inn she fortified herself with a head of corn on the cob which she hastily grilled over some glowing embers and nibbled equally quickly while supervising the preparation of some herbal tea. She had neither hemlock nor mandrake root with which to make her sedative pills, but failing these ingredients, rosemary, cloves and oriental poppies would do. She went round more or less all the houses, and rummaged through the supplies in the fort until someone told her that there was a 'herb man' on board the *Fearless*, as was the case with many ships, one of those sailors who kept a pinch of this and a trifle of that tucked away in a pocket or in the corner of a sea chest, gleaned from the four corners of the earth. She would be able to recognize the man by the black patch he wore over one eye and by the fact that he was followed wherever he went by his slave, a fellow from the Caribbean with olive-coloured skin and wearing a magical green stone round his neck on a string of cotton. The black patch would not have been sufficient on its own to identify him for there were many one-eyed men among these battling seafarers.

Some of the crew had been landed at the far western end of the main beach where they were bivouacking. 'They'll be drunk tonight,' said Madame Carrère with a knowing look. She had never stopped pouring out beer, wine, rum and brandy to the able-bodied ... Admittedly, they sometimes paid her in pearls or even in gold ducats.

The booty was brought ashore in open boats from the *Heart of Mary*, landed, numbered, laid out in rows, in barrels, casks, coffers and sacks, under the delighted gaze of sailors of every nationality who would each receive a bounty for their part in the action.

Gold Beard's vessel had the reputation of being extremely well stocked. The ship's clerks bustled around the supplies, calling out figures and affixing seals. There was tobacco from Brazil, molasses, soft brown sugar, white sugar, rice, rum, and more wine, as well as all the run-of-the-mill stores of a merchant vessel – barrels of peas, of beans, of salt pork, of biscuits plus a few delicacies: seven barrels of pigs' ears, seven pots of legs of goose, hams, cheeses, dried fruits, flasks of vinegar, oil, fruit preserved in grape juice, and finally a small studded chest, which was extremely heavy and said to contain precious jewels and the famous Caracas emeralds which Gold Beard had conquered ... Two guards were posted over this box until it could be transported to Count Peyrac's fort.

Picking up the hem of her skirt, Angélique pushed her way through the noisy crowd. Attracted by so many different sights the English Puritans from Camp Champlain as well as the Huguenots from La Rochelle were enjoying themselves hanging around the throngs on the beach, and round the fires could be heard the sound of English and French voices telling the children fantastic tales of piracy in the blue Caribbean with its endless glittering string of long white beaches fringed with palm trees where one drinks rum mixed with the cool milk of big hairy coconuts.

A child in a red dress threw her arms round Angélique's neck and, unaccustomed to such spontaneity, she almost failed to recognize her.

'Rose-Anne, my darling, how delighted I am to see you again!'

The little English girl seemed to be having a wonderful time, as were Dorothy and Janeton from Monhegan. Their Bible and reading lessons would certainly not be starting today.

At last Angélique found the herb man, with his half-naked Caribbean in tow, and bought a few items from him.

As evening fell, the gilding of the picture of the Virgin on the poop of the *Heart of Mary* glittered in the light of the declining sun. Tilting at an angle on account of the list of the ship, the reflection of its colours trembled in the harbour waters, and as the shadows grew darker, so did the faces of the Virgin and the Angels begin to look more and more like sweet, nostalgic apparitions watching over the motley crowd gathered on the shore. The whole bay smelt strongly of black iodine-steeped seaweed, for the tide had been out all day. The tangy breath of the sea borne on the wind mingled with the smell of wood smoke and tar. A woman suddenly began to dance wildly to the sound of castanets. Her full, flame-coloured embroidered skirt wavered about her like a red and gold mist and her glance was keen and provocative beneath her heavily-blackened eyelashes. Her eyes followed Angélique for a long time as she went by.

'That's Ines,' someone told her, 'Mr Vanereick's mistress. Apparently she is as handy with a sword as with the castanets.'

Angélique halted for a moment to watch the 'tigress' leaping into the air with feline grace.

There was laughter and singing and shouting that night in Gouldsboro as well as the moans of the wounded, the dying and the vanquished.

In all this feverish agitation, this tumult born of victory and defeat that muddles and confuses men's minds as much as the noisy seething of waves and wind, the Devil with his cloven hooves found many an opportunity to dance, intrigue, sow seeds of unhappiness and discord, lead his infernal ballet escorted by every invisible spirit of Evil . . .

CHAPTER SIXTY

THE MAN appeared to Angélique, towards the end of the day, in the guise of a pale creature who, crossing the bay at low tide, and leaping from rock to rock, seemed to have come on foot from the remoteness of the sea. At the time Angélique was standing at the door of Madame Carrère's inn and for the umpteenth time washing her hands in a basin beside a rainwater butt, surreptitiously trying to rub a bit of balm into the bruise on her temple. She had been unable to attend to herself during the day, and she was now utterly exhausted.

'Monsieur de Peyrac wishes to see you,' said the man, 'on that island over there; you must go immediately.'

'Are there more wounded, then?' Angélique asked, glancing down at the open bag at her feet which had never left her side.

'Possibly . . . I don't know.'

For a fraction of a second Angélique hesitated. Madame Carrère had just told her that she had warmed up a bowl of pickled pork and cabbage, to 'set her up' and as a change from those everlasting shellfish. And then there was something else too which she found hard to put a name to at that moment, something that made her hesitate to follow this man.

'Where is your boat?' she asked him.

'No need to take a boat. You can reach it on foot. The tide is right out.'

She followed him, and together they crossed the broad stretch of sand between the shore and the island that the man had pointed out. Slimy pieces of seaweed burst beneath their feet with a sharp crack and a hiss.

The reflection of the setting sun in the many pools of water dazzled Angélique and made her eyes ache.

The tiny island rose up before them at a distance of about a mile, the first of a chain of reefs, topped with the usual crown of black pines, growing straight as lances, parasol firs, green bushes and birch trees. An old-rose-coloured beach sloped gently up towards the shade of the little wood.

'Over there,' said the man, pointing to the edge of the trees.

'I can see no one . . .'

'There's a clearing a bit farther along. Monsieur de Peyrac is waiting for you there with some other people.'

His voice was monotonous and listless. Angélique looked at him. She was surprised how sickly he looked and wondered whose crew he could possibly belong to.

Slowly she made her way up the beach, her feet sinking into the damp sand, reached some grass which was short at first then grew thicker.

There was indeed a clearing among the trees, in the centre of which lay the wreck of an old vessel. The ghostly shape of the ship rose up at an angle in the green shadows, sticking up out of the tangle of grass, bushes and creeper. It was a small argosy of the previous century, little more than a hundred and twenty tons. She could make out the curving balusters, and the approximate shape of the figurehead on the prow, which was half rotted away but must once have represented the muscular torso and long-haired head of some sea god. The poop had been half buried by a fall of rock, and the masts broken off, but the mizzen, covered in red canker and black fungus, was still standing, its tip lost among the leaves.

Some tempest, some giant wave, some equinoctial tide, higher and more terrible than the rest, must have carried the wreck into this leafy haunt then retreated, abandoning it there for ever.

A bird began to sing, a pure, joyous sound, which only made the silence more apparent. The place was deserted.

At the same moment Angélique at last remembered what it was that had caused her to hesitate about following the pale man. Had she not, just a few moments before, caught sight of Count Peyrac putting in to the beach and heading for the shed where the prisoners were kept? He could not be in two places at the same time.

She turned to shout to the stranger who had brought her, but he had vanished.

Perplexed and overwhelmed by a sense of danger that made her flesh creep, she looked back towards the old ship. The only sound was of tiny waves splashing among the rocks, and the sensuous trilling of the bird that rang out at regular intervals, like a call . . . like a warning.

Angélique's hand moved to her belt but she knew she would find no weapon there.

Her breast was heavy with oppression and she dared not call out, for fear of breaking that torrid silence and provoking she knew not what horrible discovery.

Just as she had finally decided to attempt a cautious retreat she heard the sound of footsteps coming from behind the ship.

It was a heavy tread, the sound deadened by the grass and moss, but it seemed to her to shake the earth to its foundations.

Angélique leaned against the rotten keel of the ship, and her heart stood still.

Coming as it did at the end of a difficult, exhausting day which for her had followed hard upon a terrible night of pain and tears, the approach of that inexorable tread advancing towards her as slow and heavy as Destiny itself – neither her husband's, nor a sailor's, nor an Indian's tread, since both sailors and Indians preferred to walk barefoot, nor even – who knew! – that of a human being – caught her in a completely demoralized state and awoke within her all the superstitious terrors of childhood.

And when a powerful shadow appeared at the corner of the ship, standing out somewhat hazily against the bluish-green darkness of the undergrowth, she really believed it must be that of an ogre or a giant.

CHAPTER SIXTY-ONE

FILTERING THROUGH the branches, a ray of light glittered on a head of golden hair and a thick blond beard – Gold Beard!

'Is that you?' he asked.

As she made no reply, he continued to move warily towards her.

His heavy boots, whose turn-down tops exposed his big brown knees, crushed the grass dotted with dainty flowers. He was wearing short breeches, a white open-neck shirt and a sleeveless leather jerkin with a broad crossbelt slung from one shoulder. But the belt did not contain the customary four pistols, nor did his boarding sword hang from it. He too was unarmed.

He came to a halt a few paces from Angélique.

'Why did you send for me?' he asked her. 'What do you want of me?'

Angélique shook her head vehemently.

'I didn't send for you,' she finally managed to say.

Gold Beard's blue eyes scrutinized her keenly. The magic he could not resist, as soon as he found himself in her presence, was already acting upon him and he began to look less like a hunted lion as his heart softened.

'How pale you are, my lamb!' he said softly, 'and what have you done to your face? ... Were you wounded?'

He raised his hand and ran the tips of his fingers over the bruise on her temple.

Angélique shuddered from head to foot, not only on account of the pain caused by even this light touch but at the terrifying thought that had just occurred to her. She was alone on this little island with Colin! Supposing Joffrey were to find them ...

'It's nothing,' she stammered, in a frenzy of despair. 'But go away, Colin, quickly, get away ... I must not stay here.'

And she began to run down the grassy slope towards the beach, heading for the exposed stretch of the sea bed by which she had crossed the bay.

But on reaching the shore she came to a sudden halt, horror-stricken.

The transparent sheen of the sea now spread nonchalantly over the rocks which but a short while before had lain uncovered, and an arrogant wave ran bubbling and foaming up the beach.

Angélique began to run as if demented along the beach, flinging herself first on to one still unsubmerged rock, then another. A wave swirled around her feet, then a second almost threw her off balance.

A firm hand grasped her and pulled her back.

'What are you doing?' said Colin Paturel. 'Can't you see it's high tide?'

Angélique looked up at him in dismay.

'We are cut off on this island,' she murmured.

'It looks like it.'

'But I must get away!'

'There's no boat,' Colin replied.

'But that's impossible! You must have a boat. How did you get here?'

'I don't know how I got here,' he replied somewhat mysteriously.

'And what about the man who brought me here, where is he? Didn't you see him? He had a face like wax.'

All of a sudden Angélique felt faint and clutched at the lapels of Colin's jerkin.

'Colin, that was the Devil, I feel sure!'

'Calm down,' he said, taking her in his arms. 'The tide will be out again at dawn . . .'

She tore herself from his arms with a heart-rending cry.

'No! It's impossible! . . . I can't spend the whole night here . . . with you . . . Especially not with you! . . .'

And once again she rushed down to the water's edge and began to undo the fastenings on her dress. A moment later Colin was with her once more.

'What are you trying to do? Are you mad?'

'I shall swim if I have to. I don't care! I shall reach Goulds-boro naked but I shall not stay here. Let me go!'

'You must be mad!' he repeated. 'The current is very treacherous and you'll be drowned in the channels.'

'I don't care! I'd rather be drowned . . . Let go of me, I say.'

'No, I will not let you go.'

She began to shout and struggle with him, but in vain. Colin hurt her horribly with his vice-like grip about her arms, but he would not let her go and she felt utterly powerless against his Herculean strength. Then suddenly he whisked her off the ground like a wisp of straw and carried her up to the top of the beach where he continued to hold her without yielding an inch until, with frayed nerves and exhausted body she collapsed sobbing on his chest.

'This is the end of me! . . . This is the end of me . . . He will never forgive me.'

'Was it he who struck you?'

'No! No! It wasn't he! . . . Oh! Colin, it's terrible! . . . He found out! . . . He found out! . . . And now he doesn't love me any more! . . . Oh! Colin . . . What will become of me? . . . This time he will kill me!'

'Now calm yourself.'

He rocked her gently back and forth, clasping her very tightly to him in an attempt to arrest her uncontrollable trembling. When she began to grow a little calmer, Colin Paturel looked up at the first star to appear in the emerald-coloured sky.

An evening mist had come down, veiling the lights of Gouldsboro. They were really alone. Colin's eyes returned to the golden head buried in his shoulder.

'It's not as terrible as all that,' he said in his deep voice. 'For the moment we can do nothing but wait for daybreak. The tide is the tide! . . . After that we shall see. Now calm yourself, Madame de Peyrac.'

His solemn entreaty and sudden formality acted on Angélique like a jet of cold water. She grew quiet, still trembling like an animal at bay, but suddenly mindful of her dignity as a woman and as wife of Count Peyrac.

'Do you feel better now?' he asked.

'Yes, but . . . let go of me.'

'I shall let go of you when you have promised me that you will not rush down into the water, and that you will wait quietly until it is safe to cross. What do you say?'

He leant forward laying bare her face and looking at her with tender irony as if she were an unreasonable child that had to be persuaded.

'Is that a promise?'

Angélique nodded her assent.

He released her and she took a few hesitant steps before dropping down on the sand.

She was aching all over, in her arms, in the back of her neck and in her head. She felt as if her whole body was bruised and beaten. Yes, she would long remember this day and her homecoming to Gouldsboro! . . . A sudden spasm of cramp gripped her stomach.

'And I'm hungry as well!' she exclaimed angrily. 'That really is the limit!'

Without saying a word Colin went off and soon returned with an armful of dead wood, kindled a fire between three stones, and went off once again. A little later he reappeared holding a large lobster, which was waving its enormous claws indignantly.

'This customer will help to pass the time,' he announced.

Deftly he turned the lobster over and over on the red embers until it went a handsome bright red. Then he broke open the burning-hot shell and proffered the best part to Angélique. The white, firm, delicately flavoured meat comforted her, and she began to take a less tragic view of the situation.

Colin watched her eat, fascinated by her movements, which he knew so well and which had always delighted him by their inimitable grace. How naïve he must have been when he had first met her not to have recognized immediately just by watching her eat, that she was a great lady! ... The deft way she held the food, the easy grace with which she bit into it without any trace of vulgarity, were unmistakable pointers to the elegance which is learnt only at the table of kings ...

Angélique fed eagerly but her mind was so preoccupied that she was unaware of Colin's gaze resting on her.

At Wapassou she had often imagined what a delightful moment it would be, once she got back to Gouldsboro, and had the children and her woman friends about her, to roast a lobster or a crayfish in the hollow of a rock. Never would she have imagined that it would be like this in the darkness of a diabolical nightmare. Wapassou had disappeared and seemed very remote. So did Father de Vernon, alias Jack Merwin, in whose inscrutable eyes she had suddenly seen a flash of warm feeling for her, and yet that was only yesterday! ... It was only yesterday that the dreamy voice of the Jesuit had murmured: 'When the Devil's work is afoot, things go very fast ... time stands still ... Everything occurs outside of time ...'

Three nights ago she was enjoying herself and dancing at Monhegan, and her conscience was at peace. Today she realized that she was in danger of losing for ever Joffrey's love, and perhaps her life.

'I'm afraid,' she said half aloud. 'These parts are full of evil spirits. I sense them prowling about, dogging our every footstep and planning our ruin.'

Sprawled on the other side of the fire, leaning on his elbow,

Colin never took his eyes off her. She struck him as so pale in the firelight that he said not a word.

She got up to rinse her fingers at the water's edge, and the gesture reminded her of the day's exhausting tasks from which she had just emerged into the silence of the evening, stunned and still weary in every limb.

The wanton, languid movement of the waves made her feel giddy, and she came back, shaking her skirt out about her.

'My clothes smell of blood, of gunpowder, of the sweat of those unfortunate men, of death ... How many a soul has left this earth today! ... I can stand no more!'

She sat down again and realized that, without intending to, she had come closer to him.

'Tell me,' said Colin, 'what happened at Gouldsboro and in the bay? Something decidedly unpleasant, I'll wager. It was my ship they were after, wasn't it?'

'Yes indeed! And they got her. She is lying in the harbour now, half filled with water. Half your men have been killed, and the others wounded or taken prisoner ... It's the end for you, Gold Beard! You won't be troubling honest men any more ... Where were you while it was all going on?'

She was astonished to hear her own words sounding so full of peevishness and violence, and to find herself longing to strike him in her turn.

Sitting there, all on edge, with her arms around her knees, she stared out towards Gouldsboro, so keen was her desire to be back there again.

The mist was not so thick as to cut out the glimmer of the fires that had been lighted on the outermost points of land and on the most prominent rocks. Pieces of resin would be kept burning all night in those carefully sheltered bonfires to warn ships of the location of dangerous reefs.

Occasionally, when the roaring of the surf died down a little, Angélique thought she could just make out a confused murmur of sound from the port, and several times she seemed to catch a gleam of light from houses or the lanterns of ships lying at anchor, thinner and fainter than the light of the beacons.

What was happening over there? Had anyone noticed her disappearance? Were they searching for her? 'No matter what,' she told herself ... 'I'm finished ... finished!'

Colin remained silent, as if crushed by fate and the news she had just given him so abruptly.

Behind them the moon was rising, huge, shapeless and

golden, the mist forming a halo around it. Its brilliance began to spread out, whitening the languid waves, the sand on the beach, and vying with the dying glow of the fire. An owl hooted. Then Angélique gave a start of mingled fear and hope, as she thought she glimpsed human shapes moving about among the rocks, and swimming in the swell. But it was only a small band of seals, which splashed about for a bit then disappeared out to sea again, no doubt scared to discover humans on the beach where they had chosen to rest. Their short, sharp yapping cries faded into the distance and died away nostalgically.

No one would come out to the Old Ship Island that night. Angélique would have to spend with Colin one more of those lonely nights remote from the world, which only fugitives, out-cast lovers, the condemned and the hunted know, nights such as they had once shared in the desert. Nights full of sweetness, or fear, or the sense of a hostile surrounding world, that draws together fearsome hearts and trembling bodies.

Colin Paturel stirred.

'And so I've lost everything,' he said, as if speaking to himself. 'This is the second time ... no, the third ... possibly even the fourth. That's what life consists of for a gentleman of fortune and a poor sailor. Off you go ... off you go across the blue seas. Far away, over there. You win once, twice. And then be-cause you happen to pass a certain ship, or the wind changes direction, the whole of your life is wrecked, and you have to begin again ... Twelve years of captivity on the Barbary coast ... You escape, you make a new start, you rebuild your for-tune ... Then once again there's nothing left ... nothing but death to hope for ... or what other kind of life? A beach to be alone on and that's all.'

Angélique, her heart moved by some obscure remorse, listened to his monologue.

'And I have lost you too,' he went on, looking up at her with his keen blue eyes, which, in spite of herself, never failed to move her. 'Before, I always had you as a presence, a dream, a woman's face, a precious possession ... but now all that has vanished.'

'Colin! Colin!' she cried, 'my dear friend, you are torturing me. Have I hurt you that much, I who loved you so? ... Why these regrets? I am not worth it. You have idealized some mem-ory or other which you now use to torment your heart quite pointlessly. I am only a woman like other women, who happens to have crossed your path as many other women cross a sailor's path ... and I wonder what was so seductive about that miserable creature with the sunburned skin that I was then, with my dusty feet and emaciated body, dragging myself along over the stones, holding you back, encumbering you with my weakness ...'

'Don't try to destroy or to explain,' said Colin softly ... 'your poor bleeding feet, your cracked lips, your tears that left trails of salt on your cheeks, your body, growing thinner and thinner every day, more and more fragile beneath its burnous, those are the things of which I have made a secret paradise ... And in any case, you cannot be expected to understand what kind of "charm" a woman like you can have in the eyes of a simple man without means of defending himself. All that your eyes and your smile promise, your body can fulfil only too well. That is what one will never get over. Because there isn't one woman in a thousand who ... One might wander all over the face of the earth without ever finding her, without ever finding her again. After that, other women just don't count. After that, other women are hell!'

He spoke the last words with bitterness and was surprised to hear her laugh.

'That I just don't believe,' she said.

'What?' he exclaimed, straightening up, half angry.

'When you say that other women are hell, you are just dramatizing things in order to touch my heart but I don't believe you! You men are far too sensual not to take advantage of any agreeable opportunity even if you do carry an eternal love in your heart.'

'Oh! Do you think so?'

'You must understand that when we were together in the desert I regarded you as the master. You were the boss and ... I was terrified of you. Later on you became the man who carried me, protected me, and made me happy ...' her voice dropped a murmur – 'very happy! Colin Paturel, you are to beg my pardon for what you said just now. Now is the time to fall on your knees.'

He had listened to her, fascinated. Then slowly he lifted his massive body from the ground, and knelt down before her.

'Forgive me,' he said, 'forgive me, Madame.'

He saw a maternal, indulgent smile on Angélique's lovely lips.

'You are foolish, Colin.'

Her tender woman's hand brushed his rugged forehead, while

her slender fingers ran through his thick boyish hair. He caught the delicate hand in full flight and kissed the palm.

'How you do dominate me!' he whispered. 'I suppose it is because you are a great lady while I am nothing but a poor bumpkin.'

'No, you are a king, Colin.'

'No, I am a bumpkin.'

'All right then, you are the king of bumpkins, there!'

The two of them began to laugh gaily, and a moonbeam flashed on Angélique's teeth. They were so close together, linked by such a tender complicity, that the slightest movement would have brought their lips together.

Angélique knew that Colin's head was beginning to swim. And she withdrew her hand from his as if she had been burned, a gesture that stirred him to the very marrow.

This recoil of hers was a homage to him, for with it she had given him back a strength he had doubted for so many years.

Then he stood up and walked a few paces away. So he really did have the power, he, Colin, to stir that haughty, magnificent, regal body, and the happiness he had given her was not a tissue of lies. Of course, in Meknès he had shown a lack of prudence and discernment, in spite of the fact that his captive subjects willingly conceded that he 'had an eye for these things'. In spite of the Moorish veils that enveloped her when she was a prisoner in the harem, he should immediately have guessed from her bearing, from her slender wrists and ankles, her beautifully inflected voice, her well-chosen phrases with their occasional touches of boldness, from her delicacy, her patience ... and her moments of impatience, the way she had of always striking exactly the right note with everyone, and from her courage too – the hereditary courage of noble families – he should have known he was dealing with a great lady and not with a country wench.

He had paid dear for his mistake.

What a terrible awakening, afterwards, in Ceuta! What a blow!

'Now, my good man, away with you! This woman appears to be none other than the Marquise du Plessis-Bellière! One of the most illustrious names in the Kingdom, my good man ... widow of the Marshal of France ... a very great lady ... and, so it is whispered, she was ... not long since, the favourite of His Majesty ... The King himself has sent for her. Leave her now ... Let us take her to the Governor's apartments ...'

And 'they' had snatched her from his arms . . . and 'they' had taken her away, inert, taken her from him – his own heart! His dear love! His beautiful creature, his desert sister, his adored child . . . and he had remained there, covered with sores, sweat and sand, motionless, stupefied, for hours, just as if 'they' had torn his heart from his living breast, torn his guts from his belly, leaving great, bleeding holes where they had once been . . .

What a ghost to carry with him across the world, the ghost of such a woman!

Then he had found her again. She had not changed. She was still lovelier, still more of a woman. She still possessed that patrician grace that hid such courage and . . . such spirit.

Yesterday she had been Madame du Plessis-Bellière. Now she was the Countess Peyrac. Still on the move, still inaccessible. Away with you, my good man. And he remembered with an inexpressible rending of his heart how good she could be and how tender. And how gay . . . and how merry and caressing she was when he made love to her. She was the most natural woman in the world, the most straightforward, closer to him than anyone he had ever held in his arms . . .

But if it was true that she did not despise him, he could find it in him to eclipse himself, to go away, still possessor of the past, his treasure, and he would leave her to the other man. Had she not begged him to help her to keep her sacred oaths?

CHAPTER SIXTY-TWO

'COLIN, HOW is it that you come to be on this island? Who brought you here? And why were you not on board your ship at the time of the battle?'

The sound of Angélique's voice drew him from his reverie. Her voice was vibrant with emotion and he worshipped the fact that she was trying to create a diversion in order to ward off temptation.

He came and sat down beside her and filled in the picture of the suspicious events that had happened to him during the day. He was forced to admit that some evil forces seemed to have conspired to confound them and lure them into this trap.

That morning at dawn, while lying at anchor in one of the little inlets of the isthmus of Schoodic, where he had been hiding for some days with the intention, he freely admitted, of mounting a new attack upon Gouldsboro, a small boat had appeared with three sailors in it. They claimed to bear a message from Madame de Peyrac who had allegedly sent them across from Gouldsboro to ask Captain Gold Beard to meet her, as she needed his help in some matter. The whole thing was to remain a close secret and he was not to take any of his men with him.

'Did these strangers not give you a written message – or an alleged message – from me, or some object as a token?' Angélique asked him in astonishment.

'No, actually they didn't. And it never occurred to me to ask them for one. I admit that where you are concerned I forget my customary caution. I knew you were close, in Gouldsboro and ... I was longing to see you again. So I left the ship in charge of my lieutenant, and jumped down into their boat without any further explanation. The fog was so thick that I don't think I should ever recognize the island they took me to, where they claimed you had arranged to meet me. We began to wait and went on doing so for a long time. I thought that the fog must have delayed your arrival. Then, when towards the middle of the morning I heard the sound of gunfire, I began to get worried. I had a feeling that it was my ship that was under attack. I asked the men to take me back to it. They beat about the bush and delayed things until eventually I lost my temper. There was a fight. I am not at all sure that one of the men hasn't seen the last of this world, but I myself was dealt a blow that knocked me cold, and the back of my neck is still aching from it. When I came to I found myself on this island, stripped of my cutlass, my sword and my pistols. Night was falling. Then a little later, when I began to feel better, I began to explore the island and ... came across you near the old wrecked ship.'

Colin had stood up and was pacing up and down as he talked. Finally Angélique got up too and joined him, and they walked slowly side by side up and down the little beach that shone like a bright jewel in the setting of the night-dark trees. Their two shadows stretched out across the sand, fantastically drawn out and black as ink.

'What did they look like, these men who came to fetch you?'

He gave a shrug.

'Just sailors, such as one might encounter here or in the Caribbean. More or less any nationality, and speaking more or less any language . . . and yet no, I don't think they were foreigners. They were almost certainly French.'

Angélique had been full of anguish as she listened to him. She found it hard to resist an oppressive feeling of certainty that they had been the victims of evil spirits, which were making sport of them in order to destroy them. Events had been so precipitated and had become embroiled with such malicious cunning, that she no longer knew which thread she should seize to begin to disentangle the skein.

'Colin, did you know who the man was you handed me over to in Casco Bay? The English skipper of that boat?'

'The Jesuit?'

Angélique stared at him, stupefied.

'So you knew?' she exclaimed.

Colin halted and stared thoughtfully at the dark horizon.

'He appeared that morning,' he said. 'He moored his boat to the bollard and climbed on board. He spoke English so I took him for the skipper of some ship. He asked to speak to me and when we were in my cabin he revealed his true identity. He said he belonged to the Society of Jesus and had been sent on a secret mission; he asked me to hand over Madame de Peyrac to him. I had no reason to doubt him; he had an abrupt way of talking and looked at me with those penetrating, black eyes of his that could not possibly have been lying.

'Then I realized that this was my chance to enable you to leave, a helping hand God was holding out to me, and it was precisely because he was a Jesuit that I thought that it must be God's way of sending me a sign. Had it not been for him, had it not been for that Jesuit turning up like that, I . . . I think I would not have let you go. I had kept on saying to myself since the day before that I would have to give you up, but I could not . . . It was worse than in Ceuta . . . almost worse. Had you remained on board, I think I should have tried to win you back again . . . and I would have been the cause of your undoing . . . so this way out seemed best. I said: "All right, I understand. Let it be as you wish." Then he told me not to tell you who he was, but to let you think that he was the skipper of the boat, and an Englishman. I felt somewhat uneasy about this, but I have always bowed to the will of priests. I reckon they are fighting on the side of Good and that they know what they are doing. But I felt uneasy about it. I could not help feeling that someone was seeking to harm you . . .

'Did he do you any harm?'

She shook her head.

'No!' she murmured.

Now she understood what had gone on in the mind of Jack Merwin, the Jesuit, as he stood on that rock watching her die.

At Maquoit Point, he had captured her in order to conduct her back to other people who wanted to see her cut off, isolated, brought into question, utterly destroyed. And then at Monhegan the cruel sea seemed to have taken upon itself the task of getting rid of her. Everything had been simplified. He must have thought 'This is God's will!' and he had folded his arms across his chest and refused to offer her a helping hand.

But it was one thing to say of a fellow human being: 'This person must die' and quite another to watch him as he struggles with death.

He had just not had the heart to watch her death agony to its bitter end and to see her disappear beneath the waves never to appear again.

He had dived.

'My backers in Paris and Caen belong to the Company of the Blessed Sacrament,' observed Colin. 'I have undertaken to serve the missionaries in the new countries where I was going to establish myself. But I did not think that it would be such a difficult matter. I had been assured that the Gouldsboro region was clear of English settlements.'

'We are not an English settlement,' said Angélique. 'This territory belongs to my husband by virtue of his being the first occupier and of having promoted its prosperity.'

'Why did you marry this lord of Gouldsboro?'

Angélique hardly had the heart to give him an answer. It was too long a story, and besides everything relating to the intimacy of her life with Joffrey was an extremely delicate topic for her. She was reluctant to put into words things that concerned them alone, Joffrey de Peyrac and Angélique de Sancé – their dreams, the drama of their early relations, their ordeals, their struggles and weakness, their final happiness, and all that established between them this intangible bond: their life in common, their own private ship which was ceaselessly imperilled and storm-tossed and on which for so long they had been intertwined with one another in a way that made it impossible for anyone ever to separate them. No one, no, no one, she thought, gazing passionately up at the sky with its night clouds fringed with gold by the moon. And for the first time since the previous evening she suffered atrociously as if the blow she had received in her face had at last reached her heart, after a long period of wandering in the unconscious regions of hope. Joffrey! It was all over ... He despised her, he detested her, he no longer believed in her.

'Why did you marry him?' insisted Colin. 'What kind of a man must he be for a woman like you to want to link her existence to his and be willing to follow him even to these remote lands?'

'What does it matter?' she said dejectedly. 'He is my husband and he is more than anything in the world to me in spite of my latent weakness which sometimes betrays me.'

For a long time neither of them spoke.

'You know exactly the line to take with me,' said Colin Paturel at last with bitter irony. 'Respect for sacred vows! ... That was what you hit upon and it was the one thing which could stop me. I have remained true to it in spite of my own weaknesses ... One does not shed one's blood for twelve years in order to remain faithful to one's God, without finally becoming more attached to Him than to anything that one might find admirable on this earth. Let Him make but a sign ... "Stay, Colin! Thy Master has spoken." '

And he added almost below his breath, and with profound faith:

'And I know how to recognize Him when He makes a sign.'

Angélique, who was less simple than Colin and who had wandered on more diverse paths, was less willing to admit this intrusion of the divine into the logic – or the illogic – of her actions.

'Are we so strongly attached to the teachings of our childhood that we continue to let ourselves be governed in spite of ourselves, precisely, in fact, because it is in spite of ourselves?' she asked. 'Is it possible that we are merely frightened of things that we have learnt?'

'No,' said Colin, 'it is not only things that we have learnt which govern us. Fortunately! But there are times when man finds himself, whether he wishes it or not, in the fairway of truth. It would be as difficult to prevent him from following it as to prevent a star from passing across the sky.'

Noting an abstracted expression on Angélique's face, 'Are you listening?' he asked gently.

'Yes, I am listening to you, Colin Paturel. You are such an eloquent talker. How many things you have taught me which have remained engraved upon my heart ...'

'I am happy to hear it, Madame, but the words which I have said are, if I remember rightly, those I learned too from the Grand Eunuch, Osman Faraji, the tall dark fellow who guarded you in the harems of Mulai Ismail. Often at Meknès, the king would summon me and make me sit in my squalid rags on his gold-trimmed cushions. And together we listened to Osman Faraji. What a sage that Negro was! What a splendid fellow! He influenced my soul more strongly than any other being in the world. He was a seer.'

'How I liked him! How fond of him I was!' Angélique exclaimed, moved by a poignant nostalgia. 'He was a greater friend than any other.'

She broke off, moved to the depths of her heart, for from the limbo of memory came back to her the fact that it was Colin's hand that in order to save her, had killed the noble eunuch with a stab in the back.

'Enough of all this,' said Colin softly, 'enough of all these hurtful memories. You are tired and we are now far, very far from those places and farther still on the road of our lives. If at least I could say that I had made progress, that I had advanced towards something in the course of the years which followed upon Ceuta ... It is not merely that I have fallen back, but rather that I have spoilt all that I had garnered up in the prison hulk of God.'

'One always progresses when one suffers and yet does not give in, does not succumb, does not turn one's back decisively on good,' said Angélique fervently.

Thinking of the long tunnel full of stumbles and recoveries that she herself had passed through when she was far from Joffrey's side, she felt she had earned the right to encourage Colin.

'You are not as sick as you were making out a moment ago, Colin, my dear, dear friend. I know it. I feel it. From moment to moment it seems to me that the old Colin is going to reappear before me in his grandeur, laying aside the cheap frippery of Gold Beard, and I see him greater even than before, stronger, ready to fulfil the task that awaits him ...'

'What task? ... unless it be to have myself hanged high and dry like a common pirate.'

'No, not you, Colin! That will not be. Fear nothing, fear no more. I do not know how it is to be done, but I do know that God will be faithful to you, you will see. He cannot abandon you, you who were so cruelly crucified for Him ...'

'But he has abandoned me for so long.'

'No, no, do not doubt any more, Colin, you who were such a firm believer – that is the very essence of your being ... It is not for nothing that He has placed in you so many invaluable qualities. You will see ... For my part I do not doubt you.'

'Oh you are adorable,' said he in muffled tones, and he took her in his arms.

Angélique trembled from the roots of her hair to the soles of her feet.

In her infinite longing to carry Colin, as a wave might have done, towards the shore on which he would at last rediscover himself, she had spoken with fire, lifting up towards him her face radiant with that wonderful look in which he could read the sentiment more precious to man than all the hazards of the Universe – the trust of a woman. A trust in him, in his strength, in his grandeur, in his power, in his transcendental destiny.

And now pressed up against him, in the magic circle of his embrace, she felt this wave of tenderness changing into a wild voluptuous current which she recognized with deep dismay. For Colin's arm in the hollow of her back, that steely arm too often unaware of its own strength, was welding her to him with irresistible passion, and from this contact there surged up once again a strong attraction to him, which was like a ground wave, a torrential sweet and delicious longing.

Standing pressed close to him from head to foot, she threw back her face in the moonlight, her eyes closed as if she were going to die ...

'Do not be afraid, my love,' he said in his deep low voice, with a note of teasing in it which appealed so strongly to her heart and emotions, 'do not be afraid of me any more. This is the last time ... I promise you, it is the last time that I will hold you thus pressed close to my heart. But I would still like an answer ... did you cry, tell me ... did you cry, Madame du Plessis-Bellière, when I parted from you at Ceuta, when I turned my back on you to leave you for ever?'

'Yes, you know very well that I did,' she breathed. 'You know it very well. You saw ...'

'I was not sure ... for years I have wondered ... those tears, those tears that I saw shining in the eyes of that great lady, were they real? ... Were they for me? ... Thank you, thank you, my love ...'

He pressed her closely to him then released her and pushed her gently away. He refused to see her half-open lips trembling, offered to him. He straightened up and stood to his full Herculean height under the moonlit sky.

'Now I know what I wanted to know. I have received all the answers. And from your mouth! From your mouth! ... I seem to be able to breathe more freely. Thank you, my dear one. You have restored to me what I had lost. Now go, go and rest. You are exhausted.'

And as she hesitated, he took her by the shoulders, pressing her against him with infinite tenderness and led her back to the fire that he had lit earlier on. She dropped rather than sat down on the sand. He stirred the flames a little, then went off to the other end of the beach, where he lay down, visible in the shadow of the trees, in order to rest a little at a distance from her.

Shortly before when she had been walking along the beach, a higher wave than the rest had lapped her ankles. Her shoes were damp. She kicked them off, drew her feet in under her skirt, and resumed her former somewhat chilly posture, her arms folded around her knees. The nearby fire did not warm her and she was still trembling. 'How weak my body is, when it comes to love!' she said to herself bitterly and ashamedly. 'I have been wrong to neglect prayer for so long. It gives the grace to resist such impulses.'

She was very angry with herself and despised herself somewhat. For one whole part of the night she had felt very reasonable, capable of holding at bay the temptation roused by the revival of her memories and the proximity of Colin, and then quite suddenly had come this hot, greedy wave! ...

When things had reached that point, even if one stepped aside in time, there was an element of betrayal. A burning blush swept over her face and she hid it against her knees. How long the night was! 'Forgive me, Joffrey, forgive me, it is not my fault. It is because you are far away ... I am weak. You have cured me and revived me only too well, my wizard. Ah! how far off those days are when I could not suffer a man to even touch me without having convulsions ... It is your fault too. You have given me back my taste for kisses, for ... everything ... Today I am weak!'

She was talking to him in a low voice, in order to banish fear. And it was to the lover, to the adorable and adored husband that she spoke, to the man who had pressed her tight to his heart in the great bed at Wapassou, through all the length of the winter, and she held this image before her in order to forget the terrifying man who the evening before had seized her by the hair and struck her so harshly.

'If he finds out . . . if he finds out about this senseless meeting, on this island all night long . . . all night long with this pirate who for him is nothing more than Gold Beard, he will kill me. I shall never escape . . . that is certain. He will kill me before I have had time to open my mouth . . . And that I would be incapable of ever doing, just as I was last night . . . Oh God! How helpless and frightened one is when one loves too much . . . Help me, God, help me . . . help us. I am frightened and I do not understand any more what is happening. I do not know what to do any more . . .'

In spite of her present distress she was unable to regret entirely the chance which had brought Colin and her together again that night, alone on the little island of the old ship. Since she had seen him stand up as he said 'Thank you, my dear one, you have restored to me what I had lost,' she had felt a sensation of relief, a lightening of her conscience, she was going through a period when it is a duty to rid oneself of the burdens of the past. Thanks to God if, before one finally forgets, one is given the chance to make good the omissions of the past.

In the fullness of the gifts which had made her a woman, she was reaching that extraordinary age at which for each and every woman, life, while continuing its headlong course, seems to grow lighter, to grow purer, and to be renewed in the apotheosis of a liberty of mind and soul, which has been hard won but is all the more precious for that, when the weight of the mistakes which were often no more than the apprenticeship to the harsh trade of living, becomes less irksome. It is permissible to leave behind along the way the burdens of the past, to forget what can be forgotten, to remember only the richness of that imperfect and difficult adventure of the full time of life.

She realized that she had for a long time borne within her unconscious remorse about Colin, her desert lover.

Now he was safe.

The one thing which he would never know was that she had carried a child of his in her womb. The too intimate bonds between them must be dissolved. How difficult it was for human beings to help one another!

A spark of humour flashed in her numbed mind – she knew well the ways of that droll bird, ever ready to take flight within her in her darkest hours – and the idea occurred to her that she would like to be an old lady. Old age enables one to help one's neighbour, one's friends, without complicating their life or one's own.

It makes it possible to follow the impulses of one's heart in all their sincerity, and to give unselfish, and effective help to one's fellows. It gives one the right to live frankly, in the company of one's own heart, such as it is, without becoming involved in the perpetual conflict of caution, retreat, advance and retreat, which the seductions of the flesh impose upon emotional life.

'How good it will be to be old one day!' Angélique told herself, and began to smile, then to laugh to herself. She was shivering, and her feet were frozen and her forehead hot. The sound of approaching footsteps, crushing the sand and breaking the gentle silky rustling of the waves, put her on the alert. Colin was returning.

'You must sleep, my little one,' he said softly stooping over her. 'There is no sense in staying curled up like that, mulling over your thoughts. Lie down and you'll feel better. It will soon be day . . .'

She did as he bade her, putting herself in his hands as she used to do, experiencing once again the firm patience of his hands as he tucked her up carefully in her cloak and placed his own buffalo-hide jerkin over her feet.

She closed her eyes. To her aching body, the passionate adoration that emanated from Colin was like a balm, something to appease her heart, worn down with anxiety and grief, and which now, as it began to emerge from its state of shock, was becoming increasingly aware of its own pain.

'Go to sleep now,' Colin whispered, 'come now, you must sleep.'

And as she let herself slip into the black waters of sleep, she thought she heard a voice murmuring through the solitude of those nights in the Magreb . . .

'Go to sleep, my lamb, go to sleep. Tomorrow we have a long way to go, both of us, across the desert.'

Perhaps he really was murmuring those words.

CHAPTER SIXTY-THREE

AND COLIN was there once again, silhouetted against the brilliant dawn sky as he shook her gently.

'The tide is going out.'

Angélique raised herself on one elbow, brushing back her hair from her face.

'There is still a thick mist,' said Colin. 'If you hurry you can get across the bay without being seen.'

Angélique was on her feet in a flash, shaking the sand from her clothes.

It was indeed a favourable moment to cross. The haze hung over the bay some distance from the shore, one of those light mists full of brightness, that nevertheless formed a protective screen between the island and Gouldsboro. The wind had not yet begun to blow; it was the hour of calm in which the cooing of the turtle doves mingled so sweetly with the silence that it seemed to make it even more profound and overwhelming. The seagulls, tiny alabaster figures poised on the brown tips of exposed rocks, were of the general immobility of dawn, and when they did move it was only to glide slowly and silently, flashes of white through the pink and gold mist.

A strong smell of kelp filled the warm morning air, an indication of the vast stretches of mud and seaweed uncovered by the outgoing tide.

Angélique began to hope that she might manage to reach Gouldsboro without attracting attention and that by some miraculous set of circumstances her absence might have gone unnoticed. For, in fact, who would be concerned whether she had spent the night in her room or not? Apart from her husband ... who, in view of their cool relations since the previous day, had probably not bothered to inquire. With a bit of luck, her chance escapade might well have gone unnoticed.

She hastened down to the beach, with Colin close behind, watching her as she tested the first stones of the ford with her foot.

'And what about you? What is to become of you?' she asked suddenly.

'Oh, me! ...'

He pointed in a vague general direction.

'I shall try to find the men who stole my knives and pistols, and then I shall try . . . to get away . . .'

'But what then?' she cried. 'Colin, you are all alone! You have nothing left!'

'Don't worry about me,' he said sarcastically. 'I am no babe in arms. I am Gold Beard . . . don't forget that.'

She remained undecided, one foot poised, unable to make up her mind to leave him.

She sensed the terrible state of abandonment in which Colin found himself. He no longer even had any weapons. She could see him standing on the shore of some desert isle, a giant with empty hands, and, once the fog was dispersed, nothing better than a hunted animal, a ready target for the sharp eyes of his enemies, who would hunt him down among the islands.

'Go on, go on!' he said impatiently. 'Go on.'

She thought: 'I must go and find Joffrey . . . I must tell him everything . . . so that at least he will give Colin a chance to escape, to get away from Frenchman Bay . . .'

Then one last time she turned towards him so that she could carry away in her mind's eye a picture of him with his Viking's head and his two eyes as blue as small pieces of sky.

It was the sudden horror he saw in Angélique's eyes that warned him of the approaching danger.

He swung round, turning to face it in a single leap, his hands powerfully out-thrust, ready to grasp, to strangle, to strike, to kill.

A man in black armour leapt upon him, then four more, six, ten. They seemed to come from everywhere, as they leapt from the cover of the little wood behind the rocks.

Angélique recognized Joffrey de Peyrac's Spaniards as if in a nightmare, as if they had been devils hiding their ferocious features beneath a familiar face.

They had moved forward and crept up on him without disturbing the silence by a single sound, by the slightest crunch on the sand.

Even at the moment when she had seen them bearing down upon Colin, she had not understood. It had been like a crazy vision, a figment of her frightened imagination.

She had forgotten that these men, chosen by Peyrac, had once fought in the Peruvian jungle, had been trained to act with all the cunning of serpents, to move like cats, to be as cruel as the Indians, and that Moorish blood ran in their veins.

Pedro, Juan, Francisco, Luis .. she knew them all but at that moment she could not recognize them. They had become the incarnation of an evil, wild force, in hot pursuit of Colin, while in their efforts to overcome him their teeth gnashed and glistened, ridiculously white in their tanned faces.

Colin fought like a lion attacked by a pack of black Salukis. He fought them bare-handed, cutting himself on the crest of a steel helmet, and wrenched himself away from them so furiously that on several occasions he managed to drag along and hurl to the ground the men who were clinging to his clothes.

His knees finally gave way beneath their weight. His shoulders were seized from behind and he was tipped over backwards. Someone raised a pike over him.

Angélique cried: 'Do not kill him!'

'Do not fear, Señora,' came the voice of Don Alvarez. 'We only want to stun him. Our orders are to take him alive.'

The dark eyes of Don Juan Alvarez, haughty and heavy with solemn reprobation, fixed upon Angélique. His long ascetic face, still a little yellow, was framed as usual by a ruff, quilled in the old-fashioned way.

'Would you be so good as to take a seat, Señora,' said he in formal but commanding tones.

She realized that if she refused, he would not hesitate to use force. He was responsible to Count de Peyrac, and, having lived several months in the compulsory intimacy of Fort Wapassou with them, she knew that for Don Juan and his men the orders of the Count were sacred.

A nameless terror opened a dark hole within her and as yet it was only fear of realizing the precise meaning of what had happened.

In the eyes of Don Juan Alvarez, she read her condemnation. To him, this woman that he had honoured as the wife of the Count de Peyrac had been found in the arms of a lover. It was the collapse of everything that mattered. There was sorrow written on the proud features of the old Spaniard.

Angélique glanced towards the woods from which they had emerged, as dark as night in their black steel breastplates, their lances pointed towards Colin's back, and she was quite prepared to see him appear, 'him', the master, the man who had given orders for Gold Beard to be seized and for her to be brought back as a captive, an accomplice of the pirate, a contemptible woman. But the sinister masses of leaves remained closed, stirred only by the breath of the wind.

Then she clutched at the hope that 'he' did not yet know, that it was mere chance which had brought the Spanish guards to the island. Was it not the case that the archipelago had been combed since the previous day in order to find Gold Beard? . . .

'You must follow me, Señora,' repeated the commander of the guards.

He laid his hand on her arm.

She shook herself free and passed in front of him. It would be useless to attempt to justify herself in the eyes of a man like Alvarez. As far as he was concerned she was guilty, and guilty she would remain. And she fully deserved the penalty of death.

Wapassou was far away – the place which had bound them together in calm friendship, when they were all in the cold grip of winter.

A succession of uncontrollable and fiendish events seemed to have cast them into an eddy in which self-respect, mutual respect, and gladness had all gone under.

There was blood flowing from Colin's forehead.

He had drawn himself erect and, closely surrounded by his guard, he was saying nothing and making no further attempt to defend himself. His wrists and his forearms had been drawn behind him and were tightly bound, and his ankles had been put in shackles. A short length of cord between them allowed him to hobble along slowly.

Turning their backs on the distant prospect of Gouldsboro, whose wooden houses and pink cliffs were beginning to emerge in the light of the morning, the small company escorting Angélique and the prisoner passed across the island close by the hulk of the stranded ship. On the other side the rocks were steeper. Two small boats were waiting in a small cove. Low tide had left a channel giving access to the open sea.

Inviting Angélique to take her place in one of the boats, Don Alvarez held out his gloved hand to assist her. She disdained to take it.

He sat down beside her. She noticed that he was even more yellow than usual and that his spasmodic tic, the ferocious expression which made him suddenly bare his teeth, one of his permanent features since his torture by Atakap Indians, was troubling him particularly. It was the first time that she had noticed grey threads in his old-style Spanish beard. The truth was that during the last two days Don Juan Alvarez had aged ten years. Angélique's gaze met his in passing and what she saw moved her deeply.

Divided in mind between his loyalty to Count Peyrac and the loyalty which, in his own despite, the noble Countess had inspired in him in memory of the harsh winter which she had so heroically shared with them, the noble Spaniard was suffering the torments of the damned.

He took up his stance before her as a solemn guardian and custodian of the law. Sailors and mercenaries who were waiting on the beach took their places on board and pushed the boat out into the current. Another craft took on board the rest of the detachment.

Angélique found herself thinking, 'I'm going to die; when he finds out he will kill me.'

It was perhaps a childish notion but she could not shake her mind free from this persuasion. It was as if her brain were paralysed. The fatigues of a trying day caring for the wounded and a too short night had destroyed her defences and made her incapable of resisting anxiety. She felt ill and in actual fact she was ill.

She was pale to the lips and shivering in spite of the rising warmth of a summer day, but she tried to put on a good countenance. The hostility of those about her was tangible, like a kind of leaden cloak weighing down upon her.

'But I used to carry round warming drinks to all these men,' she thought somewhat resentfully.

But now she was a woman who had dishonoured her husband, and in the eyes of these males, fanatically attached to a punctilious code of jealousy, she deserved death. It was a senseless act but in this harsh, savage, virgin land everything appeared possible and as if dictated by the intransigence of nature herself. Anger, fury, jealousy, hate and the gestures of death were woven into the very fabric, sensitive and subtle as it was, of this splendid summer morning, and glowed like burning coals of fire in human hearts.

In the rising wind of the open sea blowing into her face, she felt the same breath fanning the passions of the human creature forced back on his own strength. With a kind of painful intuition she sensed their solitude as men and women, without nation and without laws, set down in the midst of an untamed nature and the way in which, in spite of themselves, as day after slow day passed by, the wildness of this continent penetrated to the depths of their being. In such circumstances a single man, a leader, meant everything. And on him and on his actions and his feelings depended life and death. Such is the law which has governed tribes and peoples since man has wandered over the face of the earth. What she had felt of Joffrey's secret strength, even in his gentleness and tenderness, was today leaving her almost without hope, in proportion as they drew nearer to the goal, more and more profoundly shocked and terrified.

But where were they going? The boats had veered towards the east, hugging the coast. The point of a peninsula was at a few cables' distance, and then they had rounded the cape and come almost immediately upon a rock-sheltered beach at the nearest point of which could be seen a number of armed men. It was a hidden place, remote from Gouldsboro and from any houses.

As they drew nearer to the group she made out Joffrey de Peyrac's tall form with his wide cloak billowing in the wind.

'He will kill me,' she kept on telling herself, petrified but in a way resigned. 'Without even giving me time to open my mouth. He could never have loved me, after all, since he cannot understand. Oh, how pleased I would be to be killed ... If he does not love me what is the point of living?'

The lassitude which possessed her was largely responsible for the disjointed thoughts which flashed through her mind.

'And what about Cantor? What will Cantor say? My son should not be involved in all this!'

The boats reached the shore. The surf was fairly violent and this time Angélique was obliged to accept the helping hand which Don Juan Alvarez held out to her in order to get ashore. In any case she would have been glad to accept it for her legs were scarcely capable of supporting her. She found herself at Colin's side, both of them closely surrounded by Spanish soldiers, while the sailors were busy making the boats fast.

Stepping out from the distant group Count Peyrac came towards them. Angélique would never have believed that the sight of her husband could cause her so much apprehensiveness, especially after those long months of love and comradeship which they had spent together in Fort Wapassou – still so close in time ... But ... but all that was gone with the wind of the shores and it was no longer the man that she loved who was advancing towards her. It was the master of Gouldsboro, of Katarunk, of Wapassou and sundry other places, a leader and at the same time a husband that his wife had flouted in the sight of his men and one might even say of his people.

'Is it he?' said Colin in a muffled voice.

'Yes,' murmured Angélique with a dry throat.

Count Peyrac was in no hurry. He was advancing with an off-handed haughtiness which in the circumstances was an insult and underlined the contempt but also the threat in his bearing. It would have been better if he had come forward mad with rage, as he had been on that recent evening. Angélique would have preferred such a paroxysm to this horrible waiting, this approach like that of a wild beast gathering itself to spring.

She was overcome once again by a panic which emptied her mind of all thoughts as she came face to face with him, just as it had done over and over again since Colin's fate had been at stake. It was partly a sense of guilt towards her husband, partly a desire not to lose him and partly loyalty towards Colin, but it paralysed her and deprived her through excessive fear of her best capacities – including the gift of speech, and of movement. Instead of running towards him, she remained rooted to the ground, struck dumb. Nevertheless, her eyes took in almost unconsciously every detail of Peyrac's dress, which was clearly a ridiculous thing to do in such a moment, and could be of no assistance to her in resolving the inextricable dilemma in which they all found themselves.

It was a green velvet costume. She had seen him wearing it on board the *Gouldsboro* the year before; it was one of those dark, sumptuous colours he liked to wear, whose subtle shades were heightened by a trifle of Flanders lace at the collar and revers, the points of which, embroidered with silver thread, covered his shoulders. The same lace picked out in silver formed the cuffs of the jacket, and adorned the tops of his knee boots of fine English leather. A short-haired black beaver-skin hat with a cluster of white feathers tossing in the wind, covered his thick hair. He was not carrying weapons in his belt that day, but had slipped his two silver-handled pistols into slots on his silver-embroidered crossbelt which ran across his doublet from shoulder to hip and held his sword. He came to a halt a few paces from them.

Angélique made a slight movement, she knew not to what end. Colin growled:

'No, don't get in front of me, I won't have it.'

The Spaniards clung to him, restraining him with considerable difficulty.

Motionless, Count Peyrac continued to scrutinize him from a distance with great concentration.

With his head held slightly on one side, the lord of Goulds-boro stared intently at the Norman filibuster, and Angélique, unable to take her eyes off her husband, saw his eyes grow dim. Then a sardonic smile twisted his scarred cheek on which the old gashes seemed even more prominent that morning, as if Peyrac's inner tension had made them whiter.

With his left hand he doffed his hat and advanced towards the prisoner. On reaching him, Joffrey de Peyrac raised his hand to his brow then to his heart in an oriental greeting.

'Salaam aleikom,' he said.

'Aleikom salaam,' Colin replied automatically.

'Greetings to you, Colin Paturel, King of the Slaves of Meknès,' Joffrey de Peyrac went on in Arabic.

Colin, taken aback, scanned his face closely.

'I recognize you too,' he said finally in the same tongue. 'You are Rescator, Mulai Ismail's friend. I often used to see you sitting at his side on embroidered cushions.'

'And I often saw you chained to the gallows in the market square, with vultures for company . . .'

'And I am still in chains,' Colin said simply.

'And in all likelihood soon to be hanged from some gallows,' the Count replied with the same icy smile that made Angélique tremble.

She still remembered her Arabic and had been able to follow the gist of this extraordinary conversation.

Almost as tall as Colin, Joffrey nevertheless seemed, from the lordly way he bore his slender body, to dominate his massive adversary. They were two utterly different types, from two entirely different backgrounds. Finding themselves face to face like this was nothing short of terrifying. And a long, heavy silence ensued as the Count appeared to think.

He had shown no sign of violence, even restrained violence, and his eyes had not even flashed menacingly. But Angélique felt that she no longer existed for him. Or, if she did exist, it was a mere object, a nuisance whose presence he wanted at all costs to ignore. Whether it was detachment or scorn, she knew not, and she found the situation inconceivable, unbearable. She would have preferred him to kill her, to strike her. But this was worse. By his attitude he was forcing her, in spite of herself, into the position of the woman she did not want to appear to be, the woman *she was not*, an adulteress, a dishonoured wife, cast out from her husband's heart as she stood beside her 'guilty lover' awaiting a verdict. But even that was gradually becoming a matter of indifference to her. She felt indifferent to those who surrounded them, indifferent to the background in her desperation for a single glance from him, some sign from him, no matter what it was.

Now that he knew who Gold Beard was, would he understand a little . . . her weakness? . . . She wished she had the courage to open her mouth and say: 'Let us have it out . . .' But the presence of the soldiers and sailors cast a chill upon her, as did that of all the gentlemen gathered around them in a silent circle, concealing their curiosity beneath a mask of indifference, and stiff formality – Gilles Vanereick, the Flemish corsair, Roland d'Urville, another Frenchman whom she did not know, and even the English admiral, very finely turned out, and his second-in-command, still more beribboned.

Why had Joffrey brought them all here to this tragic encounter, in which his honour as a husband risked being so sorely tried?

But above all she felt fear. Fear inspired by this stranger who was yet so close, Joffrey de Peyrac, the Magician, the Man of Mystery, her husband! . . . People are afraid when they love too much. They lose their self-confidence.

She felt sure that he would not throw a single glance.

So distressed was she that she did not see that there was someone who looked at her – Colin. Glancing surreptitiously at her, he noticed her expression of anguish, the pallor of that beautiful face disfigured by the great blue bruise, and what he read in Angélique's eyes – her feelings for the man who had struck her – made him bow his head, heartbroken.

He had glimpsed the truth of the situation.

It was that man standing there, and he alone, that she loved. That man Rescator he had seen at Meknès, as he entered the city accompanied by his splendid escort. Another renegade whose presence was an insult to the wretchedness of the slaves. Gold and silver gave him unequalled prestige and Mulai Ismail had loaded him with honours.

And now he was the man Angélique loved. It was he who possessed her heart. It was that dark nobleman, as slender and vigorous as a Moor or a Spaniard who possessed her, that ugly man with the alarming features marked by the sabre slashes of duels, yet handsome with the radiance of his spirit shining from his sparkling eyes. It was this great nobleman with the full weight of his heritage and grandeur behind him who possessed her.

And he did possess her ... to the marrow of her bones, to the innermost corner of her being ... to her very heart. It was obvious. He only had to look at her ... to see that devouring expression, that childish confusion he had never seen in her before, courageous creature that she was ... But when a woman's heart has been reached, she has neither shame nor pride, nor anything else left. She becomes a child again. He understood.

He, Colin – Colin the Norman, Colin the captive – he was nothing to her, in spite of the womanly weakness she had once shown towards him. He need not deceive himself about that.

Face to face with that man there, in her eyes he was nothing. And what did it matter anyway? He was going to die. This deserted place, this lost corner of the American continent, this would be the end of his journey!

And his generous heart longed to do something more for her, for Angélique, his sister in captivity, who had been the only light – warm, heavenly, dazzling – in all his hard existence.

This at least he owed to her. And he would do it since this was the only thing which mattered to her.

'My lord,' he said, raising his head proudly and looking straight into Peyrac's impenetrable eyes, 'my lord, today I find myself in your hands, and after all, it is according to the fortunes of war. I am Gold Beard, and I had chosen this place for my raid. I had my reasons and you had yours for stopping me. Let the most skilful and the swiftest man win, I say. I lost! ... I defer to you – you must do with me as you will ... But before you begin the process of trial and conviction, I want everything to be made clear, so that if you hang me it should only be because I am a pirate and one of your enemies, a bandit on the high seas to your way of thinking, a filibuster whose trade is an obstacle to yours, a man who has lost this particular game, but ... NOT FOR ANYTHING ELSE, my lord! There is nothing else, that I swear.

'Just memories, nothing more. You must know this, since you recognize me. People remain friends when they have shared captivity on the Barbary Coast ... and when they have made their way together back to Christian lands. Those are things that can never be forgotten ... between those whom the hazards of life have brought together again. You must understand this. But each man has his destiny. And I can swear to you under oath, my lord, that it was neither my doing nor hers,' he nodded towards Angélique – 'that the unfortunate occurrence of last night happened. The tide is not to be treated lightly in these parts, as you know as well as I; and if you are surrounded on an island, there is nothing for it but to be patient and wait.

'But once again I give you my word as a seafaring man, before your men here and before these gentlemen who are listening to me, that nothing happened during the course of this night which could possibly damage the reputation of your wife, Countess Peyrac, nothing which could stain your honour as a husband.'

'I know that,' Peyrac replied in his hoarse monotone, 'I know that. I was on the island.'

CHAPTER SIXTY-FOUR

THIS TIME, Angélique was seized with a rage that shook her like a tempest, and there were moments when she told herself that she hated Joffrey de Peyrac with all her heart and soul.

The blow had struck her full in the heart, dragging her out of her anguished stupor as, with an ironical grimace, he had murmured: 'I know, I was on the island!'

Then turning away, he had given the signal for all to set off back to Gouldsboro.

He had refused to see the expression of horror on Angélique's face, an expression she had been unable altogether to repress on hearing his revelation, and as they all moved off in a heavy silence, along the rough track at the edge of the sea, he strode on, his head held high in his customary manner, his full cape flapping in the wind, with never a glance back at the prisoner who was being pushed along by the Spanish soldiers, nor at the young woman who walked alone, wrapped in her own thoughts, and occasionally stumbling without noticing it, on the rough ground.

Had he looked into her green eyes, he would have seen nothing but a woman's exasperated rage. It dominated all else, this rage that sprang from her burning humiliation, from a sense of shame whose origin she had not analysed.

In her agitation, she did not realize that above all she was wounded in the privacy of her feelings. Her friendship for Colin, her tenderness for Colin, these he had seen. He had seen her lay her hands on Colin's forehead, and laugh with him, and to that he had no right. That was hers alone, it was her secret garden. A husband, however dear he may be, has no right to see everything, to know everything. Besides, he was no longer a beloved husband to her, but an enemy.

In her sudden introspective state she rediscovered the age-old image – man, the essential enemy of woman – more profoundly hated still because deceptive and disappointing.

Then a surge of anger and bitterness helped her to regain her footing and to go forward with her head held high.

That he should have insulted her, that he should have struck her, she could accept, and she bowed before the violence of righteous anger. But the horror of this Machiavellian deceit discredited him in her eyes, in proportion to the utter confidence and boundless esteem in which she had held him. Everything was ruined! Everything! He had played with his wife's heart, with her senses whose fragility he well knew, and he had driven her into the arms of another man . . . in order to see! . . . In order to see! . . . To amuse himself! Unless it was that in his jealous fury and his wounded pride he had sought, in launching her into a new temptation, a pretext for killing her . . . KILLING HER! . . . Her! His wife! Who had believed she had a privileged position in his life and in his heart! . . . Bitter sobs welled up in Angélique's throat. With a superhuman effort she succeeded in shaking them back and in controlling the flood of tears which was rising to her eyes. She tilted her chin defiantly.

Such was her inner turmoil that she did not wonder what was going to happen. Would he lock her up, have her guarded in the fort? Would he drive her away? Would be exile her? In any case she would not allow herself to be bullied and would know how to plead her case this time. On the other hand, Colin's fate appeared to her inevitably tragic, and when, as they reached the outskirts of the establishment, a babel of shouts and cries went up from the woods like the blast of a gale, her own feelings faded into the background leaving only a sense of acute fear for Colin's life. She summoned up her strength, ready to defend him by word and deed against all and without concern for herself; for this could not be, she would never tolerate this shocking thing, to see Colin hanged, butchered, to see Colin Paturel's life destroyed because of her.

She would throw herself down on his body, she would defend him like one of her children. Had he not carried her on his back in the desert? . . .

The shouting from the woods was that of a mob ready to kill.

Warned by the invisible messenger which is said to pass on the wings of the wind in savage climes, the entire population of Gouldsboro, swollen by foreign sailors, Acadians in transit, and Indians who had come to barter, was racing to meet them, tumbling down the slopes, crossing the spaces laid bare by the retreating tide, and the white bonnets of the women mingled like a flock of seagulls with the dark, motley, surging mass of the men. The people of La Rochelle and the sailors from the ships had been joined by English refugees, and by Indians, always in search of excitement and diversion and quick to take up the cudgels on behalf of their friends.

'Gold Beard! Captured! . . .'

And 'she' was with him. That too was already known. She had spent the night with him, on Old Ship Island. 'They' were being brought back in chains.

Cries, howls and insults created an immense uproar which came to meet them as they advanced, and when the crowd, wildly excited, emerged from the forest and the beaches, the Spanish soldiers were obliged to form a barrier, with levelled pikes, in order to prevent the prisoner being overwhelmed and falling a victim to the frenzy of the mob.

'Kill him! Kill him!' they howled. 'There you are, Gold Beard! Bandit! Pagan! . . . You wanted our property, now you are in chains! Where are your emeralds? And your ship? . . . It's our turn now! Ha! Ha! Your golden beard will not save you. It will serve to hang you with as a punishment for all your plundering raids!'

In the swirling mass of seamen and settlers, all seething with anger and united in a common execration of the enemy who had come within an ace of ruining them when he had laid siege to the little community, just emerging from the rigours of the winter, this man was today nothing more than a colossus finally vanquished, after the violent skirmish of the previous day, which had resulted in the death of several of their people. In their cries of hate, their need to heap insults upon his head, there was a blend of triumph, relief, and a kind of regret. Their victory was too dearly bought. Their wild hearts were somehow touched.

At Gold Beard's side was the Lady of Gouldsboro, the Lady of the Silver Lake, the Fairy with the healing hands. So it was true what they said about her and the pirate! How dreadful it was to find that the allegations were confirmed!

This low-born plunderer had destroyed what had been for them a precious source of strength in their grim exile – the respect which they had come to pay, in spite of themselves, to two superior beings – the Count and the Countess of Peyrac.

In the tumult of execration and hostility surrounding them, Angélique missed the only look which Joffrey had deigned to cast upon her that morning.

If she had seen it, perhaps the pain which was tormenting her would have been somewhat eased. For the glance was to make sure that she was protected by the Spanish lances.

'Ungodly man! Woman-stealer! Gallows-bird!'

The boos and sarcastic cries kept bursting out in volleys. Colin, his hands bound, shoved, pushed and battered, kept on advancing as well as he could in the midst of the soldiers.

The wind ruffled his long hair and his tangled beard. With his clouded brow and his bristling eyebrows and his eyes fixed in the distance above the bobbing heads of the mob, he was like Prometheus, son of the Titan, bound powerlessly to his rock and abandoned to the vultures.

On entering the village the group was obliged to halt once more by the thrust of the crowd which neither d'Urville's injunctions nor Vanereick's threats nor the forbidding aspect of the Spanish guard could control.

A stone whistled through the air and struck Colin on the temple. Another rolled at Angélique's feet and from somewhere another cry went up: 'She-Devil!'

The anathema hung in the clear morning air. And suddenly, as if terrified by its own violence, the mob fell silent.

They were then able to hear the Count's voice, whose calm manner and hand raised as a sign of peace did not fail to act upon their over-excited nerves.

'Order!' came his voice, which was hoarse but calm, solemn and firm. 'Your enemy, Gold Beard, has been captured! Leave him now, leave him to my justice!'

With bowed and submissive heads the crowd withdrew. The fort was near. Angélique heard orders being given for the captive to be taken to the guardroom and locked up under double vigilance.

Before the palisade gate there opened for her the refuge of the apartment in the keep. But she stopped and suddenly turned round to face the close-packed, scowling crowd, which was watching her. In the front ranks there were the Protestants from La Rochelle.

Angélique realized that, if she adopted the attitude of a guilty woman and buried her fears in the apartment in the fort, she would never be able to come out again without risk of being stoned by the mob. She knew the uncompromising character of the people of La Rochelle, the superstitious impulsiveness of the seamen, which was exceeded only by that of the English. Once she and her husband became the butts of malicious gossip, each of these groups of people, in accordance with its own particular beliefs, would arm itself with holy water or muskets as the case might be, just as the people of La Rochelle had done during the mutiny which had taken place on board ship during the crossing from Europe. The only way to quell these oversensitive consciences was to assert oneself, to discourage gossip by showing that one's own conscience was clear, and since there was no hiding away this face of a woman taken in adultery with which she was credited, to have the boldness to display it to all and sundry with its pallor, the rings around the eyes, and the ignominious marks of the blows she had suffered during her conflict with her husband.

She shook off the hand – perhaps that of Don Alvarez – seeking to guide her in the direction of the interior of the building. She would not passively accept being put on trial or being held a prisoner and, if that was what they wanted, force would have to be used and it would be clearly seen whether Joffrey was prepared to add this new indignity to all those he had already inflicted upon her.

Adulterous woman! So be it! Well then, how should an adulterous woman behave in order to avert the flood of calumnies and preserve her own dignity and that of her husband, to save what could be saved? Surely by facing the music, by acting as if nothing had happened, as if nothing were known, 'just like before'.

'I would like to examine the men wounded yesterday,' she said in a loud voice and as calmly as usual, to the woman standing close to her. 'Where were the men from the *Fearless* put?'

The woman turned away roughly, but Angélique marched boldly on through Gouldsboro, as one might walk on water, her mind firmly made up to show what she was and what she intended to remain in the eyes of all.

On a sign from the Count, two of the Spanish guards fell into step behind her. To that too she was indifferent. She would assert herself, and gossip would die away at her approach for lack of fuel to maintain it. Angélique was determined that the youthful mind and heart of her Cantor should not be disturbed either.

All these things were going round in her head, which felt strangely empty as a result of hunger and fatigue, but she would not rest until she had regained control of Gouldsboro, and she went tirelessly from one wounded man to another. The majority of the complement of the *Fearless* had gone back on board their ship, which was anchored in the roadstead, but the most seriously wounded and the sailors from the *Gouldsboro* were being nursed in private houses. Angélique went into the houses, called for water, cloth, salves and assistance, and the people of La Rochelle, both men and women, found themselves assisting her in spite of their feelings.

The wounded greeted her with impatience and hope and she felt calmer as she handled the dressings wet with blood and pus. These gaping wounds in the healing of which she saw the reflection of her own power gave her back her sense of dignity.

All this unshaven and sick humanity was in fact less receptive to the rumours circulating at the expense of the beautiful noble lady, whom they had met in the wild antipodes of the Americas on a day of battle, than they were to the relief they felt at her coming and because of her presence.

'Madame, will you be able to save my eye?' ... 'Madame, I couldn't sleep all night because of the gnats and mosquitos ...'

The wounded pirates from the *Heart of Mary* had been put with the able-bodied prisoners in the corn barn, surrounded by a cordon of heavily armed sentries. Furthermore, the building was covered by the guns of the corner bastions of the fort; and these precautions were by no means superfluous, for the sentries told Angélique that their prisoners had been in a state of high excitement since they had heard of Gold Beard's capture, and that it would be risky to go among them.

Two sailors proposed to escort her inside, with levelled muskets and lighted matches, but she refused their services.

'I know these people, and I am not concerned!'

She ordered the two Spanish guards to stand outside with such an imperious expression that they did not dare disobey her. Divided as they were between the authority of the Count de Peyrac, which was sacred to them, and that of this fascinating woman, poor Luis and Pedro had never been so distressed as on this harsh day.

Angélique was not afraid of being alone with the pirates from the *Heart of Mary*. On the contrary, she felt herself more at ease, for today they were very much like her – unhappy and in peril.

The wounded were in dire need of care and the comfort of a hand which they knew to be skilled and soothing. As for the able-bodied prisoners, they concealed their anxiety about their unenviable fate, which was rapidly drawing nearer. Was this the last morning that they would see? The conqueror, the master of Gouldsboro, had come to inspect them on the previous day, fixing his eagle eye on their hang-dog faces.

'Monsieur,' the Chevalier de Barssempuy had ventured to ask, 'what fate have you in store for us?'

'A rope for the lot of you,' replied Peyrac roughly, 'there is no shortage of yard-arms on the masts of our ships.'

'Just our luck!' the pirates grimaced. 'We've fallen into the hands of an even more bloodthirsty fellow than Morgan!'

Being men of blood themselves for the greater part, and having to their account many tortures, severed hands, poor victims hanged or roasted alive in the islands – for the Caribbean sun sets the taste for evil ablaze in the heart of man – they expected no mercy for themselves. The better elements among them no longer congratulated themselves on having wished 'to settle down and turn over a new leaf'.

'And we wanted to become settlers and family men! This last campaign has been our undoing.'

In their black despair or grey resignation, which they felt alternately, Angélique's appearance was a ray of light. It is a hard world, particularly for gentlemen of fortune. No crack in the rough shell of a life spent cutlass in hand, a thirst for gold in one's heart, and a thirst for rum in one's throat. Suddenly a woman was filling a void in their hearts, passing among them, a woman who was neither booty nor a whore, and there was not time to wonder what she really was before she took you in hand and you found yourself once again under her sway, with no alternative but to respect her and obey her humbly.

For all of them it was a relief to see her coming in once more, when Gold Beard had been captured, into the barn, her bag of lint and medicines in her hand, and kneeling down at once at the bedside of these sick and wounded men and beginning to dress their wounds and nurse them without further delay. A few put forward the suggestion that she should be seized and held as a hostage in order to save their skins; they would negotiate on that basis with the Gouldsboro swine and, according to the results achieved, they would send a finger, an eye, a breast of the lovely lady to her husband, the 'bloodthirsty rogue' who wanted to kill them all, and it would be highly surprising if they did not succeed in getting out as a result of this manoeuvre. What about it? In such an extremity was it not the right thing to do, as indeed they had already done in the past more than once? But the plan got no further than that. Glittering eyes followed Angélique's fair hair as she came and went in the stench of the half darkness, but no one said a word or made the slightest move. Only young Barssempuy dared to break his silence to ask her a question:

'Is it true, Madame, that Gold Beard has been taken?'

Angélique nodded without speaking.

'What will happen to him?' went on the lieutenant in an anxious voice. 'He can't be executed, Madame . . . He is such an extraordinary man! We are devoted to our leader, Madame.'

'His fate depends on the decision of Monsieur de Peyrac,' replied Angélique dryly. 'He is the master.'

'Yes, but you are the mistress,' piped Aristide Beaumarchand in his reedy voice. 'From what they say. . .'

Immediately, under Angélique's withering gaze, he curled up, his arms folded across his belly which he constantly nursed as a pregnant woman who fears to be beaten protects her precious burden.

'You would do better to hold your peace,' she said coldly, 'I'll cut your throat for you one of these days.'

The others chuckled with a sudden sense of relief. Having finished her work she left them. She felt in no mood to laugh and chat with these ruffians. But when she had closed the door behind her, she no longer felt any sense of resentment towards them.

Try as she might, she always ended up by allowing her heart to be touched by the wounded and the vanquished. Bandits or soldiers, highwaymen or sailors, as soon as she had nursed them she could not help loving them. This irresistible attachment was the result of the knowledge she acquired of them as she attended to their sufferings.

A sick man is so vulnerable. At such times he lowers his defences and reveals his inner character, and, if he resists, it is easy to circumvent him. Through the armour of an embittered, cruel and inflexible character, which in its state of weakness had lowered its defences, Angélique always succeeded in reaching in the end the simple and childish heart. When they were up and about again, she kept them under her spell. They felt, sometimes with dismay, that henceforth she knew them better than they knew themselves. Outside, she gave orders for gaming boards, playing-cards and tobacco to be taken to the prisoners to help them pass the time of their captivity.

CHAPTER SIXTY-FIVE

STANDING UP to the ladies of Gouldsboro was quite a different kettle of fish! No quarter and no faltering to be expected there, she well knew. Their virtue exuded a sense of self-righteousness and condemnation of others and seemed possessed of an infinite capacity for virulence.

But it was up to her to shut them up too before the wave of bitterness engulfed them all and ruled out the possibility of ever making a new start.

Before pushing open the door of the 'Inn-Beneath-the-Fort', where she expected them all to be forgathered, Angélique paused briefly and instinctively prayed to Heaven. Naturally there they all were, in their dark skirts and white bonnets. Madame Manigault, looking more imposing than ever, was presiding, Madame Carrère was bustling about, Abigail Berne was standing on the far side of the chimney place, pale and dignified, a resolute expression on her beautiful face, which reminded one of a Flemish madonna. Angélique's entry seemed to have interrupted an argument, in which Abigail must have incurred the displeasure of her companions because of the moderation of her opinions.

'Madame Carrère,' said Angélique, addressing the proprietor of the establishment, 'would you be so good as to have dinner brought to me in the apartment in the keep? And I should also be grateful if you would heat me a basin of water so that I can wash.'

'All the waters of all the rivers on the earth cannot wash clean a guilty soul neither can any earthly food nourish those who are dying for having offended the Lord,' Madame Manigault declared in a loud aside.

Angélique received this Parthian shot, but she had been expecting it.

Over and above her exasperation, and the irritation she felt towards these gossips, she knew that these women, whom she could not help considering as friends, were torn between two opposing views.

Behind the uncompromising attitude of these Gouldsboro ladies towards Angélique's presumed scandalous conduct, lay a feeling of indignation at the betrayal of a man for whom more or less all of them felt a profound admiration, even a trace of something warmer. It was a repressed, disguised sentiment but a sentiment all the same, for the hearts of these Huguenot ladies were susceptible beneath the layer of frigidity imposed by their early upbringing.

Madame Manigault's 'I always said as much' came into its own now, spreading out like the bands of calico hung across the streets on the Papist feast day of Corpus-Christi! Had she not always considered Angélique, Master Berne's servant, a dangerous troublemaker!

To which Abigail retorted that Madame de Peyrac's present conduct just went to show that she had a clear conscience.

'That's only pride!' Madame Manigault replied. 'I always said as much!'

'And in any case, what did anyone know about what had actually happened?' rejoined those who remained faithful to Angélique ... Gossip, allusions, hints ... The Swiss had been drunk when he said those outrageous things about her, as Master Manigault and Master Berne would bear witness ...

And now Angélique herself had appeared holding her head high among them, and had replied to Madame Manigault's aspersions with a slightly disdainful smile.

She was close to them, and very different from them, just as she had been when she had shared persecution with them in La Rochelle.

And they remembered how Angélique had run with them over the moors to escape from the King's Dragoons, how she had rushed them away in order to save their lives ...

'That is a fine pretext, an impressive piece of truth,' said Angélique, eyeing the august lady calmly, 'and I think it was intended for me to meditate on, wasn't it, dear Madame Manigault? Thank you for the thought, but just for the moment, my soul, guilty or not, is less in need of food than my body. It is two days now since I reached your settlement in Gouldsboro, ladies, and I would just like to point out that the only thing that has passed my lips from its well-stocked larders has been one cob of Indian corn, which would not be saying much for your hospitality were I not aware of all the worries and tasks you have been overwhelmed with since yesterday, what with the battle and the wounded men to care for. When I asked for water and food I was only expressing an extremely natural need which you too, ladies, seem also to feel.'

It happened that some of the worthy ladies from La Rochelle were in fact sitting down to a tasty looking stew accompanied by goblets of wine. Having divided their time since the previous day between the care of their houses, their children, their farms and the men wounded in battle, they too were feeling exhausted and had taken advantage of a lull to obtain some sustenance from Madame Carrère's cheerfully welcoming inn. Caught in the act of regaling themselves, they sat abashed and confused, their spoons in mid air.

'Please, I beg you,' Angélique insisted condescendingly, 'do not put yourselves out on my account. Please continue. I am in no way casting stones at you. You are quite right to take some refreshment, my dear friends. But pray allow the Countess of Peyrac to do likewise. So please send me something as soon as possible, Madame Carrère . . .

'Abigail, my dear, could you come with me for a moment? There is something I would like to say to you in private.'

With one foot on the first step of the stairs that led to her room, Angélique looked up at Master Berne's wife, her gaze frank and free of all deceit.

'Abigail, do you doubt me?'

The bold front she had put on was breaking up, her exhaustion was beginning to tell. Abigail felt an impulse of affection for her.

'Madame, nothing can ever change my feelings of friendship towards you, as long as you do not find them offensive.'

'You have got things the wrong way round, my gentle Abigail. It is I who has always found your friendship a precious thing. Do you think I shall ever forget how kind you were to me when I came to La Rochelle with my child in my arms? You never despised the poor servant girl I was then. So please don't be so reverential towards me – it is quite unfitting between the two of us. And thank you for what you have just said. You have given me back my courage. I cannot yet explain to you what is going on but none of it is as serious as some nasty-minded people would have you understand.'

'I know in my heart of hearts that this is true,' Abigail agreed.

How charming Abigail was, the pure, chaste girl from La Rochelle, in the radiance of her approaching maternity! Happiness had ennobled her still further. Her blue eyes pledged her affection. Angélique weakened, and, feeling she could not bear it any longer, let her forehead fall on Abigail's shoulder.

'Abigail, I am frightened, I feel as if I were caught up in some infernal whirlpool . . . as if I were hedged about by threats . . . If he doesn't love me any more, what is to become of me? . . . I am not guilty . . . not as guilty as people say . . . but everything seems to have conspired to condemn me.'

'I know what an honourable heart you have,' said Abigail, running a soothing hand over Angélique's brow. 'I am on your side and I am very fond of you.'

Hearing the sound of footsteps Angélique straightened up abruptly. No one but Abigail must see her weaken. But Abigail's kindness to her had renewed her strength.

She gave her friend a meaningful wink.

'They would like to see the last of me, wouldn't they?' she said. 'They have already had enough of having to put up with the presence of a sinner like me in Gouldsboro! But don't worry, Abigail. I have come here to help you at the birth of your baby and I shall stay with you as long as you need me, even if they make life hell for me.'

Alas, nothing had turned out as she had foreseen it. She had dreamed of sitting in her friends' houses, exchanging news with them. Then they would have gone a tour of the recently established facilities of the township. They would have checked accounts and organized celebrations to which they would have invited the crews of all ships docked in the harbour. There was always something to celebrate during the summer months. Quickly, oh how quickly the mild season went by! They had to live their lives at double or treble speed, to gather in, store up, exchange, while hordes of people rushed down to the sea and there was feverish activity everywhere. Quick! Quick! Winter would soon come close in upon them again.

But nothing was as she had dreamed it. Far from being a period of celebration, these summer days ran on like a muddy torrent, carrying with them passions, griefs, despair, swelling hourly with a new flood of obscure dangers.

CHAPTER SIXTY-SIX

WHAT WAS Joffrey thinking? What decision had he reached about her, and about Colin?

This silence, this absence were becoming intolerable to her.

Throughout every moment of that day which seemed to last for centuries she feared and hoped alternately that he would send for her. She would be brought to justice before him, admittedly, but anything was preferable to the uncertainty in which he had left her. Had she been able to cry, to storm, to implore, to beg, or to accuse him in turn, this would have given her a new lease of life.

Her fury, her pride, and her instinct of self-preservation which had kept her going that morning, were beginning to weaken as the hours passed. By driving her away, by ignoring her, he was torturing her in a way that so completely sapped her inner strength that she could scarcely swallow a few mouthfuls of the meal she had ordered Madame Carrère to send her.

That afternoon, she went in search of Cantor whom she found busy down by the harbour.

'Pay no attention to any of the gossip you may hear about me,' she told him earnestly. 'You know how superstitious all these people are. I have already been called a She-Devil in Quebec, haven't I? A woman only has to be taken prisoner by a pirate for a whole web of calumny to be spun about her. Gold Beard behaved chivalrously towards me and one day I'll explain to you who he is and why he happens to be a friend of mine.'

'In any case I shan't be here to see him hanged,' declared Cantor, who seemed not to want to dwell any longer on these matters. 'I am off today at high tide on the *Rochelais*. Father has just told me I must go.'

He straightened up, sufficiently proud of his reponsibilities as a fifteen-year-old skipper not to show overmuch concern for the underlying tensions dividing the little colony. He was pleased that he had got back in time to take part in the naval battle, and still more delighted to be setting sail again, in command of his own ship, across the sea to lead the kind of busy existence with which he was familiar. He stuck out his chest and added, full of self-importance:

'I have to take some goods as far as Houssnock which will then be taken on as far as Wapassou by Kurt Ritz and six recruits whom I am taking on board with me.'

'What!' Angélique exclaimed. 'There's an expedition leaving for Wapassou in a few hours and no one has even told me? ... Laurier! Laurier!' she called to the little boy who was going by, 'Quick, come and help me collect some shells for Honorine.'

She only just had time to scribble a note to the Jonases and the Malaprades.

'Hurry, hurry, the tide won't wait,' Cantor enjoined.

Kurt Ritz was standing on the harbour breakwater, halberd in hand, inspecting the bundles of goods being loaded into the sloop, and his men who, like himself, were of German or Swiss origin, wore their full dress regalia – a survival of the sixteenth-century German infantry costume with the short, tight-fitting doublet with huge full sleeves slashed open to reveal the shirt, and full, buttercup yellow cloth breeches, tucked in at the knees and sewn with perpendicular bands of scarlet ribbon that hung slack, giving them the appearance of petticoat-breeches, and, in accordance with the improper and boastful fashion of the previous century, a codpiece shaped like a cocoon of golden-yellow satin.

One thing only was different: soft bands had replaced the goffered ruff.

They wore great broad hats, a cross between the ancient toque and the broad-brimmed modern felt, decorated with short, red ostrich feathers. A gilded steel helmet hung from each belt, and with their pikes, they made an impressive display.

Kurt Ritz fulfilled all the conditions of the manual which requires a sergeant to be 'a man at once learned, valiant, wise, courteous, who has had many encounters with the enemy, and where possible, is tall and good looking'.

He also carried a sword, a sign of the noble rank he had been given in the service of the King of France, in Austria, against the Turks.

Angélique had not seen him since that night when she had surprised him clinging to the poop of the *Heart of Mary*, apart from their brief encounter in the dark on the evening of her return, and she glanced round for him for a moment, not recognizing him.

Someone pointed him out, and she handed him her message for the Jonases, taking no notice of his haughty, disdainful look. Of course, he would always despise her, after what he had seen of her on board ship. But would he mention it at Wapassou? She could not stoop to ask him to keep quiet, but as she spoke to him in a steady voice, adding, as she suddenly thought of them, several important instructions – for instance, that she hoped they had not forgotten to pick the fir-tree buds to make herbal tea for chest infections! – her intuition told her that this stranger was a sound man. He might be rough and cold, with that lordly look characteristic of mountain folk, but he was not a petty man. Never again would this man mention the secret he had stumbled on by the light of a candle, that night when he had made his escape from the pirate ship.

Catching sight of Count Peyrac walking down towards the harbour with Roland d'Urville and Gilles Vanereick, she hastened away.

Why had she run away? From him? From her husband?

She wandered among the new houses of Gouldsboro, deserted by their owners who had also gone down to the harbour to see the yacht set sail . . .

She had lacked the courage this time to hold her ground, only a few paces from him, mingling with this crowd that was busy watching them. She should have been there, she told herself. She should have been waving her scarf while the little ship, under the command of that valiant young man, Cantor de Peyrac, spread its sails . . . but she had been incapable of it. It was her first moment of serious weakness since that morning.

He would triumph over her. But how would the battle end?

As long as she remained uncertain about Colin's fate, Joffrey would be a threat to her, his arm raised to strike, and in her heart of hearts, he would be the enemy she could not overcome.

How many a time in the past had Count Peyrac stated his implacable resolution to kill anyone who tried to steal his wife from him?

And she, sick at heart, could think of nothing but those words he had spoken to Pont-Briand and to Lomenie.

Colin was condemned, less for being a plundering pirate than Joffrey's rival. But this was impossible! Not for so little! Not just because of her! Oh! God! Do not allow this to happen!

CHAPTER SIXTY-SEVEN

THAT EVENING, back at the fort, to which, after once more going the rounds of all the wounded, she had returned as night fell, worn out with fatigue and care, she nevertheless noticed two chests in her room that had not been there before.

One contained dresses, clothes, lace, underclothing, gloves and shoes, while the other held various luxury items to make day-to-day life more agreeable.

The clothes and other things smelt of Europe. Joffrey de Peyrac must have ordered them from Erikson before setting off in the autumn, and the *Gouldsboro* had just arrived with them. They represented all the refinement, the prettiness and beauty of a lost world.

Angélique scarcely touched them, just turned them over almost indifferently as if they were the last remains of a love that had died.

Why they had been brought to her room that evening was a mystery to her, and in the state of mind she was in, they were more of a source of anxiety than anything else, for she feared a trap.

She turned her back on these sumptuous presents as if they were a mockery of her present misery, and tried to sleep a little.

She trembled at the thought of what might happen while she was unconscious; would she, when she awoke, catch sight of Colin's body dangling from the arm of some gibbet in the dawn light?

With the coming of twilight, her courage had returned, and she had done her best to find her husband. But she had been unable to find him anywhere. Some said he had set off for the interior, while others informed her that he had taken the chebec out to meet some ship or other. In sheer desperation she had decided that she must try to get some rest.

But her anxiety remained, and after a brief, heavy sleep, she awoke in the depths of the night, and unable to sleep again, began to toss and turn, tormented by gloomy thoughts.

The rest had re-awakened her anger towards her husband. Yes, she was deeply hurt by the way he had behaved like an intolerant and suspicious master.

Had not Joffrey abandoned her to her fate for a period of years, yet now he wanted everything, even her faithfulness in the past? Had he been so scrupulous when he was away from her about taking his pleasure with other women? ... But that didn't stop him tearing roughly aside the veil covering secrets which were hers and hers alone. And he was demanding from her an account of herself, attributing considerably more to her of these activities, incidentally, than she had in fact indulged in during the grass-widowhood which haunted his jealousy.

For her part, when she thought over the memories of the fifteen years she had spent apart from him, what she saw above all was a long succession of lonely, chilly nights during which her youth, beauty and femininity had been consumed in weeping for him, calling up his image and missing him ... and in sleeping too, fortunately, alone and soundly. She had always slept as soundly as a child and it was this gift which had been her saving. When she had been running the Inn of the Red Mask in Paris, she had gone back night after night to a narrow bed, weary to the bone, and dawn had found her ready to face a day's work in which there would be hardly any place for love, unless one was prepared to count throwing out an over-cheeky musketeer; and at the time when she had kept the chocolate shop Ninon de Lenclos had teased her for being something of a prude.

Like luminous points of light, flickering and rapidly extinguished, there had been here and there a night of love, in the arms of a Parisian poet hunted by the police, and even in those of the man who was hunting him, Desgrez. Both of them had been too preoccupied with their cruel little game to bother about her overlong.

At Court, in spite of the erotic atmosphere prevailing there, could her amorous life be considered more sensual? Hardly, and perhaps in fact rather less so. The King's passion had isolated her. And her personal ambition, combined with her persistent longing for a beloved ghost to whom she never ceased to hold out her arms, had kept her away from light adventures and trivial affairs which would very quickly have become unbearable to her. What then had remained of all these things?

A few nights with Rakoczy, the persecuted prince. A fleeting embrace one evening after the hunt with the Duke of Lauzun – a mistake which had very nearly cost her extremely dear. And with Philippe, her second husband? Twice, perhaps three times.

Scarcely more. And then Colin, and the comfort that had come to her in the desert . . .

All in all, she thought, she had made love less frequently in fifteen years than any prudish middle-class wife of a lawful husband in three months, or than she herself had done in Joffrey's arms in a much shorter time. Was that an adequate reason to hold her up to public obloquy, to put her in the pillory, to credit her with the amorous temperament of a shameless Messalina? . . . It would be useless for her to try to bring these realities home to Joffrey, even if she were to reconstruct for him an account in detail which would enable a man of science like him to understand the logical scope of such matters. Alas! She sensed that even in the case of a scholar and scientist like Peyrac, one could hardly expect to count upon his detachment in matters of the heart, and he was liable to react like all other men when their proprietary instincts are at stake. In such cases men lose control of themselves and even the most intelligent refuse to understand.

But why such a lot of fuss about a kiss?

What is a kiss after all? Lips that meet and merge. And hearts that are touched.

Two lost creatures intertwined within a divine sense of security, warming one another with their breath, recognizing one another in the darkness of a night where for too long they have walked alone. Man! Woman! Nothing else, that is all.

And what is an embrace, but the prolongation and a fulfilment of that supraterrestrial state so rarely enjoyed by the human creature? . . . In some cases never enjoyed!

Well, if that was what a kiss was, Joffrey would be right to begrudge the one which she had exchanged with Colin, Gold Beard, or was that really so?

Life was a work of art, a difficult artistic task. The most difficult point for Angélique was to face the fact in her pride that ostracism, contempt and the anger of other people, the force of whose attacks she felt to the depths of her consciousness, were justified by her own conduct, which at times she herself knew very well was inexcusable.

In order to re-establish her balance, she would have needed to give this blunder, this accident, its just place, and she was incapable of doing so entirely on her own. Alternately she condemned herself utterly or saw in her brief abandonment nothing more than a pleasant intermission that a pretty woman has every right to steal from life from time to time.

The coming of a damp misty dawn released her from this eternal round of thoughts. She emerged weary and aching from her tossing on her cold deserted bed. Uncertainty about Colin's fate tormented her.

The restless, pinkish-grey dawn brought the tireless singing of the turtle doves in full, swelling, insinuating notes. The sickly-sweet, cloying sound of this cooing would be intolerable to Angélique for the rest of her life. Henceforth it would always remind her of this short, distressing season spent at Gouldsboro, which in her memory she would call the accursed summer.

It was a season of subdued horror and foreboding in which every warm morning, every tragic dawn was punctuated by the monotonous cooing of that bird.

Behind the mists, the sounds of the fort and the waking village were echoed and amplified. There was a sound of hammering! Was a scaffold being erected?

There came the lilt of a seaman's voice singing the lament of King Renaud:

> 'And in the middle of the night
> The soul of Renaud took to flight.
> Ah! tell me, tell me mother dear
> What is that hammering I hear?
> The carpenter, 'tis nothing more,
> A' hammering of the old barn door.'

Angélique shuddered. A scaffold, or perhaps a coffin ... She must rush out to act. But the day passed, and the wind blew unceasingly, and nothing happened.

And now it was evening again, and the darkness was already profound and without a trace of light, for the sky, swollen with rain, hung low over the sea and merged with the tops of the trees.

Clinging to the wooden framework of a window, Angélique watched two men facing one another. A moment before she had crossed the courtyard and headed for the council chamber intending to have it out with Joffrey face to face:

'Let us have it out ... What are your intentions?'

Then, from outside, she had caught sight of them – Joffrey and Colin standing face to face in the council chamber. They were alone and did not know that they were observed.

Colin had his hands behind his back, doubtless because his wrists were bound. Joffrey de Peyrac was standing beside the

166

table on which were laid out scrolls of parchment and maps. He was unrolling these documents one by one, slowly and methodically, and reading them attentively. From time to time he would take out of a coffer standing open before him a precious stone and examine it in the candlelight with the eye of an expert. The green sparkle of an emerald twinkled elusively at his finger tips.

When she saw his lips moving, Angélique guessed that he was questioning the prisoner and that the latter was answering briefly. At one moment Colin moved and his finger pointed out a place on the map. So he was not in bonds after all . . .

She began to be afraid for Joffrey's sake. If Colin were suddenly to seize him impulsively by the throat . . . Was Joffrey not aware of the tremendous physical power of this Gold Beard standing so close to him? But no. He was pretending to be quite impervious and indifferent to such considerations. How imprudent! This constant challenge of his to events, to the elements and to men, this constant resolve to go further, to press on beyond the extreme limits of experience, to see . . . One day death would pounce upon him like a swooping eagle. 'Joffrey! Joffrey! Take care!'

She trembled as she clung to the window frame, powerless, feeling instinctively that she had no right to intervene between these two men. She must leave fate to decide, and let these two powerful wills confront one another in a combat in which she could have wished to see neither victor nor vanquished. Her eyes passed from one to the other anxiously, and fastened greedily as if drawn by a magnet on the tall, powerful, angular figure of her husband. Separated from him by the wall of silence of the window panes as she was, it was like catching him unawares and watching him as he slept . . . This she had never been able to do without feeling a mixture of excitement and fear, tinged sometimes with a sense of acute jealousy, because at such times he had as he slept an expression on his face which seemed to symbolize his enigma to her as a man, a mystery into which she could not penetrate.

There was a touch of silver at the edges of his brown temples, which had a suggestion of gentleness about it, but that was a mere illusion. He remained distant, hard and unattainable. And yet every subtlest detail of his person was familiar to her, his wife, and tugged spontaneously at her heart strings as she contemplated him. Detail by detail she reconstructed in her mind all that she knew of him – his caution and his dash, his skill and self-control, his intellect, his knowledge, overlaid by so much human simplicity, and if the meditative expression on his face hinted at his genius as a thinker, Angélique nevertheless remembered as she followed the movement of his muscles under his dark velvet clothes, his energy, his vigour and an extraordinary amorous health which he had always shown and which pulsed through his tough indomitable frame.

Then her eyes went back to Colin. Rising up out of the mists of the distant years, it was the image of the King of the Prisoners of Meknès that stood there in the narrow room. The motley costume he had worn in his role as Gold Beard seemed now no more than a disguise. This particular evening his eye had its sovereign shade of blue, the great Colin's blue eye, accustomed to gaze into the distance of the desert and to read in the depths of human hearts.

In spite of herself, because she was the woman, and as such belonged to a race which for many thousands of years had been downtrodden and humiliated, Angélique could not help being on the side of the weaker of the adversaries in this silent duel – Colin. Knowing them both, she knew that Joffrey was much stronger than the Norman. Learned as he was in the great philosophies and sciences of the world, and concerned with the subtle and infinite passions of the intellect, he could endure anything, or almost anything, without flinching – even the wounds of the heart. Colin, on the other hand, was an uncultivated man in spite of his native intelligence, a man who did not even know how to write, and he was helpless before unforeseen blows.

And it was she who had inflicted them upon him. She felt remorseful, and her heart was torn seeing him there helpless and conquered in advance, in spite of his undeniable physical strength.

Suddenly her heart quailed. She saw Joffrey push the heap of parchments aside and advance upon Colin. Her dread was as great as if she had seen him pointing his pistol at Colin and firing straight into his heart. It took her a moment to persuade herself that the Count's hands were bare. Nevertheless, her fear remained. On the other side of the window a decisive moment had come. She felt it in the trembling of her flesh, in the tension of her mind, and in the straining of her senses, trying to catch what was said, trying to understand. Something decisive was going on. But it was happening in silence. It was happening in words that she could not hear, and that sprang from the lips of the two men like the blows of sharpened daggers ...

Joffrey was speaking, standing very close to the prisoner, his flashing eyes fixed on Colin's hard, attentive face. Little by little a sombre fury and profound indignation marked the Norman's face, and Angélique saw his fists opening and closing, rising even, and trembling with powerless rage. Several times, he shook his head, meeting Joffrey de Peyrac's words with the pride of an indomitable lion.

Then Peyrac left him. He began to walk up and down, like a caged animal, and to circle round and round Colin, darting quick, penetrating glances at him, like a hunter trying to decide the best point at which to strike. Then going up to him again he seized the big man by the collar of his jacket and drew him close to him as if to speak confidentially to him, and this time he spoke in a low voice. There was now a kind of dangerous gentleness on Joffrey de Peyrac's face, and a subtle ambiguous fold at the corner of his lips, and Angélique could almost sense the insinuating charm of his tone. He was wearing his most charming expression, but there was a little flame dancing in his pupils that frightened her. What she was afraid of was occurring – Colin was succumbing to Joffrey de Peyrac's ascendancy.

Little by little the rugged determination faded from his face, and was replaced by an expression of confusion and despair, and even a fleeting panic. Suddenly, he let his head fall forward in a movement of weariness or avowal.

What had Count Joffrey de Peyrac succeeded in saying thus to vanquish Colin Paturel, who had never bent his back before Mulai Ismail and all his tortures?

Joffrey de Peyrac stopped speaking, but he continued to hold Colin and to watch him closely. At length, the heavy blond head was raised. Colin gazed straight ahead, fixedly. Angélique was afraid that he had glimpsed her through the window. But Colin saw nothing outside, his gaze was turned in upon himself. And suddenly she saw in him too the kind of naïve innocence which he had in his sleep, an expression of face which was like that of Adam as he must have been in the first days of creation. His blue eyes, with something drowsy in them, turned towards Peyrac once more, and the two men stared at one another for a long time without speaking. Then Colin bowed his head again and repeated the gesture several times. This time it was a mark of agreement, of acquiescence.

Count de Peyrac went back to his place behind the table. Shadows moved in the back of the room. Several Spanish guards came in and stationed themselves behind the prisoner. Angélique had not heard them summoned. They went out, taking Colin with them.

Joffrey de Peyrac remained in the room. He sat down.

Angélique drew back, fearing that he might suspect her presence. But she stayed there, fascinated. Just as he had spied on her the other night, in the shadows of the island, without her knowing it, she also wished to discover him naked and unaware of the fact that he was being observed. What feelings would he betray? What mask might he let fall which could reveal him to her and which might enable her to guess at his thoughts and his decisions?

She saw him stretch out his arm towards the coffer of emeralds, the famous Caracas emeralds, plundered from the Spanish by Gold Beard. He picked up an exceptionally large one between two fingers, and holding it up to the light of the torch he became absorbed in contemplating it. And he was *smiling* as if watching in the transparency of the precious stone some pleasurable spectacle.

CHAPTER SIXTY-EIGHT

THE FOLLOWING day was a Sunday. There was a wailing call of a conch in the distance, and the sprightly tinkling of a bell in the little wooden belfry, calling the Protestants to divine service. Not to be outdone, the chaplains and Father Bauce, joined by another Recollect father, recently back from the woods, decided to hold a solemn Catholic service on the clifftop, with monstrance, procession and all.

Through the mist the rival hymn singing went on all morning, but the religious ceremonies were completed without incident.

When divine worship and Mass were both over, the people strolled down to the harbour, where new arrivals were being announced. Soon, mingling with the foghorn came the sound of more literal bellowing. A small cutter from Port Royal on the peninsula was bringing in two cows and a bull, long promised in exchange for a gift of fresh food and ironmongery that had saved the lives of a French colony abandoned by the remote administration in Quebec. The unfortunate animals were unloaded by suspending them from a system of ropes and pulleys, and they were landed without undue difficulty amidst the acclamations of the population.

The arrival of the cattle created almost as much interest as the imminent hanging of Gold Beard. Would it be today?

Amidst all this hustle and bustle the arrival of a small ship bringing John Knox Mather, a doctor of theology from Boston, with his chief curates, went unnoticed. The jovial, noisy Acadians, followed by their red Mic-Macs, giants with square, copper-coloured faces, rubbed shoulders with the honourable Puritan gentleman without even noticing him.

He wore a 'ruff and a full, long, dark Genevese cape that reached to his heels, which he wrapped about him right up to the eyes to protect himself from the wind, while the crown of his hat, with its severe silver buckle, seemed higher than the others.

'I wanted to meet you,' he said to Peyrac who came down to greet him. 'Our Governor reminded us, at a recent synod, that after all Maine belongs to England, and he asked me to inquire from you whether the situation still remained the same ...'

He had been casting anxious looks about him.

'The place reeks of saturnalia to me ... I say, it is rumoured that you are living with an enchantress ...'

'Absolutely right,' Peyrac replied. 'Come ... let me introduce you to her.'

John Knox Mather went pale and began to tremble like the surface of a pond at the approach of a storm. He grew uneasy, and he had good cause. The Protestants had got rid of the Virgin Mary and the saints, as well-disposed intercessors in the Other World, and they were left with nothing but demons. So any intrusion of an evil spirit left them disarmed and helpless. They could count only on their own spiritual strength. Fortunately the worthy Mather possessed plenty of this; he stiffened and prepared to face the ordeal of meeting the enchantress.

Angélique, on learning that Count Peyrac had urgently requested her presence, left a man whose wound she was dressing and set off with beating heart to the encounter, only to find herself face to face with a sombre monolithic monument, called a doctor of theology from Boston, who examined her with a stony gaze. Actually he was as astonished as she was; this she realized, bade him welcome and dropped him a brief curtsy.

She gathered from his conversation with Count Peyrac that he would be staying in Gouldsboro for several days, and that on this Lord's Day they intended to hold a feast to thank Him for His blessings.

The arrival of all these people at Gouldsboro put off the settlement of the bitter matters that hung over the towns-people, tormenting their hearts and their consciences, and she did not know whether to be glad or whether the suspense would be just too much for her. She wanted to have done with the anxiety, to finish the game they were all playing. She wanted to cry out, to beg them: 'Let us put an end to it, let us know! . . .'

But Joffrey de Peyrac's inflexible hand kept them all in sus-pense and expectant, awaiting his good pleasure, forcing them to play their part to the point of exhaustion. Since her hus-band had introduced her to the guests, she would have to preside at the festivities.

She went back to the fort to select a dress from the chests that had arrived from Europe.

Soon afterwards there was a sharp shower of rain and the sky cleared. The delicious smell of the preparations for the feast down at the inn began to permeate the air and dominate the powerful tang of the sea.

Voices took on a resonant lilt, and several blasts of trum-pets rang out. Gouldsboro already had its own well-established traditions. Angélique did not know that these trumpet blasts were intended to call the population together on the esplanade before the fort, but, intrigued by the sound, she went outside.

There, everything was glistening as if varnished by the recent storm, while thin trickles of mud poured down the cliffside, hollowing out little channels down to the shore. The women-folk lifted their skirts to leap over them.

The people gathered, like the torrents, at first in thin, isolated streams issuing from the ships, the houses and the woods, emerging from all sides and converging on a single point to form a compact mass, a heterogeneous gathering of sailors, settlers, Huguenots, Indians, Englishmen, soldiers and noblemen, finally united by the temporary but unforgettable feeling of all belonging to the same remote American shore and looking for-ward to witnessing a rare spectacle.

Those who had come on horseback from Camp Champlain along the lupin-lined road, and those who had come down from the tiny hamlets up the coast along the anemone track, carried muskets or blunderbusses and formed a tight guard round their women and children. Everyone was under strict orders never to go more than half a league beyond the range of the cannons in the fort without being armed. With the summer months upon them, the season of Iroquois raids had begun, and in addition no one was immune from the possibility of a sudden Abenaki attack upon any Whites against whom their suspicions might have been aroused.

The open space in front of the fort was black with people.

Children rushed hither and thither and Angélique heard them calling:

'They say they're going to hang Gold Beard!'

'And before that, they're going to torture him . . .'

Her blood ran cold. The moment she had never ceased to dread since Colin's capture had come.

'No! No! I shall not let them hang you,' she told herself. 'I shall scream, I shall cause an uproar, but I shall not let them hang you! Joffrey can think whatever he likes!'

She came forward in all her finery as far as the square, and heedless of the eyes that followed her, made her way to the front of the crowd. By now she felt completely unconcerned about what people might think of her and heedless of any remarks her presence might occasion. Inwardly she was trembling but managed to show a pride that both intrigued and disconcerted.

She had selected, almost without thinking, a dress that was both severe and sumptuous. It was an unusual black velvet dress covered with spidery lace and studded with tiny pearls, and she had thought to herself: 'A dress to wear at a king's funeral.' But she had made up her mind that she would not be attending Colin's funeral, for she intended to save his life!

At the last moment with a hasty finger, for there was no time for meticulous care, she had rubbed a little alkanet rouge on her pale cheeks.

She looked ghastly, but never mind!

If anyone noticed her feverish pallor, no one said anything. Her flashing green eyes froze any unkind words on people's lips.

'Look at her,' Vanereick whispered to Lord Sheringham in English. 'She is fascinating. What nobleness of bearing, how superbly proud she is! Very English, old chap. She is as good as Peyrac any day. She is holding her head high in spite of all glances, hostility and reprobation, and she could scarcely have shown greater arrogance had she been wearing the letter A embroidered in scarlet in her bosom, a penalty imposed – as you undoubtedly know, sir – by your Puritans in Massachusetts on adulterous women.'

The Englishman – an Anglican – gave a disabused smile.

'Puritans have no sense of the *nuances* in these matters.'

He gave a sidelong glance at Knox Mather, who was busy discussing with his curates the theological implications of hanging a man on the Lord's Day. Was it a breach of the Sabbath to haul on a hangman's rope? Or, on the other hand, might not the choice of this day allow the Lord greater leisure to receive this new soul He had to judge?

'We men of the world,' the English lord went on, 'must admit that we find it easy to forgive so lovely a woman for having sinned a little.'

'How much do you wager that she will defend her lover with as much fire and passion as Lady Macbeth?'

'I'll stake you twenty pounds ... Shakespeare would have liked this country which is English not only by right, but also in spirit ...'

Lord Sheringham raised to his eyes his beribboned spectacles – all the rage that season in London – which were suspended from his brocade coat.

'And what about you, Vanereick, how much will you wager that, in spite of her slender appearance, that lady is full of delightful curves when she slips out of all that finery, like Venus rising from the waves?'

'Let us not wager, sir, for I am already aware of that particular state of affairs, for I have had my arms about her. You English lords are indeed men of good taste. You guessed right, my lord. When you actually get your hands on that sylph, she is as well padded as a featherbed.'

'For goodness' sake hold your tongues, you lewd rakes!' burst out Gabriel Berne, the Huguenot from La Rochelle, who, overhearing their ribald conversation was unable to contain his indignation.

There followed an exchange of insults in English, and Lord Sheringham spoke of a duel. But his lieutenant pointed out that one could hardly fight with common men like these, whereupon all the settlers from La Rochelle rose like a single man to this insult and began to close in upon the beribboned admiral with clenched fists.

The guards and militiamen who stood around the platform were on the verge of intervening, but fortunately the amiable d'Urville appeared and managed to calm everybody down. But he could not entirely still the storm that was brewing among the Rochelais, who, their attention diverted from their English guests, turned upon Angélique, 'the apple of discord' whom they considered far too conspicuous and shameless on such a day. People began to dart furious glances at her, the murmurs grew louder, and comments could be heard all round her until finally they reached her ears through the mists of her distracted mind.

She glanced at the sombre crowd moving towards her, in which she saw the flash of accusing eyes.

'It's your fault too,' Madame Manigault shouted at her, seeing that at last she had come down to earth. 'How dare you show your face among honest folk?'

Monsieur Manigault stepped solemnly towards her.

'Yes indeed, Madame,' he continued, striking a further blow, 'your presence here at such a time is an insult to all laws of honourable behaviour. As head of the Protestant community of Gouldsboro I must ask you to leave.'

She stared at him with eyes that seemed suddenly to have grown pale, and they might well have thought that she had not heard them.

'And what do you have to fear from me, Monsieur Manigault?' she inquired softly, at last breaking the breathless silence.

'You must not side with that bandit,' cried Madame Manigault, unable to keep out of it any longer, 'And don't try to wriggle out of things or put on airs of innocence. We all know there's something between the two of you. It's a most disagreeable and deplorable business for us all, and you should be ashamed. Not to mention the fact that we owe it to ourselves to get rid of this scoundrel who caused us so much trouble last month and would have killed the lot of us had we not fought to the death. And here you are, ready to intercede for him and ask for his pardon. We know you.'

'Yes indeed,' Angélique conceded, 'I think you have good cause to know me.'

It was not the first time she had had to face the wrath of Calvinists. In the long run she had ceased to be impressed by these jousting matches between them. She drew herself up to her full height and looked at them.

'A year ago, on this very spot, it was your lives I begged for, begged for on my knees ... and for crimes which, according to the law of the sea, merited hanging even more than those which Gold Beard has committed ...'

In spite of herself her lips began to tremble and kind-hearted Vanereick thought she was going to burst into tears, which he could not have borne.

'I knelt ...' she repeated, 'I did that for you ... for you who cannot even kneel before God Himself. For you who no longer even know your Gospel.'

Then she abruptly turned her back on them.

A superstitious silence hung over the crowd.

CHAPTER SIXTY-NINE

THE PRISONER came out, hands behind his back, on to the balcony of the fort overlooking the esplanade.

He was closely surrounded by the Spanish guards in their gleaming cuirasses and red-plumed morions.

Colin Paturel was bareheaded. He wore a chestnut-brown cloth doublet with gold-braided revers, fetched for him from his wardrobe on board the *Heart of Mary*.

This simple costume, worn with short-clipped beard and hair, made a considerable impression, for the terrible, flamboyant Gold Beard was not recognizable in this dark-clad giant prepared for death. They had not thought him so tall!

Joffrey de Peyrac appeared almost immediately behind him, dressed in saffron-yellow satin in the French fashion, with an open jerkin over a long embroidered jacket which was a marvel.

A cry of astonishment and admiration went up from the crowd and a wave seemed to travel across the sea of faces. Even the Huguenots were affected by this further sensation produced by the nobleman from Aquitaine, who was a personality outside their normal range of experience and quite beyond their comprehension, but who had been thrown by a stroke of fate into their hitherto reasonable lives, and who now held them all under his spell.

His presence checked the jeers and dangerous excitement that lay close to the surface and were about to burst forth as the other prisoners, the pirate crew of the *Heart of Mary*, were led forth, in chains or with rope bonds. Closely encircled by a ring of muskets, they were pushed forward in a troop to the foot of the platform.

Some of them pulled faces and gnashed their teeth villainously, but most seemed resigned like men who, having gambled and lost, know that they have reached their journey's end and that the hour of reckoning has come.

Count Peyrac did not need to lift a little finger to impose silence.

Impatient for the verdict which was about to be announced, the crowd held its breath. And all fell silent. Not a sound could be heard save the lapping of the sea. The Count advanced to the edge of the balcony, leaned over, and directly addressing the group of Protestants from La Rochelle who stood at the front of the crowd, forming the compact nucleus, sombre, incorruptible and indefectible, of his settlement.

'Gentlemen,' he said, pointing to Colin Paturel who stood there between his guards, 'gentlemen, I present to you *the new governor of Gouldsboro.*'

CHAPTER SEVENTY

IN THE thunderstruck, incredulous silence that followed this announcement, Joffrey de Peyrac took time to turn up his delicate lace cuffs.

Then, quite unperturbed, he went on:

'Monsieur d'Urville, who for a long time has discharged this most difficult responsibility, is to become admiral of our fleet. The number and size of our ships, both merchantmen and men-of-war, continues to increase and multiply, and the time has come to appoint a professional naval man to take charge of them. Similarly, the way in which Gouldsboro has developed over the past months, thanks largely to your activity and industry, gentlemen of La Rochelle, makes it imperative for me to choose as a governor someone who has had experience both of the sea and of governing a wide variety of peoples and nations, since, as our port is gradually coming to occupy a more and more important place, a unique place, in the area we have chosen to live in, we shall find that henceforth we shall have the whole world on our doorstep. Now, I would like to make it clear to you that I know of no one more capable of dealing with the many tricky problems that such a position will entail for all of us than the man whom I have designated to you today, the man into whose hands I place with the utmost confidence the fate of Gouldsboro, its repute, its prosperity and its future greatness.'

He broke off, but not a single voice echoed his words. The crowd before him was as if turned to stone.

Among them Angélique was by no means the least dumbfounded. Joffrey's words entered her ears as a string of disconnected sounds and their meaning did not penetrate her mind. Or rather, she tried in vain to see a meaning in them, some other meaning that would signify that Colin was to be hanged.

Before the sea of open mouths and staring eyes, Joffrey de Peyrac gave a sardonic smile, then he went on:

'This is a man whom you have known under the name of Gold Beard, a Caribbean corsair. But allow me to inform you that before that he spent twelve years as King of the Christian slaves in Meknès, in the kingdom of Morocco on the Barbary coast, the sultan of which dealt harshly with the Christians, and that in this capacity this gentleman, Colin Paturel, ruled for twelve years over a nation of thousands of souls. These people, from every corner of the globe, speaking every language, practising many different religions, abandoned to their wretched fate as slaves in a strange, hostile, Moslem land, slaves with no possibility of escape or relief from the burdens that oppressed them and the evil that seared their souls, for twelve years these people found in him a sure and indomitable guide. He knit them into a powerful, dignified, united people, who together fought against the temptation to despair and abjure their baptismal faith.'

Then Angélique began to realize the truth – Colin would not be hanged. He would live. He would rule again.

It was of him that Joffrey was talking when he said: 'He will guide you with his wisdom . . .'

Then peace came back to her, accompanied by an underlying pain. But first and foremost she felt peace, and she literally drank in the words that fell from her husband's lips, seized by an emotion that quite overcame her and at last brought tears to her eyes. Was it this he had been asking of Colin so insistently that previous evening in the council chamber, this that Colin had so passionately refused? Then he had bowed his heavy head and had assented.

'Although we are not slaves here like the Christians in

Meknès,' Joffrey went on, 'we do nevertheless have to face similar strains – a sense of abandonment, doubt, mutual animosity, and the constant peril of death. He in his wisdom will be able to help you to face these things, just as he will know how to guide you in your dealings with neighbouring peoples, for he speaks English, Dutch, Spanish, Portuguese, Arabic and even Basque, which the Indians understand. He originates from Normandy and is a Catholic, and will prove equally valuable to you in your relations with the Acadian French. Monsieur d'Urville, would you be so kind as to repeat through your megaphone the salient points of what I have just said so that each man may hear it and think it over at his leisure?'

While d''Urville did as he was bade, the Protestants at last began to emerge from their stupor – which, it must be admitted, was not without cause.

They began to grow restless and mutter among themselves.

As soon as Peyrac's announcement had been repeated, Gabriel Berne stepped forward.

'Monsieur de Peyrac, you have already asked us to stomach many an affront, but this one, I warn you here and now, will never be accepted. Whence do you have such detailed information about this dangerous man? You have let yourself be taken in by a lot of chit-chat from a vagabond with the gift of the gab, as they all are, these pirates who live on the property of others.'

'I myself saw the work of this man when I was in the Mediterranean,' Peyrac replied. 'I saw him tied to the whipping post, taking upon himself the punishment of his brothers who had made so bold as to attend Mass one Christmas night. On another occasion he was crucified by his hands on one of the city gates. I realize that Monsieur Paturel is not anxious for me to bring up all these details of the past, but I am telling you of them, gentlemen, so that you may rest assured as regards your faith. I am putting at your head a proud Christian who has already shown that he can shed his blood for his beliefs.'

The protests of the men of La Rochelle grew louder. Martyrdom endured for the Catholic faith had no value in their eyes and this was no way to win them over. On the contrary, they saw in it the obstinacy of narrow-mindedness, clinging to superstitious and diabolical beliefs.

A confused murmur broke out and began to swell:

'Hang him! Hang him! Treachery! We cannot accept this . . . Hang Gold Beard!'

Colin who, until then, had stood impassively aside from the debate, keeping his place between the Spanish mercenaries, stepped forward and posted himself beside Joffrey de Peyrac.

With his hands on his hips, he looked down at the seething crowd with his penetrating blue eyes.

It was as if they all recoiled before his massive presence, and the calls to hang him slowly died down, finally fading away in a stupefied silence.

Berne reacted with his customary impetuosity. He rushed forward.

'This is madness,' he cried, one hand reaching to the sky as if calling it to witness to the folly that possessed them all. 'You should hang him twenty times over, Monsieur de Peyrac, if only for the harm he has caused Gouldsboro. And you yourself, Count, have you forgotten that he has dishonoured you, that he has . . .'

With an imperious gesture, Peyrac cut short the accusing sentence that would have dragged Angélique's name into the mud.

'If he did deserve to be hanged, it would not be for me to lead him to the scaffold,' he declared in a quiet voice that nevertheless brooked no reply. 'The debt of gratitude I owe him would make that impossible.'

'Gratitude? . . . *Your* gratitude? Yours?'

'Yes indeed, my gratitude,' the Count insisted. 'Allow me to tell you why I feel like this. Among the exploits that Monsieur Paturel has to his credit, not least is that of his escape – attempted in company with several other slaves, that brought them face to face with the most terrible dangers, in order to get away from Morocco – an escape which proved successful.

'Now it happened that among those whom he helped in this way to reach Christian territory there was a woman, a prisoner of the Berbers, whom in this way he managed to save from the terrible fate reserved for unfortunate Christian women who find themselves in Moslem hands. This was at a time when my own exile and my wretched fate kept me ignorant of what had happened to my own family and made it impossible for me to come to their assistance when they too were in danger and abandoned by everyone. That woman was the Countess of Peyrac, my wife here. Monsieur Paturel's devotion saved the life I valued above all else. How could I ever forget that?'

A thin smile creased one corner of his scarred lip.

'And that is why, gentlemen, forgetting our present misunderstandings, we, the Countess of Peyrac and I, can consider this man, the object of your hatred, only as a friend, a worthy recipient of our complete confidence and esteem.'

Among these last words, to which she had listened in a kind of trance, one phrase had struck Angélique, rousing her like the crack of a whip, had almost stung her like an urgent appeal from that hoarse and apparently serene voice, enjoining her, ordering her to submit to his decision in this entire matter.

'The Countess of Peyrac and myself.'

In this way he encompassed her in his plan, making it impossible for her to escape, and his hidden intentions became clear to her, namely to wipe out the insult. To wipe out the insult that his wife and Colin had inflicted *publicly* upon him. What had there been between them? Nothing more than memories of friendship and gratitude which he deluded himself that he shared with them. Thus he managed to confuse everyone about the nature of the passions that were rending the three of them, presenting them with a travesty of the truth.

Had she not, instinctively, in her own pride, adopted the same attitude?

Would the Protestants be taken in?

They had to be! Let everyone behave as if they were. Joffrey de Peyrac had decided that Colin Paturel was worthy of a place at his side in governing his people, and that the only feelings he could entertain towards him were those of gratitude and friendship.

The crowd would simply have to submit to this image he was imposing on them.

Who could ever resist the unbending will of a Peyrac?

Never had Angélique felt so conscious of his steely hold over all of them, that literally grasped them and moulded them according to the laws of his personal authority.

She felt a sense of awed admiration, which had nothing to do with warmth or affection, and her suffering grew all the more intense, all the more penetrating.

He had just given an order to the 'Countess of Peyrac', but he had never even glanced at her throughout the course of his long explanation, and at no time had his voice registered those tender inflexions which once he had been unable to restrain whenever he spoke of her, even to a stranger.

Everyone looked from her to the two men standing there side by side on the platform, and Angélique's trembling looks, the astonishment which in spite of herself could be clearly seen in her eyes, disconcerted and dismayed the bystanders . . .

Colin went on staring impassively into the distance, over the heads of the agitated crowd, his arms folded on his chest. Such was the imperiousness of his countenance, such its extraordinary nobility, that he was no longer recognizable as the same man.

They began to look elsewhere for Gold Beard, the coarse pirate, hung about with weapons and stained with bloody misdeeds. Standing there beside him, as if protecting him and sheltering him beneath his own power, Count Peyrac, disdainful but half smiling, contemplated curiously the effects of his sensational announcement.

'Look at the three of them,' cried Berne, panting for breath, pointing first to the two men then to Angélique. 'Look at them! They are making fools of us, they are deceiving us, they are making fun of us . . .'

He kept on spinning round on his own heels, like a man demented, half crazed, beside himself. He tore off his hat and threw it as far as he could.

'Just look at them, the three hypocrites! What are they planning now? . . . How much longer are we to be gulled by people like them? Have you forgotten that Papists are without shame! That they will go to any lengths in order to carry out the intrigues of their tortuous, idolatrous minds. It's unthinkable! Brothers, are you going to acquiesce in these iniquitous decisions, this ridiculous trial? . . . Are you going to agree to be placed at the mercy of the most vile individual we have ever had to deal with up to now? Are you going to agree to admit within our walls a criminal, debauched mob which he intends to foist upon us as settlers? . . .

'What about your crimes, Gold Beard?' he shrieked, turning upon Colin full of hatred. 'And those of the ruffians in your crew?'

'And what about yours, Huguenot!' Colin replied, leaning down over the balustrade so that his steely blue eyes looked straight into those of Master Berne.

'My hands are not tainted with the blood of my fellow man,' the Protestant replied emphatically.

'Oh no? . . . No man here can claim to have hands untainted by the blood of his fellows. Think carefully, Huguenot, and you will remember those you have sacrificed, killed, or strangled, men whose throats you cut with your own hands. However far off, however deep you have buried this memory, search well,

Huguenot. You will see them floating back to the surface of your conscience, those crimes of yours, with their dead eyes and stiff limbs.'

Berne stared at him in silence. Then he staggered as if struck by lightning and backed away. Colin Paturel's deep voice had cast in his face the memory of that subterranean struggle that had been going on among the Protestants in La Rochelle for over a century. Once again he smelt the acrid scent of the darkness, the stink of decaying corpses down those wells that led into the sea where they used to tip the dead bodies of *agents provocateurs* or Jesuits.

'Oh yes,' Colin went on, narrowing his eyes to a slit through which he observed them, 'I know. I know, it was self-defence! But it is ALWAYS self-defence when people kill one another. To defend oneself, one's family, one's life, one's aims, one's dreams. He is a rare man indeed who kills out of sheer evil impulse. But as far as indulgence for the sinner goes, God alone can share that, for He alone can read into our hearts. Wherever a man goes, he will always find a brother who says to him: "You are a murderer, and I am not!" There is not a man alive in this day and age who has not killed. In these days, a man worthy of the name always has blood on his hands. I might even go as far as to say that killing is a mission and an inalienable right we receive at our birth, we males, for our age is still the time of wolves prowling on the face of the earth, although Christ has come. So give up saying of your neighbour: "You are a criminal, I am not." But since you are obliged to bring about the death of men, at least work on behalf of life ... You Huguenots from La Rochelle have saved your skins and escaped from your tormentors; are you going to refuse to others, to condemned men like yourselves, the same opportunities that you have had, even if you consider yourselves the Elect of the Lord and believe that you alone deserve to survive ...'

The La Rochelle folk, who had been somewhat intimidated by Colin's attack, regained possession of themselves on looking at the crew of the *Heart of Mary*. On this point, their consciences would not be led astray. Monsieur Manigault advanced to the foot of the balcony:

'Let us leave aside your assertions about alleged crimes we all are said to have on our hands. God absolves his Chosen Ones. But do you mean, *Monsieur*,' he said, ostentatiously stressing the word, 'that you intend to impose on us here at Gouldsboro, with the agreement of Monsieur de Peyrac, the company of these dangerous ruffians who formerly made up your crew?'

'You're badly mistaken about the nature of my crew,' explained Colin. 'The majority are sterling fellows who had engaged to serve under me on this campaign precisely in the hope of becoming colonists and finally settling down in a favourable place where they were promised good earth and women to take to wives. Even the right of ownership of the place where you have settled has been paid for by me on their behalf in hard cash, and contracts have been exchanged. Unfortunately it is obvious that things have not worked out as expected and I realize that I have been deceived by my backers in Paris, who expressly indicated Gouldsboro to me as a place which was unencumbered and belonging to the French. On parchment we have no more right to it than you refugee Protestants, and Monsieur de Peyrac has recognized this, but the pompous ignoramuses in France seem to have forgotten that the Treaty of Breda left the region under English jurisdiction. This I recognize and accept on my side too. One can do what one likes with documents; land is another thing. Enough good men have been sacrificed for the sake of a fool's plunder – or it might be more exact to put it down to ill will – by which we have been duped.

'Of all these matters Monsieur de Peyrac is ready to supply evidence, and to discuss them with you in private. But with regard to the decisions which we have both taken and the contracts with one another into which we have entered, all that is fixed and settled and there is no going back upon them. All that remains to be settled is what all of us are going to make of these matters for good or for ill . . .'

His voice, which was both inflexible and persuasive, was taking effect and checking the protests which rose to the lips of his listeners; and at the same time his gaze held their attention.

'He's done it,' thought Angélique, an irresistible tremor running through her whole body, 'He's got them, he's got them in the palm of his hand . . .'

Colin Paturel's powerful eloquence, his grip on the mob, had always been his strongest weapons. He had brought them to bear with masterly dash.

Leaning towards them, and speaking confidentially but in a voice which carried to those standing at the back of the crowd, he resumed:

'There is one thing that I want to tell, that I learnt when I was a slave among the Saracens. It is how much the sons of

Christ, the Christians, hate one another. So much more than the Moslems and Pagans! ... I'll tell you what I realized – that the whole lot of you – Christians, schismatics, heretics or Papists – are all alike: sharp-toothed jackals ready to devour one another for a mere comma in your dogmas. And what I want to state to you is that Christ, whom you claim to serve, did not want that, and that He is not happy about it ... Now, I am warning you, from this day on, Protestants and Papists alike, I'm going to keep my eye on you Gouldsboro people, and I'm going to see that you live together in peace, and on good terms with one another, just as I established peace among the slaves of Meknès for a period of twelve years.

'If there are genuine thugs among you, I shall find them out. But I don't think there are many of them, except in my most recent cargo, two or three characters that I tried to get rid of but who continue to stick to my legs like Malacca leeches. They had better keep quiet or it'll be their turn to dangle at the end of a rope for good and all.'

He shot a glance that was far from reassuring in the direction of Beaumarchand, who had dragged himself to the front row supported by his 'brother' Hyacinthus.

'And now,' Colin went on, 'I am going to establish three institutions of function from this day forth, the first day of my governorship of Gouldsboro. The first is that I am going to provide the port and settlement of Gouldsboro with nightwatchmen, one to every thirty households, the expense to be borne by my salary as Governor. We all, I think, have happy memories of that aspect of life in our French towns and villages – being able to go to sleep with the knowledge that the nightwatchman is going his rounds in the streets keeping an eye on things. Here we have an even greater need for such a watch, for if fire breaks out in the wilderness it spells the end – ruin, winter, and death. And in a port where there is a constant throughtraffic of disorderly and drunken people, an alert guard is required to keep an eye out for the mischief such people may get up to. Finally, there is the ever-present danger of an attack by Indians or anybody else who might take it into his head to dispossess us.

'The nightwatchmen will be appointed by the Governor and their maintenance and equipment will be paid for by him. This is a gift to mark my assumption of power at Gouldsboro.'

He was about to go on when a woman's voice rose up in the heavy silence.

'Thank you, Governor,' said the weak, thin but energetic voice. It was Abigail's.

There was a commotion in the crowd, and a babble of voices in which timid expressions of thanks mingled with the protests of the majority of the men. So they were giving in! ... They wanted to make it clear that they had still not given their approval to Colin's establishment in power and that they were not to be bribed with nightwatchmen.

Abigail looked Master Berne straight in the eye. Colin Paturel gave the young woman a slight smile and went on, holding out his hand to demand silence:

'The second institution is particularly appropriate after this amiable lady's remark. We hope to hold a meeting every three months of women, or rather mothers, although a woman old enough to be in charge of a family but who has no children would be allowed to attend. Monsieur Peyrac suggested the idea to me and I thought it a good one. Women always have a great many relevant things to say with regard to the good management of a city. But they don't say them because they are afraid of their husband's sticks.'

The remark was greeted by laughter.

'There are to be no sticks or husbandly interference in this matter,' Colin went on. 'The women will discuss matters among themselves and then send on their views to me. Monsieur de Peyrac has been telling me that the Iroquois govern themselves in this way, and that no war is entered upon unless the Mothers' Council considers it necessary for their nation.

'Let us see if we can show ourselves at least as wise as the Redskins.

'The third measure I propose to take was suggested to me by the colonists of New Holland. I believe that we should never hesitate to borrow ideas from our foreign neighbours to make our life more enjoyable. It is their custom to make a present to every young man getting married of a "pipe", that's to say 125 gallons, of Madeira. One third is to celebrate his marriage, another to celebrate the birth of his first child, and the third is to console his friends on the day of his funeral. Do you like the idea and do you agree to its adoption here at Gouldsboro?'

There was a temporary shock, a pause of supreme hesitancy, and then a unanimous clamour arose, consisting of mingled applause, approval and laughter. Angélique realized that Colin had won through.

There he stood with his hands on his hips, calm and dominating, while the ovations rained down upon him, just as he had stood when they had booed him. Colin Paturel, King of the Slaves, the outcasts, and the persecuted, was showing himself to be the strongest man present, and was standing out before them with his strong figure erect under the cloudy sky, as invincible as a rampart in his essential honesty, the straightforwardness of his simple heart, and the incredible toughness of his resourceful mind.

They had recognized from the very outset that he would be their permanent protector, their just and unbending Governor, and that they could rely on him utterly and completely.

The man, the sovereign that he was capable of being, had been raised up before their eyes by Joffrey de Peyrac. In this calloused hand Joffrey had set the sceptre which it was intended to bear. And all was well, Gold Beard no longer existed.

'Long live the Governor!' shouted the young people and children of Gouldsboro dancing and jumping up and down. The young people were the most enthusiastic, then the women, then the seamen of all nations, and last the transients, whether English or Acadian, who thought very highly of the decisions which had been announced, but were resolved to turn them to their own utmost advantage as neighbours.

The Indians, always of a cheerful disposition, added their own peculiar ebullience to this merry tumult, and the sour faces of the notables of La Rochelle disappeared from view, overwhelmed by the tide of general approbation.

'Hurrah! Hurrah! Bravo for our Governor,' bawled the prisoners from the *Heart of Mary* waving their arms exultantly and setting up a great clanking and clattering of chains.

Joffrey called to the Spaniards to unbind them.

'Do you know I'm tempted to settle here!' said Gilles Vanereick to the English admiral. 'The intentions of the new Governor strike me as highly entertaining. Did you notice, my lord, how he handled those sourpusses of Huguenots? And how cleverly he got himself unanimously acclaimed as Governor? Too late for them to back out of it now... And as for Count Peyrac, what a delight to see the inscrutable expression on his face ... like Mephistopheles getting the souls to dance at a Witches' Sabbath ... He's a juggler with sharp knives, a man who never hesitates to juggle with his own fate, with his own heart, in order to achieve his ends. But he has always been like that. I knew him well in the Caribbean ... Although, if that superb wife of his were my property, I would never have had his cheek ... to place my wife's lover on my right hand, on the same throne! ...'

With a lump in her throat, Angélique now realized why she was so distressed in spite of the happy outcome of the dilemma. Count Peyrac, because he was a man and Head of State, had had the power to save Colin's life, where she had not. He had made full use of it. And yet it was not just this subtle form of jealousy that rent her heart: she would have despised herself for it. It was rather the fact that he had excluded her from his discussions that proved that she no longer meant anything to him, and that it was not on her behalf that he had acted as he had. No! He had done it for Colin ... and for Gouldsboro!

The solution he had devised was admirable. It solved all their problems. But as for her, he did not love her any more.

'My dear Abigail,' said Joffrey de Peyrac, stepping down from the stage and bowing to Gabriel Berne's wife, 'would you allow me to escort you to the banqueting hall? And you, my lord Governor, will you take Madame de Peyrac's arm? Let us form a procession, shall we? ...'

The blood rushed to Angélique's cheeks on hearing her husband's suggestion.

As if through a haze she saw Colin's tall figure advance towards her, bow, and offer her his arm, on which she laid her hand, and together they walked off behind Joffrey de Peyrac and Abigail while the rest of the procession formed up behind them. Madame Manigault, furious at being ousted by Abigail from her position beside their lord and master, joined Master Berne, who was utterly dejected.

Monsieur Manigault somehow found himself with the lovely Ines on his arm, while the English admiral had a pretty Acadian girl as his partner. The Reverend John Knox Mather, whom the atmosphere was making more and more relaxed, was simultaneously favoured by the ravishing Bertille Mercelot and the charming Sarah Manigault.

Flanked by these two pretty girls, the respectable doctor of theology strode proudly along the sandy track leading from the fort to the inn.

Miss Pidgeon, full of blushes, walked arm-in-arm with the Reverend Patridge.

Bystanders lined the way, acclaiming and applauding the notables as they passed.

'So this is what that diabolical man has thought up to make

us all play his little game,' Angélique muttered between her teeth.

'It was quite a feat, wasn't it,' Colin replied. 'I still haven't got over it myself. His strength of character quite overwhelms me.'

'How could you have agreed to his terms?'

'I didn't want to, but he availed himself of an argument that forced me to agree to his plans.'

'What did he say?'

'I can't tell you yet,' Colin replied meditatively. 'Maybe I shall one day...'

'Oh, indeed! I am no doubt considered too stupid to share the grandeur of the visions and projects that you gentlemen have thought up!'

She clenched her fingers on Colin's sleeve.

'It is obvious that you two have become as thick as thieves; I should have guessed as much. How stupid I was to have worried so much on your account, Colin Paturel! Men always come to an understanding at women's expense! ...

CHAPTER SEVENTY-ONE

TRUMPETS WERE sounding and banners flying in the wind. The hall adjoining the inn, which was already so popular that it had come to be known by the name destined to be famous for a hundred leagues on all sides – 'the Inn below the Fort'.

Outside, along the beach, around the port and the bay, game hung roasting on spits, and barrels were being broached for the seamen, the common people and the Indians.

As the guests began to take their places around the huge banqueting table, Angélique slipped away to the kitchens.

She must have a drink, or she would never get through the evening. She did not know whether she wanted to laugh or to cry, and she had never felt so close to breaking down completely. Joffrey had gone beyond all bounds and was making a fool of her.

'Give me a pint of that wine,' she said to David Carrère, after sniffing the contents of the barrels in the store.

'A pint!' the boy exclaimed, wide-eyed. 'For you! That's white Bordeaux, you know, Madame, as powerful as the sun.'

'It's exactly what I need!'

With her pint mug in her hands, Angélique went back to the kitchen where the spits were turning over the fire, and cast a scathing glance at the ladies of Gouldsboro who were busy titivating.

Madame Manigault, Madame Mercelot and all the others had come back into the kitchen under the pretext of lending a hand, but more particularly to check that their coifs were straight.

'Well,' Angélique asked them, 'what do you think of your new Governor?'

And she threw back her head and burst into peals of laughter.

'I can see what's upset you, my good ladies! After all that gossip about me, this was not at all what you expected to hear! There's the answer to all the talk about no smoke without fire. Gold Beard turns out to be a friend of mine who saved my life once on the Barbary coast. Is one to disown a man who has saved one's life— Was I not within my rights to embrace him when by pure chance I found myself face to face with him again? But that was enough to stir up gossip and calumny, to turn a friendly meeting into a vile betrayal, an apple of discord. ... And you were all too keen to see evil where it did not exist...'

The Countess of Peyrac's sardonic laughter humiliated them all.

Although she knew that what she said was only half true, Angélique almost believed it. She went on taunting them. Kurt Ritz was far away, the poor man! No one would ever ask him to bear witness in public to what he had really seen – or thought he had seen – by the light of that smoky candle, on the night of his escape.

'So you see, my dear friends, gossip will be the ruin of the New World just as it has been of the Old,' Angélique concluded drinking down the last drop of her white wine.

Someone put a head round the door.

'Madame la Comtesse, your presence is requested in the banqueting hall.'

'I am coming immediately.'

'Now it is my turn to offer everyone here a gift to mark this joyous inauguration,' said Angélique as she took her seat at the banquet table.

Then, having aroused their curiosity, she went on:

'A cask of pure Armagnac which was given to me last week by a gallant Basque captain.'

Her announcement called forth a further ovation.

'Please fetch Adhemar,' Angélique bade one of the men serving the meal.

When the soldier arrived, still as bewildered looking as ever, she instructed him to go to camp Champlain to fetch the things she had left there since the evening of her arrival. After Adhemar's departure, the appearance of this curious soldier of the King of France having caused considerable comment, Angélique related the history and exploits of the good fellow, thus starting off a round of gay conversation accompanied by innumerable anecdotes.

Dish after dish was passed round, abundant and tasty. A pig had been slaughtered, for these early settlers regarded oysters, lobster, turkey, salmon and game as food for the poor, because they were their daily fare.

Angélique found herself sitting on Colin's right hand, while he presided at one end of the table, and Joffrey at the other, with the gorgeous Ines on his right and Abigail on his left. Madame Maigault was sitting opposite her. A little farther along sat Gilles Vanereick, his fiery black eyes in his round, Flemish face never leaving Angélique. There was a generally fair balance of the sexes among the guests gathered round the table, French and English, people in dazzling livery or wearing dark, sober clothes with white bands, to whom were added as isolated figures, a Recollect friar, Father Baure, the Breton almoner of the *Fearless*, the Abbé Lochmer, a somewhat rough and ready man but jovial with it, and in no way concerned to have as his neighbours Pastor Baucaire and Pastor Patridge; an Acadian gentleman, Monsieur de Randon, who had disembarked that very morning from Port-Royal, talking with his blood brother an important Mic-Mac chieftain, who, in spite of the fact that he wiped his mouth with his hair, nevertheless seemed to dominate the entire gathering by reason of his regal stature.

While his presence among them astonished and even scandalized the Anglo-Saxons, they accepted it as one of the consequences of the French eccentricity that often makes them bristle but seems nevertheless to exist in order to enable foreigners to taste the joys of licence, of extravagance and even of sin, without forcing them to take the initiative themselves. At that moment the strict John Knox Mather had no sense of offending against the virtue of temperance while gaily emptying his pewter tankard, *for the wines were French ones.*

Their host was French, and likewise their hostess, which authorized her to be beautiful, dazzling and sumptuously dressed to delight the eyes of men, and never mind if so much dangerous provocation inevitably led her to sin against the Sixth Commandment, for even in God's own eyes, a French sin is a half-forgiven sin; and if the Spanish lady exuded the scent of jasmine, a perfume as sultry as the look that follows from those two velvety eyes half hidden behind her black lace fan, all the fear and horror such an association might have called forth elsewhere was attenuated by the fact that they were sitting at a French table on French land.

Does not the genius of this giddy, thoughtless race lie precisely in the fact that they are able to impart to all situations a touch of their own levity?

Is it not true that the very daring of the astonishing mixtures which the French produce in their colonies, instead of leading to a blood bath as might be expected, produce no more than a mild euphoria that enables one to dream for the space of an hour that men are brothers and that damnation has been abolished? . . .

The English admiral declared:

'Gouldsboro will soon have become the most luxurious establishment along the whole of the American coastline. I am not even sure that the Spaniards in their fortified cities in Florida lead such a merry life as you do here. It is only fair to say that you gentlemen filibusters don't give them much chance,' he said to Venereick.

'But they hit back pretty hard. That is, incidentally, why I am here. I share your opinion that it is a better place to live than anywhere else.'

'By what genius do you manage, Monsieur de Peyrac, to bring out of a situation apparently irremediably evil, something that is good and acceptable? For it is not enough just to will the good; the good must – how shall I put it? – be capable of materialization,' said Knox Mather, whose numerous libations were inclining him naturally in the direction of his governing interests, which were intellectual and theological.

'I do not think it is a matter of genius,' Peyrac replied, 'but rather of giving one's preference to life. Occasionally it is necessary to inflict death – one is obliged to by the imperfections of the world – but I consider that the only good is to be found in life.'

Mather frowned.

'Hum! You would not be by way of being a follower of that man Baruch Spinoza the philosophers speak of, the Jew from Amsterdam, so strangely out of line both with Judaism and Christian doctrine? . . .'

'I know that he said: "Whatever favours the persistence of the individual in Being, that is to say Life, is called Good, and whatever impedes it is called Evil . . ." '

'What is your opinion of the vague, disturbing sayings that seem to me to deny God his position of sovereignty?'

'I think the world is changing! But it is a slow and painful gestation. It is the common lot of all idolaters, to whom all of us here belong by our origins, to be unable to change their graven images. You gentlemen of the Reformed Church have already made an effort in that direction by destroying the statues in churches, and you English gentlemen have taken a step towards the liberation of mankind by beheading your kings, but take care, a step forward is often paid for by two steps backwards.'

'Gentlemen, gentlemen,' Father Baure exclaimed, in considerable agitation, 'what are you saying? I should not be sitting at your table. Your remarks have a smell of brimstone about them. . . . Beheading kings! Destroying statues! . . . come, come! Have you forgotten that we are God's creatures and as such have an obligation to obey His laws, and to bow before the authorities He Himself has set up on earth, such as the dogmas of the Holy Church first and foremost, and the decisions of rulers who govern us by divine right. Cut off their heads! What are you thinking of? . . . Hell awaits you. Things are being said here that make me shudder! . . .'

'An excellent wine is being drunk here, too,' Vanereick cut in. 'Drink up, my dear Father. The most shocking remarks are forgotten at the bottom of a glass.'

'Yes, drink up,' Angélique insisted, smiling at the priest to help him regain his composure. 'Wine is also one of God's gifts and there is nothing more likely to help the French to unite and forget their differences.'

Adhemar poked his head round the door:

'I've got your keg, Madame la Comtesse; and the Baron's box of English scalps, what am I to do with that?'

CHAPTER SEVENTY-TWO

ANGÉLIQUE BROKE into peals of hilarious laughter.

Her pint mug of white wine and the spicy warmth of the food had made her very animated. Adhemar asking what he should do with Baron Saint-Castine's coffer full of English scalps was the last straw.

By some miracle the simple-minded soldier's question had passed unnoticed in the uproar of conversation, and Angélique's light, airy laughter diverted the attention of the guests from Adhemar and concentrated it on this sudden outburst of delightful gaiety, so charming and so welcome.

Seeing that she had become the object of all eyes, Angélique led her guests on through a regular hail of jokes, witticisms and puns by which she tried to justify her excessive hilarity.

'Are we not plunged into the depth of licence, profligacy and dangerous depravity, brothers?' John Knox Mather asked his fellow Puritans, his eyes shining ecstastically like those of a martyr surrounded by the flames of the stake.

'It is by skirting such precipices without falling into them that the strength which the Lord gives his elect can be recognized,' the Reverend Patridge replied, his cavernous voice booming out over the pearls of laughter.

Never had they been so happy to draw so close to the shores of licentiousness, and so satisfied with their own ability to resist temptation.

Angélique began to laugh more and more, and sometimes, in her effort to restrain herself, she was almost weeping. Borne along by the liberal supply of drinks, most of the guests found no difficulty in keeping pace with the general merriment.

It was too bad if her gaiety seemed inopportune and misplaced. The master of Gouldsboro had forced her to play this role, before them all, without a thought for her bleeding heart and her distress. He had decreed that she had to be the Countess of Peyrac. Without a crack in her armour. The drama between the two of them must be buried, must be denied. No doubt this mattered less to him than to her. She no longer knew what he thought. She would almost have preferred the violent outburst of the other night to his apparent indifference, the kind of detachment that made her nothing more than a pawn to move about his chessboard, that carefully contrived set-up which he manipulated for his own personal ends. And he had carried his Machiavellism to the point of seating her on Colin's right hand.

If Colin had been less noble he would have disturbed her less. He would have kindled less warmth in her heart. Now, her nerves on edge, she felt a perverse desire to destroy the understanding that existed between him and Joffrey, to reach out towards him again, once again to try out her power over him. Her shining eyes sought his out, and she was furious to see, when he turned towards her, nothing but serene impassiveness, deliberate but unassailable. Joffrey had cut her off from him, too. He had taken everything from her, seized everything she possessed and cast her out with nothing.

Thus did her heart and her distracted mind torment themselves, while she offered her guests a vision of exquisite vivacity, like an apparition of light and luxury at that rustic table at which a group of exiles attempted to reproduce in spite of their poverty the sumptuous display of the Old World.

Alone among them all, Joffrey de Peyrac sensed the tension and slightly forced note of over-excitement in Angélique's laughter.

Like his guests he had caught from Adhemar's rambling remarks some vague story about 'English scalps', which had provoked Angélique's mirth, but also like them, inasmuch as Adhemar's words had been drowned by the general babble of conversation, he had preferred not to inquire more closely into the matter. There was time to look into that later. This was not the moment for dubious inquiries.

She was laughing, but she was also suffering. Inwardly moved by her brilliant beauty, roused by her boldness, the provocation of her slender chin proudly raised, of her lovely eyes turned towards Colin, and being, in spite of himself, filled with admiration at the promptness with which she had taken up his challenge, and faced up to the humiliations that he had inflicted upon her, he could not succeed in guessing the source of the suffering that he felt vibrant within her.

As a result of his having turned her roughly away and cast her into the darkness, her woman's heart was becoming impenetrable to him again. He had lost that special gift of reading openly in it. The capacity to see and understand one another exactly as they were had been lost.

He did not dare to think that she was suffering precisely on his account. The bruise marking her lovely face, which she could only imperfectly disguise under her make-up, made him cautious in his approach. Angélique had pride, the pride of all high-born women, a mixture of self-confidence, of consciousness of value and rank, which, even if throughout their childhood they have eaten wild chestnuts and run about barefoot, makes them so difficult to handle and to tame. It is a sense of their lofty descent, and it is in their very flesh. Could Angélique ever forget the way he had treated her? A sense of anxiety which he was unprepared to recognize for what it was had been tormenting him since he had discovered the state of her face the morning after that terrible evening. He had been overwhelmed with dismay: 'I did not think that I had struck her so hard,' he had murmured in his distress. He realized that no woman had ever been capable of making him lose control of himself so completely. 'I might have killed her!'

Being furious with himself he resented her all the more, and, paradoxical as it might seem, she attracted him all the more . . .

When he set eyes on her, he felt a great tide welling up within him, both sentimental and sensual, which bore him irresistibly towards her with the desire to take her in his arms. For too long his arms had been empty of her. Gilles Vanereick might well have been right when, passing off his quite considerable philosophy as a good-humoured joke, he had advised him to take an indulgent line: 'Believe me, Monsieur Peyrac, your wife is one of those women who are "worth while" forgiving . . .'

He could not help reflecting that in spite of her apparent misery, she had not failed to fulfil her role as the Comtesse de Peyrac, which circumstance demanded of her, and had shown herself to be his worthy companion in every undertaking during those three painful, decisive days. And for this he would always be secretly grateful to her.

As he contemplated her surreptitiously, he could not help noticing all the qualities that made it 'worth while' to forgive her. Not only her beauty and the perfection of her body – an appalling temptation, to which he would have been loathe to succumb – but the things that constituted her very essence, the things he regarded as a priceless treasure.

Just when he thought he hated her, he found himself caught in the trap of those secret, unique qualities Angélique possessed.

On the morning of the terrible fight on board the *Heart of*

Mary, he had made a pause, breathless from so much fighting, finally certain of victory, but seeing just how bloody the battle had been, and he had found himself thinking spontaneously: 'Fortunately *she* is in Gouldsboro! . . .'

As soon as they had learned that *she* was in Gouldsboro, the unfortunates who had been wounded took heart, even those who only knew her from hearsay. 'The Lady of the Silver Lake! The Frenchwoman with the power of healing! The Lovely Lady! The woman who knows all the secrets of the herbs . . . their healing virtues . . . There is witchcraft in her hands, so they say . . . She is on the beach, so they say . . . She will come . . . she will save us . . .'

All the men adored her. There was nothing to do about it.

At that moment her throaty laugh inflamed and tormented him alternately and subjected him, as it did all the other men present, to a charm that inclined him towards indulgence, and abject surrender.

As he chatted with his guests at the banquet table, the faces of two women came and went, mingling in his mind's eye. Angélique's weaknesses could not detract from those human qualities which had finally won him over – he realized this in the light of the test to which they had been put – a feeling that was so intimately bound up with his pleasure in her, that he was unable any more to dissociate it from that other aspect of her female nature, treacherous and changeable, which aroused his wrath. He wanted to hate this woman for the weakness of her flesh and her contemptible fickleness, while passionately desiring the presence of the other woman, his friend, his companion, his confidante, his sensual, blissful haven of refuge.

His arms had missed her for too long. His body cried out for her with insistence that left him with a sense of abandonment.

Their sudden quarrel had wounded him, and through this wound he felt some of his essential strength ebbing away. He had slept badly during these impatient, troubled nights. Where are you, my smooth, gentle, white-skinned, soft-fleshed wife?

Where is your bare shoulder on which I love to lay my brow? Where are your delicate fingers, your magical fingers which used occasionally to dare to take my face between two hands and draw it down towards you to kiss my lips, in a movement full of the irresistible desire of a lover, but also of that warm, possessive tenderness that dwells in mothers' hearts, and which always occupies a unique place in men's memories! You were just beginning to feel less nervous of me, and then everything was destroyed.

Count Peyrac suppressed a sigh.

What was she thinking there at the other end of the table? He no longer knew.

During the past few days, he had found himself hesitating about what decisions to take, he had experienced self-doubt.

The only thing he had never hesitated about was what to do with Colin Paturel. Colin, the King of the Slaves, was the very man he had been waiting for for so long. And as soon as he had recognized him, he had ceased to see him as a rival, and had decided that no 'woman trouble' was going to prevent his close association with so influential a man, such an obviously born leader of men.

And yet his was the rugged brow with the leonine mane, which, with his own eyes, he had seen Angélique stroke with her delicate hand.

On that island, what a torment it had been to him to think that the moment of betrayal had come. And yet, from where he stood hidden among the trees, as soon as his eyes had fallen upon the figure of the pirate, he had recognized him as the King of the Slaves of Meknès. This explained everything, and this made everything more serious, more tragic. He had always know that Angélique had loved this man, in a way that could not fail to make him intensely jealous.

For Colin deserved to be loved by such a woman.

This memory sent the subtle poison filtering back once more again into his heart. The plot he had hatched and set in motion against all of them now seemed to have become too big for him to manage.

Now her lovely eyes were fixed on Colin, seeking a glance of understanding from his as he sat there, rigid, through loyalty to Peyrac, pretending not to understand the provocativeness of her dazzling smile. He could hear her fascinating voice, a trifle mocking.

'My lord Governor, I seem to recollect that when we were in Barbary you used to call me Angélique. Should we not keep up the fraternal customs of the Christian slaves here?'

The little trollop! Not only was she turning a bold face to her shame, but here she was fighting back devastatingly.

How foolish he was to feel sorry for her. If she was unhappy, well let her be unhappy! She deserved to be taught a lesson.

He turned his attention once more to his neighbour on his left, Ines y Perdito Tenares, the voluptuous product of Caribbean, Spanish and Portuguese blood, whose black eyes were keeping a jealous watch on her Gilles, whom she considered to be far too fascinated by the charms of their laughing hostess.

Peyrac laid one finger on the chin of the pretty half-caste, to turn her head away from the distressing sight and to make her look at him.

'Let us console one another, Señorita,' he said to her softly in Spanish.

CHAPTER SEVENTY-THREE

'COLIN, HE doesn't love me any more! He is flirting with that woman Ines. He's tired of me.'

In the dark corridor Angélique staggered against Colin's shoulder. The feast was drawing to an end. A golden sunset sky with clouds scudding across it cast its tormented light on the noisy groups along the beach, dancing and laughing for joy. Some still sat in the banqueting hall, glued to their stools. A great deal of mutual support would be needed to get everyone back to their ships or their houses.

In the darkness of the corridor, Angélique staggered against Colin's shoulder.

'He doesn't love me any more ... I shall die ... I could never bear him to love another woman!'

'Calm yourself. You are drunk,' said Colin indulgently.

And he, fairly tipsy himself in spite of his resistance to alcohol, found it hard not to view the world through a slight mist and not to succumb to the temptation of taking her in his arms. He had left the banqueting hall to go and inspect his crew, saying that he must keep an eye on 'the lads'.

But Angélique had followed him. And now she clung to him obviously very much under the influence of her repeated samplings of the cask of Armagnac, but also overcome by unhappiness.

'He is well disposed to you who led me into temptation, whereas he rejects and despises me ... It's not fair! ... It's a shame!'

She was hiccuping slightly and stressing every word.

'Listen, my child!' said Colin. 'Go and take a walk in the fresh air. It will make you feel better.'

'That's right! You men are always hand in glove when it's a question of humilating a woman, of mock … mocking her! You have betrayed me too!'

'Oh stop it! … Everything's all right now. Don't get in a state. There!'

She felt that Colin had become the true Colin once more, capable of being as intransigent as Joffrey and, like him, if he so decided, of controlling the most violent physical desire.

He pushed her firmly away from him, looking at her, and his expression grew a trifle melancholic.

'You love him too much,' he murmured nodding his head. 'It is quite obvious that his hold over you is complete. He dominates you. That is what hurts. That's what's got under your skin. Come on now, go and take a turn outside, my dear … my pretty one.'

He accompanied her down to the beach, where he left her and she headed off in the direction of the promontories to the east of Gouldsboro.

Colin was right.

The brisk evening air dispelled her giddiness and she began to walk with a firmer tread towards the rocks, hoping that she would not meet anyone.

Her mind was in a ferment like a wine-press at vintage time, full of noxious fumes.

Joffrey was flaunting his aversion for her.

That she could not stand! Never would she tolerate seeing Joffrey take another woman in his arms, seeking his pleasure in her, and, who knows, worst of all … forming an attachment to her and confiding in her. If that was how he wanted to punish her, he would succeed only too well. She would die for it … or she would kill the other woman!

She felt outraged that he found it easier to forgive Colin for having attempted to seduce her than her for having allowed him to.

The complicity between the two of them in their male sensuality exasperated her. It was useless to attempt to reach an understanding with men. They always managed to deceive you or to confound you with some argument or other. She had had enough of men and their demands.

Tending those wounded in their wars, feeding and bringing up the children that resulted from their pleasure, polishing their weapons, and, year in and year out, wiping their footprints off the floors of their houses, cooking the game from their hunting parties, gutting the fish that they had caught. Their work had dignity and status, whereas women's was mere drudgery!

A week ago she had been dancing on Monhegan Island, leaping over the Basques' fire, raised aloft by the joy of living and big Hernani's strong wrists.

Although separated from Joffrey at that time, she had felt closer to him than she did now. For three days they had not spoken, and seemed to have ceased to exist for one another.

In a matter of a few days, less than a week, a chasm had opened at their feet, a wall had sprung up between them, an impregnable rampart. Everything had conspired to produce a situation in which their love for one another would be destroyed, had possibly already been destroyed.

A voice seemed to whisper to her through the wind:

'He will separate you . . . you'll see! You'll see! . . .'

She gave a shudder and halted at the end of the promontory. She thought again of the combination of circumstances that had led to the public humiliation of the man she adored. There was something diabolical in it all. An interweaving of pure chance and bad luck which seemed explicable only if one attributed it all to the ill-will of evil spirits bent on their destruction.

She was gripped with fear, the same fear she had felt the evening the stranger with the white face had led her off to the island. She was beginning to believe in the Devil . . . like everyone else in this god-forsaken land.

She turned towards Gouldsboro. 'There are places where the spirit blows . . .'

Was Gouldsboro one such? Had it really been predestined, as the nun visionary in Quebec claimed, to be the setting of a supraterrestrial drama?

'But I am not the She-Devil,' Angélique told herself, almost aloud. 'So what then?'

In spite of herself she recalled the nun's prediction which had caused so much agitation among the Canadian population.

'I was standing on the seashore. There were trees growing right down to the edge of the sand . . . The beach had a pink sheen. On my left stood an outpost built of wood, with a high palisade, and a turret with a flag on it . . . The bay was crowded with islands like sleeping monsters . . . At the top of the beach, below the cliffs, stood a number of houses built of light wood

'... and in the bay two ships lay at anchor ... At the far end of the beach, some distance away, perhaps a mile or two, there was another hamlet of small huts surrounded by roses. I could hear the screeching of seagulls and cormorants...'

The wind tore at Angélique's hair which twined around her like some crazed being, leaving her at one moment, binding her fast the next, whispering words of terror in her ear.

Standing rigid and motionless on the point of a rock, Angélique gazed back towards Gouldsboro.

The beach was tinged with pink and there were the sleeping emerald-coloured monsters, the islands, and the 'wooden outpost with its turret and a flag on it', and the hamlet of camp Champlain where the roses were coming into bloom.

'Then suddenly an extremely beautiful woman rose up out of the sea and I knew she was a She-Devil. She remained there, suspended above the water, in which her naked body was reflected ... Then a unicorn loomed up over the horizon, its long pointed horn glittering like crystal in the light of the setting sun. The She-Devil leapt astride the animal and bounded off through the air. I knew she was going to destroy Acadia, that beloved land we have taken under our protection...'

Angélique stared desperately at the scene before her. It was as if some secret lay behind those sybilline words. Now she was sure of it. The irrational element in human nature that makes us sensitive to the meaning of symbols sounded the alarm and held her in a state of suspense as she gazed at the panorama before her eyes.

Yes, there were ships lying at anchor in the bay, there were seagulls and cormorants, and light-coloured wooden houses under the cliff.

She gave a sudden cry as a memory came back to her.

When she had disembarked here, a year before, THERE HAD BEEN NO LIGHT-COLOURED WOODEN HOUSES under the cliff. Those houses had been built by the Huguenots from La Rochelle during the course of the winter and spring.

She began to pace up and down in agitation, her mind confused by the wind and the wine she had drunk, while her thoughts jostled one another feverishly. She muttered:

'I'll tell them ... I'll tell them all ... I'll tell them in Quebec that I am not their She-Devil ... You see, there were no light-coloured wooden houses when I arrived ... and now there are ... So now is the time that the She-Devil should appear!'

She stopped short, as if an icy hand had clutched her throat, an impulsive terror. The words she herself had just uttered struck her as insensate, and yet inescapably true.

Apart from the number of ships – of which there were many that day and not just two – the whole scene described in the prophecy lay there before her very eyes.

She must be raving! Had she been able to run to Joffrey, he would have shared or dispelled her fears, he would have laughed at them . . .

But henceforth she was on her own, and to her alone, behind the cloak of appearances, had been revealed the threat of the succubus, the She-Devil, that dazzling creature who was to rise up out of the sea, astride a unicorn, to bound off into the air over the land of Acadia, to ravage and destroy everything in her path . . . even to the depths of men's hearts!

I have had too much to drink! . . . And I'm so weary! Am I going mad? I must sleep, and not think any more.

Such were Angélique's thoughts on the evening of that proud day in the annals of Gouldsboro when the colony had celebrated the accession of its first governor.

As night fell, Colin had spoken once more from the platform and had ended his speech by throwing a hundred pounds worth of gold pieces into the crowd.

Everyone seemed happy. Only Angélique felt the threat behind the appearances. Ever since the 'revelation' she had had down by the sea, to her misery at being separated from Joffrey was added her fear that they might all be the victim of some evil spell.

On all sides she saw tangible signs of her foreboding, and the laughter, the singing, the dancing, and the general hilarity all shocked her, seemed insultingly misplaced in face of the misfortune that she thought she saw advancing upon them – that might already be among them! Like a worm in the fruit. A succubus on the prowl amongst them, gibbering and sniggering. The screech of a nightjar sounded like the She-Devil's laughter to her ears. To whom could she turn in her anxiety?

'I had too much to drink! I'll feel better tomorrow . . . Tomorrow I shall go and see Joffrey. He will have to agree to see me. He will have to tell me what he intends to do with me, whether he intends to send me away, or to forgive me. But things cannot go on like this . . . because this way we are weak, and the She-Devil will get to us . . . But no, I'm raving. There is nothing, truly, nothing coming towards us over the water!

That terrible thing! We shall prove stronger than her ... but we must not be separated ... I think I am feverish. I have had just about my fill for today. Goodbye gentlemen, I leave you to your grandiose projects.'

She went from one group to another, finding that they were still singing around the fires lighted along the beach in the night, and they all gave her a cheer as she went by. She then made her way to where Joffrey de Peyrac and Colin Paturel were standing side by side below the fort, receiving the respects and congratulations of the assembled company. In silence she dropped them a curtsy and retired.

Her step was unsteady as she made her way along the path to the fort, unaware of the fact that the two men, in spite of themselves, followed her with their eyes.

Beneath her windows in the central courtyard of the fort, some sailors were talking together as they drank one last tankard.

'Meanwhile, we've been done,' said one of the men from the *Heart of Mary*. 'It's all very well being a settler in a pleasant spot, but all I can see here by way of women are either Huguenots or squaws. Working hard for your living in America is all right, but not on your own. We thought we'd have our dinner waiting for us when we got home and a white Christian woman waiting for us in bed, that was what we agreed! THAT'S the part of the contract I liked.'

Lieutenant Barssempuy gave the man a dig in the ribs with his elbow.

'Don't be too greedy, my boy. You've seen another sun go down, although this was the day you were supposed to die. Tonight the loveliest woman you'll hold in your arms is Life. The other kind will soon come up over the horizon, you may be sure of that!'

'That doesn't alter the fact that there's no sign of them for the time being.'

'Pray, brothers,' Father Baure interrupted, 'pray, and God will provide.'

'Avast there, monk,' one of them said. 'Without wishing to contradict you, can you see how God could possibly make twenty or thirty marriageable girls spring up out of the sand between now and tomorrow, fit to be married to gallant gentlemen of fortune like us?'

'No, I cannot see how,' the Recollect father replied quietly, 'but God is great! And anything can happen by His hand. So say a prayer, my sons, and He will grant you these women.

'God is great. God is all powerful, let it be remembered.'

And this is how these converted filibusters from the *Heart of Mary* were granted wives the very next day after all these strange events.

CHAPTER SEVENTY-FOUR

A MAN CAME running along the path leading from Blue Creek to Gouldsboro. Gusts of wind and rain tore at his cloak, but he hurried along, puffing and blowing. It was the papermaker Mercelot, whose mill stood at some distance from the village.

He reached the fort and called to the sentries:

'Quick! Make haste! A ship has gone aground at Blue Creek.'

Angélique, who had slept like a log, was awakened by lights in the courtyard of the fort. It was scarcely dawn and she thought at first that the festivities were still continuing, then all the stir and bustle made her realize that there was something strange going on. She dressed quickly and ran down to find out what it was.

By the light of lanterns, Mercelot was pointing at a map held by the Count.

'They must have struck the reefs of Bleak Monk at the mouth of Anemone Bay and then been driven inshore in Blue Creek.'

'But whatever were they doing in those waters?' exclaimed the Count.

'The storm . . .'

'But . . . *there is no storm.*'

It was indeed surprising.

The wind was in fact blowing hard and the sea was rough, but for once the sky was clear and ships at sea must have had a perfectly clear view of the coast with its guided beacons.

'Is it a cod-fisher?'

'How can one tell? . . . It's still too dark to see, but they are crying for help fit to make your hair stand on end. My wife and daughter are already down on the beach with our servant-girl and our neighbour.'

Thus it was that the inhabitants of Gouldsboro, scarcely recovered from a day of festivities, found themselves, still half-asleep and tormented by anxiety, standing in the wind-swept dawn on the beach of Blue Creek, listening to distant cries of terror that came tragically to them through the grey murk through which from time to time they glimpsed, just above the surface of the waves, the masts of a half-submerged ship.

Angélique was there with most of the other Gouldsboro ladies.

The wreck was submerged up to its rails. Strangely enough, it still did not sink, and the currents at the mouth of the bay were battering it back and forth between the two promontories of land lying at the entrance. Every time this occurred they expected to see the vessel crash against the rocks and explode like a heavy, over-filled barrel; but then off it would go again, its three masts swaying aimlessly, its sails flapping and its shrouds hanging uselessly.

If only they could hold on until the chebec and the cutter from Gouldsboro arrived with Joffrey de Peyrac and Colin Paturel, who were at that moment rounding point Yvernec to get to them by the sea route.

Borne on the wind came heart-rending shrieks and cries for help, all the more distressing because over the crests of the waves no one could be seen on board the wreck.

The gang of sailors and fishermen who had come by the overland route from Gouldsboro were armed with boathooks, gaffs, anchors, ropes and lifelines.

Under the instructions of Hervé Le Gall, three of them got into the Mercelot's fishing smack and pulled out as hard as they could row.

The others spread out along the rocks ready to help out of the water any of the shipwrecked people who might try to swim for it.

'I shall go and get blankets, soup and hot drinks ready,' said Madame Mercelot. 'Come on, Bertille.'

Angélique had brought ointments and lint to dress any injuries there might well be, and a flagon of rum. She was just about to follow Madame Mercelot when, only a few cables' length from the shore, a kind of raft made of wooden planks and barrels hastily lashed together came surging up before their eyes from the hollow of a wave, with a group of dishevelled creatures clinging screaming to it.

'Women!' Angélique exclaimed. 'Oh! Lord! The breakers are driving them on to the rocks. They will be smashed to pieces!'

No sooner had she spoken than the raft, as if driven by some inner malice, canted up on one end and crashed against a particularly jagged rock, where it ripped apart, bursting and scattering into hundreds of tiny splinters and shamelessly tipping its entire cargo into the sea. Fortunately the beach was near, and Angélique and her companions dashed into the water up to their waists to rescue the drowning women.

Angélique seized a head of long hair just as its owner disappeared beneath the surface of the water down into a deep bed of seaweed.

She managed to keep the half-drowned woman's head above the surface and to tow her back to the shore.

It so happened that she was an enormous woman who must have weighed at least sixteen stone, and as long as Angélique was pulling her through the water, she did not notice how heavy she was, but as soon as they reached the sand she suddenly found herself dragging a weight like a sack of stones and was quite incapable of shifting the inert mass a single inch.

'Come and give me a hand!' she called out to the bystanders.

A sailor sprang forward, then a second, then a third and a fourth.

'In Heaven's name, whatever was a woman like this thinking of to put to sea?' they complained. 'Such hefty creatures should never go near a ship, they should remain on land like cannons in a fortress.'

Meanwhile Madame Mercelot, her daughter, their maid and their manservant had helped the six other women ashore. Some of them were shivering dreadfully, their teeth chattering uncontrollably, while others were crying. One of the girls fell on her knees and made the sign of the cross.

'Thank you, Blessed Virgin, for saving our lives,' she said fervently.

They were all French but to judge by their accent they were not Canadian.

'There's Delphine still caught out there!' one of them cried, pointing to a young woman who had succeeded in clambering on to a rock. No doubt she was exhausted, for she lay there half conscious, and at any moment another wave might have swept her away.

Angélique ran round the edge of the promontory to where the girl was and helped her back on to firm ground again.

'Put your arm round my shoulders, my dear,' she told her. 'I will support you and take you to that house yonder, where we shall soon have you in front of a good fire.'

The shipwrecked girl, a pretty brunette with intelligent-looking eyes, seemed to come from a good family. She found the strength to murmur, through her deathly pale lips, with a faint smile:

'Thank you, Madame. You are very kind.'

'Here they come!'

A cry of hope went up at the sight of the white sails of the chebec and the cutter as they rounded Cernek Point. The two ships made their way swiftly towards the wreck.

'Are there still many people left on board?' Angélique asked the young woman she was supporting.

'At least twenty of my companions, I think, and some members of the crew. Oh God, let's hope they're not too late!'

'No, they aren't! Look, our ships have already reached the wreck and taken up position on either side of it.'

Dawn had broken and they could now follow the stages of the rescue operation.

Le Gall, returning with his boat full of women, said that those still out there stood a good chance of being saved.

The wreck was certainly sinking, but slowly enough to allow time to get the survivors on board the chebec. Some of the Indians from the hamlet had also put out to sea in their canoes and were bringing some of the women back, no more chilled and terrified by their ordeal than by these redskinned faces and befeathered heads. They also brought in a cabin boy with long hair.

Then suddenly the masts began to go under, rapidly dwindling from sight as they plunged beneath the waves. The white sails of the two Gouldsboro ships could be seen tacking back and forth like birds hovering over the doomed ship in its death agony. On the shore, the women refused to leave the beach and stood with their eyes riveted upon the last moments of their ship.

When it had completely vanished they began to sob and wail and wring their hands.

CHAPTER SEVENTY-FIVE

DAME PETRONELLA DAMOURT – 'with a *t*', she insisted – the fat woman whose life Angélique had saved, laced into some of Madame Manigault's spare clothes – the biggest they had been able to find in the place – was sitting facing Count Peyrac and

Colin Paturel, trying to explain to them in a series of long speeches interrupted by equally prolonged bursts of weeping, what their exact position was.

She had been entrusted with the task, she said – 'for £600 cash,' she added proudly – of acting as escort to a contingent of some thirty 'King's Girls' being sent out to Quebec as wives for the unmarried settlers, soldiers and officers there, in order to people the colony.

'But your ship was not making for Quebec, my good lady,' the Count remarked. 'You are in fact a very long way from it.'

'Is that so?'

She turned to Colin whose simple features intimidated her less than the Spanish-looking gentleman who had saved their lives. Colin seemed to her more likely to understand the torments of an ignorant and simple heart.

He confirmed what Count Peyrac had said:

'You are not on the route to Quebec.'

'But where are we then? The lights of a town had just been sighted when the ship went aground.'

She looked from one to the other, her face full of terror and incredulity, and tears streamed down her fat cheeks.

'Whatever will the Duchess of Baudricourt, our benefactress, say when she hears this? ... Oh, but I was forgetting, she has been drowned. How dreadful! Oh no, she can't be! Our dear benefactress. A saint! What will become of us?'

She began to sob still harder, and Colin handed her a handkerchief as big as a duster, for sailors are prepared for all eventualities. She dabbed her eyes, and at last succeeded in controlling herself.

'Poor dear lady! She who so longed to give her life for New France!'

She resumed her story from a much earlier point. For her the adventure seemed to have begun when she became a chambermaid in the service of the Duchess of Baudricourt d'Agenson. A few years later the Duke of Baudricourt had died at the age of seventy-five after an extremely debauched life, having nevertheless contrived to leave his widow a handsome fortune.

The noble widow, Dame Ambroisine de Baudricourt d'Argenson who throughout her married life had patiently borne the affronts, vexations and infidelities of her husband, found that at last the time had come when she could do what she herself wanted to do, namely to retire into a convent of her choosing and there to await death in prayer and mortification, and also, under the guidance of learned men and astronomers, to give herself up to the study of mathematics for which she had a decided gift.

So it was that she entered the convent of the Augustinians in Tours as a canoness. But two years later her confessor persuaded her that her considerable fortune should be used in the service of the Church rather than in the pursuit of mathematics, and persuaded her to leave. He it was who had fired her with enthusiasm for the welfare of New France and the conversion of its savages.

However, the widow had continued to hesitate, until one morning when she was already fully awake, a tall woman dressed in a white serge dress appeared to her and said quite distinctly:

'Go to Canada. I shall not forsake you.'

She was convinced she had seen the Blessed Virgin, although she had not been able to make out her face, and from that time on she had dedicated herself to the succour of these distant territories. Having a good head for business and being fully conversant with the way of the world, she was able to contact various ministers, obtain authorizations and form a company called the Society of Our Lady of the St Lawrence, which had the advantage of being partly a commercial venture, partly a religious one, and which, by placing its services at the disposal of the King, the Governor and the missionaries, ensured its own subsistence.

Dame Petronella, who had become very attached to the good lady and had even followed her into the convent, wished to remain in her service in spite of the increasing hazards associated with the Duchess's projects.

The inevitable had to be faced. One cold morning in May she had clambered on board that shifting world of planks and canvas known as a ship, and loaded her sixteen stone of flesh into the monster's hold – there to die a thousand deaths, less on account of the stormy seas than the peevishness of the girls in her charge. But how could she have left the poor Duchess alone and unaided to face the unknown with all its dangers? For the Duchess of Baudricourt, after inquiring what were the colonies' most pressing need, had learned that wives were wanted for the colonists.

Indeed, all young men in the colonies were required, by order of the King, to marry before reaching the age of twenty. Failing this, the fathers of the recalcitrant young men were to pay a fine and present themselves every six months before the authorities to justify their sons' non-compliance with the regulations.

Recently the administrator of the Province, Carlon, an energetic man, had ruled that all unmarried Canadians should be forbidden to hunt, to fish, to trade with the Indians or to move inland into the forestlands under any pretext whatsoever. From Europe the Minister of the Crown, Colbert, had added to this ordinance the decree that any man objecting to marriage would have to pay a special bachelor tax. These men would be ineligible for any kind of distinction or honour and would be required to wear, prominently sewn to their sleeve, a special badge as a mark of their disgrace.

Following the publication of this decree, out of the thousand bachelors living in Quebec, eight hundred had taken to the woods.

Peyrac was familiar with this situation since he was acquainted with Nicholas Perrot, Maupertuis and his son, and even l'Aubignière, who were among the immediate victims of these laws.

As for the two hundred faithful men who had remained in Montreal and Québec, resigned to their fate, they needed wives, and Madame de Baudricourt had wished to add her contribution to this noble aim. She herself took charge of a convoy of young women known as 'the King's Girls', gave them all dowries, and, in emulation of the royal 'gift' which the administration was expected to give each of the girls, undertook to pay their expenses to the sum of one hundred pounds apiece, namely ten pounds for recruitment expenses, thirty for their outfits, and sixty for their fare. In addition to this she had given each girl a small trunk with a lock, four chemises, a full set of clothes – cloak, skirt and underskirt – shoes and stockings, four neckerchiefs, four mob-caps, four bonnets, two pairs of cuffs, four pocket handkerchiefs, one pair of skin gloves, one coif, and a black taffeta square, not to mention a brush and comb and other small items of haberdashery.

In this way they would all be well equipped to please the submissive bachelors awaiting them on the quayside at Quebec, formed up in two lines, wearing their best clothes and their heavy shoes, for the ladies to process between.

After a small reception and some refreshments to smooth over their first meeting, they were to be housed in a convent in the city – of which there was no lack – where, during the following days, they could receive the young men in the parlour, watched over and advised by the priests, nuns, and lady bene-factress.

'As you must know, Monsieur Colbert is very exacting about the women chosen to come to Canada,' Petronella Damourt stressed. 'And like him, we took great care about recruitment. The girls we have brought were all born in wedlock; some are orphans and the others come from families that have fallen upon hard times.'

In addition to all this, Madame de Baudricourt had chartered a ship; the King had donated a banner decorated with his mono-gram and the Queen had given holy pictures, statuettes and the like to adorn a church.

Dame Petronella burrowed in her pockets for documents to prove to these alarming strangers how piously and carefully the expedition had been organized.

She wanted to show them her precise accounts, for she her-self had itemized every article for every girl, had had the docu-ment countersigned by a commissioner for oaths, and had kept it carefully filed away in a waterproof envelope together with the letter from Monsieur Colbert ...

When she remembered that the clothes she was wearing were not her own and that all these goods and chattels were now at the bottom of the sea, she burst into floods of tears once more.

They could not get much more out of her beyond the fact that, having embarked early in May on a small 150-ton ship sailing for Quebec, she found herself shipwrecked in these first days of July on the coast of Maine in Frenchman Bay.

'And what was the name of the captain of the wreck?'

'Job Simon. So charming and gallant a man!'

'But a poor navigator, it would seem,' Peyrac interjected. 'And where is your captain at the present moment? Where are all the crew? I know the ship was only a small one, but it must have had about thirty men on board to man it. Where are they?'

It soon became only too clear. The sea began to wash up bodies mutilated from being dashed against the rocks. They were found in every creek and inlet, and the Indians brought them in on their backs, and laid them out on the sand in Blue Creek. Joffrey de Peyrac set off to identify them with the ship's boy, a Breton lad who knew only a few words of French. The boy considered himself lucky to be alive and still in possession of his carved wooden spoon, the sailor's most important pos-session. He told how he had heard the hull split open on a reef. Then the mate had launched the longboat with a number of men and women on board, intending to seek help from the harbour of the nearby city.

'What city?'

'We saw lights, and we thought we had reached Quebec.'

'Quebec?'

'Yes, of course!'

CHAPTER SEVENTY-SIX

MEANWHILE ANGELIQUE had worked ceaselessly throughout the day to bring some comfort to the poor survivors from the shipwreck in Blue Creek. First it had been the survivors of the battle in the harbour, now it was women. Then it had been the tanned, hairy flesh of the pirates she was obliged to deal with, now it was soft, smooth white flesh. But this difference apart, she would always remember the period of confusion that had followed her first return to Gouldsboro as one reminiscent of a visit to the infernal regions where Dante had described the damned writhing in torment, their naked bodies intermingled.

First it had been wounded men, now half-drowned women. After the groans and oaths of the men had come the tears and whimpers of the female sex.

Angélique began to think of her quiet, pleasant life in Wapassou as if it were some unattainable paradise.

The 'King's Girls' were aged between fifteen and seventeen. Some of them were peasant girls, but most came from Paris, where they had been chosen from among the inmates of the State Orphanage. Angélique recognized their lively, cheeky style of speech, which brought these remote regions of America the flavour of the narrow winding streets behind the Chatelet or the Quai aux Fleurs, the smell of the Seine, the whiff of cookshops, and butchers' stalls, and made one remember the rumble of coaches over the round cobbles.

There were among them four 'young ladies' of good birth, intended as brides for officers, a Moorish girl with skin the colour of burnt toast, and one called Julienne who was manifestly a whore.

From the outset this girl boorishly refused all help from Angélique although she was evidently in pain, and dragged herself to a place away from the others. Her companions gave her the cold shoulder, for she was quite out of place in this convoy of brides-to-be, who, according to the directives of Monsieur Colbert, were always to be 'biddable, attractive, hard working, industrious, pious young women'.

Delphine Barbier du Rosoy, the attractive, plucky brunette stressed this fact by way of explaining that Julienne should never have found her way into their company. Madame de Baudricourt's over-generous heart had been taken advantage of in this case.

'You can talk, you young ladies,' shouted Julienne, who had overheard her, 'you can talk when it comes to generosity! ... You must have satin at twenty pounds a length for your clothes while we girls from the orphanage have to make do with Troyes cloth at thirty sous a time.'

In spite of her vulgar outburst, her attempt to create trouble misfired, since all the other orphanage girls were in fact affable, modest and well behaved in spite of their poverty, for they had been brought up by nuns in the orphanage, and the shipwreck had drawn them closer to their more distinguished and better-off companions. It was Delphine du Rosoy who had had the idea of building a raft and had encouraged and sustained them throughout the worst of their ordeal.

Angélique had no other means of housing her protegées than to install them in their turn in the grain store, now vacant again since the release of the prisoners who had gone back to their quarters on the *Heart of Mary*.

And now the men were on the prowl around the barn, examining the lines hung with petticoats and bodices flapping in the wind.

Lieutenant de Barssempuy appeared carrying a pale, inert form.

His eyes shone with feverish excitement.

'I found her,' he explained, 'I found her over yonder, there among the blue rocks, like a wounded seagull. She is just like in my dream. It's her, I'm sure. I have often seen her in my dreams; look how pretty she is!'

Angélique glanced at the bloodless face dragged back by the weight of its long blonde hair heavy with seawater, sand and blood.

'My poor fellow, the girl is dead ... or as good as dead.'

'No, no, I beg you, save her life,' implored the young man. 'She is not dead. Do something for her, Madame I beseech you,

you who have miraculous hands, care for her, bring her back to life, make her better ... She cannot die, she is the one I was waiting for.'

'That's Marie,' said several of the 'King's Girls' bending over the inanimate, blood-stained body. 'Poor girl! It would be better if she did die. She was the maid-in-waiting to Madame de Baudricourt and looked on her as her mother. What will become of Marie without her?'

While Angélique, assisted by old Rebecca, did her best to bring life back to the poor battered body, the other girls discussed how the Duchess had lost her life, and came to the conclusion that it must have been when she went back to the 'tween-deck to fetch Jeanne Michaud's baby boy who had been left behind there.

Jeanne Michaud was weeping in a corner. At the age of twenty-one she was the oldest of the women. She was the widow of a coppersmith and had so moved Madame de Baudricourt's generous heart that she had encouraged her to come to Canada with her little two-year-old son, Pierre, where she would find it easier to obtain a new husband than in France. She had a certificate from her parish priest stating that she was of good character and had no husband alive in France. She remembered nothing save that she had been woken up in the midst of darkness and the sound of shrieks and wails and searched in vain for the child that had been sleeping beside her.

She went on, moaning:

'It's all my fault. My child is dead and our benefactress lost her life trying to save him. She was a saint, and died a martyr's death!'

'And I think you're making a devil of a fuss of that damned Duchess,' Julienne shouted coarsely. 'That benefactress of yours, let me tell you, was nothing but a boring old bitch! Let the angels in heaven have her, if they want her, say I; I put up long enough with her and her mean ways.'

'You're only saying that because she made you go to Mass,' Delphine said severely, 'and made you say your prayers and behave yourself.'

The girl burst into a raucous cackle, then gave Delphine a sly glance.

'Oh I see. You let her harpoon you, too, Miss du Rosoy. She got you too in the end with her paternosters. And yet you didn't like her any more than I did at the beginning. But she got round you all right.'

'Julienne, you loathed her from the start because she tried to save you, and you hate all goodness.'

'Her kind of goodness? I'll say! I'll have nothing to do with that. Shall I tell you what sort of a woman she was, your Duchess? . . . She was a baggage, a trollop.'

The end of her sentence was lost in a chorus of shouts and cries while three or four of the 'King's Girls' hurled themselves upon Julienne in a paroxysm of indignation.

Julienne struggled with them, gesticulating wildly, and biting the hands they tried to place over her mouth to keep her quiet.

'I'll damn well say what I think . . . and it's not the like of you that are going to stop me, you bitches!'

Her voice grew faint, and faded away, and she collapsed on the ground in a faint.

Her assailants were disconcerted.

'What's happened to her? We hardly touched her.'

'I think she was hurt when the ship went down,' Angélique intervened, 'but she wouldn't allow anyone near her. Now she will just have to let us attend to her.'

But no sooner had she bent over the unruly girl, than the latter sat up again with her eyes full of hate.

'Don't touch me, or I'll kill you!'

Angélique gave a shrug and left her, and Julienne went off into a corner, where she remained cowering like a wild animal.

'A girl like that ought never to have been included in a convoy for Canada,' the girls repeated once more. 'Because of her, people will think we're like those good-for-nothing thieving wenches they sent to St Christopher Island . . . We may be poor, but we aren't convicts.'

Marie opened her eyes, lovely periwinkle-blue eyes between golden eyelashes, now filled with unspeakable dread.

'Demons,' she murmured, 'I can see them, I can hear them screaming in the night . . . They are striking me . . . . demons! . . . Demons! . . .'

CHAPTER SEVENTY-SEVEN

THAT EVENING, when Angélique was down on the beach again, her mind running once more on the mystic prophecy and its relation to Gouldsboro, she sensed a presence behind her.

She turned round and felt her knees grow weak.

It was the mythical animal!

The unicorn.

It was standing erect, proudly arching its gilded neck, and its long nostrils 'glittered like crystal in the light of the setting sun'.

The beach was a tiny one, shaped like a half-moon, hemmed in by clumps of trees whose roots extended boldly down to the very edge of the seaweed. It opened into the narrow inlet known as Anemone Creek, because of the fact that multicoloured anemones bloomed there throughout the summer. And now, above the smooth white sand, rose the long neck and head of the unicorn.

Angélique thought that she must be dreaming and could not summon up the strength to cry out for help.

Then a hairy creature, bellowing like a seal, loomed up out of the water and rushed forward, his shrieks filling the bay and echoing around the cliffs. He swept like a whirlwind past Angélique and threw himself down before the unicorn, with arms extended.

'Don't touch her, you wretches! Don't touch my beloved. I thought she was gone for good ... Don't touch her or I'll kill you all! ...'

The man was huge. Blood and water streamed from his hideous, bearded face and trickled off his ragged clothes, while from his eyes shone an elusive, terrifying fire.

The men who had come running from the direction of Gouldsboro, their attention attracted by the shouting, clutched their knives or swords in their hands and watched the man apprehensively.

'Stand back, you wreckers, or I'll strangle you.'

'We'll have to shoot him,' said Jacques Vignot who was carrying a musket. 'He has gone mad.'

'No,' Angélique intervened, 'leave him. I think I understand. He is not mad, but he is in danger of becoming so.'

Then she went up to the unfortunate man who towered over her like a crazed giant.

'What was the name of your ship, Captain?' she asked the man gently. 'Your ship that was wrecked on the rocks last night.'

The sound of her voice penetrated to Job Simon's befogged mind, and tears began to pour down his shaggy face. He fell to his knees clasping the gilded wooden figurehead from his lost ship – a figure that was almost as tall as himself.

'It was *The Unicorn*, Madame,' he murmured. 'My ship that went down was called *The Unicorn*!'

'Come, I will find you some food,' she said to Job Simon, laying one hand on his arm with a gentleness that soothed the wretched man's troubled mind like a balm.

'And what about her, what shall we do with her,' he stammered, pointing towards the gilded wooden figurehead rising out of the sand. 'No one must hurt her, my unicorn . . . she is so beautiful!'

'We shall move her somewhere else . . .'

'We shall move her to where she will be safe from the sea . . . Then later you can put her on the prow of another ship, Monsieur.'

'Never! Never! I am ruined, I tell you . . . but at least I have her, my unicorn! Isn't she lovely? Real gold leaf on her, that was! I put the horn there myself on her head, that beautiful horn from a narwhal that I harpooned myself. Beautiful pink ivory just like a corkscrew . . . You should have seen the way it glistened in the sun . . .'

He talked on, unburdening himself to the unknown woman who guided him, quite unaware of what was happening around him. He let himself be led like a child.

When they reached Madame Mercelot's house she sat him down at a rustic table. In every settler's house in America there is always a pan of broth or soup simmering on the hearth, and Angélique gave the man a bowl of mashed pumpkin and stuffed oysters.

The man began to eat voraciously, sighing as he did so and picking up visibly at each mouthful.

'Well, there it is. I'm ruined,' he concluded on reaching the bottom of a second bowlful. 'At my age, I might as well say I've had it. A graveyard's the nearest thing to a ship I'll ever find to rest my bones in. I said to the Duchess: "I don't give much for our chances, in all this," but nothing doing! She does exactly what she wants to, that woman! I was sure that no good would come of this voyage, but at my age you take whatever comes along, don't you? Girls for cargo, that was what I was reduced to, settlers' girls for America.'

'It can't have been easy, a voyage like that with so many women on board!'

Only the whites of the captain's eyes were visible.

'It was hell!' he sighed 'If you want my opinion, Madame, women shouldn't exist at all.'

He stuffed a huge hunk of bread into his mouth, along with a piece of cheese she held out to him, and, as he chewed away vigorously, he watched her with his little sharp eyes.

'And all that to lose one's ship on a strip of coast full of wreckers,' he growled. 'And yet you don't look like a bandit, do you? You look to me more like a good, honest woman, you do. You ought to be ashamed of yourself. Allowing your men to become wreckers and murderers.'

'What do you mean by that?'

'I mean drawing ships on to your filthy rocks, and bludgeoning to death the poor wretches who try to escape, do you call that an honest livelihood? God and the saints in Heaven will punish you.'

Angélique felt quite incapable of showing indignation at this outrageous accusation. She had had her fill of madness during the past three days from all the despairing and hysterical men and women about her. It was all understandable, coming from people who had almost lost their lives at sea.

So she replied without any sign of anger:

'But you are wrong, my good man. We are just ordinary settlers, making our living from trade and the work of our hands.'

'Well then, why would I have run the blasted ship on to that reef of needle-sharp rocks,' he roared, leaning towards her, 'if I hadn't seen those lights flashing through the night? I know perfectly well how wreckers go about it – how they wave lanterns about on the cliff tops to sink ships by making them think there is a port there.

'Ushant's the port I hale from, at the tip of the Breton Peninsula.

'So little was I expecting to run aground that I was thrown into the water. Then when I reached the shore and began to clamber up, "they" struck me there, and there . . . look. It was no rock that did that.'

And he tossed back his shock of hair, which was like that of a sea god, all sticky with salt and seaweed.

Angélique's eyes widened and her heart missed a beat. 'What do you say to that?' the man asked in triumph, delighted to see her so pale and dumbfounded.

But Angélique was less concerned by the wound she saw on the man's skull than by the appearance of a large red birthmark which Job Simon had revealed on his temple.

'When you see a tall captain with a red birthmark, your enemies will be close at hand! . . .'

Who had said this to her? ... It was Lopez, the little Portuguese buccaneer on the *Heart of Mary*, when they had been together on Maquoit Point.

But where was Lopez now? He had been killed in the battle on board the *Heart of Mary* ...

CHAPTER SEVENTY-EIGHT

SHE LOOKED at herself in the mirror. Night surrounded the cold surface of Venetian glass with its dark shadows, while the last glimmer of the sunset, coming in at the window, cast a pallid light on the mirror itself. Her face appeared to her like that of a ghost with flashing eyes.

Her hair, that lay like a silvery halo round her head, seemed to have gone mad. The wind had tossed it and entangled it when she walked up and down the beach and had encountered the unicorn, and she had grown tired of its endless flapping round her temples, which by now were throbbing with pain.

'I shall plait my hair,' she decided.

So she took it in great handfuls, twisted it, divided it, and brought some order into its gold and pearly sheen. The rich, heavy tresses now lay across her shoulder like a shining fur. But she threw it back again, undid it, made it up once more, lifting it and knotting it at the back of her head after twisting it three times around itself. The weight of it against the nape of her neck, just above her shoulders, made her head feel heavy, but it did bring her a sense of relief. She ran the tips of her fingers over her forehead.

Who was it who had said to her: 'When you see a tall captain with a red birthmark, your enemies will not be far away?'

Earlier on she had remembered who it was. Ah, yes, it was the Portuguese half-caste, Lopez, back at Maquoit Point in Casco Bay.

But young Lopez had died in the battle on board the *Heart of Mary*.

Angélique threw herself down fully dressed upon the cold bed but failed to get the rest her exhausting life required. When all the sick and wounded had been attended to, she had retired for the night as Abigail had entreated her to do, for she was the only one who seemed to care about the exhaustion resulting from Madame de Peyrac's exertions of the past few days.

Had she even caught sight of her husband in the course of the day? She no longer knew. She no longer had a husband. He had become a stranger, indifferent to her suffering. She was alone as she had been before, in an alien world, with an invisible menace slowly advancing towards her. She was all alone, struggling through a chaotic heap of naked bodies, men and women covered with blood, with open wounds, their repulsive flesh tangled inextricably together as in Dante's Inferno, a vision from which the stench itself had been eliminated, shot through from time to time by terrifying *symbols*: the gilded figurehead of the unicorn, the captain with the portwine stain gobbling his food, and the light-coloured wooden houses along the dawn-tinted shore.

Had Joffrey been there, she would have told him of her wild thoughts, and he would have made fun of her and reassured her.

But she was alone . . .

'. . . It seems to me as if the stage is now set,' she would have said to him, 'and that terrible things are about to happen.'

'What terrible things, my love?'

'I don't know, but I'm frightened!'

She could hear Father de Vernon's voice saying: 'When diabolical things begin to happen . . .'

She turned over on the cold bed, longing for some haven, some warmth. She would get up and seek him out and would say to him: 'Forgive me! Forgive me! I did not betray you, that I promise, but please, please don't go on rejecting me . . .'

But she could see him, implacable, sombre and distant, as in the days when he had been Rescator, and she found it impossible to imagine that he had ever been capable of caressing her as he had done, or that their life together, every moment of it, could have been so precious and intimate.

'Oh my love! We were such gay lovers, such serious lovers. All those fantastic nights . . . so much laughter, so much unclouded joy, when we could look upon one another ceaselessly, distractedly, without shame.

'And at the time of the smallpox epidemic, you remember? And especially . . .' at this point her eyes filled with tears, and she could see him, his tall figure bowing before the minute little creature that was Honorine, whom Cantor had offended. 'Come, young lady, let us find some weapons for you.'

'I used to think then that our love would last forever . . .

Fool that I was! Watch therefore, for ye know neither the day nor the hour ...'

Angélique began to toss in her sleep. She dreamed that her golden plait had grown to a monstrous size and was sliding down her body, binding her fast. All the signs of the zodiac writhed and twisted about her like her plait, suffocating her. Then a demon appeared with a cruel grin on its face which reminded her of Wolverine's.

She gave a horrible shriek, and awoke with a bitter taste in her mouth.

The sound of her cries still rang in her ears. And yet her body was still transfused with a sensation of voluptuousness, for she had dreamed that she was making love with some hazy creature, both frightening and strangely gentle.

She remembered her shriek, but it was not she that had given it.

For now she heard it again, piercing the early morning mist, the sharp shriek of a woman.

Angélique leapt out of bed, ran towards the open window and leaned out.

A mist still lay over the ground, like trails of pink smoke, a sea mist that hid the early beginnings of a July day that would undoubtedly be stifling hot. Even the silence of those first hours had something about it that was opaque and crushing.

Angélique's heart thudded irregularly in her breast, unable to resume its normal rhythm. So complete was the silence and so clammy the mist that once again she thought she must have been dreaming.

But then a third cry rang out; it came from the barn where the shipwrecked girls were sleeping.

'Good God!' she exclaimed. 'Whatever is going on now?'

She rushed out of her room, shook the drowsy sentry and got him to open the gates of the fort, summoning one of the Spanish guards in a postern-gate outside to accompany her. The ground in front of their feet was barely visible.

Outside the barn a crowd of people moved aimlessly about like so many souls in limbo.

Angélique reached them just in time to position herself between two stalwart men armed with cutlasses who, notwithstanding the fact that it was impossible to see an adversary at a distance of three paces, were about to set about one another in single combat.

'Have you gone mad!' she cried. 'What are you doing fighting here? You should be on board your ships!'

'It's because of them as are trying to steal our wives,' one of the combatants explained, and she recognized him as Pierre Vanneau, the quartermaster of the *Heart of Mary*.

'What do you mean, your wives?'

'Blow me, the ones inside the barn there.'

'And what gives you the idea that they are your wives, since they only got here yesterday?'

'Blow me, because the Good God sent them specially for us, didn't he, for us folks on the *Heart of Mary*. It was in our contracts, and Father Bauce told us to pray, so we prayed, and ...'

'So you know all about God's intentions for you, do you? And you imagine that all He has to do is to work miracles on your behalf? And under this pretext you consider you can dispense with any sort of respect for the poor unfortunate girls whom the storm has thrown up on our shores ... That's pitching it strong! I am astonished, you hunchback there,' she went on, staring him full in the eyes, 'that you had the nerve to lead your men into an escapade like this. When the Governor, your captain, hears about this, you'll be for it.'

'But, Madame la Comtesse, I would like to point out ...'

'Nothing!' scolded Angélique. 'What are all these crazy notions running through your heads? ... It will be the cat for you, Vanneau, let me tell you, not to mention the loss of your command.'

'But Madame, it was because of the others.'

'What others?'

The mist was beginning to disperse, and Angélique noticed a group of men from the *Fearless*, Vanereick's filibuster ship, consisting of the most sinister-looking members of the crew. The fair Ines, wearing yellow satin, with a coral necklace round her gold-brown neck, seemed to be urging them on to fight.

'When I learned that those scum from the *Fearless* were trying to pester our ... well, those ladies, I and some of my companions came to their rescue,' Vanneau explained. 'We couldn't let those pirate pigs, those gingerbread filibusters, those gallows-birds, lay hands on them.'

'What's it got to do with you, you great lump of pickled pork?' his adversary retaliated, still holding his long, shining dagger in his hand, and speaking with a heavy Spanish accent. 'You know the privateers' law: in the colonies all women belong to sailors passing through. By all means let us fight over them, but we have just as much right as you to that particular booty.'

Vanneau made a threatening gesture, which Angélique quelled with a single look, without a thought for the sharp blade that whistled through the air only a few inches from her face.

Grumbling and growling, two groups of men surged angrily around her, exchanging threatening glances, muttering insults between their teeth in every language under the sun.

Ines began to incite her troops to rebellion in Spanish, but she too was promptly reduced to silence by Angélique, who suspected her of having led the men on this expedition in order to create trouble for her, Angélique, through childish jealousy. The insolent air of the little Spanish woman did not impress her. She knew the type and how to handle her. They were not really bad at heart beneath their fiery exterior, the only danger lay in the way they might incite men to do all kinds of stupid things.

Her intelligence lay in her senses; beyond that she had the brains of a humming bird. Angélique knew exactly how to deal with bold creatures of that kind.

With a single look she checked Ines's harangue in full flight, then tweeked her pretty ear with its gold earring, giving her a mocking, indulgent smile. Finding herself treated in this almost maternal manner, the girl lowered her head, for she was in fact only a young half-caste who had been taken away from her Indian background and had never received any other form of attention than what men offered her, always through self interest. She was in fact a rather pitiful courtesan from the islands, and Angélique's haughty but friendly condescension caught her so much off her guard that suddenly she became nothing more than a somewhat baffled child.

Deprived of the support of their hot-blooded champion, who had persuaded them that they ran no risk whatever in embarking on this adventure and that she would see that everything was all right with their captain, Vanereick's men began to waiver, to exchange glances and to appear far less cocksure.

At that moment the last of the mist cleared and the scene was revealed in all its brilliance, including fat Petronella Damourt, her scant hair uncovered and both eyes blacked, for the poor lady had done her courageous best to defend her charges. And if she was not exactly lively on her legs, at least she had weight on her side. Behind her, two or three of the more curious girls, in their petticoats, stared anxiously round the door, while the others had sought refuge at the furthermost end of the barn.

Delphine Barbier du Rosoy, very pale, her naked arms black with bruises, was trying to cover her bosom with the torn shreds of her bodice. It was her terrible cry, on being brutally seized by a pair of lewd hands, that had awakened Angélique.

A man lay at her feet – one of the sailors from the *Gouldsboro*, who had been placed on sentry duty at the barn door that night, and whom the men from the *Fearless* had knocked out before battering down the door. This dastardly action, which bore full witness to their evil intentions, put Angélique in a fury of indignation, all the more so when she noticed among the ruffians some of 'her' wounded who, in spite of their dressings, their wounds, and the state of their arms or legs, had nevertheless found the energy to participate in this gay expedition.

'This is too much!' she exclaimed, beside herself with anger. 'You all deserve to be hanged. You are nothing but a lot of scum. I've had enough of you. Enough, I say! If you carry on like this any more, I shall wipe my hands of the lot of you, for all your blind eyes and spilled guts, your pus and your pox! You can all rot as far as I care ... You can die of thirst under my very eyes, and I wouldn't give you as much as a drop of water!

'How dare you behave yourselves like this in our country? Have you no sense of honour? Not a shred of it! You're nothing better than vermin, scarcely worth feeding to the cormorants ... and I'm sorry I didn't do just that when I had the opportunity.'

They were subdued by Angélique's wrath and the violence of her language, intimidated by her gaze, which was like that of an angry queen, and by her imperious air, emphasized on the present occasion by the severity of her hair style, and her dark violet robe of heavy silk and the way she had of drawing herself up to her full height and wrapping her sealskin cloak about her – as she looked them up and down like so many clodhoppers which, after all, was what they were. Thus cut down to size – and pretty poor specimens of humanity they were – the men from the *Fearless* found themselves tongue-tied, and Hyacinth Boulanger and his friend Aristide began to sidle away.

'Monsieur Vanneau, you were quite right to intervene,' said Angélique. 'Would you be so good as to go and fetch Father

Baure and the Abbé Lochmer whom I can see over there, probably on their way to say their first Mass.'

When the priests had come up and Angélique had told them of the sailors' behaviour, she went on:

'I leave them to you, Fathers. Try to make them understand that they have behaved as no Christian should, and that they deserve a severe penance. I must now go and inform Monsieur de Peyrac of what has happened.'

The Breton chaplain called down curses upon them all, warning his flock that all the torments of Hell awaited them, and the Recollect Father decided to take both the crews off to Mass, after hearing their confessions.

Then the sailors bowed their heads, sheathed their knives, and with heavy, repentant hearts and dragging footsteps, followed the two priests to the top of the hill.

CHAPTER SEVENTY-NINE

IN THE CABIN on the *Gouldsboro*, Joffrey de Peyrac had just concluded a business discussion with John Knox Mather, his assistants and the English admiral. Colin Paturel was in attendance as well as d'Urville, Berne and Manigault. Guttering candles bore witness to the fact that they had been at work since before dawn, for the ship for Boston was sailing on the tide.

Angélique got Enrico to announce her. She had had some difficulty in finding out where her husband spent his nights. Now she knew it was on board the *Gouldsboro* in the den he had occupied in his Rescator days.

On the whole she felt pleased that events were forcing her to act, and resume her position in their male lives. Since he had not cast her out, she would take her place once more, and he would have no choice but to speak to her again. This would enable them to have matters out and to clear up their misunderstandings. In those early morning hours Angélique felt at her best and ready to take control of her own destiny once more.

On seeing her, all the gentlemen stood up, wondering and silent, for each one of them in his own particular way had a place in his most secret thoughts for this uncommon woman, and each time she appeared she brought a new savour to their lives.

After greeting them she told them in clear and even tones about the incident that had brought the two crews to blows, one group having decided that the women were their legitimate booty, the other taking the view that the Lord had sent the girls most opportunely to become their lawful, wedded spouses.

'What a splendid idea,' Peyrac exclaimed, turning towards Colin. 'Of course the miraculous presence of these women could well provide the solution to the discontent of some of your men who feel frustrated on this score. Governor, that is a decision which you must take. We cannot entertain the idea of sending those girls on to Quebec, even if that was supposed to be their destination. We have neither the time nor the means at our disposal. I had thought of sending them to Port-Royal, but isn't the solution your men have in mind probably the wisest and best for all concerned? It was a private company that sponsored them and it is quite possible that none of the French settlements of Acadia – which in any case are impoverished – would feel inclined to assume responsibility for them. If they would like to stay here, good, we shall welcome them as wives for our French settlers. I leave you to work out the details of the agreement.'

Colin Paturel stood up, rolling up maps and pieces of parchment which he packed away into the huge pockets of his jerkin. He was now dressed with a sobriety and correctness that did not exclude a few concessions to finery demanded by his new position. His jabot and the frills at his wrists were extremely neat and the cuffs, collar and pockets of his russet-coloured coat were picked out with embroidery, the coat itself being cut away to reveal a pearl-grey underjacket of brocaded linen. With his trimmed beard and his grave, intent expression, Angélique had difficulty in recognizing him. He had already become another man, whose broad shoulders seemed to carry lightly the responsibilities laid upon them.

He tucked his round beaver-skin hat with the black feather beneath his arm.

'For my part, I am also in favour of keeping the girls here,' he declared, 'but Quebec may take umbrage at our welcoming their expected guests, and the powers that be may regard it as a seizure. Are we not running the risk of still further poisoning your relations with New France, Monsieur de Peyrac?'

'Leave that to me. If they complain, I will point out that they ought to entrust their convoys to pilots who don't lose them in the Antipodes. And in any case, our relations with New France

227

are already so strained that one incident more or less isn't going to make much difference. Anything, at any time, may serve as a pretext for war, or for peace. But one thing is certain: that now I no longer fear them, and that it is for me to decide whether or not to remain on good terms with them; and my view is that if the winds of fortune blew this charming cargo in our direction just when we needed it, we ought to regard it as a sign from heaven. I am in entire agreement with your men on this matter.'

'By the way,' Angélique remarked, 'I wish that man Gilles Vanereick, his Ines and all his crew would get to the devil out of here. They are causing endless trouble and if they have nothing better to do than to amuse themselves at our expense ... I managed to put them under the charge of the chaplains. I suppose they won't get up to any mischief for the time it takes to say Mass, but what after that? ... I am terribly sorry, Captain,' she went on, realizing that Vanereick was present, 'I am sorry I spoke so bluntly to your face, but you know as well as I do that your Caribbean seamen are no choirboys, and that a little of them goes a long way in well-ordered communities ...'

'All right! All right!' the privateer groaned. 'I shall go, I have been struck to the heart,' he added, resting an agonized hand on his breast.

'Let us go back on shore,' said Peyrac with finality.

Angélique, walking up the beach beside Vanereick, tried to soften the effect of her blunt remarks.

'At any other time, believe me, Monsieur, I would be delighted by your company, for you are most charming. And I know that my husband values his friendship with you. You stood with him in many a battle, and only just now again ...'

'In the Caribbean, we were Brothers of the Coast. That is a thing that binds men together for all time.'

Angélique, examining the somewhat portly although extremely agile figure of the French adventurer, thought that here was yet another man who had been part of Joffrey's unknown life. The two of them shared many memories, from which she was excluded. He also knew Cantor and often spoke affectionately of him as 'the lad' or 'the boy'.

Of course at some other time, as she assured him most sincerely, she would have been delighted to chat with him about her husband and her son's past life, but now she just could not cope, she had to admit it.

'I am worn out from nursing all those people. I am deeply concerned about their fate, and live in constant dread lest some fresh quarrel should still further swell the list of the wounded.'

He gave her a knowing glance.

'And you might add that your little heart has been wounded and that's what's upsetting you, isn't it? Yes! Yes it is! As if one couldn't see ... Come, come! I know women. Tell me, young woman, aren't you and your husband soon going to make up your quarrel? Come, come! What is so terrible about a little bit of fun like that? That Swiss fellow blabbed, that I agree! If he hadn't happened to be there at the wrong moment the whole thing would have blown over in a trice. It's no more than a peccadillo, if you think of it. So you tore a little hole in the marriage contract? ... Well, so what! What a fuss! You are far too attractive, my lovely lady, to be able to prevent things like that happening from time to time, here and there. You ought to go and see him and explain matters to him.'

'How I wish,' Angélique replied bitterly, 'that my husband shared your serenity of feelings. For it's true that he is dearer to me than anything else in all the world, but he is not a confiding man and even I ... sometimes feel frightened of him.'

'It is perfectly true that where you're concerned he is as dour as an Englishman and as jealous as a Saracen.

'Although you are suspicious of me, I would like you to know that I am a good friend of yours to the extent of having tried to convince Monsieur de Peyrac how ill-founded his anger is, or rather how unreasonable it is where you are concerned. I have tried to get him to see that there are certain kinds of women whom men, even men of honour, must needs forgive. "Take my Ines for instance," I said to him ...'

'Oh, come' Angélique protested with some annoyance, 'don't confuse me with your Ines.'

'And why not? I know what I'm talking about. For all that you are a fine lady and she is nothing but a little pest, popped out of some sea-shell in a sultry sea, you both of you belong to that exquisite strain of women who on account of their beauty, their skill in love, and that mysterious something known as charm, are capable of making men forgive the Creator for the aberration of mind He suffered the day He decided to make Eve from Adam's rib.

' "Now you must realize," I said to him, "you must realize that there are some women to whom we men must forgive certain lapses, for if we do not we run the risk of finding ourselves even more harshly punished than the guilty woman herself. The point is that when one is lucky enough to have been dealt an ace in the game of Love, one should make the most of it and thank the gods that be. For so many others go through life with nothing but second-rate cards in their hands ..." '

'I can imagine how my hot-tempered husband must have greeted your specious and immoral arguments,' Angélique replied with a melancholy smile.

A little while ago, back in the cabin on the *Gouldsboro* he had once again pretended to ignore her, and by adopting this attitude, she felt that he was striking her still harder than he had previously done. This encounter had taken the heart out of her and already she was feeling exhausted; what would it be like by the evening, after a day that brought her no relief, and when all her fears assailed her.

It was all so much more serious than Vanereick imagined.

What he did not know was that she could never endure being rejected by Peyrac. She would die of it. And the fear of this risk checked her spontaneity.

'But whatever have you done to him to have got under his skin like this?' Vanereick cried, scrutinizing her with his shrewd, coal-black, sparkling eyes. 'It's inconceivable! ... I would never have thought a great pirate like him could be so vulnerable, with all his experience of life, of science, of philosophy and of the ups and downs of fortune! He made a terrific impression on us all in the Caribbean on Tortuga Island and in the Gulf of Mexico, and the women were all the keener on him because he never seemed to care a jot for them. But I can see that, as soon as he laid eyes on you, he succumbed. Making love to you must really be something ... unforgettable, prodigious ...'

'Captain, please keep your imagination under control,' Angélique interrupted, laughing. 'I am only an ordinary mortal, alas!'

'Too much so! Too much of an ordinary mortal. Just what we men need. Good! I have managed to make you laugh. All is not lost. Now listen to my advice. Say no more about all this business, think no more of it! Go to confession. It is a good thing to begin by seeking God's forgiveness. And as for your husband's, just slip into his bed one night without warning him, choosing the right moment, and I guarantee your absolution.'

'I am beginning to think you really are a true friend,' Angélique told him, feeling much more cheerful. 'Now, having said that, my dear Vanereick, if you have nothing better to do round here than to repair broken hearts, once again I would suggest that you set sail. There is a good wind, the fog has lifted, and I for one have had enough of spending my days from dawn till dusk dressing the wounds of men bent on cutting one another's throats. If you don't sail on the next tide, there will be more bloodshed caused by your hotheads from Tortuga.

'Those of your crew who were wounded are well on their way to recovery and I can safely hand them back to you now, quite fit enough to join in your future expeditions.'

Dame Petronella Damourt came rolling rather than running towards them, her hair still tousled and her eyes full of tears.

'Oh, Madame, please help me, the girls have gone mad! I simply can't control them. They are talking of running away from here and of setting out across the forest on foot, goodness only knows where to!'

CHAPTER EIGHTY

'WELL NOW, girls, do you or do you not want to get married?'

Colin's voice, booming out as his tall figure appeared on the theshold, put a sudden stop to the weeping and lamentations that filled the barn. Had not Angélique been beside him the more excitable girls would have died of fright. As it was they rushed towards her and clustered in a group round her, finding reassurance in her female presence.

'Well, my dears, whatever's going on? Why all this noise?' Angélique asked with her most conciliatory smile.

'Tell me everything,' said Colin, striking his broad chest. 'I am the Governor here and I promise you that the wretches who frightened you, gentle ladies, will be punished.'

They immediately launched out into a description of their impressions, all speaking at once, which went from 'I didn't hear anything, I was asleep' to 'A beastly man grabbed me by the wrist and dragged me outside ... I don't know what he wanted from me ...'

'He stank of rum,' Delphine Barbier du Rosoy ended up with a grimace of disgust, for as bad luck would have it she, one of the 'young ladies', had been the most roughly handled in the scuffle. Her dignity obliged her to fight back her tears of humiliation.

Angélique drew a comb from her belt and did her best to tidy the poor girl's hair. Then she wiped swollen noses and eyes, smoothed folds on neckerchiefs and bodices, and decided to call for a large pot of broth and some good wine, which, in the eyes of the French is the best panacea of all ills.

Meanwhile, Colin Paturel continued to question them and listen to their complaints, stooping his tall frame down towards the young creatures as they spoke. His rough, kindly appearance coupled with the attention he paid towards them eventually reassured them and even Delphine, although offended that he should have included her among the 'girls' when he first addressed them, looked up trustingly at him.

'Oh, please sir, please have us taken to Quebec, we beg you!'

'But it must be by land! We never want to set foot on board a ship again, never in our lives. . . .'

Poor girls! It was obvious they had no idea of the sort of place Canada was, any more than they had ever heard mention of Acadia or Nova Scotia, even supposing that a single one among them even knew that the earth was round or had ever set eyes on a map.

Bearing these things in mind, Colin, after promising them that all the unpleasant characters who had pestered them that morning would have left the neighbourhood before dusk, began to tell them about the settlement of Gouldsboro to which the Lord seemed to have guided them by some inexplicable miracle – but everyone knew that miracles were by nature inexplicable – at the very moment when a number of worthy French sailors, having decided henceforth to lead the healthy, courageous lives of settlers, were lamenting the fact that they had no valiant wives at their sides to assist them and make their lives more pleasant.

It was a lovely part of the country, never frozen up in the winter, and the climate was far less severe than that of Canada.

And when they learned that the 'King's gift', which they were so distressed about losing was a mere pittance compared with what this kindly Governor of such handsome appearance was prepared to offer to newly-married couples in the settlement of Gouldsboro – nor would they need to set sail again across the fury of the deep, nor journey through forests infested with Indians and wild beasts – their smiles returned and they began to exchange glances, tempted to accept the offer. There were, however, a few protests, more for appearance' sake than anything else.

'My three friends and I had been promised officers,' Delphine said with grave modesty. 'In the convent we were taught how to run a house, how to receive important guests, how to make conversation and curtsy to royalty. I feel sure that the husbands intended for us in Quebec didn't reek of rum.'

'Yes, you're probably right,' Angélique agreed. 'They would be more likely to smell of rye or maize whisky. An excellent drink, be it added, especially welcome during the long, hard winters. Come, ladies,' she added with a laugh, 'if you're going to make a fuss about every trifle here in America, how will you ever face the Iroquois, the storms and the famines, and all that awaits you in the New World? And that's as true of Canada as of here. In fact, if anything, it's worse there, as it's a more remote and less civilized place.'

'And what about me,' the Moorish girl inquired, 'won't I be treated like a slave as in the West Indies, as I was warned that people with dark skins are treated there? I was brought up in a convent at Neuilly where a great lady came regularly to pay for my board and lodging. I can read and write and embroider on silk.'

Colin took hold of the girl good-naturedly by the chin.

'You'll find a taker, my pretty one, if you are as gentle and sensible as you seem to be,' he assured her, 'and I myself will make sure you get properly settled.

'In any case we shall allow you plenty of time to think over these proposals and to discuss them with your chaperon. And if they don't suit you, Monsieur de Peyrac will have you sent on without any further ado to one of the Acadian settlements on the other side of Frenchman Bay, where you will certainly be well received.'

Dame Petronella was in a dreadful quandary. She was much better informed than her companions and far more level-headed than she appeared, and she was well aware that these French settlers, interspersed as they were with a fair number of Englishmen, without being wreckers as Job Simon alleged, were hardly among the King of France's most devoted subjects. Moreover, she too found it hard to grasp her precise geographical situation, and the maps Colin and Count Peyrac had unrolled in order to convince her that Quebec was not just next door had only succeeded in adding to her confusion.

'Oh, if only our dear benefactress was here!' she sighed.

'Then we'd be able to set up a regular whorehouse!' Julienne rasped out in her vulgar voice. 'She was as well up in the running of whorehouses as she was in saying prayers and that ...'

Antoinette, her sworn enemy, grabbed her by the hair, and when they had been separated, Colin turned to Julienne and said:

'You, girl, come here!'

She was the only one to whom he had spoken with such familiarity, showing that he was under no illusion about what kind of a girl she was.

'I can't keep you here,' he told her after he had taken her off into a corner. 'Not because you're common, but because you are unwell, and I don't want any of that for my men.'

Julienne immediately began to shriek her head off in protest without worrying in the least about creating a scandal.

'Me, not well? It's not true! Not so long ago I was examined by a doctor at the Chatelet who told me that I was as fresh as a rose. And since I spent all my time after that locked up in the orphanage, what men do you imagine I could have caught anything from, you and your illnesses! Madame Angélique, come and help me! Listen to what he says ... He says I'm rotten!'

'This woman is unwell,' Colin reiterated, calling Angélique to witness, 'just take a look at her.'

Indeed, the girl's chubby face was an unpleasant waxen colour and there were dark rings round her eyes as if she had blackened them with kohl. Moreover, the excessive brightness of her eyes indicated that she was running a high temperature.

'I don't think that she is sick,' said Angélique, 'but I'm sure that she was hurt in the wreck. But she has consistently refused to allow me to treat her, and her wound is getting worse. Come on, Julienne, let me attend to you, or your life could be at stake ...'

'Oh go to hell ...' the girl replied coarsely.

Angélique slapped her twice across the face, sending her tumbling to the ground. In fact the unfortunate creature could scarcely stand anyway.

'Let yourself be seen to,' Colin concluded, 'otherwise there'll be no quarter. I shall pack you off this very evening with the men on board the *Fearless*.'

Lying there on the ground Julienne looked vanquished, a pitiful sight. Her wild eyes darted hither and thither in panic, seeking a way out.

'It's that I'm frightened,' she moaned, unable to think of any better argument. 'You'll hurt me when you cut me up.'

Aristide Beaumarchand's grating voice was heard suddenly behind them, for somehow or other he had managed to slide into the barn.

'Not with her, you won't, my lovely! She won't hurt you, that I guarantee. There isn't anyone who'll make you better with a lighter hand. Just cast your peepers on this piece of handiwork. Hand-stitched, I assure you.'

With deft fingers he undid the laces of his breeches for Julienne, fascinated by his authoritative manner, to examine his wretched pale belly traversed across its full width by a long purple scar.

'Just take a look at that! Well, it was her, Dame Angélique, who sewed me up with a needle and thread, yes, that's exactly what she did, my lovely. All me guts was lying on the sand. I'd had it, and that's a fact.'

'It's impossible!' cried Julienne, accompanying her exclamation with many a heartfelt oath.

'It's as I say. Well now, look at it today. And what's below *that* is still in good trim and at your service, my lovely!'

'Enough of your broad jokes,' Angélique interrupted, seeing the turn the demonstration was about to take. 'Aristide, you are a good-for-nothing, and I wouldn't encourage the devil's daughter herself or the lowest trollop on earth to have anything to do with you. It would still be too good for you and too bad for her.'

'You are offending me; I have my dignity,' said Aristide, slowly lacing up his breeches again . . . 'I'd even go so far as to say you are insulting me.'

'That's enough,' Colin intervened, moving the man away. 'You've no call whatever to be in here.'

And he seized him by the collar and propelled him in the direction of the door.

'Upon my word, you're harder to shake off than vermin. I shall have to drown you with my own hands in the end.'

Julienne was roaring with laughter, greatly cheered up.

'I likes him, I do! He's a rare one that, a real man, I calls him.'

'Well, I'm pleased to hear you think so. But I warn you that he's the worst scoundrel in the two hemispheres.'

She knelt down beside the miserable, limp creature who nevertheless still managed to summon the necessary cheekiness to crack jokes and distribute insults. A typical child of the Court of Miracles in Paris.

'I know why it is you don't want me to dress your wound,' she whispered to the girl.

'You can't possibly know,' the girl protested with a hunted look.

'Yes I do! I can guess ... It's because you have been branded with the fleur-de-lis! ... Listen, I promise to say nothing to the Governor, but on condition that you behave yourself and do exactly as I say.'

The terrified expression on poor Julienne's face was tantamount to an admission.

'Honest, you won't tell on me?' she whispered.

'I swear it,' said Angélique.

Then crossing two fingers and spitting on the ground, she twice repeated the secret sign of recognition used among members of the Paris underworld.

Completely dumbfounded, Julienne never so much as made a squeak, allowing Angélique to lay bare her swollen ribs, and apply poultices to them, and she docilely swallowed potions and drinks of herbal tea, so preoccupied by the deep mysteries that awaited her in the land of America, that she even forgot to wail. Reassured about the girl's condition, Angélique propped her head up and tucked her up comfortably in her corner, giving her a friendly tap on the cheek before leaving her.

'That man Aristide you've taken such a fancy to, I bet he has a fleur-de-lis branded on his back too, just like you. Get better quick, my lass. We'll have you married too ... and what a fine pair you'll make! ... That I'll swear.'

Julienne's eyelids were beginning to droop over her fiery eyes which, through sheer weariness, were at last losing some of their fierceness. Calmed by the medicines she had been made to take, she was falling asleep.

'What a funny lot of people you do have here,' she whispered, 'and who are you, Madame? Lady of America ... you can see things that are hidden from other people. That plait of hair suits you ... You look like those holy queens you see ... on missals. Surely a poor rough girl like me could never be *that* lucky...'

CHAPTER EIGHTY-ONE

THE FLAGS were flapping in the wind and the sails ready to catch the breeze.

Once again everyone was down at the quayside.

'Won't you even kiss me goodbye?' asked Vanereick, holding out his arms to Angélique. 'Not even when I'm going away?'

She ran to him and kissed him on both cheeks, feeling the comfort of his manly arms about her, and utterly heedless of the presence of the entire population assembled along the harbour side watching their demonstrations of friendship.

Let them think what they wanted, jealous lot that they were! She had the right to kiss anyone she liked.

'Keep your courage up!' Vanereick whispered in her ear. 'You will win! But remember my advice. First to confession, then to bed . . .'

He waved his big, feathered hat and jumped aboard the boat that was to take him out to his ship.

The *Fearless* stood quivering with the surge of the tide, its yard-arms black with sailors ready to spread the sails, tugging at its anchor like a thoroughbred horse at its halter.

Cheers and bravos mingled with the terse words of command that came from the bridge in Gilles Vanereick's voice.

'Prosper Jardin, are you standing by?'

'Aye aye, sir,' the quartermaster replied.

'Miguel Martinez, are you standing by?'

'Aye aye, sir,' the leading topman replied.

And when he had been through the whole list, 'Stand by. Cast off ship!' he cried with a sweeping gesture.

The ropes were released, the sails filled out, billowing and dazzling white against the blue sky, and slowly the *Fearless* began to get under way, tacking between the islands, escorted by the fly boat and the small cutter which Count Peyrac and Colin Paturel had boarded to escort their guests as far as the exit from the narrow channel.

On the poop deck, the fair Ines stood waving her fan and yellow satin scarf in Angélique's direction. Reassured about her Vanereick's feelings towards her, now that she was setting sail with him again, the little half-caste adventurer felt able to show her friendship towards the woman whom she had considered her main rival.

When the ship was no more than a distant white triangle on the horizon Angélique returned to the fort. On the way back she met the herb man and his Caribbean slave, sitting side by side on the sand chewing cloves. For some complicated reason they had asked to stay on for a while. There had been a certain amount of swopping after the sharing out of the loot: precious stones, bolts of cloth and merchandise, in which – a unique case in the annals of privateering – the captain of the prize ship, Paturel, formerly known as Gold Beard, had himself participated. In exchange for two priceless emeralds, Vanereick had agreed to take on board the buccaneers regarded as undesirables. Despite their idleness and untrustworthiness they would serve as replacements for the men he had lost in battle, provided they were kept up to scratch with a touch of the rope's end.

So it was that Hyacinth Goulanger had been parted from his Barbary Coast brother, Aristide, who, claiming that his stomach was still weak and swearing by all that was holy that he would behave himself, had begged to stay on in Gouldsboro. 'And I've made a hit, you see,' he whispered in Hyacinth's hairy ear; 'a smashing girl called Julienne. When I've got where I want with her, I'll let you know and you can come back and fetch me . . .'

So it was no good thinking they were done with the *Fearless* for good! They would see her back again with her cargo of black patches, wooden legs, toothless grins and breath reeking of Jamaica rum; they would see the gay dogs from Tortuga once more, with their feathers, their ribbons, their print turbans, their belts stuffed full of cutlasses, daggers, sabres, pistols and frightening-looking hatchets.

The summer was only just beginning.

And they would also be seeing again the English and Bostonian ships which had sailed at dawn, and the Acadian sloops that had set off full of Mic-Macs and – purchased with some of the proceeds of the sale of the cattle they had brought – a selection of luxury goods to delight the hearts of the ladies of Port-Royal over on the other side of Frenchman Bay: lace, velvet, trimmings, soap and perfume, arms and ammunition for the defence of the French fort, embroidered banners, and a magnificent windfall in the form of a ciborium and monstrance of silver-gilt seized from the Spanish booty of a converted pirate. Surely God would be doubly honoured in the poor church of the oldest of the French colonies founded by Champlain?

A strange calm seemed to fall on the village, whose inhabitants dispersed in silence to their wooden houses.

'Oh look!' young Séverine suddenly exclaimed, 'there are only two ships left lying at anchor in the bay, the *Gouldsboro* and the *Heart of Mary*. After that great forest of masts swaying about there these last few days, how empty it looks!'

'Two ships lying at anchor in the bay' ... whispered the voice of the visionary nun in Angélique's ears.

CHAPTER EIGHTY-TWO

'I SHALL GO to you, my love. I must go to you ...' she kept on repeating to herself. 'I am frightened. You are a man; your two feet are firmly on the ground; your sleep is deep and nothing can trouble its mystery; whereas I am a woman ... and because I am a woman, I can read the meaning behind symbols. And what I see there is terrible! I can no longer sleep.'

In spite of the fact that peace had returned once more, in spite of the songs the sailors hummed as they hung about in the vicinity of their promised wives:

> Ten maids one day I chanced to spy
> When o'er the meadows I did hie
> One was Dine and one was Chine
> One Claudine and one Martine ...

In spite of the more relaxed atmosphere that had followed upon the days of distress and anguish, a change of which all the settlers in Gouldsboro were conscious, Angélique found that she could not share in the enjoyment of it.

July came sizzling in, rising to the surface of the world in a puff of scorching heat. It made people's heads swim with the chirping of crickets, the buzzing of bees, the heavy scent of flowers, resin, and overheated sap. The tall candelabra of pink, blue and white lupins, rising up thickly in banks of fairyland beauty, vied with the splendour of golden rod, monuments of pure metal carved into a thousand arabesques, that stood along the edge of the woods. Wild eglantine mingled with the roses against the houses, and clouds of delicate poppies covered the riverbanks right down to the sea.

The sea birds, in their long, white lines, glided through blue air tinged with pink.

The bay, too, was pink like an open flower, like surrendered flesh . . .

> Catherine and Cath'rinette
> Comely, dimple-cheeked Suzette
> The Duchess of the Maine,
> And Montbazon, I saw them plain . . .

For Angélique alone the fabulous languor of each dazzling day, with its evening full of mauve clouds fringed with fire, was like slow poison.

The day after the departure of the ships, after yet a further sleepless night, she decided to get herself some weapons, for she had lost her pistols at the time of the attack on the English village.

Yann le Couennec used his key to open the door to Count Peyrac's study in the fort, for Angélique had met Yann near the armoury and he had told her that the *Gouldsboro* had brought in a large stock of pistols, arquebuses and muskets, and that the Count had had the best and most up-to-date models placed in his study so that he could examine them at his leisure.

Yann took the guns out of a chest where he had put them himself, and spread them out on the big table on which lay goose quills and ink stands; then he opened the narrow window to let the light in. The little narrow room was full of Joffrey's familiar smell, the smell of tobacco and sandalwood oil, an Eastern perfume with which he impregnated his clothes. It was a strong yet subtle perfume, somewhat disconcerting in its originality which did not seek to please but was in perfect harmony with the distant yet seductive personality of its user.

'When you see Monsieur le Comte, would you please tell him what I require,' Angélique asked Yann. 'I have not seen him yet this morning.'

Would he respond to this appeal that she was making to him in everyday words, but with a trembling heart; would he come?

She bent to examine the handsome new weapons, and absorbed in their contemplation forgot her cares. Some of the English gunlocks showed interesting improvements. The gunlock was the mechanism by which the charge was ignited and varied in its details according to the country of origin. In these English pistols the battery was combined with the cover of the pan which admittedly increased the risk of accidental discharge, but was compensated for by a little catch at the bottom of the hammer known to initiates as the hammer-lock or dog-lock.

But in spite of this undoubted advance, Angélique still preferred the French type of lock – no doubt because it was familiar to her. Her eye was caught by a long-barrelled Scandinavian gun with an ivory stock set with amber, the elegant appearance of which pleased her. Its firing system was rather antiquated but it did have the advantage that it could be armed with any flint picked up at random, whereas other types of locks required carefully cut and calibrated flints which were too complicated to produce in a more or less uncivilized land like this.

She was busy turning the pistol over and over in her hands, examining the cocking mechanism, the capacity of the magazine, when she sensed that Joffrey de Peyrac had entered the room and was standing behind her.

'I came to select some pistols,' she said, half turning her head in his direction; 'I lost mine at Newehewanik.'

She could feel the weight of his glance on the nape of her neck and once again she realized just how weak she felt, how in spite of everything a secret joy rose up within her at his very presence.

From behind he had almost failed to recognize her, although Yann had warned him that Madame de Peyrac was in his study.

The deeply pleated, violet taffeta dress and the pale gold plait she wore in a coil at the nape of her neck made her look different. He had thought for a moment that some unknown noblewoman, some great lady must have arrived ... but where from? ... Still, so many people kept on disembarking at Gouldsboro these days, that anything was possible!

A fleeting impression, but how piquant! But it was by the dexterity with which the 'stranger' handled the pistols that he had recognized HER. There was only one woman in all the world who could do so with such utter familiarity – Angélique.

Likewise there was only one woman in all the world with such beautiful shoulders.

He drew closer.

'Have you found anything that suits you?' he asked her in a voice he sought to make neutral, but which to her seemed icy.

'Actually,' she replied, forcing herself to remain calm, 'I cannot make up my mind. Some of them seem excellent for shooting, but are cumbersome; others are elegant but have defects of design that could be dangerous.'

'You are hard to please. These arms bear the seal of the best workmen in Europe: Thuraine of Paris, Abraham Hill of England, and this ivory pistol comes from Maestricht in Holland. Look at that warrior's head carved into the end of the butt ...'

'It is certainly handsome.'

'But you don't like it.'

'I had grown accustomed to my old French pistols, with all their bits and pieces – screws, keys, flints – that one had to keep in one's pockets and that could easily go astray but that allowed for quite a lot of finesse.'

She felt that they were like two actors speaking their lines in a play. Neither of them had their minds on what they were saying but they still went on working away at it.

Count Peyrac seemed to hesitate then turned and walked over to the half-open chest. Returning, he placed before her a long box of inlaid mahogany.

'This was what I got Erikson to bring back for you from Europe,' he said briefly.

In the centre of the lid the letter *A* had been inlaid in gold, its scrolls and curves forming a medallion of intertwining enamelled and mother-of-pearl flowers. The same flowers formed a posy on either side of the letter, the craftsmanship being so fine that she could make out the minutest details of each flower, down to the delicate pistils in silver or gold filigree work, and the veins on the green enamel leaves.

Angélique laid her fingers on the ironwork lock. The lid opened to reveal a green velvet-lined case containing two pistols and their accessories – a powder horn, a pair of tongs, a priming box and a bullet mould.

Everything was made of the finest materials and bore the same stamp of elegance, delicacy and beauty.

At a glance Angélique could see that these weapons had been conceived, designed, and made for her.

Executed with minute care, every detail pointed to the fact that the gunsmith, ironsmith and engraver who had worked on these beautiful weapons had striven to delight the woman for whose use they were intended. And that woman was she, Angélique, a woman on the other side of the world.

They had doubtless received special, carefully prepared instructions and must have worked from detailed plans and drawings prepared by Count Peyrac, which had been taken over the ocean and been given to them in their workshops in Seville or Salamanca, or Rivoli or Madrid. And inasmuch as the instructions were accompanied by leather purses bulging with gold doubloons, they had been careful to give their wholehearted attention to the execution of this unusual order – pistols for a woman's hand.

'Such a lovely gift,' thought Angélique, 'which he had thought of specially for me ... with love ... with love! A present he intended to give me this spring in Gouldsboro! ...'

Her hand trembled as she lifted out the magnificent pistols one after the other. It would have taken days to take in all their refinements. They had been designed not only for her to fire in self-defence with the maximum speed and the minimum of discomfort – loading a firearm with delicate fingers was not always a simple matter – but also to appeal to her particular tastes.

How could she fail to be delighted by those inlaid bunches of flowers that likewise decorated the shining butts, fashioned out of wood the colour of red amber.

The barrels were long, of Spanish steel, an extremely rare product, given a bluish tint by the addition of oil so as to eliminate tell-tale flashes of light when the user was waiting in ambush. Inside they were rifled to ensure accuracy of fire but were smooth at the mouth.

'How well he knows what I like, how well he knows what gives me pleasure!'

And as for the lock, it was a marvel! By combining the battery and the cover of the pan in a single part, it was possible to eliminate four moving parts, thus simplifying the mechanism and ensuring that the touch-hole could only open at the precise moment of impact of the flint on the battery. Hidden between two silver scrolls lay the main spring, and the fact that this was fixed outside the gun and not, as previously, inside, was bound to make it exceptionally powerful. The difficulty of setting the spring was offset by the presence of a ring on the threaded screw that regulated the vice. Not only was this ring exactly the size of Angélique's index finger – this she verified there and then – thus enabling her to set the main spring without effort, but she could also adjust the vice by hand, obviating the necessity to carry around a cumbersome screwdriver or similar tool, which was often liable, as she had had occasion to note, to go astray.

Finally the cock had a little projection at its base against which the spring acted directly without need for an intermediate tumbler, thus eliminating one further part. And behind

243

this assembly, which had been designed and put together with clockwork precision, there was a sliding bolt, which very few gunsmiths had had the daring or skill to make up to that time, enabling several shots to be fired one after the other quite safely and without reloading.

Behind the quality of so handsome a present Angélique had a picture of her husband bending over his files last autumn, secretly, just before the ship set sail, dashing off rapidly and peremptorily with his customary inspiration, outline drawings complete with calculations and masses of figures that compressed the essential points of this masterpiece into a few strokes of the pen.

He must have wondered what material to use: metal – copper or silver – ivory or bone? ... He had opted for wood, which was lighter than metal and less brittle than ivory, and it must have been he who had specified the Turkish-style curved butt, which grew narrower on the curve to give a better grip to the fingers and enable the pistol to be held firmly without fatigue.

She recognized his hand in the double action of the 'vice' which, stripped of its flint and suitably tightened, could serve as a hammer with which to strike, in a specially constructed cavity, a charge of gunpowder, the secret of whose manufacture was known to the Count alone, and which constituted a completely new method of firing.

As for the ornamentation and the inlaid work, IT WAS FOR HER that he had chosen flowers.

A lump rose in her throat, and she asked herself why he had chosen to give her this gift that morning? Was it a mark of reconciliation? Did he want her to understand that the period of ostracism he had imposed upon her was coming to an end?

Standing before the window, Joffrey de Peyrac, with a look he could have wished to appear less avid, sought to read Angélique's thoughts in her sensitive face.

A pink wave had mantled her over-pale cheeks as she raised the lid of the box, followed by an expression of wonder on discovering the beauty of the pistols. He had been unable to resist giving her this pleasure. He so longed to see her happy on his account, even if only for a brief moment!

She was biting her lower lip and he saw her long eyelashes flutter.

Then at last she turned and looked at him with those admirable eyes and murmured:

'How can I ever thank you, my lord?'

He gave a start, for the words reminded him of the first occasion he had made her a gift in those far-off days in Toulouse – an emerald necklace – and she had possibly thought of it, too.

He replied dryly, almost haughtily:

'I don't know whether you have noticed that the lock is of the Miquelet type. The exterior spring gives considerably more force to the shot, and the hand is protected by a special flange.'

'So I see.'

The flange was decorated with a salamander, or a long-tailed lizard, whose tongue of golden filigree shot out towards a red enamel poppy on the butt. Actually it was definitely a salamander, for the creature's ivory body was dotted with spots of jade. At the back, the metal of the gun-lock was embossed with a round posy of May flowers, of incredibly delicate workmanship, and the hammer, known as the 'dog', which the craftsmen had carved with the same minute care into the shape of the snout of a fierce-looking little pug, was adorned with an eye of gilded glass which blazed with light.

But beneath all this prettiness and refinement lay hidden the responsive, implacable tension of the mechanism.

And while with her deft fingers, and the familiar light touch she brought to the most unexpected tasks, she handled the different parts of the gun-lock, he was rapt in contemplation of her beauties, and the contrast between her femininity and the businesslike way she handled the guns made him catch his breath.

Through the open neck of her bodice he glimpsed her pearly skin, all the more luminous for being surrounded by shadows and for melting so softly into a warm, dark hollow full of mystery.

The milky softness of this woman's flesh, this fragile, smooth, swelling corolla, it was in this that he saw the symbol of her weakness, the vulnerability of her sex.

A tender-breasted woman, that was what she was, that was what she remained however formidable she might appear with a gun in her hand.

'She has borne my children within her,' he thought, 'my only sons. I never wanted to have children by any other woman.'

The spell of her charm emanating from her entire being overcame him, intoxicated him, made him grow numb, filled him with the desire to clasp his hands around her slender waist, to rest them on her hips and feel her warmth through the amethyst-coloured taffeta of her bodice. For too long now his arms had been empty of her.

He drew closer and said in a slightly hoarse voice, pointing to the pistol she held in her hand:

'Load it! Cock it.'

'I am not sure I would know how. I am not familiar with this kind of lock.'

He took the gun from her hands and promptly loaded it with bullets, gunpowder and primer. She followed the movements of his brown hands, longing to stoop down and kiss them.

He handed the gun back to her saying: 'There!' And added with a caustic smile:

'You could kill me now ... and be rid of your troublesome husband.'

Angélique turned deathly pale. She felt as if she would never recover her breath, and she had the greatest difficulty in laying the pistol back in its case with a trembling hand.

'How could you say anything so foolish!' she at last managed to say. 'You are incredibly unkind!'

'Ah! So you think you are the victim?'

'At the moment, yes ... You know perfectly well that in saying things like that you are tormenting me appallingly.'

'And undeservedly, no doubt?'

'Yes ... no ... yes, more undeservedly than you think ... I have not done you as great a wrong as you want to think ... and you know it well ... But you are insanely proud.'

'And you are fantastically dishonest and impudent!'

And he felt, as he had that other night, an insensate desire to pummel her, to strike her down, and at the same time to luxuriate in her perfume, in her warmth, as in some heady incense, and to lose himself in the brightness of her green eyes, now flashing with anger and love, with despair and tendernesss.

For fear of succumbing, he made off towards the door.

'Joffrey,' she cried, 'are we going to allow ourselves to fall into the trap?'

'What trap?'

'The trap our enemies have set for us.'

'What enemies?'

'The enemies who have made up their minds to separate us in order to strike us down more easily. And now it has happened. I don't know how it was all contrived at the beginning and what tricks were used to bring about our downfall, but I know that it has happened. You see, it has happened. *The fact is that we have been separated.'*

She glided over to where he stood and laid one hand upon his heart:

'My love, are we to allow them such an easy victory?'

He drew away from her with a violence that betokened his fear of giving in too quickly.

'That's rich. You behave in a completely senseless manner and then accuse me of acting illogically. For example, at Houssnock, whatever gave you the idea of setting off for the English village?'

'But you yourself sent me orders to do so.'

'I! Never on your life!'

'Well then, who did? . . .'

He stared at her speechless, suddenly struck by a terrifying presentiment.

Although of very superior intelligence, Peyrac nevertheless was typically masculine in his approach to the world. Men proceed by leaps of the intellect, whereas women are guided by an instinct of cosmic foresight.

Men bound forward like the big cats. For a long time they remain motionless, sometimes stagnant, causing anxiety by their refusal to move, then suddenly they leap forward, rending the skies, discovering, in a single flash, all that the eye can see, and penetrating still further, pushing back the limits of the horizon.

That was how Peyrac felt as Angélique's voice unleashed within him a series of passionate impulses, and he saw everything about him transformed, taking on a new signficance, a different aspect. Yes, they were faced with a grave peril, and yet his male logic rejected the onslaught of the occult.

But Angélique was not mistaken. She had a greater feeling for the mystical than he, and he was well aware that *that mattered too.*

He kept up the struggle.

'Stuff and nonsense, all these feelings of yours,' he grumbled. 'It would all be too easy.

'All adulterous women would have to do would be to claim that demons were involved. Was it they, Madame, who were our enemies, or was it chance that brought your erstwhile lover to Casco Bay, ready to fold you in his arms? . . .'

'I don't know. But Father de Vernon said that when diabolical things were afoot, chance was always on the side of evil, that is to say on the Devil's side, on the side of destruction and unhappiness.'

'And who is this Father de Vernon?'

'A Jesuit who took me in his ship from Maquoit to Pentagouet.'

At this remark Joffrey de Peyrac seemed thunderstruck.

'You fell into the hands of the French Jesuits?' he cried, in a strange voice.

'Yes! At Brunswick-Falls I only just avoided being taken off to Quebec as a prisoner.'

'Tell me about it.'

And as she briefly described adventures since her departure from Houssnock, he saw in his mind's eye Outakke, the great Iroquois chieftain, saying to him:

'You have a treasure! They will try to take it from you ...' Had he not always feared that it would be through her, Angélique, that they would attempt to strike at him? She had spoken rightly.

Enemies were lurking about them, more cunning, wily and subtle than the 'Cowardly Ones', the spirits of Air.

Could he deny that he had suspected this himself, inasmuch as he still had in a pocket of his doublet the anonymous message an unknown sailor had brought him on the evening after the battle with the *Heart of Mary*, a scrap of parchment on which the following words had been penned:

'Your wife is on Old Ship Island with Gold Beard. Land on the north side of the island so that they do not see you, and you will be able to catch them in one another's arms.'

Infernal spirits, without a doubt, but spirits which, lurking among the islands, were capable of taking pen in hand to ensure that such a damaging denunciation reached the intended quarter.

He drew a deep breath. Everything seemed to have changed, to have taken on a different aspect, and in the tumult, Angélique's infidelity no longer appeared to him to have been so odiously calculated. She had been caught up in a web of plots, further complicated by a series of coincidences. It was inevitable that so feminine a woman should reveal the vulnerable side of her nature, but beneath her weakness he had seen evidence of an extraordinary courage. He thought back to that night in the island, when he had watched Colin and Angélique from afar and had seen clear signs of their struggle against temptation.

Of course, it was not pleasant for him to have to admit that she could be tempted by another man, but in this he knew that he was behaving as unreasonably as a young boy.

What did remain was the loyalty towards him which she had shown that night. And as for what had taken place on board the *Heart of Mary*, he did not particularly want to know the precise details, although various things that Colin Paturel had said had hinted at what had occurred.

Sometimes he even thought he would more readily forgive Angélique for giving her body than for a single passionate kiss, for he knew by heart every aspect of her responses. For her, a kiss had always seemed to commit her entire being more completely than the impersonal surrender to physical intimacy. That was how she was, his unpredictable goddess! She would more willingly give her body than her lips. And he would have been prepared to bet that with 'the others', it had always been thus. He would have liked to think that his were the only lips she enjoyed, but once again, in his demand that this should be so, he was displaying ridiculous, adolescent feelings. This was what she had brought him to, after a life in which, on grounds of well-considered policy, he had sought to give women an attractive and important place, but one which should never be allowed to affect his own inner being.

But what was the point of dwelling on what had been?

Far more serious were the risks she had run, the traps which had been laid for her, and this must all be sorted out.

He paced up and down in front of her, glancing at her from time to time, looking at her, as she thought, somewhat more gently, then his eyes would harden again under the influence of his thoughts, his fears and his suspicions.

'Why do you think Father de Vernon allowed you to go free?' he asked.

'Indeed, I have no idea. Possibly because, during the three days we spent at sea, he had become convinced that I could not be the She-Devil of Acadia as everyone seemed to imagine.'

'And what about Maupertuis and his son? Where are they?

'I imagine they have been taken back forcibly to Canada.'

The Count exploded:

'This means war!' he cried. 'I've had enough of their underhand methods! I shall send my ships against Quebec!'

'No, don't do that! We should be wasting our strength and I would be accused more bitterly than ever of spreading misfortune. But we must not be parted! Do not let them prevail against us by tearing us apart, by hurting us . . . Joffrey, my love, you know that you are everything to me . . . Do not reject me or I shall die of grief. Now and henceforth I am nothing without you! Nothing!'

And she held out her arms towards him like a lost child.

She was in his arms and he was crushing her to him. He still had not forgiven her but he did not want her to be taken from him. He did not want anyone to threaten her, to make attempts on her life, her precious, irreplaceable life.

His iron embrace crushed her and she trembled, overwhelmed with joy, her cheek against his hard cheek. The sky reeled, dazzling bright.

'A miracle! A miracle!' cried a voice from afar off in the distance of space. 'A miracle! A miracle!'

They could hear the sound of voices outside, growing louder and louder.

'A miracle! A miracle! My lord, where are you? Come quick! A real miracle!'

It was Yann Le Couennec's voice in the courtyard beneath the window.

Count Peyrac released his grip on Angélique and drew away from her, as if regretting the impulsive gesture he had made in opening his arms to her. He went over to the window.

'What's going on?'

'A real miracle, my lord! The benefactress . . . the noble lady, the patroness of the "King's Girls", who we all thought had been drowned . . . well, she wasn't. Some cod fishers from Saint-Malo picked her up on an island in the bay with her secretary, and a sailor, and a boy whose life she had saved. They are coming by boat . . . They are just arriving in the harbour.'

CHAPTER EIGHTY-THREE

'DID YOU HEAR that?' Peyrac asked, turning towards Angélique. 'The benefactress! It looks as if the sea found the honourable duchess and her pen pusher too much of a bellyful.'

He glanced at her, hesitant and perplexed.

'We shall see one another again later,' he said, looking away irresolutely. 'I think it's my duty to go out and welcome the poor woman thrown up by the sea like Jonah by the whale, on our lawless shores! Will you accompany me, Madame?'

'As soon as I've put away these guns, I shall join you down at the harbour.'

He went off.

Angélique stamped her foot.

That girl Julienne was right. This benefactress was an un-qualified pest. After being deemed drowned for three days, she could at least have waited a few more hours before sur-facing again! Instead she had to choose the very moment when Joffrey de Peyrac was opening his arms to Angélique, but when he had still not lowered all the defences of his proud heart.

She had sensed his impulse of concern for her but was also aware that his pride still bristled. Then suddenly fate seemed to have turned against her once more.

In spite of the memory of that all-too-brief embrace, a deathly chill crept in Angélique's veins, and dashed her spirits.

She felt like rushing after Joffrey, to call him and beseech him to return.

Her feet felt heavy and she could hardly move them, like in a nightmare.

She staggered against the doorway and almost fell. There on the floor sat a demon, with grinning jaws and flashing eyes, looking up at her.

Her flesh crept and she suddenly felt sick.

'Oh, it's you, Wolverine! How you frightened me!'

The wolverine had not followed Cantor up the Kennebec but had been prowling round the village, his body heavy, supple and snakelike, like a giant weasel.

He stood looking up at her.

'Go away! Go away!' she whispered with a shudder. 'Go away! Go back to the woods!'

Then a huge, hairy shape, moving among the silky green leaves of a tree, caught her eye.

Once again it was only a mirage of threatening danger: it was only the bear, Mr Willoughby, waddling along, sniffing the scent of fruit on the soft, warm wind.

With one paw he turned over a stone, revealing a swarm of ants which he lapped up with a few rapid licks of his tongue.

Angélique strode mechanically down to the beach, guided by a distant babble of voices that sounded farther off as she moved towards it. The stifled voice of a white ghost-like figure called to her as she went by.

'Madame de Peyrac! Madame de Peyrac!'

'What are you doing there, Marie? Be careful, now! You should not have got up with your wounds . . .'

'Let me lean on you, please, dear lady, so that I may go to meet my benefactress.'

Angélique put a sustaining arm round the frail, supple waist of the girl with the radiant face. Her feet seemed to carry her forward in spite of herself, and from time to time she turned round to see the bear and the wolverine still following her, and shook her fist at them, saying:

'Go away! Go away, you dreadful creatures!'

CHAPTER EIGHTY-FOUR

EVERYONE HAD gathered on the beach. That beach! It was a theatre facing a stage to which each day brought some new spectacle.

Now a boat was making its way up the harbour towards them, and over the sea of heads Angélique could hear shouts, sobs, and cries of joy and devotion.

'She's alive!' Marie kept on saying as she wept. 'May God and all the saints in Heaven be praised!'

Angélique stood back a little, at the point where the ground began to slope down towards the water; in this way it was possible to get a better view of what was going on, and she saw the boat reach the shore and Yann wade out into the water to steer it in and prevent it jolting as the stem touched the bottom.

Straight away all the 'King's Girls' raced towards it screaming hysterically.

In the midst of all this activity Angélique failed to identify the Duchess, although her eye was caught by the unexpected presence of a very young woman whose elaborate costume gave a touch of colour to the prow of the boat.

In spite of the distance that separated them Angélique could see that she must be quite exceptionally beautiful. In contrast to her dark hair, her complexion was as bright as a lamp, or rather reminded one of an exotic flower – a camellia or magnolia – brilliant in the shadows with all the delicacy of a perfumed petal, pure white tipped with pink.

A flower. Or a bird if you thought of the brilliant colours of her costume. Although this was as daring as the latest fashion allowed – her peacock-blue coat-dress opening over a short yellow satin skirt, with a paler blue bodice above, inset with a scarlet modesty-vest – it formed an astonishingly elegant ensemble that suited her to perfection.

The only discordant note was the wretched-looking child she was holding in her arms.

'You have saved my boy's life! God bless you!' came Jeanne Michaud's trembling voice rising above the hubbub, as she stretched out her arms and took her Pierre into them.

Relieved of her burden, the woman in the bright clothes laid her hand on that of one of the bystanders and sprang nimbly ashore holding her yellow satin skirt high to prevent it getting wet.

At that moment, what Angélique noticed was to remain engraved in her memory for a very long time, assuming a disproportionate importance, incomprehensibly so, in fact, until the day when, haunted by these unconsciously registered memories, she was finally to discover the key to many a mystery.

She noticed the young woman's scarlet stockings and her dainty little clog-shaped shoes of carmine velvet, trimmed with white leather and decorated with golden satin rosettes.

Angélique heard herself asking:

'But . . . who is that woman?'

'It's SHE,' Marie replied with a sob. 'Our benefactress! Madame de Baudricourt! . . . Look at her! isn't she lovely! Adorned with all the virtues and graces! . . .'

Slipping free from Angélique's sustaining arms, Marie mustered all her strength to make her way towards the newcomer and fell to the ground at her feet.

'My dearest lady!' . . . You are alive!'

'Marie, dear child!' came the reply in a soft, deep voice – a moving contralto – as the duchess bent down to Marie and kissed her forehead.

A man dressed in dark clothes, somewhat corpulent, with a pair of spectacles on his nose, had managed to climb down from the boat without anyone paying the slightest heed to him and was vainly attempting to bring a little orderliness into the effusive exchange of greetings.

'Come, ladies, come,' he urged them. 'Please, ladies, please allow the Duchess to receive the respects of the lord of these parts.'

Joffrey de Peyrac stood waiting a little higher up the beach, his brocaded cloak flapping in the wind, and if he too had been surprised at the unexpected appearance of the duchess, this was revealed only by a faint touch of irony in his smile.

'Make way, ladies,' the bespectacled gentleman insisted, 'have some consideration for her Grace's fatigued state.'

'Monsieur Armand!' all the girls cried out, finally deigning to recognize him too. Friendly and welcoming, they clustered round him, and Madame de Baudricourt was able to move a few paces towards Count Peyrac.

Now that she could see her closer to, Angélique realized that the duchess's clothes were stained with seawater and torn in places, and that her feet, in their delicate white leather and velvet shoes, seemed to be having great difficulty in walking across the sand, whose shifting surface added to her problems, and that, in spite of their gracefulness and the slenderness of her ankles, thrown into relief by a gold band round one of them, those feet seemed heavy and weighed down, just as Angélique's had been shortly before when she made her way down to the harbour.

Either those feet were lying shamelessly, or else it was her face that lied. She was less young than she had seemed from a distance but still more beautiful. In fact the Duchess Ambroisine de Baudricourt must have been about thirty, and possessed all the ease of manner, the assurance, and the verve of youth – at once animal and refined – of that splendid age.

And yet it was becoming more and more obvious to Angélique's practised eye that this dazzlingly beautiful woman who strode boldly up the beach was at the point of collapse. Was it exhaustion, or fear . . . or some overwhelming emotion?

And Angélique could not understand why she herself found it quite impossible to rush forward towards the exhausted woman to welcome and sustain her as she would have done to any other human being.

Joffrey de Peyrac swept the ground three times with his plumed hat, bowing low as he did so before the beautiful woman, and kissing her outstretched hand.

'I am Count Peyrac de Morens d'Irristru . . . a Gascon by birth. Welcome to you, Madame, welcome to my American settlement.'

She gave him a warm glance through her eyelashes.

'Oh, Monsieur, what a surprise! You wear your cloak more elegantly than any courtier at Versailles.'

'Madame,' he replied gallantly, 'allow me to tell you that there are more gentlemen of noble birth on this beach than in the King's antechamber.'

Then he bowed low over her white, ice-cold hand, and turning to Angélique who stood motionless a few paces away, went on:

'And this is the Countess Peyrac, my wife, who will see to it that you are given whatever refreshment you may desire after your cruel journey.'

Ambroisine de Baudricourt turned towards Angélique, her eyes now as dark as night in her lily-white face. A smile full of pain flitted across her lips that had suddenly become drained of all colour.

'And surely, in the whole of the Palace of Versailles, there could not be a lovelier woman than your wife, Monsieur de Peyrac,' she graciously added in her deep voice that almost seemed to sing as she spoke.

She grew still paler and her eyelids began to quaver. Then a sigh, a faint moan, escaped her lips.

'Ah! Please forgive me, Madame,' she murmured, 'I am dying . . .'

And there, in all her dazzling clothes, like some magnificent bird struck down in full flight, she fainted away and slid gently to the ground at Angélique's feet. For a brief instant Angélique had the sensation of being alone in a strange, unreal place.

Her mind petrified and seized with some unspeakable fear, she asked herself: 'Is this she? Is this the woman who is to rise from the sea? . . . The woman who is to come among us in the service of Lucifer?'

A series of glittering fifteenth-century
romances in the lusty, turbulent tradition
of Angélique.

JULIETTE BENZONI

One Love Is Enough 30p (6/-)
Violet-eyed Catherine Legoix knew only
too well the violence, terror and
sensuality of the Hundred Years 'War.
At twenty-one, a tantalizing and
dangerous beauty, she was virgin wife,
unwilling mistress, and in love with a
man she could not hold.

Catherine 35p (7/-)
Braving the dangers of war-torn France,
Catherine seeks Arnaud de Montsalvy,
the nobleman who has scorned her
passion—and threatened her life.

Belle Catherine 30p (6/-)
The tempestuous heroine's search for her
lover brings her face to face with torture,
lust, imprisonment and the Black Death ...

Catherine and Arnaud 30p (6/-)
As the ravishing Catherine seeks
vengeance against her arch-enemy,
La Trémoille, her beauty is at once her
keenest weapon and her greatest danger.

Catherine and A Time for Love 35p (7/-)
To rescue her husband, Catherine braves
the perilous journey from medieval
France to Saracen Spain.